MW01633624

Philip Roth Loves Me

Nancy Bagshaw-Reasoner

For Dulcie

"It is a poor sort of memory that only works backwards."

Lewis Carroll, *Through the Looking-Glass*

Prologue

a Summer day in 2020

My mother has been dead for twenty-six years. Yesterday I heard her voice. She actually spoke to me. I was alone, taking one of my daily walks around a lake near the house where I live with my husband. I was admiring the border of native plants along the shoreline. It is high Summer now, and a cluster of miniature daisy-like blooms caught my eye. My mother was an avid gardener all her life and had an encyclopedic knowledge of wildflowers in particular so without thinking I said aloud, Mother, what is the name of this one? And before I could catch myself for talking to a dead woman, I heard my mother answer, as clear as day, "Feverfew." It was her voice, no mistaking that voice—very feminine and bell-like—and so close to my right ear, like she was standing behind me leaning over my shoulder, examining the bushy plant, that I gasped and turned, fully expecting to see her. When I got home I searched online through wildflowers for a photo of the one I had seen at the lake. Miniature daisies on a slender stalk. A fringe of stiff, white petals surrounding a tiny sun. There it was. Feverfew.

In the days that followed, I kept replaying my exchange with Mother. I was, of course, thrilled to hear from her after all these years, but I must confess the biggest reason for my excitement was the prospect it offered of communicating with others beyond the veil. I knew immediately who

I'd choose next. I choose you, Philip Roth. I have always wanted to meet you. I've read all of your novels. I've studied your interviews. I think we are kindred spirits. I, too, am a writer and, like you, the American Dream is my project.

I was heartbroken when you died in 2018 because we had never had the chance to connect. But now that possibility exists and I'm not going to hesitate a second longer. So, Philip Roth, let me introduce myself. My name is Leanne. I am 71. I am married. I have adult children; they are married. No grandchildren. Just dogs. Grand dogs.

You're lucky, Philip, that you've missed this pandemic. The governor declared a lockdown and that has meant that we are all now isolated in our houses. Our groceries are delivered to the front step. The TV is kept on all day so we can keep up with the death counts by state. Only the foolhardy risk exposing themselves to their neighbors, their friends, even their family. When it becomes necessary to see one another, we stand six feet apart on the front lawn or talk through closed windows. At all times we wear a mask. I should clarify that not everyone is cooperating. The news last night reported that a maskless man deliberately spat in the face of a two-year-old who was standing next to his mother at the pharmacy. The man said it was his right as an American to spit. He said it was in the Bible. I am reminded of one spectator during the French Revolution who reported, "You'd have to eat a live toad for breakfast in order not to run into something more disgusting during the day."

You would be shocked, Philip, at the rancor in our country at this moment. All the snakes that reared their heads in the 1960s—racism, classism, homophobia, misogyny—that seemed to have been conquered or at least suppressed by the 80s, have returned with a fury tenfold. Our current president is a scary clown—unabashedly shameless, corrupt, and criminally vengeful who will not agree to step down if he loses the up-coming election. He traffics in grievances and has unleashed an army of his followers, men and women who used to live anonymously in our fail-ing rural towns, but have, in the last four years, found their "five minutes of fame" and are quite drunk on the attention. The country is so violent; many of my friends are looking to get out. In fact, my two best friends have already left. One bought a place in Portugal and the other a place in a village in Mexico. A village in Mexico is preferable to living in America in this year 2020. Let that sink in. Oh, Philip, you would be in your element right now. You always said that you loved a society in turmoil.

Anyway, I'm spending these lonely pandemic days in reflection; I'm writing a memoir. But I want to go back to the past with clear eyes. I'm no longer interested in romanticizing my youth. I see it now as fore-shadowing for our current times. That's where you come in. You were a flawed and complicated, sexy and funny man, Philip Roth. And a wise interrogator of American identity. You would be good company on this journey. And a great character in my story. Therefore I've decided to take you along.

Let's begin....

Part One — Summer 1964

they were all blonde …

Chapter 1

I met Philip Roth on a Summer evening in 1964. I was fourteen and he was thirty-one. Philip had recently moved into a house in the upscale development where I lived with my mother, father and two younger brothers, in the quiet, eighteenth-century village of Pennswalk, an Eden of apple orchards, sparkling creeks, and cobblestone streets forty miles northwest of Philadelphia. There were so few streetlights then that you could see the stars at night. And best of all, it was an easy commute to New York City and Philadelphia. It's what they called a "bedroom community."

Philip Roth was renting the Williams' house for six months while the Williams family accompanied Mr. Williams to Ireland for his sabbatical, which he spent researching the history of peat; he was a professor of history at Bryn Mawr. My father was also a professor—of economics—at the University of Pennsylvania. And Philip Roth, the suddenly famous and very handsome author of *Goodbye, Columbus*, which had recently won the prestigious National Book Award, was the professor of desire. He was here in Pennswalk to write his next novel away from the righteous anger of rabbis who had taken issue with Philip's satiric take on modern assimilated Jews living in the American suburbs. Not to mention his dirty mouth.

My parents, Beverly and Thomas Hughs, weren't Jewish. They were WASPs, which meant they were White and Episcopalian although we only went to church at Christmastime and for the occasional wedding. Mother and Daddy commingled easily with Jews and with educated Blacks, although you had to go into Philadelphia if you wanted to meet non-White people. Pennswalk was uniformly Christian and White. Politically, Mother and Daddy identified with the Rockefeller wing of the Republican Party although they had each voted for John Kennedy in 1960 and were devastated when he was assassinated last November. My father loved Jack's witty press conferences and Mother loved Jackie's clothes.

My parents had read Philip Roth's new book and liked it. They were thrilled to have an acclaimed author living down the street. They had invited him to a backyard luau that night in honor of Hawaii's becoming a state, which had actually happened five years before in 1959, but Mother had only recently found the time to plan a luau. She was a busy woman. Not only was she a full-time homemaker and not only was she overseeing the rearing of three active children, she also volunteered for the Pickering Manor Nursing Home Foundation and Planned Parenthood as well as serving as co-chairman of the PTA and the president of the Pennswalk Historical Society for the coming year. Everyone was expecting that last fact alone would mean that this year's Friendship Day would be particularly memorable. Friendship Day was the annual celebration of the history and spirit of Pennswalk. It occurred at the end of the Summer on the second Saturday in September and it was a big deal.

My mother was mainly known in town for her fabulous dinner parties and for her sense of style. She was popular and able to enlist the help of her many girlfriends in any project that captured her devotion. And she was pretty. Which is something that surprised and delighted Philip Roth when she appeared at his front door with her dazzling smile, carrying a loaf of still-warm banana bread. She asked how he was "making out." She filled him in on the neighborhood. "Everyone here is really nice." And she

invited him to the luau. "Bring your swim trunks, Philip. We have a pool."
He had a weakness for blondes so he thanked her and said he'd be there.

THE NIGHT OF THE luau, I was in the master bathroom, playing with my
mother's eye makeup when I looked out the window that overlooked the
backyard and saw Philip Roth standing between Daddy and Mr. Landers
who lived next door. Philip was among the first guests to arrive. He was
the handsomest man I had ever seen in my life other than Sean Connery
whom I had seen at the movies the weekend before as Agent 007 in *Dr.
No*. Now I really didn't want to go downstairs and "make an appearance," as my mother expected me to do, to say hi to everyone at the party
before retreating to my room and my new Beatles album. I was already
self-conscious about my breasts, especially around my father's friends,
but around Philip Roth? He was even handsomer than Mr. Taylor whose
wife Ginger was my mother's best friend. Mr. Taylor often looked at me
when he thought I wasn't aware. And when he thought Ginger wasn't
aware. But I was always aware. At fourteen, I was beginning to notice
men.

I had been on the high school swim team that year and my school
still made the girls wear these god-awful knit jersey suits from the 1940s
that hung like a sack and showed EVERYTHING. Darlene Estes had an
outie belly button and now everyone in the school knew! So my breasts
… well, you can imagine the talk. The worst part was that they didn't
develop in gradual stages so that I, along with all the boys in my class,
could get used to them being in the room. No, they emerged almost
overnight. D cups before I knew what had happened. I went from a 32A
bra to a 34D in six weeks. And in the eyes of the boys in my school, I
might as well have turned into a breast. They no longer noticed my face.
Even when I was speaking directly to them, their eyes never left my chest.
Even Franz Kafka didn't capture the true horror of that metamorphosis.
The most troubling part for me though was that Philip Roth apparently
liked small breasts, if the heroine in *Goodbye, Columbus* was any indication. Brenda Patimkin had small breasts. Still, I hoped that maybe Philip

would eventually like big breasts more when he got to know me as a whole person.

On this night, the night of the luau, I was a virgin of course, but my mother had always been fairly candid about her own personal sexual happiness with my dad so I wasn't put off by sex. I had an idea that despite the mystery that surrounded it, sex was actually a lot of fun. Adults certainly seemed to like it, especially my parents. There had been many mornings when I would be awake before the others in my house and would descend the stairs to the first floor only to find Mother's underwear—her panties, stockings, bra—tossed on those same stairs. I'd picture my parents the evening before, after my brothers and I were sound asleep, in an urgent embrace, stumbling up the stairs, ripping off their clothes so that they were naked by the time they entered their room where they yanked the bedside table aside and shoved the twin beds together and started French kissing, which had been described to me by Audrey Wexler who sat next to me in homeroom. Plus Mother sometimes shared intimate gossip with me. "Annie, did I tell you that Mr. Landers has never seen Mrs. Landers naked? Yes, it's true! Mr. Landers told your father over drinks after their golf game last Saturday. They have been married longer than Daddy and me. They have three kids! And yet he has never seen her naked body! It's unnatural, Annie. Men love to look at a woman's body. It doesn't even have to be perfect. No wonder Mr. Landers drinks so much. Ye gods—he must be beyond frustrated at this point!"

If that wasn't enough of an education, I had accidentally read *Lady Chatterley's Lover* last Winter. In one sitting. I borrowed it from Mr. and Mrs. Williams' bookshelves while I was babysitting their kids. This was before they moved to Ireland for his sabbatical. Mrs. Williams had always encouraged me to borrow anything I wanted to read, and *Lady Chatterley's Lover* sounded so romantic. I flushed scarlet now thinking of Philip Roth being in the very house, maybe sitting in the very chair, where I first read about fucking. But I remembered that my best friend Candy had told me that the word FUCK is an acronym. It stands for Fornication Under the Consent of the King. Candy and I agreed that didn't sound dirty at all. It actually sounded more legal.

I CHANGED OUT OF my shorts and t-shirt and into a simple cotton sleeveless shift. It was hot pink with aqua-ball fringe around the hem. It was tight in the bust but otherwise fairly shapeless. I left my feet bare. My ten-year-old twin brothers were gone for the night, staying with a friend. I would normally be hanging out with Candy on a Saturday night, but Candy was babysitting for the Bobbins who were coming to the luau. I figured I'd call her once the luau got going. I returned to my parents' bathroom and looked out the window again.

Guests were arriving now in a steady stream. The women were, for the most part, dressed for a luau. And they were all blonde. That was due to the alchemy of our new neighbor, Arlene Swenson, the former Arlene Giampaoletti, a hairdresser from South Philly who married an IBM computer programmer whose car broke down in front of the salon where Arlene worked, thus enabling Arlene to keep him company while he waited for a tow. To kill time, she had read his palm with such intensity, describing how he was going to meet a tall woman with dark brown eyes and marry her on New Year's Eve, that by the time the tow truck arrived, she had Mr. Swenson convinced that Fate had brought them together, and they were married six months later. On New Year's Eve. Last Spring, they moved into the Linton Hill development in Pennswalk where she met my mother and then Mother introduced her to the other women in the neighborhood. Arlene was shy at first; she told the women she felt completely "outclassed" by them, which made the women feel protective of her. She soon became a regular at Mother's weekly Koffee Klatches.

I started skipping school on Wednesdays so that I could attend Koffee Klatch and hear Arlene tell her incredible rags-to-riches story. Mother always let me skip school at my own discretion. Sometimes she'd even ask me to take a day off from school so that we could go to Philadelphia and attend the Flower Show together or go shopping at Wanamaker's or to an early movie. We called it "girl time." Over the past five months, we had seen *Gidget Goes to Rome*; *Move Over, Darling;* and *Hud*. We saw *Hud* twice; my mother really loved Paul Newman. She said he was part Jewish which made him very sexy. Mother always gave me a note for the teacher the next day, saying something to the effect of "Please excuse Annie's absence. She had a sore throat." Mother knew that was a lie, but

I was an A student and no one at school cared why I was missing so many days. In fact, Mother had confessed to the principal after a PTA meeting that she often kept me out of school when an educational opportunity in Philadelphia came up. Like a special exhibit at the Philadelphia Museum of Art. The principal told Mother she thought it was charming that she took such an active interest in cultivating her daughter's aesthetic taste. Of course what Mother didn't tell her was that we were more likely to spend those days trying on shoes or eating Junior Mints at a movie theater in Society Hill.

Candy thought it was weird. "Your mother treats you like a friend instead of a daughter." It was true. My mother's friends also tended to think of me as a friend. They never hid their conversations from me and welcomed me to Koffee Klatch each Wednesday where I, like all of them, got to hear the details of their marriages as well as the story of Arlene Giampaoletti Swenson's rough upbringing in an inner-city Italian neighborhood in South Philadelphia. And how she finally escaped.

Here's the gist of it: Arlene was born into an extended family that to this day spoke Italian at home and lived "cheek by jowl" in cramped apartments along the same street. I loved imagining what that would be like. My parents had grown up in neighborhoods where they were surrounded by family, where they could walk a half block to see a garrulous Great Uncle who would tell stories about the First World War and toss them a nickel to spend at the candy store. They could stop at their Nana's house after school for a piece of cherry pie. And they could play a pickup baseball game with the neighborhood kids, among them their own cousins, every day of the week until snow fell.

The extended family had long ago left the old neighborhoods and now lived in suburban communities across several states. I rarely saw them. It was a long car drive to visit anyone. We still gathered on special occasions, Thanksgiving and Christmas, and at the beach in Summer where we'd vacation together for two weeks and marvel at how much we looked alike, how much we sounded alike. It was a strange sensation. I think my parents missed their families terribly, but believed it was a necessary sacrifice if they were to achieve financial and social success, which my parents had done to a greater degree than the others. My mother compensated for the loneliness by making intense friendships. She and Ginger Taylor became inseparable. My father never found the deep male bonding that he had experienced in his youth with his cousins and brother, so he turned to Mother for intimacy—emotional as well as sexual. I sensed from an early age that husbands would be lost without their wives.

Arlene Giampaoletti's life would eventually take her on a similar trajectory. She was never a good student, but had a flair for styling her hair so when she graduated from high school, her widowed mother got her a position at Jimmy Calaruso's famous South Philly hair salon. As Jimmy's oldest and most loyal customer, Mama Giampaoletti felt entitled to demand, "Give my ungrateful, fat daughter a job so at least I won't have to look at her for eight hours every day." The women at the Koffee Klatch gasped at the cruelty of Arlene's mother in these stories. But Arlene explained that she and Mama Giampaoletti accepted their relationship—it was destined. They were unfortunately simply the latest victims of the family curse, a curse so poisonous that all of the women descendants of Great Grandmother Lucci were born not trusting their own mothers! To compensate, the women in Arlene's family went out of their way to attract the love and friendship of other women, non-relations. And, as it turned out, working at Jimmy Calaruso's gave Arlene a first-class education in how to do just that. Jimmy, himself, was confidante to every woman within a four-block radius of his salon. And in time Arlene would also claim a large clientele, loyal only to her. Even Jimmy would eventually concede that Arlene "had gotten quite excellent with women." But after twelve years of working at Jimmy's, Arlene was still unmarried and yearning for a life beyond the confines of South Philly. She had begun to dream of Pennswalk. She imagined herself among the serene and elegant women she'd see coming out of the shops when she visited the pretty village on weekend drives into the countryside north of Philadelphia. Then of course, she met Mr. Swenson and her personal American Dream came true. She finally escaped her family and left the old neighborhood behind. That brought everyone up to date on her story. Mrs. Landers actually applauded when Arlene laughed and stuttered, "Th—that's all, folks!"

ON MY LAST DAY of school that year, I walked home with Candy as always, dropping her off at her house along the way and then continuing on to my own home six houses further along Linton Hill Drive. I walked through the back gate and found Mother and her friends gathered by the pool. Some of the women swam and some sat on the diving board and swung their feet over the water. It was only the first week of June and already hot, in the 90s. Mother and Ginger Taylor, were sitting side by side huddled over a hair style magazine that Arlene had brought along that day. Mother looked up and smiled as I approached. "Well, there you are! You're late. Did you have a little homeroom party after school to celebrate the end of ninth grade?"

"No, Candy and I stayed after to do some orgasms down at the tennis court."

Mrs. Taylor giggled. The other women smiled. Mother said, "Show me, Annie. Show me an orgasm."

I stood very straight and extended my arms to the sides. Then I bent my arms at the elbows and tucked my fists under my arm pits to create wings. I flapped them up and down, slowly, and deliberately with great concentration. All of the women watched.

Mother nodded and then said, "We call that a bust exercise."

I frowned. "I thought that's what orgasm means."

"No," Mother said. "Orgasm means another thing entirely."

Ginger Taylor held out her arms. "Kiss … kiss. Give me a kiss, sweet girl."

I obediently went to her and leaned over offering her my cheek. Mrs. Taylor was my godmother and I thought of her as an aunt. She kissed me and patted my arm.

Mother said, "Don't forget to practice the piano."

"Can't I skip one day?"

Mother gave me a cool look. "No," she said.

Last Winter I had happened to mention to my father that I wished I had a piano and the next day a piano was delivered to the house. That's the way Daddy was. Anything I wanted I got. And it annoyed my mother. She thought it was unfair of me to take advantage of Daddy's weakness for his children. So she decided to "teach me a lesson" this time. She hired a man who had been a concert pianist in Cuba before he escaped the communists and came to Philadelphia. He started giving me weekly lessons with hard exercises, like he was preparing me for the concert stage. But I stunk and I hated the lessons. I would eventually prevail on Daddy to give the piano to the Pickering Manor Nursing Home so that old people could have "the pleasure of music."

I went upstairs to my bedroom and opened the dictionary which I kept on my nightstand. I read the definition of *orgasm* and said aloud— "well, I'm highly unlikely to ever use *that* word in a sentence, but it's good to know what it means." I would of course share this definition with Candy later. Candy thought we were doing orgasms on the tennis court after school that day, too. In fact, she introduced me to the word.

When I returned to the pool, Mother was squealing. "Guess what, Annie? Arlene's going to cut our hair! Each of us is going to get a brand new hairdo and she's going to bleach us blonde, too!" Arlene grinned and turned to me. "You, too, Babycakes. I'll make you a Summer Blonde." The reinventions began the very next day.

Ginger Taylor was the first to go blonde. She was the vainest of the group and therefore the most susceptible to flattery. Ginger actually owned two identical wardrobes, one in a size 6 and the other in size 8. She only wore the size 6's when she was certain that she wouldn't need to sit down at any time during the evening. Mother would point it out to me during one of my parents' many cocktail parties. "See," she'd say, "Ginger is wearing her standing up pants tonight." And sure enough, Mrs. Taylor would be standing with the men at the bar in the corner of the family room, while the other women sat on couches by the fireplace. Mrs. Taylor never made any bones about it. "I just saw the snazziest little number over at the mall," she would say. "But they only had it in a size 8. And of course, I need it in a size 6, too."

So Arlene began with Mrs. Taylor's long, dark brown hair. She cut a sweep of bangs to toss over Ginger's eternally tanned forehead and then bleached them a tawny golden blonde, a color she had invented for Ginger alone. Those blonde bangs were striking against her dark hair, setting off her chocolate brown eyes. Arlene christened the color "Desire on the Riviera," and the rest of the ladies flipped coins to see who would be next.

Eleanor Bobbin won the toss and giggled like a schoolgirl as Arlene pinned a towel around her broad shoulders. Mrs. Bobbin was a large-boned woman with a sharply upturned nose and a little-girl voice. For her, Arlene chose a short sassy pixie cut, which she then lightened to a movie star platinum she called "Mitzi Gaynor." So delighted was Mrs. Bobbin with being a blonde that she actually plucked out her eyebrows and replaced them with two thin lines of lavender pencil. Oddly enough, they matched her hair pretty well, especially when she was in the glow of artificial light.

Over the course of the next two days, the rest of the women were transformed. Arlene's gift, apart from her way with cut and color, was to access a woman's fantasy. Arlene just intuitively understood how each woman wanted to be seen. And Arlene nailed them all.

Kitty Landers, whose husband had never seen her naked, went for a strawberry blonde ponytail. Arlene named her color "Irish Lassie." Regal Laura Armitage went for a honey-blonde pageboy, "Grace Kelly." Ambitious Dinah Matthews who was the only one of Mother's friends to have a job outside the home—she was a very successful real estate agent—succumbed to an ash blonde "bubble cut," which Arlene named "Tycoon." Somewhere along the way, my mother exchanged her chestnut-brown French twist for a golden-blonde chin-length bob, which Arlene called simply "Debutante." And as Arlene had promised, she added some California girl highlights to my own dark-blonde hair. She called my color, "Leanne." Everyone called me by my nickname Annie, but my real name was Leanne. I cherished the fact that Arlene had noticed that about me.

When everyone was freshly coiffed, they passed Mother's sterling-silver hand mirror around and around. No one spoke. They were mesmerized by their reflections. They felt renewed. They had all been down in the dumps this past six months since President Kennedy's head exploded during a visit to Dallas, Texas, on November 22, 1963. It was an assassination that shocked the nation all the more because it had been viewed in real time and filmed, so for weeks after, it was played again and again on the evening news. It began to seep into everyone's dreams. It was followed within days by the murder of the suspected assassin Lee Harvey Oswald by a man named Jack Ruby who owned a night club. That was caught on film, too. It didn't feel like justice had been served. It only added to the general sense of danger in the air. Americans wondered what was happening to their country. Who were our fellow citizens? Even in Pennswalk, people started to lock their doors at night.

All that Winter, there were regular stories in *Ladies' Home Journal* and *McCall's* as well as other publications that featured the devastated former First Lady and her heroic attempts to hold things together for the benefit of her small children. Mother and her friends would actually cry when they read these articles. Then came the rumors that Jack Kennedy's own brother Bobby was going to leave his wife and kids for Jackie. That made the women sick at heart. Mother decided never to vote for a Democrat again. In Mother's view, Democrats just always seemed to push the envelope a bit too far. I reserved my judgment. Even at my age, I imagined that love could overwhelm conventional mores.

Now Mother and her friends were ready to turn the page on this sad time. On this June day in 1964, as Mother surveyed her friends, their blonde hair almost blinding in the sunshine, their eyes sparkling with good fortune—in that moment, Mother knew that these were the best years of their lives. And it was at that moment that she decided it was finally the right time to celebrate Hawaii becoming the fiftieth state in the union. She announced to her friends that there would be a luau the following Saturday night. And she added, "I'm going to invite Philip Roth."

THE AFTERNOON OF THE LUAU at five o'clock, Mother came out of her bedroom and ran down the stairs into the living room, calling my name. I was on the phone in the kitchen. "I'll call you back, Candy." I walked out into the living room and Mother twirled and giggled. "Well, what do you think?"

"That's so fab! You look like a native!"

Mother had gathered a piece of brightly colored fabric around her slender figure. It was tucked and sewn in place that very afternoon. Her shoulders were bare and so were her small feet. She had bracelets of silk flowers on each ankle and a lei of the same around her neck. She said, "I probably could have been a model for Gauguin. Except of course, my skin isn't brown." Her eyes met her own eyes in the mirror over the Bombay chest and she stood very still for a long moment as if she was remembering something that happened a long time ago.

Then she started to play with her hair. Arlene had provided Mother with a long fall of human hair that she had bleached to match her golden bob. The fake hair was anchored at her crown behind her bangs and a large silk star lily was pinned behind her left ear. She flipped the long hair behind her shoulders, then thought better of it and pulled it forward over her left shoulder. "I don't know," she said. "What do you think?"

"Forward. It's sexier."

Mother gave me a playful shove. "Annie!"

"So how's Daddy?"

Mother rolled her eyes and inhaled deeply, "Oh, brother."

Right on cue, Daddy came down the stairs and stood before us in the front hallway. He wore a short skirt in a fabric that matched Mother's dress. It was knotted and tucked at the waist. Underneath he wore a pair of white tennis shorts. He wore a white V-neck undershirt, white athletic socks, and cordovan loafers. And a lei.

Mother gasped, "No, no, no, Tom. That's all wrong. Bare chest. No shirt. Honestly...."

"You're nuts," he said flatly.

"Well, at least take off your shoes and socks. That looks silly!"

"You get colds through your feet. The flagstone gets chilly after dark."

"Oh, for Pete's sake! Well, how do I look?" Mother twirled flirtatious-ly.

"You don't look like yourself," he said, defensively.

"That's the idea!" she snapped and stomped into the kitchen, muttering under her breath.

My father looked at me and shrugged.

"At least get rid of the socks, Daddy. "

"Okay," he said and kissed me on the forehead.

I COULD SEE AND hear everything at the luau from my perch at the window of my parents' bathroom. I had decided to take careful note of each detail so that I could write a story about it all. Maybe for the school newspaper. I'd call it "The Evening I Met Philip Roth." I ran back to my room and grabbed my diary, a pen, and the *Roget's Thesaurus*. I returned to the bathroom window in time to see Dinah Matthews come through the gate into the yard. Wearing an orange bathing suit top and a grass skirt, she was the first to yell "Aloha." Mr. Matthews followed her, after he parked the station wagon on the street. He wore a plastic lei over his polo shirt. The Matthews joined Philip Roth and Daddy and Mr. Landers at the portable bar that was set up near the large buffet table. Next the Bobbins arrived— Mrs. Bobbin in a lavender floral shift that matched her eyebrows. "Aloha," she squealed in her weird high-pitched voice and her husband looked embarrassed. Mrs. Landers arrived from next door, breathless, in an aqua shirtwaist dress and a polka-dot scarf tied around her ponytail. She waved to her husband. "I made it, Honey!" The Armitages came through the gate next. Mrs. Armitage whispered "Aloha" in her sultry voice and kissed Mother on the cheek. Her husband, Dr. Armitage, held her hand. He gave a bottle of wine to my father and said in his deep voice, "Everything looks perfect, Tom. Thanks for including us."

Now the Taylors arrived, fashionably late as always, entering the party like movie stars. Ginger Taylor stepped out of her husband's red sports car and tossed her blonde bangs across her forehead. She wore a skin-tight floral band across her bosom, creating a deep cleavage between her plump breasts. Her tummy was bare, and her wrapped skirt sat low on her hips, split over one thigh to reveal a perfectly tanned leg. Her dark hair was swept up high on her crown and pinned in place with a cascade of tiny white orchids that framed her golden bangs. Her hips swayed as she walked slowly into the backyard. Every head turned. "Aloha," she purred at Mr. Bobbin, who was still standing by the gate, debating whether to leave. He suddenly seemed more interested in the party and headed for the bar. Mr. Taylor followed wearing a floral loin cloth, no shirt, no socks, no shoes. No lei. Just a beach towel draped around his shoulders. He snapped his towel at Mr. Matthews as he passed him and yelled, "Fucking aloha, everyone!"

Arlene Giampaoletti Swenson and her husband arrived unnoticed by everyone but me. Arlene seemed restrained, almost timid. She wore white slacks and a simple taupe-colored shirt. Mr. Swenson wore a suit and looked bored.

Mother came out of the kitchen, walked through the screened-in back porch out onto to the flagstone patio. She passed the fountain with the little bronze girl pouring water out of a pitcher and moved gingerly down the stone steps to the pool level, all the while balancing a basket of potato chips on top of her precious cut-crystal coleslaw bowl which held the Hawaiian poi that she had special ordered at the local market. It was completely authentic although Mother had seasoned it with smoked paprika just before the party to give it "a little color." She threaded through the guests to the portable buffet table where she carefully deposited the poi and chips. When she finally noticed Arlene, she hula-danced over to greet her. "Arlene," she said. "Where's *your* sarong?"

"Oh, Bev, I don't have your confidence or your figure."

"Now you stop that," Mother whispered. "Lack of self-confidence is unappealing in women our ages." Then she turned to Mr. Swenson and extended her hand, "This must be Eric." He took it and flashed a brief smile. Mother said, "Shall we join the party?" They turned towards the pool, just in time to see Mr. Taylor leap onto the diving board, rip off his loin cloth to reveal skintight bathing trunks, then yell "Aiiiiiyeeeeee" and jump into the water.

I looked for Philip Roth among the men now leaning on the split rail fence around the perimeter of the yard, sipping from sweating glasses of scotch or bourbon. But I didn't see him. My heart sank. *Did he leave? Did he come for just one drink to be polite?* I was on my way back to my bedroom when I ran into him in the hallway. Literally. "Oh, gosh! Excuse me!" I looked up into his eyes and staggered backwards a step. He was even handsomer in person than he was in his photo on the book jacket. And tall! Over six feet. He took my arm to gently steady me and smiled warmly. "I'm looking for a bathroom?" he said.

"There," I pointed to a door across the hall. "There's also a bathroom downstairs off the family room."

He kept his eyes on me. "Oh, I'm sorry ... I should have...."

I shook my head. "No, it's okay. I mean you can use this bathroom or there's another bathroom back there, my parents' bathroom. My brothers have a bathroom upstairs. We have a lot of bathrooms." I laughed. "This one is mine but you can use it. It's fine."

I studied his face. His penetrating eyes would have been intimidating were it not for his brows. Dense and black and perfectly arched, they were his most playful feature. Even when his face was in repose, his eyes steely, those brows were animated—lifting, tilting, and registering everything his senses were signaling—like needles on a seismograph ever alert to the rumbles beneath the surface of the moment. He had a formidable nose. And a sensual mouth. A cleft beneath his protruding bottom lip produced a deep dimple at the midway point that made his lips seem always on the verge of posing a question or stealing a kiss. I felt lightheaded but not nervous. Not a bit. I liked him immediately and he seemed to be in no hurry to move on.

He smiled and said, "You must be Annie. Your father said...."

"Leanne...."

He leaned down as though he couldn't quite hear. His face was next to mine. "I'm sorry … I thought...."

"They call me—well, everyone calls me Annie—but my name is Leanne. And I prefer to be called that."

He smiled. "Then I will call you Leanne." He offered his hand. I took it. We shook and he pulled me slightly closer. I didn't resist. "I'm Philip. It's nice to meet you, Leanne."

"Yes, I know who you are. I admire your writing."

His eyebrows lifted. "You've read my work?"

"Yes, I read *Goodbye, Columbus.*"

"And your parents are okay with that?"

"Yes. I'm wise beyond my years."

He noticed the diary and thesaurus that I was pressing against my chest. "How old are you? If you don't mind me asking."

"I'll be fifteen in August. How old are you?"

"I turned thirty-one last March. So I guess I'm almost thirty-one and a half now."

I grinned. "Very funny."

He laughed. He continued to watch me so directly that I was tempted to look down at my feet, but I resisted. I kept my eyes on his face. After a long moment when neither of us spoke—when I found myself holding my breath but unable to stop looking into his dark eyes—Philip finally said, "So, Leanne, what do you think of my book?"

I rolled my eyes to one side and exhaled. "I think it's a scream." And then I laughed bending forward at my waist. That made Philip laugh, too. I added, "Actually, Brenda's family sort of makes me think of mine. Except we're not Jewish."

"Uh huh."

"And my mother and I don't fight. We're good friends."

"I see."

Pause.

"I'm going to be a writer when I grow up."

He pointed to the diary and thesaurus and said, "It looks like you're already writing."

I nodded. "I record my observations every day. But I haven't actually written a story yet. That's my goal for this Summer. May I ask you something, Mr. Roth?"

"Philip."

"Philip." I blushed at the feel of his name on my tongue. "How do you get a story idea?"

He inhaled deeply "Well, often the story will come to you in the form of a question. "*What* would happen if … or *why* did this happen? *Why* did my mother put paprika on the poi?" He grinned. I pursed my lips. I often felt defensive about my mother. I knew that she could seem shallow at times but she really wasn't. She was naturally smart and thoughtful and I loved her. Philip watched these thoughts play out across my face and said, "I'm not being a wise guy, Leanne. There really is a story in that question. The Russian writer Anton Chekhov—have you heard of him? Well, I'll lend you some of his work so you can become acquainted with him. He's a masterly storyteller and a good model for any writer. He said that the writer's job is the proper presentation of the problem. That's the hard part. You have to discern the problem—the desire in the heart of each character. You dip into what you know about desire. You dip into your own experience of living and you select two sticks of reality and then you rub them together until you create fire. And then you write, write, write."

I looked into his eyes. "Thank you. I will be ruminating about that in bed tonight."

We stood quietly smiling at each other. I felt like I'd known him all my life. And Philip seemed to be experiencing a familiar feeling about me as well. Finally he said, "Well, I should get back to the party."

"Did you still need to use the bathroom?" I gestured to the door in the hall.

"No. Actually, I was just curious about the pretty face in the window upstairs. You are visible from the yard, you know."

I blushed. "Oh … see … I'm just taking notes on the luau. For a possible story."

Philip leaned in close to my face and whispered, "So am I." He turned and crossed to the stairs, stopping to add, "Come visit me some afternoon. After four. I stop writing at four."

Chapter 2

I met Candy the morning she and her family moved into their new house on Linton Hill Drive. That was in March, just three months ago. Dinah Matthews had been their realtor and tipped my mother off to the news that the Doyles had a daughter my age, so Mother sent me down to their house that morning with a loaf of banana bread to introduce myself. The freakiest thing happened just as I approached the Doyles' driveway. It had been raining all that morning and suddenly at 11:06, according to my watch, the rain stopped, and the sun came out creating an actual rainbow across the pasture behind the Doyle's new house. I pointed it out to Candy and said, "I think this is a sign that we're destined to be friends." Candy said, "Well, I'm not superstitious. I'm Catholic. But the rainbow is one of God's traditional ways of signaling harmony so it certainly appears that God is advocating for us to be friends." In the days that followed, we were rarely apart. I liked everything about her. "You have *je ne sais quois* in spades, Candy," I would say to her. And she'd return the compliment. "And you are so sophisticated,

Annie Hughs, that it's hard for me to believe that you were born here in dopey little Pennswalk."

Candy was from Levittown and she told me that her elementary school had been bigger than my whole high school so she had dreaded moving here right up to the moment she met me. "But you, Annie, are the coolest girl I have ever known. This is Kismet," she said. I immediately introduced Candy to my friends—Lark Kennedy, Betsy Spencer, and Gaye Parsons, who had been my best friends since kindergarten. I assured Candy that while I would always be loyal to all of my girlfriends all my life, she would "henceforth be my *very best friend.*" And Candy agreed. "Best friends forever, Annie."

The morning after the luau, Mother and I were in the kitchen unpacking the dishwasher. I was sharing some of the ways in which Candy and I aligned. "It's just uncanny, Mother. We have everything in common. First of all, she's a straight A student like me. And she reads good literature. Like me. Her favorite book is *To Kill a Mockingbird.* And as you know, that's my favorite book."

Mother went to the fridge and removed a bunch of fresh radishes from the crisper. I continued, "Candy's favorite nail polish color is Pink Sand! Just like me. And she loves the Beatles of course! Her favorite is George whereas my favorite is Paul. But that's okay. Of course we will have minor distinctions between us. That's healthy. Besides that way, when we pretend we're married to Beatles, there won't be any conflict."

Mother smiled and said, "Well, that's true." She rinsed the radishes, patted them dry and began to carve them into little "roses" to garnish the platter of leftover ham that she would be serving for dinner that night. I leaned on the counter and watched her fingers move the radish around the knife. I continued, "Oh, let's see what else … Candy is a terrific writer like me and she is enlarging her vocabulary every day just like me. We share words. And she *loves* Black music. And she's for Civil Rights, Mother. Same as me."

Mother placed the finished radish "roses" in a small bowl of ice water to keep them crisp and placed it in the refrigerator. "There that's done. They're all ready for tonight." She turned to me and said, "Always take the extra time to make sure your food is presented beautifully, Annie. Remember—we eat with our eyes first."

"She's such a fabulous dancer. And she thinks I am, too. We're going to go to all the dances at the Youth Center this Summer." I sighed. "Well, I'm off to Candy's. We're going to sunbathe together today. And maybe … you know … polish our toenails."

"Okay, Honey. Ginger and Eddie and the boys will be here at five. Make sure you're back before then."

CANDY AND I SAT on the floor of Candy's large bedroom, listening to the radio and paging through the newest *Sixteen* magazine. Candy turned a page and shrugged. "Judy Fesmire says she's going to see *A Hard Day's Night* six times this Summer, Annie. Her cousin's driving her to Philly to see it. So I told her my sister Susan is going to drive you and me to see it, too."

"WHAT?" I jumped to my feet. This was news to me.

"Well, I mean … Susan and Darlene are going on Thursday and I'm going to *ask* Susan if we can ride along."

"Oh." I sat on the floor again. So it wasn't a done deal. "Honestly, Candy, I just don't *understand* why it takes so *long* to get new movies in this stupid town. The Pennswalk Plaza just got *West Side Story*! I mean ye gods—that movie is three years old! It will be years before *A Hard Day's Night* gets here and I don't want to have to have my mother take us into Philly to see it. Gosh, this town is so dumb." I rolled onto my back.

"Well, don't be so moribund. Maybe my sister will come through." Candy picked up a *Seventeen* magazine from the stack on the floor and opened it. "I think Ricky Nelson has sexy eyes."

"Mr. Roth has sexy eyes, too. I mean Philip. I met him last night at the luau. He's really nice. And gorgeous. Oh my gosh! He told me to call him Philip. He said I can visit him if I want. And I'm going to. Someday."

"You're boy crazy, Annie." Candy put her magazine down and lowered her voice. "Mrs. Bobbin was crying when she and Mr. Bobbin got home from your parents' luau this morning at like … 2:30! I was sleeping on the couch and I heard them come in. Then I heard them arguing in the hall. I was afraid they would wake up the kids again, but they slept right through."

I sat up. "Mrs. Bobbin and Mrs. Taylor had a fight."

"Get out! At your parents' party? Did you see it?"

"No, but my mother told me about it this morning. They were playing some dumb game where you have to lay down your driver's license and if anyone challenges the weight you have on your card, you have to get on the bathroom scale in front of everyone. Mrs. Taylor came up with the game and Mrs. Bobbin was embarrassed. But my mother said Mrs. Bobbin started it. She had asked Mrs. Taylor if her maiden name was Jewish. Of course, they were all pretty drunk."

Candy snorted. "Donna told me that everyone at the Community Pool calls Linton Hill 'Liquor Hill.' Some of the girls won't babysit in our development because their parents won't let them."

I shrugged. "My mother says Pennswalk is experiencing growing pains."

"All I know is that every time your parents have a party, I make big babysitting money because they go on until the early morning hours. Ka-ching!"

My parents never invited Candy's parents to their parties. Mother said the Doyles couldn't eat meat on Fridays and that's when Mother often served Steak Diane or Pork Chops Diablo to her guests. Mother didn't want to risk embarrassing them. For her part, Candy didn't seem to care. Her parents still saw their old friends in Levittown every weekend. She turned up the radio and we sang for a while.

Suddenly Candy jumped to her feet. "Hey, I got us some more of those Violets." She reached into her sock drawer and took out a small oval tin printed with old fashioned violet flowers. She opened it and offered the contents to me. I plucked out one of the pastel-colored candies and popped it in my mouth. Candy took one as well and closed the tin and slipped it back under her socks. "We have to take one every morning and every night, Annie. They're aphrodisiacs and their effect is cumulative. They will make us irresistibly sexy. We are going to get boyfriends this year. We're *not* going through our sophomore year of high school without boyfriends."

I nodded and said, "You know … I think the Violets might already be working because … because I mean … well, I think I *feel* sexy. And we've only been taking them a week."

"See." Candy's tone turned serious. "Gaye Parsons says they're very powerful. She says we're playing with fire."

We sat quietly letting the floral-tasting tablets dissolve on our tongues. I closed my eyes and focused on the sensation. "You know at first I thought these tasted like soap. But I'm getting used to them."

Candy nodded. "Gaye says nobody knows how amazing these are except us. Everyone thinks only old ladies buy them for their breath. But Gaye said that in Victorian times, ladies took these to get over being … you know … shy with their husbands about … you know."

"Mrs. Landers should get these. She needs them," I said thoughtfully.

"Why?"

"She won't be naked with Mr. Landers. Poor woman, she's very shy."

Candy inhaled sharply. "How do you know that?"

"My mother told me."

"Wow!"

"Maybe I should tell Mrs. Landers about them," I added, furrowing my brow with concern.

"Are you crazy? She'll tell your mother you're taking aphrodisiacs. Then your mother will tell *my* mother! Jeez, Annie! We'll be grounded for a month!" Candy stood up and retrieved the tin out from under her socks again. She opened it and offered it to me. "Just one more."

On my way home later that day, I passed Philip who was at his mailbox sorting through a stack of letters. He looked up and said, "Good afternoon, Miss Hughs. What have you been up to today?"

"I was sunbathing with my friend Candy." I was covered in a homemade concoction of baby oil and iodine that Candy and I used to intensify our tans. Philip let his eyes travel over my moist, bare arms and legs. I noticed the stack of mail in his hand. "My, you certainly get a lot of letters."

Philip nodded. "Fan mail. Well, actually it's hate mail. People who like my books tell their friends. People who hate my books tell me."

I gasped, "Don't read them!" I put out my hand. "I'll discard them for you if you like. I'll put them in our trash can so you won't ever have to see them again."

Philip's eyebrows lifted. "Oh, I have to read them, Leanne. They fuel my rage and give me the impetus to keep writing."

I considered this reasoning and said, "Well, then if I were you, Mr. Roth, I'd read them on a day when I was feeling completely sanguine. That's my advice. That way they won't leave you feeling so … depleted … emotionally."

Philip leaned towards me and looked in my eyes. "I want you to call me Philip. Remember?"

"Oh, that's right. Philip." I smiled at him.

"By the way, I like your fragrance, Leanne. You smell wonderful."

"Thank you. It's Canoe." I pronounced it Cah-noo-way. "It's a men's cologne."

Philip's eyebrows danced. "Oh yes. I know that one. But I think it's pronounced Canoe." He used the traditional pronunciation. Cah-noo.

"My friend Candy and I think it sounds French our way. Cah-noo-way. We think that sounds more discerning."

Philip looked into my eyes and said, "You know, now that I hear it again, I think you're right. Cah-noo-way does sound better than Cah-noo."

"Candy and I are very open minded about everything. We are children of our own time. And we aren't limited by labels. I mean when you think about cologne, I mean it's just a fragrance made from the essence of flowers. Flowers aren't masculine or feminine. That's just an empty designation. It inherently means nothing."

"I like the way you think, Lea—."

"I like the way *you* smell, Philip!" I said suddenly breathless, interrupting him. "I like your voice!" There was a moment of surprised silence during which Philip never took his eyes off my face. Then he said, "Would you like to join me on my patio? I can offer you a Coke."

I shook my head. "Thank you anyway. The Taylors are dining with us tonight. I need to dress for dinner." I started to step away, then I turned and faced him. "May I have a rain check, Philip?"

"Absolutely." Philip remained at the mailbox watching me cross the street. I could definitely feel his gaze on my back. My sunburn felt radioactive. I considered turning around one last time to wave goodbye so that I could study him a bit longer, but it wasn't necessary. I'd already memorized his face last night during our discourse. I could summon his visage at will now whenever I closed my eyes.

I entered our backyard through the gate and saw Mother and Ginger sitting side by side down at the pool studying swatches of fabrics that an interior decorator had dropped off last week. Mother was planning to have new slipcovers made for the couches in the family room. Daddy and Mr. Taylor were in the water playing with the Taylor boys—eight-year-old Evan, and six-year-old Matt—and my ten-year-old brothers, John and TJ. Evan Taylor waved happily and called, "Annie! Come, play with us!"

"I have to take a shower."

I noticed that Mr. Taylor was watching me with a strange expression on his face. I had heard Mother and Mrs. Taylor talking about him one afternoon last week. Mrs. Taylor had said that he was anxious about the Zoning Commission meeting in September. They were giving him a hard time about expanding the Pickering Manor Nursing Home into a new complex of individual apartments for older residents. Mr. Taylor and another man who lived in New Jersey had purchased Pickering Manor last Summer. After seventy-five years, it was in major need of repairs. And Mr. Taylor and his partner intended to completely rebuild it and make it the nicest, most modern facility for old people in the country. And then they would follow up with other "senior living residences" in other towns and states. Mr. Taylor thought it was a wise investment because people were living longer than ever and there would be an increasing demand for nice places for them to live when they got tired of cutting grass and changing out the storm windows in their houses but still didn't want to live out of the guest room in their kids' houses. This generation of old people wanted their "independence." So this was "an idea whose time had come." But the Pennswalk Zoning Commission was very conservative and frankly alarmed at all the changes happening so suddenly in and around the town. They were balking at giving the project approval. Unfortunately, Mr. Taylor had already purchased the adjacent plot of land, and now Mrs. Taylor said they were "cash-strapped." She said Mr. Taylor couldn't sleep most nights, and he was starting to lose his hair. I thought he still looked fine, but I felt bad that he was having to worry so much.

I hurried up the stone steps, across the patio and into the house, stopping in the kitchen to pour a glass of tea from a freshly brewed pitcher on the counter. It hadn't completely cooled yet and melted the ice cubes in my glass. Candy and I had polished off the whole tin of Violets while we were sunbathing and now, I felt queasy—like if I burped I would blow bubbles. But my encounter with Philip seemed to suggest that the Violets were having an impact. At one point I thought he might kiss me. I really wanted to be kissed. I thought about it a lot now.

I showered and dressed in fresh shorts and a pale blue cotton shirt. The phone rang. It was Mrs. Matthews.

"Hi Annie. What's up?"

"Nothing." For a fleeting second, I wanted to tell her about how Philip and I had spoken together twice now. And how it excited me. And how it seemed to really excite him. I trusted Mrs. Matthews. She and I would often talk about men, especially when she was at one of my parents' parties, and she was a little tipsy. She'd sneak up to my room and we'd tell each other secrets. I knew for example that she was thinking of divorcing her husband. She knew that I loved Paul McCartney.

"Listen, is your mother around?"

"Sure. I'll get her. Hold on."

"Excuse me for interrupting, Mother. Mrs. Matthews is on the phone."

Mother jumped up from her chair, knocking the blue and yellow floral cushion to the ground. She brushed past me, calling over her shoulder to Ginger, "It's probably about the next meeting at the Historical Society. I nominated Dinah for treasurer! We're taking over this town, Ginger. We're going to drag Pennswalk into the twentieth century!"

When she was gone, Mrs. Taylor patted the chair Mother had just vacated. I replaced the cushion and sat. Mrs. Taylor took my hand. "Every time I look at you, Annie, I remember the first time I set eyes on you. I was your mother's delivery nurse as you know. You weren't even one day old and I had already memorized your sweet face."

"I know … you always tell me that story."

"Your mother had had some difficulties with your birth so I had planned, as her nurse, to visit her a lot anyway. But that first day … gosh, your grandparents hadn't even seen you yet. And I brought you in to see your mother, but she was sleeping. So I just held you and waited for her to wake up. I kissed your dear little forehead and chin and sang to you. *I love you … a bushel and a peck....* And you loved it. You smiled at me. The very first day. I saw your first smile, Annie."

"I know, you told me ... I know."

Mrs. Taylor swallowed hard; her nose ran. She fumbled in her beach bag and pulled out a tissue. "Oh, this always makes me so emotional."

I heard my brother TJ at the other end of the pool calling "Marco" and Daddy answering "Polo!"

Mrs. Taylor resumed her story. "See I was trying to get pregnant back then."

I nodded. "Yes, Mrs. Taylor. You told me.... "

"It took five long years, Annie! And all that time I was working as a maternity nurse. That was so hard." She sniffed again. "So I wanted to take you home that day and hide you and raise you myself. Scary, huh? I was crazy! Instead I made up my mind that I'd just have to be your mother's best friend so I could watch you grow up. Nothing was going to separate us. Ever. Ever. So we moved into Linton Hill and here we are." Mrs. Taylor's eyes were liquid now like melted chocolate. She patted my hand. "You know, from the time you were born, you entered every room like you were expecting to be loved. And you have been. You're loved, Annie. You are the All-American Girl. Smart, pretty and adored. The world is your oyster."

I nodded. "Daddy says I have congenital confidence."

Mrs. Taylor laughed, a girlish cascade that sounded like singing. I had heard her version of the story of my birth often over the years. Always a slightly new variation. I hadn't heard the part about Mrs. Taylor wanting to kidnap me before; that was new. But the part about being an American girl with the world as my oyster was a consistent part of the telling each time. How could I not be confident?

I changed the subject. "Mrs. Taylor, have you ever heard of Violets? They're an old-fashioned … well, they are sold as candy. But apparently, they were used in Victorian times as aphrodisiacs."

Mrs. Taylor's eyes glistened. "No, I haven't heard of them. Why?"

"I just wondered. Mrs. Carey has them in her store on State Street. My friend Gaye did some research."

"I see," said Mrs. Taylor. "Maybe I should pick some up for Mr. Taylor? He's turning forty next month. And he's already becoming an old fuddy-duddy." She winked at me. Then she stood and stretched. "I better go help your mother pull dinner together." She walked up the steps and disappeared into the house.

Mr. Taylor walked briskly to where I was sitting and grabbed a towel out of his wife's beach bag which was leaning against my chair. I sat very still and studied the diving board, only watching him in my peripheral vision. He didn't look directly at me either. He dried his hair and shoulders, then wrapped the towel around his waist leaving his chest bare. Candy said that her sister Susan thought Mr. Taylor looked like the movie star Jeff Chandler. He was definitely handsome. In a conventional way. Tall, blonde, square-jawed. I, of course, preferred Philip's looks. Mr. Taylor said, "Annie, can you help me with something? I picked up some fruit at Yamamoto's this morning. It's in the trunk of my car. I want to give it to your mom. Strawberries. You like strawberries, right?"

I followed him out the gate and down the driveway. He opened the trunk of his car and handed me a watermelon. He started to reach for a box of strawberries; then suddenly turned and grabbed me, wrapping his arms around me pulling me close to him and kissing me. We were blocked from view of the others at the pool, and I continued to cling to the watermelon because I didn't know what else to do with it, but as his kiss became more penetrating, he pulled me in closer. I thought the watermelon would burst between us or I would crack open myself, but he didn't seem to notice. I gasped and he slipped his tongue into my mouth. I closed my eyes and tried to breathe as he pulled me in tighter and tighter until I moaned. He released me. He looked like he was going to cry. "Oh, Annie, you are so sweet!" he said with sudden urgency and I staggered back a step. He grabbed a couple bags of farm-fresh potatoes. And the box of strawberries. "Annie ... I...." He shook his head. He took a deep breath and closed the trunk. We walked side by side through the gate, up the stone steps, through the porch door, through the French doors into the house and finally entered the kitchen. Neither of us looked at each other for the rest of the evening.

That night, I went into my room and removed my clothes and studied myself in the big mirror over my bureau. I had a large bruise on my torso where the watermelon had been forced against me. It didn't hurt. I thought of how my mother had often told me that I came from a long line of strong women. She said she herself was born with formidable pain tolerance. That was how she always referred to her gift. "Formidable Pain Tolerance." I figured I must have it, too. I climbed into bed, wrapped my arms around my pillow and pulled it down on top of me. I kissed it and licked it with my tongue, the way Mr. Taylor had kissed me. And then I started kissing the palm of my hand. It was a method I had invented to learn how to be a first-rate kisser. Arlene had read my palm one day after Koffee Klatch back in May and told me I was going to fall in love this Summer. So I was seriously preparing to kiss and be kissed. And I wanted to do it well. I had begun experimenting with ways I might train myself and accidentally stumbled on this technique of kissing my palm. I stuck with it because it felt so incredibly good. Seriously. I even wrote a passage in my diary so I wouldn't accidentally forget any of the steps.

June 12, 1964

How to Learn to Kiss by Leanne T. Hughs

Hold your hand in front of your face, palm side in. Close your eyes. With your lips together begin lightly brushing the periphery of your palm in a clockwise rotation. The second time around, begin to separate your lips. Do it two times more, each time pressing your lips down against the flesh of your palm a bit more. Now do it again alternately pushing out your bottom lip then your top lip so that you can feel the sculpture of your palm more specifically with your individual lips. This will make sense when you do it. Register everything you feel. Take your time. Keep your eyes closed.

Now kiss the small padded mounds beneath each finger and push your lips into the deep dimples in between them. Explore the swell of the large "Mount of Venus" beneath your thumb. Brush your lips across the hair-fine lines that crisscross your outer palm. Make yourself find them with your lips and feel them. Really feel them. Plunge your mouth into the center of your palm and part your lips and let the tip of your tongue track your Heart, Head, and Life lines. Make yourself aware of the wetness. Do this many times. Take note of how you are not only aware of the excitement of kissing your palm; you are also aware of the excitement of your palm being kissed. Two sets of sensations. Notice that kissing involves both. When you are kissing you are also being kissed back. This will feel amazing and overwhelming. That's good. You should start to feel breathless. Now take tiny bites with just your front teeth deep in the center of your palm. Just as you are feeling an overwhelming sense of excitement, kiss the inside of your wrist intensely, quickly, like seven times.

If done right, you will know what an orgasm feels like.

ON TUESDAY NIGHT PHILIP was invited to dinner. I was standing in the garage with my ten-year-old brothers when he arrived. The door was up so Philip joined us. "Hi kids," he said. "What are you doing?"

"Chewing gum," said John.

I explained. "We're not allowed to chew gum in the house."

"My Dad says it makes the house stink like a cheap inner-city bus," TJ added.

I quickly changed the subject. "Philip, these are my brothers —John and TJ—that stands for Tom Junior. They're twins."

"We don't look alike," said John. "But Mother always calls us by the wrong name anyway."

"She called me the cat's name last week," said TJ and punctuated that bon mot with a snap of his gum. "She's a piece of work, that one."

I turned to my brothers. "This is Mr. Roth. He's the writer Mother told you about."

John said, "My mother thinks you're handsome."

"Stop it, John!" I said sharply.

TJ asked, "Have you ever been on a city bus, Mr. Roth?"

"Yeah, I grew up in Newark. That's a city in New Jersey."

"Did the bus smell like spearmint gum?" John asked.

Philip scratched his chin. "I'm not sure I ever noticed."

TJ jumped in again. "Do you know any Black people?"

I sputtered, "TJ! Don't be so provincial!"

John clarified, "My dad has a Black friend. Mr. Reynolds. He teaches math at the university where Dad works. He tried to buy a house in Pennswalk but no one here will sell to a Black family because it makes their property value go down. That's rotten, isn't it?"

TJ shook his head, "It stinks like an inner-city bus."

I jumped in again. "Philip, would you like to take a swim?"

Philip ignored me. His dark eyes were focused on my brothers, encouraging them to keep talking. TJ snapped his gum again and offered this gem: "My dad thinks he has a versatile face. And that's why all of Dad's Italian friends think he's Italian. All his Irish friends think he's Irish. All his Jewish friends think he's Jewish." John picked up on the theme. In a dopey voice, he added, "All his Chinese friends think he's Chinese. All his Black friends think he's Black." TJ roared with laughter. "Good one, John!" They punched each other playfully. It irritated me the way they were each other's best audience. But Philip seemed to enjoy it thoroughly. He grinned broadly and eventually he, too, erupted with laughter. I was mortified by my brothers' stupidity at exposing my father's stupidity.

"You boys play sports?" Philip didn't think to ask me.

TJ nodded, "Yep. Baseball. We're both on the same Little League team. John's the pitcher. I play short stop."

"Great sport. I wanted to be a professional baseball player when I was growing up. Maybe I'll catch some of your games this Summer."

"That would be cool," said John.

"I had you down for basketball," said TJ. "You're one tall drink of water." Sometimes it was hard to remember he was only ten. He talked like an old man.

"Bad back interrupted everything," Philip replied.

I interjected myself, "I'm on the high school swim team."

Over a dinner of grilled chicken and corn on the cob, Mother asked Philip if he had a girlfriend. He smiled politely and answered. "I'm married."

My heart sank.

"I'm in the process of divorcing her."

My heart leaped. But Mother said, "Oh" and lightly patted Philip's hand. "I'm so sorry. Where does she live?"

"I'm not interested in talking about it." An awkward silence followed John farted and TJ laughed and yelled, "WHOA, JOHN!"

Mother snapped, "John, how crude!"

TJ said, "Well, as Dad always says, 'Better to do it and bear the shame than not to do it and bear the pain.' Right, Dad?" John, sitting beside TJ, giggled helplessly.

Mother glared at Daddy, then scowled at my brothers. "Both of you boys are excused. Please leave the table. Now."

TJ and John were still snickering as they got up from their chairs and looked at Dad who waved them off. Mother's face was bright red. "Philip, I apologize. These children know better. It's this one you know." She pointed to my father. "Biggest kid of the bunch."

Philip shrugged and said, "Believe it or not, Bev, I was once a ten-year-old boy. And I have a brother. And I well remember there was nothing as entertaining to us as our own body functions. And it only got worse in adolescence when we discovered girls." Philip winked at me.

ON WEDNESDAY, MOTHER TOOK TJ and John with her to the Taylors' house for the day. They lived up the hill at the end of Linton Hill Drive. They had a pool, too. And a new puppy. Daddy had a conference to attend in Philadelphia. And Candy was with her cousins in Levittown. Left to my own devices, I read for a while and then in the afternoon, I went down to the pool for a leisurely swim in the nude.

I removed my madras shirt and navy shorts and folded them, laying them on one of the chaises next to my beach towel. Then I removed my panties and bra and placed them with my clothes. I walked to the diving board, conscious of the sun on my skin, it was an intensely hot day. I stood at the end of our low diving board and stretched my arms over my head. I looked up, then I looked down at the water, and dove in. My mother had hired someone in the early Spring to paint the pool sky blue with soft white clouds throughout. Now on days when the color of the sky matched the color of the pool, I felt suspended between heaven and earth just lying on the surface of the water. That was the case today. *As above so below.*

I swam submerged for half the length of the deep end. Then I erupted from the depths like a dolphin, smiling and inhaling deeply. I flipped onto my back and began laps—a slow backstroke, up and down the pool. The water rippled along the sides of my body and between my thighs as I flutter-kicked my legs. The surface of the pool shimmered like silver. It made me think of mercury. No, not the planet. I'm talking about the element used in a thermometer. One Saturday during the Winter, my dad had deliberately broken the thermometer in our medicine chest to show us how mercury acts. Mother had a fit; she screamed at us not to touch it. But Dad said, "Oh, Bev—it's poisonous but not radioactive. Relax." He pulled the puddle around the kitchen table with his broad index finger and noted with amazement how the silvery liquid re-collected itself into a perfectly domed puddle again and again. "Isn't that cool? It's as if it knows itself," he said. Now I believed that everything was conscious. Everything! Even water. Especially water. I told myself that water is alive! I had already heard its voice—the ocean would call to me during our vacations at Rehoboth Beach. And when I walked along the creek that ran behind our yard, I actually felt like we—the creek and I—were conversing. There weren't words, but it was language and I understood it. I even heard water's voice when I was alone in the pool. I concluded that water is God. I will always believe that. Just think about it—nothing alive can exist without water. Hence water is the life force, hence water is the Creator. I think I'm right about this.

At that moment, the Creator was running its hand down my stomach. I locked my legs together. From my waist down, my limbs were now fused into a tail which I snapped and swayed as I dove deeply under the surface to glide along the bottom where the clouds were. I felt like a sea creature. Mrs. Williams had an index card on a bookshelf in the living room of her house. On it was written *I must be a mermaid. I have no fear of depths and a great fear of shallow living.* I had memorized that quote. I said it to myself all the time.

I suddenly heard the wind chime. It had been a gift for Mother from my brothers on her birthday back in April. Dad had hung it on a tree in the yard but Mother made him move it. "No, Tom!" she said. "Birds nest there. You'll disturb their pattern." Then he suspended it on a Shepherd's hook by the fence near a happy patch of Black-Eyed Susans and Mother again admonished him. "Tom! That will startle the bees. We need the bees to come and gather pollen." Mother had read *Silent Spring* over the Winter and had been seriously rethinking the gardens that grew along the perimeter of our yard ever since, adding specific native varieties to attract bees and butterflies, and eliminating the use of pesticides. "Bugs are our friends" had become her mantra. Except Japanese Beetles. She plucked those off the roses with her fingers and dropped them into a mason jar full of gasoline. She said it was a quick and painless death. I didn't see how that could be and on nights when I couldn't sleep, I imagined hundreds of shiny little beetles screaming in Japanese. In the end Dad fastened the wind chime to the gate. It never made a sound now except when someone entered the yard....

I turned with a start and saw Philip standing at the edge of the pool, wearing his swim trunks, carrying a towel. I was in the shallow end so I crouched down, only my head and shoulders above the water but I knew he could see everything, had already seen everything. And he hadn't turned away. After a moment during which my body froze and my mind raced, I stood up and let him look at my naked breasts. I watched him watch me. Our eyes met again. Neither of us spoke. I could hear the water cooing. I could hear rose buds opening. I had a sudden urge to laugh, and Philip finally spoke. "Your mother said I could use the pool this afternoon. She said that no one would be home."

"I guess she forgot that I'm someone."

I walked slowly up the wide steps at the shallow end of the pool and out of the water. Not rushing. Not covering myself. I retrieved my towel from the chaise and deliberately wrapped it around me knowing Philip was watching my every move. I took my time, tucked it snugly between my breasts, gathered up my clothes and walked unhurriedly past him, toward the house. I said as I passed, "It's all yours now."

Chapter 3

Nine days passed before I saw Philip again. I watched his house but his windows were dark every evening and I saw no signs of him during the day. Not a trace since I walked past him wrapped in my beach towel. I had been sick with worry that he might have left town forever without even saying goodbye to me. But I tried not to let on to anyone that I even noticed. So on Thursday, I went with Candy to see *A Hard Day's Night* in Philadelphia. Candy's sister Susan drove us. She's seventeen. Her best friend Darlene Estes came, too. It was so *fab*, even better than we expected. Candy just went crazy over George, but even though I really loved Paul, I have to be honest, I found John sexier. He seemed more grown up. And I preferred older men now.

Candy and I went to the Youth Center Dance that week. There was one every Friday night year-round except Good Friday and of course Christmas if it fell on a Friday. The admission was a dollar. My friends rarely missed a dance—especially Lark and Betsy—and we finally got Gaye to start going even though she was a pretty bad dancer. She just couldn't seem to discern the beat. But I'd always dance some dances with her—even though it was embarrassing. I didn't want her to feel left out. On the other hand, Candy was a terrific dancer so most of the time I danced with her.

Candy and I had been dancing for about twenty minutes when "The Bristol Stomp" came on. That was our favorite. At one point I twirled and when I was again facing Candy, she wasn't there. In her place was a senior boy named Jeff Wetherill. He had cut in on Candy and was now dancing with me. Candy had retreated to the side of the dance floor and was now looking at me with an expression that broadcast hurt and fear. But Jeff was smiling at me. I looked at my feet and kept dancing until the song ended. Then I turned to leave the floor, but Sam Cooke's "You Send Me" came on and the lights shifted for a "slow dance" and before I could rejoin my friends, Jeff put his arm around my back and took my right hand in his left. He smiled at me again and led me back out onto the floor. I saw Betsy, Gaye and Lark now standing with Candy, staring open-mouthed at me. The dance floor cleared of everyone except couples.

Jeff said, "You're Annie, right? I'm Jeff." "Yes, I know." "You're a good dancer," he said pleasantly. "Thank you. So are you," I said, still not looking at him. "I've just never danced with a boy before." "That's okay," he said. "As I always say, there's a first time for everything."

When the dance ended, I thanked him and walked away. I retrieved my pocketbook, and without saying a word to anyone, quickly walked out of the building and headed for home.

"Wait up!" It was Candy running behind me. "You were dancing with Jeff Wetherill! My God, Annie!"

"But he didn't ask me. He should have said 'May I have this dance?'"

Candy shrugged. "I don't think they have to ask. I think they just dance with you if they want to."

"Candy, why is everyone noticing me lately?" It was a rhetorical question. We both knew why. It was my breasts.

But Candy responded, "I don't know, but I think you better stop taking those Violets."

ARLENE SWENSON TOUCHED UP everyone's roots at the Koffee Klatch the following Wednesday, including mine. She whispered in my ear, "Come see me tomorrow. I have to talk to you." I said okay and excused myself and went upstairs and grabbed my diary and thesaurus. I stationed myself at the window in my parents' bathroom because I wanted to listen to the women talk and see if they said anything about Philip. Maybe they knew why he left.

Laura Armitage was the one doing most of the talking that morning. She had recently moved out of Linton Hill and into a very grand house just outside the Pennswalk town limits. It sat alone in the center of what had been the Stetson Farm only a year ago. Mother said that Dr. Armitage's practice was thriving. He was an obstetrician and all the new young couples who were moving to Pennswalk were having babies now that they had houses large enough to accommodate bigger families. Mother believed strongly that every child deserved a room of their own and the new houses all boasted a minimum of four bedrooms, three and a half baths. "Children need privacy," Mother said. "It's a fundamental American value."

Laura Armitage was a real professional model before she got married. She had been in magazine ads for Polaroid and Halo shampoo, and she still had an agent in Philadelphia who called her from time to time when the client was looking for an older model. Laura Armitage was the same age as my mother, thirty-eight. I thought she looked a lot like Mother even more so now that they were both blonde. But her voice was always a surprise to people who were meeting her for the first time. It was deep and unnaturally controlled. It was the voice of a powerful woman, a woman who knew what she wanted. She was doing most of the talking that afternoon. She crossed her legs. "So I decided what was good for the goose was good for the gander. I said, 'Bill—I know full well that you are screwing every nurse in your office.'"

Mrs. Matthews swore, "Oh, shit." She lit a cigarette.

Laura Armitage continued, "I know Bill hires them on the basis of their sexual appeal to him." She removed her sunglasses and her hazel eyes flickered with such intense anger that I could feel the burn in the bathroom on the second story of our house. But her voice remained calm as always. I wrote *preternaturally calm* in my diary. Laura Armitage continued, "He's been unfaithful to me since the beginning of our marriage. He's polymorphously perverse."

"Oh, mother of God," gasped Kitty Landers and crossed herself. I wrote the word *polymorphously* in my diary.

Mother had told me once that Kitty Landers had been a Catholic and that the Pope had actually excommunicated her for marrying Mr. Landers because he was a Presbyterian, which hurt her terribly because she couldn't take communion anymore. Mother said that just revealed how out of touch the Catholic Church was. It always blames the woman; not that any other religion was that on the ball which was why we didn't go to St. James Episcopal anymore.

Laura Armitage was still talking, "He says one woman isn't enough for him."

"Oh, please," said Dinah Matthews.

"So I've taken a lover," said Laura Armitage. I almost fell out of the window hearing that. The other women became preternaturally still.

Laura stood up now and walked to the shallow end of the pool. She swung her leg over the water and dipped her toes. "Mmmmm … that's nice," she said. Then she walked down the wide steps into the blue. She kept her head and chest above the surface and moved slowly in circles, caressing the water with her arms and cupping handfuls to splash over her chest. The other women moved to the shallow end and sat on the steps.

"Do we know him?" asked Ginger Taylor. "Your lover, I mean?"

Laura shook her head, "He's one of the men who's working on the new houses that are being built in that new development on Washington Lane. You know where Fleming's apple orchard used to be? The new split-levels?"

"By the school?'

"No … the other side. Next to where they built the new car dealership. Anyway, he's on the construction crew. I stood next to him at the deli counter one day and we just started to talk. You should see his arms. You should see his.…" Laura shivered slightly and sighed suggestively. There was a long silence.

"So now what?" said Mother. "Are you going to divorce Bill and marry this man?"

"No, God, no. Bill and I have to stay married. Janine has four years of high school ahead and then college. And a wedding after that. I mean eventually. Besides Bill and I still enjoy sex with each other. And we're good friends."

Kitty Landers stood up. "I'm going to have to go. I'm getting one of my headaches. It's not you, Laura. I just need to be in a dark room." She walked carefully out the gate and headed next door. The other women remained, so riveted by Laura's confession that they barely noticed Kitty leave.

Laura resumed her story. "So Bill and I have agreed to have an open marriage. That's what it's called. We are each going to have lovers. As many as we please. But we will stay married." She looked into my mother's worried eyes. "Monogamy doesn't work for everyone, Bev. Marriage between people like Bill and me—it has to be elastic. I guess I've always known that. I'm probably more like him than I ever wanted to admit. Maybe that's why I married him. He's willing to give me the freedom to explore my appetites."

"Well, you know I will absolutely support you, Laura," said Mother with complete sincerity. The other women looked less certain. Mother added, "So do you want me to invite your lovers—yours and Bill's—to my Midsummer Soiree … or…?"

Laura chuckled huskily. "I'll let you know. Let's just leave things as they are for now. Don't worry, Bev. I'm still me." She scooped up water in her cupped hands and tossed it playfully in my mother's direction.

Ginger Taylor didn't leave the Koffee-Klatch with the others that afternoon. She and Mother had signaled to each other that they needed to talk privately when they were alone. About Laura. About open marriage. About the man building the split-level just over the hill. They talked for two hours. They split a ham sandwich and a pickle late in the afternoon as they had forgotten about lunch. It was another hot and steamy day. I almost fell asleep at the window of the master bathroom upstairs. But I splashed some water from the sink on my face and continued to take notes. I had already filled one diary that Summer and was working on a second.

Finally, around four o'clock, the sun tucked itself behind the tall oak trees on the west side of the yard. The pool was shaded now, the water cooled. Mother dove in and Ginger picked up a couple of the inflatable rafts that were leaning against the split rail fence. She tossed one to Mother who climbed on top. Then Ginger entered the pool and adjusted herself on her float. The two women closed their eyes and drifted lazily around the pool, pushing off with their toes when they came too close to the wall.

"Laura … Laura … Laura," said Mother.

Mrs. Taylor sighed. "True."

I HAD NEVER BEEN in Arlene's house before. I don't know what I expected, but I was surprised by what I found there. Stainless steel tables with white upholstered chairs and couches that were almost indistinguishable from the chalk white walls. The paintings were abstracts in grey and taupe. The windows were covered in white louvered blinds which shut out the glory of that July day. There wasn't even a random piece of fruit on the counter in the white kitchen; no trace of color at all. The rooms were joyless like an abandoned gallery in an art museum. Arlene sat on a stool by the kitchen sink and sipped a diet cola. She wore a white shirt and oyster-colored capris. She looked tired but happy that I was there. "I want to show you something, Annie."

She led me downstairs to what I assumed was the family room. She flipped a switch and a number of overhead lights came on. It took a minute for my eyes to adjust. But when I could see again, I was surprised. There were three large barber chairs before me. Each faced a tall wall mirror. A counter under each mirror was crowded with jars of clear liquid that held combs and brushes in various sizes. There were trays of scissors and handheld hair dryers and curling irons. And baskets of hair pins. On the walls were framed photographs of beautiful women in the latest coiffures. Along the north wall were three hair dryers, the large commercial ones that swallowed your whole head when you sat underneath them.

Finally, there was a waiting room area with deep, red-velvet love seats adorned with assorted paisley pillows. End tables with elaborately carved legs were piled high with magazines. And, near the stairs, a tall table held a cash register and a bowl of wrapped mints.

"Welcome to my happy place," Arlene said and disappeared behind a curtain. Almost immediately, the room filled with music. I recognized Dean Martin's voice. *When the moon hits your eye like a big pizza pie....* Arlene swayed from side to side. "C'mere, I'll teach you the tarantella." I took her hand and playfully took a few steps. She swirled me around and laughed, "Okay. Another time. Sit ... sit. Try out the chairs." I hopped onto one. "So what do you think, Annie?"

"It's like a real hair salon."

She laughed. "It is a real hair salon. I'm opening for business in two weeks. I'm waiting for the rest of my supplies to come in. I want to sell a line of products that we used to sell at Jimmy's. It's first-rate, Annie, and I want my customers to have the very best. Because they are important to me. They are all my friends. That's how you build a business. Make your customers your friends. Or your friends your customers." She laughed happily.

"Does Mr. Swenson like the salon?"

"He doesn't care." She bit her lip. "Okay ... here's the thing. Eric's good to me. Very good to me. But our marriage ... it's complicated. You know?" I didn't know but I nodded and she continued. "I have to have a job, Annie. I can't be content just sitting around the house and shopping and decorating. I'm not judging. I don't want you to think I don't enjoy the girls. I love your mother. I'm telling you I worship your mother."

"Well, I think it's great that you are going to have a business. Mrs. Matthews works and she's very happy. I'm going to work when I grow up."

"Okay, here's the thing, Annie ... I'm going to have to charge from now on. You know ... for the cuts and colors. You don't think the girls will think I'm being pushy?"

"No. You have every right to expect to be paid. You're a professional. You have a career. I'll pay for you to do my hair."

"Oh, Honey—you and your mom will always get your cut and color for free. I want your mom to be my best friend. I told you I love her."

I HAD A DENTAL appointment on Friday morning with Dr. Zoeller and I was walking home along Lincoln Avenue, when I heard a slight honk and turned to see Philip in the car that was pulling up beside me. My heart jumped. The windows were rolled down. He leaned across the passenger seat and called to me, "Hey, Miss Hughs, want a lift?" He stopped the car and I got in. He pulled away from the curb.

"Philip! Where did you go?"

"I had business to take care of in New York and then I spent some time with my parents."

"In Newark?"

"No. I moved them to Elizabeth a number of years ago. It's quieter."

"Did you see your wife?"

"None of your business."

I slid close to him and whispered, "I figure we broke the ice that day at the pool, Philip. I hope you know that you can trust me with your secrets."

"Okay. Listen...." He turned the car onto a quiet street and turned off the engine. He looked at me. He was no longer smiling. "Leanne, you're an alluring girl, but you are a girl. I mean I understand how intensely you are experiencing this time in your life. I was also fourteen once. And it's natural to be curious about the effect your body has on men. And like I said I was your age once so I know how...."

"Don't put me in a Venn diagram, Philip! To see how I overlap with other kids my age! I AM SUI GENERIS!"

"Leanne—"

"I'M IN LOVE WITH YOU!!" Oh god. I said it. I looked down at my lap. I did love him and he knew it. I knew he knew it.

Philip sighed and then, in a gentle voice, said, "Leanne. It won't work. You are simply too young."

"That's stupid. Who writes the rules?"

Philip's eyes became bullets. "There are LAWS! I could be ARREST-ED! Do you understand that? You would ruin my career. Is that what you want? To ruin my LIFE! Are you THAT kind of woman, Leanne? I've already made one colossal mistake." He paused. "You're FOURTEEN for God's sake."

Tears splashed on my blouse. I choked on my words. "I'm going to be fifteen next month. How … how old do I have to be for you to… ? Sixteen? Seventeen?"

"Twenty-one," he said, calmly. He pulled a neatly folded handker-chief out of a pocket in his slacks and handed it to me. "And you must have graduated from college. Those are my terms."

I counted on my fingers. "But that's six years from now. You'll be…."

"Old? Yes, Leanne, I will be nearing forty. You may no longer even desire me."

I wiped my eyes. We sat quietly now both facing the front window. I reviewed every word Philip had said in those past couple of minutes and I quickly came to the conclusion that there was reason for hope. Philip had just clearly insinuated that he loved me back, that he was willing to wait for me. My heart pounded. My mottled face brightened. "I can wait six years," I said. "And I don't care how old you get, Philip. You don't have to worry. I will always love you. You are my soul."

Philip looked at me, an expression in his eyes that I couldn't readily interpret. He leaned toward me and I thought he might kiss me. Instead, he whispered, "Okay. Okay."

I WALKED OVER TO Candy's that afternoon and invited her to swim. My brothers had a Little League Tournament so Mother was in Richboro all day, smearing zinc oxide on their noses to prevent sunburn and feeding them grapes which she said gave you stamina because "unbeknownst to most Americans," grapes are full of iron. The Taylor boys were in the tournament, too, so Ginger and Mother drove there together.

Candy and I floated on our backs and talked. Paul McCartney had a girlfriend now, a British actress named Jane Asher. George had an actress girlfriend too, Patti Boyd. She had been in their movie. I really wanted to look like her—skinny with a flat chest and a gap between her teeth that was so adorable that it made me regret getting braces when I was twelve. But Candy said she could no longer fantasize about being George's girl-friend—now that he had such a public relationship with Patti. She added, "I would feel like a home wrecker. I couldn't do that to Patti. And anyway, George is twenty and Paul is twenty-two. They are seriously too old for us, Annie."

I didn't reply. I had never told her that I was in love with Philip. I knew she would be shocked. Maybe even grossed out because he was even older than Paul. Mainly, I just didn't feel like defending my deep feelings for Philip even though Candy was my dearest friend on earth. Someday I would tell her, of course, when we became roommates at college and she was more mature. Anyway, Candy mentioned that a new family had moved into the house up the street from us. Candy said they had a girl exactly our age. Her name was Natalie. She would attend our school in the Fall. Candy added, "And her family is Catholic! So they will go to St. Michael's like my family does."

We were lying on the chaises when I heard a car in the driveway. I got up and walked to the gate in time to see Jeff Wetherill get out of his car and wave to me. I stood in front of him, stopping him from going further toward our yard. I felt so self-conscious in my bathing suit, but Jeff just smiled and said, "Hi. I was in the neighborhood."

"You were not," I said smiling back at him. *For the first time, I noticed that Jeff looked like Troy Donahue on Surfside 6, which was my favorite TV show during junior high. He had the same blonde hair and clear blue eyes. Troy Donahue was really cute on that show.*

"I came over to invite you to a party at my house, Annie. Not this Saturday but the next."

My face reddened, "I won't know anyone."

Jeff took a step toward me. "Well, you'll know me. And I'll introduce you to my friends. Heck, I'm not going to leave you standing in the kitchen with my mom."

Out of the corner of my eye, I caught a glimpse of Candy. She had tucked herself behind a large patch of day lilies inside the gate. She was watching us.

Suddenly it was as if I were in a movie. A movie starring Troy Donahue and me. And Candy was my audience. I was playing a role. I thought of Connie Stevens, the beautiful blonde actress in the movie Parish. I remembered her scenes with Troy Donahue in that movie. And suddenly I knew what to do. I kept my chin down and lifted only my eyes to look at him. I offered him a small smile, you know coy, somewhat teasing, but mysterious. I swung my hips slightly to one side and bent one knee. Contrapposto. I took an art history class last year and we studied ancient Greek statues.

I pouted, "I don't drive. How will I get there?"

"I'll come get you," he answered, breathlessly.

I saw that something in his expression had changed. He took a step toward me. I guess I had signaled something significant. I thought I better slow this down. "I'll have to ask my mother."

"Sure," he said with a slight frown. Then he took a piece of paper out of his shorts pocket and handed it to me. "Here's my phone number."

"Thank you." *Girls aren't supposed to call boys! Jeez, Jeff!*

"So, can I have yours?"

"Yeah … It's … uh … it's uh … I forget what my phone number is!" I thought, *I'm going to faint if this doesn't end soon.*

"That's all right. I'll just look it up in the phone book." We stood there in awkward silence. Then he said, "Wanna take a ride?"

"Right now?"

"Get an ice cream cone?"

"I can't. My best friend Candy is here."

Candy stepped out of hiding. She tossed her hair, "Hi Jeff."

He greeted her pleasantly but didn't invite her to the party. Instead he said, "Well, I guess I'll hit the road. You going to the Youth Center dance on Friday, Annie?"

"Um … I guess," I said.

"I'll see you then. Nice to meet you, Candy." And he got in the car and expertly backed down our long driveway and drove off. Candy and I avoided looking at each other. "I should be going, too," she said.

THE TAYLORS JOINED US for dinner that night. The men played basketball in the driveway with the boys, then all of them jumped into the pool to cool down. I had taken a shower after Candy left and changed into a bubblegum pink sun dress. On my way down to the pool, I passed Mother and Mrs. Taylor in the kitchen, standing side by side at the sink. Mother was seasoning steaks while Mrs. Taylor wrapped baking potatoes in aluminum foil. Mother said, "I think green beans?" and Mrs. Taylor replied, "Can't go wrong with that."

Mr. Taylor got out of the pool as I was taking a seat and wrapped himself in a towel.

"Annie, come help me. I picked up some more strawberries at Yamamoto's for your mom. And some local tomatoes. I need a hand."

I followed him to his car. He popped the trunk and turned to me. He put his hands on my shoulders and smiled. "Hi, Sweetheart," he whispered leaning in to kiss me, but I put my hand up over his mouth. "I can't, Mr. Taylor. I have pledged my troth to another."

He pulled back and looked at me confused. "You what?"

I lowered my hand and repeated, "I pledged my troth. To someone else."

He frowned. "You have a boyfriend?"

I wasn't sure what to call Philip, but I nodded. Mr. Taylor looked like he might cry. "Annie, you must think I'm ridiculous."

"No, I don't. I understand...."

"I'm going through a bad patch."

"I know."

"I haven't been myself." He sighed heavily.

I nodded. "Mrs. Taylor told me you're turning forty. But older men can be very attractive, Mr. Taylor, so you shouldn't worry. And Mrs. Taylor really loves you so you're lucky. You have a good marriage."

He looked at me. "How do you know all of this?"

"The women all see me as a peer. They're comfortable talking around me."

"A peer?"

"Yes, you know. I'm accepted as one of them."

"And your mother? What does she think of that?"

"Well, she doesn't see me as a daughter. She sees me as a friend."

"That's too bad," said Mr. Taylor. "I think you need a mother." He handed me a sack of tomatoes that smelled like the earth and grabbed the strawberries and closed the hood. Then he put an arm around my shoulders and gave me an affectionate squeeze. We walked back into the yard.

Chapter 4

My parents had one of those Black lawn jockey statues in front of our house. Made of iron, he stood at the entrance to the walkway that extended from the driveway to the front door of our colonial-style house, holding an old-fashioned lantern that lit up after dark. Mother said he was painted to look like a jockey at the Kentucky Derby, in his little red jacket and cap, and that he was there to welcome Daddy home from the "daily rat race." But I insisted that he represented a nineteenth-century slave child lighting the way for his master. We fought constantly about it.

"It's sick, Mother! I'm mortified every time one of my friends sees it! Apart from the fact that it's pretentious, it's horribly racist!"

"He's not a slave, Annie! He's there to represent a friend of the family."

"We don't have any Black friends! At least let me make him Caucasian."

She finally gave in and bought me a pint of "flesh-colored" paint. I painted his face first, then each hand. I was just finishing the job when Philip arrived for his four o'clock swim. He took a seat beside me on the lawn and watched for a moment. I avoided looking at him, but I could sense that he was amused. Finally, I said, "I just couldn't stand it anymore." I carefully dabbed a second coat on his little brown hands. Philip laughed.

My brothers arrived on their bikes and joined us. "God, Annie! Now he looks like a baby pig with a little suit on," said TJ.

"Yeah, he's too pink," said John.

"I didn't pick the color. At least he's not Black."

John cocked his head to one side and studied it. "Did you know this was supposed to be a slave, Mr. Roth?"

Philip shrugged and said, "Actually, I thought it was just there to represent your father's versatile face."

My brothers exploded with laughter. "Good one, Mr. Roth," said TJ. "Good one!" echoed John. I rolled my eyes and Philip poked me in the side, "Oh, come on, Leanne, you have to admit that was funny."

Mother's station wagon barreled down our long driveway and screeched to a stop at the end. She snapped off the engine and jumped out of the car. "Boys! Bring those garbage cans back up to the garage. This minute! If Daddy sees them still at the curb when he gets home, he'll have a fit!" Then she stomped to the back door, yelling over her shoulder, "And no one goes in the house until I say so. Mrs. Knox is cleaning the bathrooms today!" She disappeared inside slamming the door behind her.

"Hellzapoppin! Who pooped in her Easter basket?" said TJ.

John turned to Philip and explained, "Mother says Mrs. Knox is White trailer trash so we can't be around her."

I said, "Just get the garbage cans, guys. And put your bikes away."

Philip walked with me into the garage where I put the paint can up on a shelf and put the brush in a jar of turpentine so that it could soak. He said, "Wanna swim some laps with me?"

"Can't," I said. "My suit is in the house, and I can't go in until Mrs. Knox leaves."

He smiled and said, "I thought you liked to swim au naturel."

I turned scarlet so fast, I almost gasped. I just wasn't expecting him to mention that. He noticed my reaction and laughed softly, "Wow, I actually embarrassed Leanne Hughs. I didn't think that was possible." He slipped his arms around my shoulders and cradled me for a long minute. "Hey … don't be embarrassed, Honey. If you want to be a serious writer, you have to be shameless. And you definitely shocked me that day. Frankly I was impressed with your courage. And your poise. And your...." He grinned naughtily. I turned redder. He took my hand now and pulled me toward the pool. "Come on. You can keep me company."

I watched Philip swim. He was tall and lean with long arms that cut through the water in powerful strokes. Inside my head, I keep replaying his soft voice calling me Honey. *Don't be embarrassed, Honey.* I wanted to take off my clothes and slip into the water beside him. But I didn't. After twenty-five laps he pulled himself out of the pool and sat next to me on the warm flagstone tile. "So—this Mrs. Knox. What's the story there?"

"She was our cleaning lady all last year, but she and her husband would fight on the phone—our kitchen phone. And she would call him names. Like shit head and deadbeat and SOB and one time she even used the F-word and my brothers were in hearing range. And Mother heard her, too."

Philip threw his head back and laughed. "My god, you upper-middle-class people have your challenges, don't you?"

"So Mother, of course, fired her. And called the agency and asked them to send someone else. Preferably someone religious. For some reason, even though my mother disapproves of religion, she thinks religious people are more polite. I, of course, bring up the oh-so-polite Salem Witch Trials and the Spanish Inquisition and Mother says, 'Whatever, Annie.'"

Philip laughed again and I continued. "Anyway, the agency sent us Tynetta and she's a young Black Muslim which Mother wasn't expecting. Well, none of us was expecting a Black Muslim. But we all sort of know something about the Black Muslims because of Muhammad Ali. Whom, by the way, my brothers and Dad admire. And I do too even though I don't like to watch him fight. I just like to listen to him talk. He's so honest. I find that sort of public discourse revitalizing. Anyway— things got off to a bad start between Tynetta and Mother and she quit halfway through the first day."

Philip's eyebrows were animated now. "What happened? Did she take offense at the slave child lighting the path to your house?"

"Probably. But that was just one of the misunderstandings that day. Tynetta wears this long black dress that covers everything from her neck to her feet. And she wears a black scarf over her hair. Obviously, it's a deliberate choice. It's like a uniform. Many of the female followers of Elijah Muhammad dress that way. I've seen pictures in *Life* magazine. But of course, my mother doesn't do any investigation; she just assumes that Tynetta has bad taste. Or that she's poor. So Mother says, *Oh, Honey, you look so hot. Why don't you wear something of Annie's at least while you're cleaning?* And Tynetta said no. And then, ignoring that, Mother went and put an outfit together out of my bureau—pedal pushers and a sleeveless blouse and Tynetta still said NO. Then Mother asked if she had a boyfriend and Tynetta said NO. Then Mother asked her if she was saving her money to go to college and Tynetta said I QUIT. So we got Mrs. Knox back. Better the devil you know, right? But now we have to stand outside until she's finished cleaning just in case she calls her husband 'a lazy fucking asshole' again."

Philip laughed so hard he startled the wrens at the bird feeder. They spiraled into the sky and departed our yard for the rest of the day. "All I can say, Leanne, is I hope you're taking notes on all of this."

"Of course, I am," I said. "Aren't you?" Philip laughed again.

That evening, my brothers and I ate Sloppy Joes by ourselves, sitting on the porch. My parents were having an extended cocktail hour by themselves at the bar in the family room downstairs. At one point I went into the kitchen to get more iced tea and overheard my father's voice exclaim, "Jesus Christ! That goddamn guinea!"

Late that night, Mother knocked on the door of my room. "Annie? Are you still awake?" She entered and sat on my bed, cross-legged, facing me. Her face was discolored like she'd been crying hard.

"Mother, what's the matter?"

"I got a call from Caroline Miller today. She's on the Zoning Commission. She wanted to give me a heads up. Apparently, Arlene Swenson has applied for a variance so that she can put a hair salon on our street.

In her house! A business! Oh my god!!" Mother closed her eyes and anxiously rubbed her temples.

"I know, Mother. She showed me the shop."

"She what?"

"It's nice! It's downstairs in her family room. She has chairs and hairdryers. It looks like a real salon."

"Oh my god, Annie!! And you didn't tell me? How could you not tell me right away?"

"I thought she wanted to announce it herself at Koffee Klatch. She's very excited about it. I thought you would be happy about it, too. She said she's going to charge everyone except you."

"Annie, do you know what that would do to our property values? To have a hair salon on our street? Do you know how people would see us after that? My God, that's what they do in Philadelphia. I mean we might as well live in an apartment. God, we'd never be able to sell our house for the price we want."

I gasped. "Are we moving?"

"No. Not any time soon. I just mean someday." Mother began to pace, wringing her hands, then twisting her diamond ring around and around her finger. "I should have known better than to try…. Honest to God. That woman! I mean I knew she wasn't our class. She didn't even go to college. And she lived in a really crummy part of Philadelphia, Annie. I'm sorry to seem so judgmental. But it's a fact." Mother started to cry. "Daddy is so mad at me."

"Oh, Mother…." She sat on my bed again and I rubbed her arm, trying to comfort her. "I'm too nice, Annie. I just … well, that's just the way I am. I introduced her to my friends. I let her cut their hair. I was trying to expose her to … Well, she didn't have a loving mother so she was lacking…. I was just trying to be a role model for her. And she betrays me like this! I even invited her and that stiff husband of hers to my luau."

Truth to tell, I didn't care for Mr. Swenson either. Mother stood up and started to pace again. "I'm sure Arlene only married him because he has money. Eric is cold but he comes from a higher class. I can always tell by peoples' nails. There's something precise about the shape of their moons. Anyway, I'm sure Arlene never loved him."

"Arlene told me she loves you, Mother. She means it. She's not doing this to upset you. She really loves you, Mother."

"Oh gosh. Well, that explains a lot." Mother stood with her hands on her hips looking pensively out my front window. "I knew a girl in college who had a crush on me." She shrugged. "It happens. Arlene's probably jealous of Ginger being that she's my best friend. That's so high school of her to act out like this and ruin our property value, but then she didn't go to college. You have to go to college, Annie. No matter how nice your upbringing is, college is the finishing touch."

I nodded. "Oh, I'm definitely going to college."

Mother continued, "I was always so grateful to my mother for setting a high bar for me and my sisters. We were expected to rise above our class. We were taught to fit in with royalty if that's where our life journey took us. You'd be surprised how many high-class women started life as middle-class or worse. But in America, you can reinvent yourself. Remember that, Annie. And if you do it well, everybody will be proud of you for achieving the American Dream. I suppose Arlene thought she could cut corners by marrying rich. That isn't the same thing. Marriage can give you status but it doesn't confer class. That you must achieve on your own."

Mother inhaled and exhaled twice. She sometimes got short of breath when she was feeling emotional. She coughed dryly and resumed her speech. "My mother always insisted that I set my sights high when it came to men. And she emphasized that I didn't have to sacrifice true love for money. So I never settled for just any rich guy. I fell in love with your father the first time I danced with him at a fraternity party. He was from a better social class than I was, but he recognized that I was a lady. His parents accepted me and we got married. Well, we almost didn't. One evening after we were engaged, Tom told me that he didn't want children and I said, Sayonara, Buster! I would never marry a man who didn't want a family. I think men who love babies are the sexiest men of all. And after one day, after Tom had thought about it, he begged me to take him back." Mother smiled. "Now you just try to imagine your wonderful Daddy without you kids. You just try." It was true; my father was always a sucker when it came to kids.

 Eleanor, had been married to a man who drank too much and beat her up. He was in the Merchant Marines so at least he was gone for months at a time. When I was three, Aunt Eleanor decided to leave him. She had three kids, my cousins—Alice, Amanda, and Albert. Alice was the oldest at seven years old. I was too young at the time to remember any of this, but Alice told me this story years later. My father said he would help them all get away while Uncle Bert was deployed on his big ship. Daddy began searching for a new home for them, driving further and further south, until he eventually landed in a pretty small town on the eastern shore of South Carolina. There were nice schools and a china painting factory where Aunt Eleanor would eventually be hired. She was highly artistic. Daddy rented a furnished apartment with two bedrooms right near the beach and then, after Uncle Bert had departed for the sea, he began moving carloads of their belongings down to the little apartment. Then two days before my uncle returned, Aunt Eleanor kissed my mother goodbye and Mother kissed my cousins and my Dad and they all piled into his car and headed for their new life. Their clothes and toys filled the trunk; everything else was waiting for them in South Carolina. It took many hours to get there and was around midnight when they finally began unpacking the car. That's when my cousin Alice realized that she had left her favorite doll behind. She began to quietly cry. Her mother said, "I'll buy you a new doll." But tears continued to pour down little Alice's face, and Daddy said, "It's okay, Honey—I'll go back and get your doll." And Daddy climbed back into the car and drove all night and all of the next day to bring the doll back to Alice. Alice told me this story when I was twelve and she said that my father was the most wonderful, the bravest, and best man she would ever know. I knew that was true even though I kind of took him for granted. A postscript on the whole episode: Uncle Bert got in a bar fight in Turkey the night before they were heading back to the United States, and he was killed. Mother said it was divine intervention.

 about Arlene Swenson and the hair salon when I emerged from my reverie. "Bottom line—you don't put a business in your home when your home costs forty-eight thousand dollars. And that doesn't even cover the cost of an in-ground swimming pool like we have. And all the landscaping. Wait till the neighbors find out. Oh my god. You think the Landers or the Bobbins or Ginger are going to be happy with this? And wait till Dinah Matthews finds out. They're all going to blame me. Arlene will be shunned by all of us. She took advantage of the wrong ladies."

Mother canceled Koffee Klatch that Wednesday, and instead the blondes, excluding Arlene, met at Ginger Taylor's pool. Caroline Davis from the Zoning Commission joined them. Caroline assured everyone that the variance Arlene had requested for a hair salon in our neighborhood didn't stand a snowball's chance in hell of being approved. "Not in Linton Hill! My goodness, the county doesn't have any interest in seeing property values decline. They want the tax revenue," she said and added that the Commission would meet in mid-September to make the decision official and final. In the meantime, Mother quietly told Arlene that she was no longer welcome at our house.

On Saturday, Jeff called to say that he couldn't pick me up for his party. "My mom says I have to be here to greet my guests. So I'm sending my brother Andy."

Mother hovered over me while I dressed. "Are Jeff's parents going to be chaperoning tonight?"

I rolled my eyes. "I'm sure they are, Mother. But Jeff isn't some agent provocateur. Candy's sister knows him and says he comes from a nice family. He's already been accepted at Cornell."

I wore my bubblegum pink gingham sundress and a new pair of pink sandals that Mother picked up for me at I. Miller in New York City earlier that Summer. Mrs. Taylor arrived and called up the stairs. Mother replied, "We're in Annie's room, Ginger!"

Mrs. Taylor came through my door already grinning. "I can't believe it! Our little girl is old enough to date now!" She hugged my mother.

"I don't think it's a date exactly," I said. "It's a party."

"Of course it's a date. He's coming to get you," said Mrs. Taylor, piling my hair on top of my head. I gently pushed her hand away. "I like it down," I said.

"Jeff's mother insists that he stay at the house and greet his guests," said Mother. "So he's sending his younger brother to pick Annie up."

"She sounds like a good mother," said Mrs. Taylor. "This is very special, Annie. You are being accepted by a Pennswalk Founding Family. The Wetherills have lived in Pennswalk for generations."

Mother smiled at me. "That's why I wanted you, and the boys to be born here in Pennswalk. So you would be accepted. Gosh, we moved in just weeks before I gave birth to you, Annie. It was close! I felt like an immigrant crossing the border to make sure her baby was born in America!" Mother laughed. "But seriously, I knew being born in Pennswalk would open doors for you someday. The children who have moved here with their parents, having been born elsewhere, will always be viewed as interlopers like their mothers and dads. Like Daddy and I are. Like Ginger and Eddie. The older families look down on us. They say we're nouveau riche. I think they're just a bit jealous."

Mrs. Taylor nodded. "Yes, but our boys will be regarded like you, Annie, as true Pennswalkians. They won't think of *you* as nouveau riche. They will simply regard you kids as well-to-do. Which is a completely different class."

Mother turned to Mrs. Taylor and said, "Jeff Wetherill has already been accepted at Cornell. He has a very bright future."

"He sounds great!" Mrs. Taylor's eyes sparkled. She, Mother, and I lined up in front of the mirror, me in the middle between them, facing our reflections. Mrs. Taylor spoke to mine, "Now remember—just a simple kiss, Annie. That's all you do on the first date. Then say thank you and step out of the car."

"I'm sure he'll walk her to the door," Mother said to Ginger's reflection. Then looking at mine, she added, "You can kiss him goodnight at the door. Your first kiss, Annie." Mother sighed.

Andy Wetherill arrived. He was shorter than Jeff with dark eyes and dark hair. And he was younger by a year; Andy would be a junior in our high school this year, one year older than me. He was so attractive I would have lost my nerve and stayed home were it not for his playful smile. He seemed so at ease in the world, happy-go-lucky. And he seemed to like me on sight. "Your chariot awaits," he said and offered me his arm. He turned to my mother and said, "She'll be home before midnight. And I'll bring her myself. I can beat my brother at arm wrestling any day of the week." He winked at me and we were off, leaving my mother and Ginger behind, wide-eyed, their mouths agape.

On the way to his house, Andy talked non-stop. About the recent KKK murders of Civil Rights workers in Mississippi. About the JFK assassination. About the banjo which he was learning to play. About the Chinese language he was learning to speak. He talked about how trees can live for thousands of years and how fish can communicate with one another just as migrating birds do. He talked about how funny George Carlin was. I responded enthusiastically to everything he said, every topic delighted me. I agreed. I disagreed. I pushed back. I offered my opinions. I laughed. He laughed. By the time we arrived at the party, we were already good friends. I hadn't had this much fun since well … ever.

Andy and his brother Jeff lived in a stately farmhouse at the other end of Pennswalk. It had been built in 1771 out of that wonderful yellow grey fieldstone that used to be plentiful in the area. Inside there were large open fireplaces and deep window seats, a haphazard assortment of overstuffed chairs, and bookcases packed with books on every subject imaginable. Deep, rich colors, cinnamon and crimson, washed the walls, mirroring the old oriental rugs that overlapped each other on the floor. Everything felt so well-loved and comfortable. Andy held my hand and didn't let go even when Jeff approached. There was an intense exchange of non-verbal communication, then Andy whisked me off to his bedroom upstairs where we sat on the floor and he played the banjo just for me. His dogs joined us, an old hound, and a young St. Bernard. They sandwiched me between them and I rubbed their necks and ears. Then his dad came in eating a hot dog and plunked down on a chair. He tapped his toe while Andy played another tune. When he had finished eating, he took a harmonica out of his pocket and harmonized with Andy's banjo. I clapped along, rocking side to side; the dogs moved with me. Then his dad demonstrated for my sake how to play the scale on a harmonica. "You blow or suck at each opening. Just remember to do it in this order. Blow. Suck. Blow. Suck. Blow. Blow. Suck. Blow." When he left, Andy turned to me and said, "Jeff and I call him Our Gentleman of Questionable Taste." And then we both fell over laughing.

Next, Andy demonstrated Chinese calligraphy. He used a large brush dipped in black ink and his hand moved gracefully, the letters looked like art.

"That's beautiful," I said. "What does it mean?"

"You really want to know?" he asked, arching his left eyebrow.

"Am I going to be embarrassed?" I said, grinning.

"Well, we'll find out. This roughly translates to 'My brother's socks smell like gorilla puberty.'"

I smiled and said, "Andy Wetherill, you are sui generis!"

"Yep. We are made for each other, Annie Hughs."

Eventually we went downstairs and mingled with the other kids. They were mostly seniors. I didn't know any of them and none of them bothered to talk to me. A couple of upper-class girls eyed me and whispered to each other. Andy said, "Want a Coke?" I went with him into the kitchen and there I met his mother who struck me as peculiar, but interesting. She looked like Katherine Hepburn, wearing a tailored pin striped jacket and skirt and a white cotton shirt. She was barefoot. Mrs. Wetherill was an artist and well known in the area for her still-life oil paintings. Her latest were distributed on three walls in the large kitchen, extending from the chair rail to the ceiling. Each one was a painting of a single russet potato sitting on a blue plate on a wooden table. In some, the potato looked robust and dirty as though it had just been pulled out of the ground. In others, the potato looked sleek and wet, like it had been washed or rained on. In several, the potatoes looked pruny, and, in the most recent, they sported delicate, root-like branches. Even in old age, these potatoes were beautiful. They were perfectly rendered in oils and reminded me in some ways of the elegant, eighteenth-century, still-life paintings in the Frick Museum in New York City. Mrs. Wetherill told me she always painted at the kitchen window and had painted these potatoes at different times of the day to capture the effect of changing light as well as advancing time. I told her I had seen the Water Lilies paintings by Monet on a trip to Paris two years before. Monet had executed a similar idea, painting his garden at dawn, noon, and dusk. Mrs. Wetherill seemed to appreciate my sincere interest in her work. She said to come back anytime. Andy beamed at me.

At 11:30, Jeff approached me swinging a set of car keys. Andy stepped between us. "I'm driving Annie home."

"She's my guest, Andy. You lose."

"Knock it off, Jeff. You're embarrassing yourself."

"I'm driving her home!"

Jeff took a swing at Andy. Andy punched back. They locked in an angry embrace and banged against the food table, upending it. Kids scattered, laughing raucously. Mr. Wetherill calmly retrieved the keys from the floor and said, "Come on, Annie. I'll drive you home."

The next morning, I called Candy and started to tell her about the party. She interrupted me. "Susan says that Andy Wetherill is a weirdo."

"No, he's not, Candy. He's smart and funny. He plays the banjo!"

"Eeuuuu—the banjo?"

"And he knows how to write in Chinese."

"I rest my case."

"And he's handsome, Candy. Okay? He's handsome and he's fun. And he's so smart. I like him so much better than Jeff."

"So are you going to date *him* now?"

"No. He's a friend. I mean I had fun with him but I'm not interested in dating anyone." That wasn't entirely true of course. I did sort of have a crush on Andy now. Not like my deep feelings for Philip, but I had time to kill—six years to be exact—before I could become Philip's lover. That's a substantial stretch of time. So I figured I could practice being a girlfriend with someone else in the meantime so that my feminine charms wouldn't atrophy from lack of use. Besides Andy would definitely be good company during the interim. And if I stayed alert and took careful notes, I could learn how to be natural around boys. That way I wouldn't be awkward with Philip when I'm twenty-one and we have sex. I changed the subject and asked Candy about the dance that week. "It was pretty great actually," she said. "There were lots of kids there. Natalie came. You know from up the street. She's a really good dancer."

"Oh? I would have gone but Mother needed me. She's upset.... "

"I know all about that, Annie. My parents have been talking about it a lot. I hate to tell you, but they blame your mom. They think your mom encouraged Mrs. Swenson to open a salon on the street so your mom and her friends could get free haircuts."

"No that's not why she did it. My mother is just nice. She wanted her to feel welcome in Linton Hill, that's all."

"Well, a lot of people think your mother caused the whole mess by being kind of cheap."

My heart was pounding. "Look, it will all work out, Candy. You'll see. The Zoning Commission is going to handle it. It will all be fine."

ON SUNDAY, I WOKE up late and carried a glass of orange juice out to the pool. Mother and Kitty Landers were talking over the fence that separated our yards. Mother had finally settled on the date for her Midsummer Soiree which in past summers had always been held in mid-July but would be held this year on the third Saturday in August because Mother had been too rattled by Laura Andrew's news about taking a lover and Arlene's plans to open a hair salon to even consider a date let alone plan the menu for the party until recently.

"I tell you, Kitty," Mother sighed. "Summers just seem to fly by faster every year. You get to July 4 and the next thing you know it's Labor Day and the kids are back in school. This Summer—whew! I'm lucky I could carve out a Saturday in August the way things are going. Little League tournaments and the end of the season banquet. And Annie's birthday is this week, then we head to the beach. And Friendship Day is just around the corner. Oh, it makes my head spin."

"I don't know how you keep up, Bev," said Mrs. Landers. "Friendship Day, Labor Day...."

"And I have bridge club this month!" Mother gasped for breath.

Mrs. Landers shook her head in awe. "And now the beach ... and Annie's birthday...."

"HAPPY BIRTHDAY, LEANNE." I was standing in front of Philip on the Williams' patio that afternoon. He had phoned and invited me to join him alone for a birthday celebration. I showered and dressed in a white piqué cotton sundress that was my very favorite of all my dresses. I only wore it on special occasions. It made me look especially tan.

"Thank you, Philip. Actually, my birthday is this Friday."

"I have something for you."

"What?" I said with obvious pleasure, removing my sunglasses. "A book?"

"Sit down. I'll bring it out to you."

I took a seat on one of the Williams' comfortable patio chairs and watched Philip slide the glass patio door and disappear inside. It was another hot day, but the wind delivered a rich parfait of seasonal scents. I inhaled the warm breeze and could taste the sweet Summer corn growing on the Fisher farm a half mile away, but I also smelled a hint of Autumn in the perfume of ripening apples wafting out of the one remaining orchard in Pennswalk.

Philip returned with a small blue box wrapped in white ribbon and handed it to me. I recognized the color right away. It was a Tiffany box in that elegant robin's egg blue. My favorite color in the whole world ever since Mother and I saw *Breakfast at Tiffany's* on one of our "girl days" a couple of years ago. We had both swooned at Audrey Hepburn's upswept hair and her astonishingly simple but striking little black dress. And her cigarette holder. That really clinched her look. I tried to talk my mother into getting one.

Mother smoked occasionally. Mainly at bridge club. When it was her turn to host, she provided cigarettes for the guests in sterling silver servers. She had received them as wedding gifts. A silver footed urn about two inches tall held the cigarettes upright, ready to be plucked. One urn sat on each of the two card tables. There was a companion silver lighter for each table as well. It looked like a genie lamp and was a perfect size to cradle in a feminine hand. There were also individual crystal ashtrays, small and rimmed in silver. Four per table, one for each player. And finally a silver Revere bowl sat at the center of each table filled with dark chocolate "Bridge Mix," which Mother bought in bulk at Woolworth's candy counter.

Each of Mother's friends would smoke a cigarette after the card game, after Mother had served the dessert and coffee. It was a ritual. They'd push back slightly from the table and cross their legs carefully smoothing their full skirts over their knees. They always dressed up for bridge, sometimes in their best cocktail dresses. Some of the women even had their hair done for Bridge Night. The cigarette urn was passed around the table and each woman selected either a Winston or a Lucky Strike. After the party, the silver bridge sets were carefully washed and dried and slipped into navy blue velvet bags to thwart any tarnish. Mother said the sets would be mine someday when she was gone. The leftover cigarettes went into the freezer in a Tupperware container. Mother would slip one out during the week and light up during the rare times when she needed to suppress her appetite to lose a few pounds.

"Leanne? Leanne?" I looked up into Philip's searching eyes. "Aren't you going to open it?" He took a seat across from me.

I slipped the ribbon off the box and sighed, "Tiffany's!"

"You strike me as a girl who appreciates the finer things in life."

"I do," I said and lifted the lid. There was a small velvet bag inside. I loosened the drawstrings and slipped my fingers in and retrieved a gold pin. "Oh my gosh! Philip!! I wanted a circle pin for my birthday! How did you know?"

Philip grinned. "I asked your mother for a suggestion."

"Circle pins are the rage this year. Oh my gosh! And it's monogrammed!"

"Your middle name is Taylor?"

"Yes. After Mr. and Mrs. Taylor. They're my godparents." I looked at the pin again. A small gold disk with swirling letters beautifully engraved on the surface. "Oh, Philip, thank you so much. It's beautiful. I'll cherish it forever."

"May I put it on you?"

"Yes, please." I stood before him. He stood up and leaned down to fasten the pin to the bodice of my dress. His face was so close to mine that I could feel his breath on my neck. Impulsively, I kissed him on the cheek. He stepped back and looked at me. I couldn't tell if he was glad

I did it but I was glad that I did it. And I boldly looked him in the eyes. "Oh my gosh, Philip, you smell so good."

He touched the pin again lightly and said, "It looks very pretty on you."

We sat again and were quiet for a moment. Then I spoke. "Would I fit in with your friends?"

"Absolutely."

"Would my parents?"

"No."

I wasn't surprised to hear that. My parents were lovely people but, to be completely honest, they weren't my type either. I changed the subject. "We're leaving for the beach on Friday. I'll be gone for a week. We go to Rehoboth in Delaware. My grandmother owns a couple of houses there. Do you know Rehoboth Beach?"

He shook his head. "Jews stick to the Jersey beaches. Have you ever seen any Jews in Rehoboth?"

I shrugged. "To tell you the truth I haven't looked for any. I did meet a girl from Argentina last Summer."

"I guarantee she wasn't Jewish."

"Anyway, when I get back, I get to celebrate my birthday again—this time with Candy. We're going to see *A Hard Day's Night* again. This time by ourselves."

"Oh, rats—I was hoping to tag along."

"Well … actually she and I have been planning this for a while and see, she's my best girlfriend, Philip, so I can't invite you, but.…"

"I'm teasing you."

"Oh." I laughed. "Well, it is a clever movie, Philip. You would probably appreciate it."

"So you like the Beatles?"

"Yes, very much. I think they're ingenious."

Philip tilted his head. "How so?"

"Well, all music is a response to the culture, you know. So in any given time period, most of it ends up sounding the same. Because all the composers are surrounded by the same culture and most of them are feeding from the same trough of influences. But the composers that break through—the innovators, like the Beatles—hear something more in their culture. They hear the future."

Philip nodded. "Is there any other music that appeals to you?

"Lately I've been discovering classical music. I listen to it on the radio at night. They don't sell classical records at the Hobby Shoppe though, just the Beatles and other popular groups; you know, the stuff that kids buy. And my parents mainly listen to Frank Sinatra and Glenn Miller and Peggy Lee records on the hi-fi. Mother says the World War Two music was romantic so it's her favorite. She said it was a very happy time."

Philip's eyebrows twitched. "Your mother thinks World War Two was a happy time?"

"No ... she doesn't mean...." I laughed. "I mean ... I think what she means is that when there's a war, our country unites. People don't worry so much about our differences. Like race and religion. They just see themselves as Americans."

"You believe that?"

"Well, everyone in our country was against Hitler."

"Actually, Leanne, everybody wasn't. There were Americans who admired him. Go to the library and look up Charles Lindberg."

We sat quietly for several minutes. Then I said, "I've also been thinking a lot about World War One."

Philip adjusted in his chair. "Does your mother think that was another happy time?"

"No, Philip," I rolled my eyes. "I think about how classical music was affected by World War One. Twenty million people died during those years between 1914 and 1918. Did you know that? And so many of them were Europeans because the war was fought there. And I think about Chopin and Beethoven and Mahler. I imagine they had grandchildren who were probably alive in 1914, and they were likely among those killed and isn't it possible that among them, there might have been some who carried the genius of the great nineteenth-century composers? Had there not been such devastating destruction and death, one or more of them might have survived and carried the family gift into a new generation and produced more of the great music of their grandfathers. Everything was ended by the war. Like all that genius was evaporated. So we'll never know what might have been when all those people died."

Philip said nothing. He studied my face like he was going to paint my portrait. His attention was so intense that I felt compelled finally to speak again. "I guess I'm just saying that when you consider all that is lost in war, the greatest loss, in my view, is hereditary artistic genius. Because I think we can afford to lose bodies, those we can replace. And most people are so ordinary. But to lose the ability to create beauty. That is the real cost of war. That's why I'm a pacifist."

Philip stood up and offered me his hand. "Come inside with me. I want to give you some records." I stepped into the dining room. I'd been in the Williams' house so many times, but everything felt different that day. The table was covered with neat piles of typewritten pages. A typewriter sat at one end. There was a bed pillow on the chair.

"Leanne, can I get you something to drink? I have ginger ale, orange juice...."

"No thank you. I'm fine. Is this where you write?"

"Yes, it is."

"Can I read something?"

"Someday."

"What are you writing about?"

"About my awful wife. But I have begun gathering my notes for a new book as well."

"What will that be about?"

"About being a boy who is fourteen. And all the intense unfiltered feelings I had about sex and girls at that age."

"Do you think about me often when we're not together?"

"Leanne, I think about you constantly. You are becoming my muse."

I RETURNED HOME LATER that afternoon just as Andy pulled into the driveway in an older model convertible. I waved. He got out of the car and strolled toward me, hands in his pockets. He was sporting a black eye.

"Did your brother do that?"

Andy grinned. "You should see his face."

"I find it hard to believe you were fighting over me."

Andy shrugged. "We're always looking for an excuse. You just happened to show up. Hey, want to get some ice cream? I want to go to that place where the waitresses dress up like pigs."

"My mother says they have the cheapest quality ice cream in the world."

"They do and they know it. But you get gigantic helpings. And if you can actually finish a bowl of that swill, they give you a pin that says I AM A PIG." He laughed gleefully. "Most people can't finish it, but I accept the challenge. And with you by my side, Sweet Annie, I will finally attain one of those pins. I have to have one. I'm obsessed. I'm a man on a mission. I want to wear it the first day of school."

"Okay … okay." I laughed. "I'll be your coach. Hold on. I have to check in with my mother." I ran inside and put the classical records Philip gave me on my bureau. Then I found Mother, Mrs. Taylor, and Laura Armitage on the back porch. "I'm going out with Andy for a while. I'll be home for dinner."

Mrs. Taylor sat up straight. "Andy? What happened to Jeff?"

I left the porch calling back to them, "I'll tell you later." I hopped into the car. Andy turned the key and said, "I hope we don't break down. This car is a piece of defecation. Oh, by the way, you look really pretty. I like that dress."

As we were driving past Candy's house, I saw her at her mailbox. I waved excitedly and called to her but she looked back, stony-faced. I wondered if she realized it was me.

Chapter 5

Saturday, August 22 arrived, the day of Mother's Midsummer Soiree. I had offered to polish the silver candlesticks, so I was in the kitchen when Mother took a call. Moments later, she hung up. She looked troubled. "That was Laura Armitage. She isn't coming tonight. She says she doesn't feel well."

"That's too bad," I said.

Mother nodded. "Ellie Bobbin called earlier. She can't make it either."

I shrugged. "Maybe there's something going around."

I noticed my mother's hair. How could I not? Her dark brown roots were obvious now.

They looked severe against the fading bleached blonde of her bob. She also needed a trim. She had told me the day before that she intended "to tough it out until the Zoning Commission meets next month and puts an end to Arlene's folly," and she had added. "All of the girls agree. Our roots are the visible sign of our resistance to this interloper coming in and trying to change our way of life."

My brothers and Dad set up three café tables in the woods. Then Mother and I set the lace place mats and sterling-silver cutlery. Mother positioned the candlesticks, two per table, and I placed a pale blue taper in each. The finishing touch—nosegays of late blooming roses tied with blue ribbon and placed in small glass vases—were centered, one per table. Mother said, "Did I tell you that I knew a girl when I was growing up whose name was Noseygay Angry? That was her real name, Annie." We walked back up to the kitchen. "So do you have a date with Andy tonight?"

"Yeah, we're going to the movies."

"Well, I'll say hi to Philip Roth for you. He's coming to the Soiree. He's bringing a date, Annie. I have to admit I'm curious to see what sort of woman he's attracted to."

My heart pounded. "Actually, we might stay around here. Hang out with TJ and John. You know … they love Andy."

"Well, be sure to wear your circle pin if you stay home. That way if Mr. Roth sees you, he will know that you are enjoying his gift."

That night I posted up in the master bathroom at seven o'clock to watch the guests arrive, in particular Philip and his date. Andy said he'd be over at eight so I had an hour to scope out the scene. All the women wore dresses in summery shades of rose and turquoise and celery green with gathered skirts that rustled and swayed when they danced with their husbands. The men wore beige suits and neckties in pastel hues. Everyone was unusually quiet. Maybe they were all exhausted; it had been a busy Summer. Or maybe they were feeling romantic; there was a full moon rising. Mr. Taylor held Mrs. Taylor tightly against him and kissed her neck. It reminded me of how he had held me that day except that she wasn't carrying a watermelon. Caroline Miller from the Zoning Board was there with her husband. After quickly downing a couple of cocktails, they moved deep into the yard and danced together awkwardly, stopping from time to time to make out. I knew that Mr. Taylor planned to dance with Caroline Miller at some point that evening to ply his charms in the hope that she would advocate for the Pickering Manor Nursing Home project. It was the reason Mother had invited the Millers to her Midsummer Soiree.

Philip arrived with a woman. I almost fell out of the window trying to register every detail of her appearance—kohl-lined eyes, dark short hair, pale lipstick, and her dress—a slim fitting black cocktail sheath befitting Holly Golightly. She was obviously not from Pennswalk. Of course, neither was Philip. His suit was dark grey and he wasn't wearing a tie. Soon he was dancing with the woman. I was relieved to see that he wasn't in love with her. They danced looking at each other and talking. I figured she must be a friend. At one point, Philip looked up at me in the window and before I could duck, blew me a kiss and laughed.

I went into my bedroom and called Candy. I started to share that Philip had brought a date to the Soiree, but she cut me off. "I have to go. I'm babysitting for someone you don't know."

"Well, let's get together tomorrow. I haven't seen you all week."

"Sure I'll call you in the morning."

By the time I joined my brothers in the family room, Philip and his date were already sitting at the game table with TJ and John. Andy had also arrived and joined them. Philip stood when I came down the stairs and introduced me to the woman in the black dress. "Leanne, this is Adrienne. She's an editor at my publishing house. Adrienne, this is the young lady I told you about." *Young lady? What am I—his niece?*

Adrienne smiled and said, "Philip tells me you're a writer, Leanne."

"Well, I'm moving in that direction," I said pleasantly, avoiding Philip's eyes.

Andy stood up and pulled out the empty chair next to him, "I saved you a seat." I sat and he leaned toward me and whispered, "So who are you? Annie or Leanne?"

"Leanne is going to be my pen name." Philip heard and winked at me.

Philip grabbed the deck of cards at the center of the table, looked at my brothers and started to shuffle. "So it was the Summer of 1941. My friends and I were eight years old and one of the boys had started a daily poker game in his basement. We called him Stinky. Cause he was stinky. We went with the obvious when it came to nicknames—my friends and I."

T J grinned, "What did they call you, Mr. Roth?"

"Handsome."

"Ha!"

"So Stinky set up this game and since it was his basement he always got to deal, and he always kept score. And by coincidence, he always won. So one afternoon, Stinky had dealt the cards as he always did. 'Read 'em and sleep, boys' he'd said as he always did and then he picked up his hand. But this time, all the other boys left their cards on the table. Fat Seymour faced Stinky and said, 'You shouldn't be keeping score, you know. You stink at arithmetic.' Then Face-Mole added, 'Yeah, Stinky, you don't even know your Times Tables.'

TJ interrupted. "What were you doing, Mr. Roth?"

"Oh, I was there, TJ. I was back-up in case things went south. Stinky was a scrawny kid but wiry. And he had a bad temper! We were all on high alert. So Stinky jumped to his feet and yelled 'Oh yeah? I'm a damn genius!'"

John half-laughed. "Whoa! Stinky was eight years old and he said 'damn'?"

Philip nodded solemnly. "I hung with a rough crowd, John. We lived in a city, you know. Where the buses smell like spearmint gum." Philip winked at me and I grinned. "So now Stinky was on his feet and swearing. He shook his fist in Face-Mole's face. But Face-Mole didn't flinch. And still no one picked up their cards. So Stinky sat back down. 'Fine,' he said, acting all cool. 'Ask me a multiplication problem. Go on. Toughest one you got. I'll show you how good I am at math.' So Fat Seymour thought for a minute and then said, 'Okay—what's nine million four hundred thousand two hundred and eighty-seven TIMES twenty billion, five hundred thousand and sixty-three?' Stinky didn't blink. Quick as a flash, he answered, 'Forty-five trillion nine hundred and thirty-six thousand and forty cents.' There was a pause. Everyone looked at everyone else. We were incredulous. Then Face-Mole turned to Fat Seymour and said, 'Wow—that sounds close.' So Stinky continued to deal and keep score. And win every hand."

Everyone roared, of course. Andy's laugh stood out, high and boyish. It soared with joy. My brothers nearly passed out laughing. I watched Philip. I watched how he watched my little brothers with such affectionate delight, laughing harder at their laughter. I wanted to throw my arms around Philip's neck and kiss his wonderful lips and the dimple at the center beneath his lower lip. Philip dealt the cards now. "Five card draw," he said. 'Jokers wild." TJ picked up his hand and said, 'Read 'em and sleep!"

I looked at my cards and said, "I wish I could tell a joke well."

Philip looked surprised. "You can't?"

TJ laughed, "No, she's terrible. She always gets the giggles before she gets to the punchline and then no one can understand what she's saying."

Andy leaned against me. "I'll teach you."

We played a few hands. Then I went upstairs and made popcorn. Andy followed me and gathered Cokes out of the fridge. When we returned, I announced "Andy is learning Chinese. He can speak it and write it."

Philip was incredulous. "Seriously, Andy? Okay, tell me what would lead a teenager in Pennswalk, Pennsylvania to learn Chinese?"

Andy was thoughtful. "I just felt like I already knew this language, like it was already inside me and that I just needed help releasing it." Andy explained that he had been studying with a Chinese man in Philadelphia for two years now. The man had escaped from Mao Zedong's China a number of years before. He had been a prisoner in a reeducation camp because he had been caught in his home reading *A Tale of Two Cities* in English. Now he taught mathematics at Temple University. But he gave Andy private language lessons in his home on Saturdays. He said it was important to him to retain his native language and teaching Andy was a way of doing that.

John said, "Hey Andy—say something in Chinese. Say *I am smart.*"

"Wǒ hěn cōngmíng." Andy added that he was also learning Japanese. Then he took my hand. Philip took note; his eyebrows twitched.

I said, "Andy, I wonder if you are an incarnated member of the court of an Emperor from one of the great Chinese dynasties. Maybe that's why these languages come so easily to you."

Andy nodded. "I have come to accept that reincarnation is a possibility. That's the thing about learning a foreign language; it opens you up to their culture. I don't think you can truly understand any culture unless you speak the language." He looked at me and said, "I learned this week that there's no word in Mandarin for privacy."

Adrienne said, "That's fascinating!"

Philip asked, "So what are you going to do with this talent of yours? Teach? Become a translator at the United Nations? Be an ambassador?"

"I'm not sure. Actually, I'm in contact with some folks at Hamilton College in New York."

Adrienne smiled, "That's a fabulous school, Andy. My nephew goes there."

I said, "They are offering to create an international studies program just for Andy, one that is focused on Asia. They're hiring specialists in the field to be his instructors."

TJ now came around the table and draped an arm around my shoulders. "You should go to Hamilton, Annie. You're the smartest girl in the world."

Before I could reply, Andy said. "Sorry, Annie. It's an all-men's school."

I countered. "You should remind them that Confucius say women hold up half of heaven."

Andy grinned at me. "Maybe I'll make it a condition of my attending their college that I get to bring you along."

I blushed. There was an awkward silence. Andy continued to look in my eyes as though no one else was in the room but I was very aware that Philip was watching us. The conversation then moved to books. Everyone wanted to know what was next for Philip Roth. He replied, "I'm writing another dirty book."

TJ yelled, "WHOA, Nellie!" And Philip grinned. "Don't tell your mother."

"Don't tell me what?" Mother was suddenly there in the room.

Philip stood politely and said, "That you have great kids, Beverly."

Mother beamed. "Thank you, Philip. I do indeed."

I WAITED FOR CANDY'S call the next morning but then I remembered that she went to church on Sundays with her family. When I hadn't heard from her by lunchtime, I phoned her. She said, "Oh, yeah. C'mon over. Natalie's here."

We sat on the floor in Candy's room. I showed the girls the new record my cousin gave me for my birthday. It was the German version of "She Loves You." "Sie Liebt Dich." "This is so neat. The Beatles are actually singing in German! My uncle found it in a shop in the airport in Toronto when he was on a business trip, and he knows how much we love the Beatles and...."

Natalie scrunched up her nose. "Ugh. The Beatles."

Candy jumped in. "Natalie's into the Beach Boys."

"They're *Americans*," said Natalie. She looked at me with disdain. Candy studied her fingernails.

After a stunned moment, I said, "Natalie, you don't like the Beatles at all? But they're so talented."

"We have better talent here in our own country. *American* talent. Besides I'm into surfing."

I noted Natalie's pale white skin. She didn't look like she spent any time at all in the sun. "Where do you surf?" I asked, trying to seem interested.

"At the beach. Geez, where do you think?" She laughed dismissively.

A tortured silence set in. Then Natalie turned to Candy and, with exaggerated enthusiasm, said, "Candy, I almost forgot to tell you. You know Beth from CYO?" Natalie briefly turned to me, "That's our Catholic Youth Club." She turned back to Candy. "Anyway, you know Beth's the one who LOVES Jan and Dean so much, it's crazy? Anyway, she can recite the lyrics of "Surf City" backwards. It's so FUNNY, Candy! I'll have her do it for you tomorrow night at CYO."

Candy stood up and said, "Listen, I have to get ready to go over to my grandmother's. I have to say goodbye for now."

I got up off the floor and left the room without saying a word to either of the girls. Natalie remained seated on the floor. Candy followed me down the stairs. "Annie? Annie, maybe we can do something on Tuesday. Okay?"

"Sure. I'll call you." I was confident that Candy saw what a rude girl Natalie was. She was probably just trying to be a friend because Natalie was new in Pennswalk and didn't have any others yet. Candy was thoughtful that way.

Later that afternoon, I was stretched out in a chaise that I had pulled close to the pool. I was writing in my diary when I heard the wind chime on the gate ring. I looked up and saw Philip. He had arrived for his afternoon swim. He crossed to me and sat on the edge of my chaise. "Leanne, I'm moving back to New York earlier than planned."

I sat up alarmed. "Why?"

"I have to begin working with my editor. I've finished a good draft of my book."

"The one about your awful wife?"

Philip laughed. "Yeah, that one. Listen, I'm going to give you the address and phone number for my apartment. I want us to keep in touch. Maybe you can visit me some weekend? I mean it."

"Can't Adrienne come down here and work with you in Pennswalk?"

"Frankly, Honey, this place is distracting. Far more distracting than I anticipated."

"Am I distracting?"

Philip leaned in and kissed me on the forehead. "I'll be here until mid-September. So I'll get to see you return to school. I imagine you and Andy will set that place aflame this year. I'm so glad you have him in your life. He's a terrific young man."

"He's not my boyfriend, Philip. I'm saving myself for you," I said earnestly.

Philip removed his loafers and his shirt. He avoided my eyes. "So what's going on with your mother's hair? And Ginger's?"

I filled him in on the details of the hair salon war. I ended by saying, "It's really sad, Philip. And I think it's my mother's fault. I mean I love her, but I think she overreacted. Now she and Mrs. Swenson aren't speaking to each other and her friends are picking sides. Mrs. Bobbin doesn't come to Koffee Klatch anymore and skipped the Midsummer Soiree. Mrs. Armitage didn't come either. Every day seems to bring a new betrayal." I thought of Candy. And then I added, "I swear this town should be renamed Perfidy."

ON TUESDAY I CALLED Candy, and I wasn't surprised to hear that she couldn't get together. This time it was a babysitting job. "It's going to be an all-day thing," she said and added, "Listen Annie, why don't you see if Lark or Gaye wants to go to Philly with you to see *A Hard Day's Night* again. Or maybe Betsy. I really don't think I'm going to make it. I'm so busy."

"Do you still like the Beatles, Candy?"

"Of course. I think they're fab. You know that."

I walked down to State Street later that morning and entered The Ladybug Shoppe. My grandmother had given me money for my birthday, and I had my eye on the Fair Isle sweater that was displayed in the window. I had a choice of two colors—soft heather blue or a heather green. I chose the blue and Mrs. Jacques who owned the store showed me the matching A-line skirt. I said yes to both. While she was wrapping my packages in tissue, I showed her my circle pin. I was wearing it that day. She said, "Oh, Annie, what a very special piece! You are a lucky girl. And won't it look lovely on your new sweater!" I didn't tell her that it had been a gift from Philip Roth.

I left the store and headed toward the Hobby Shoppe to see what new records had come in. And then I saw them. Candy and Natalie coming out of the Hobby Shoppe. They were laughing so hard that they had to lean on each other to catch their breath. I froze and they saw me, standing directly across the street. Candy turned scarlet. Natalie smirked. And I immediately started walking in the other direction. Faster and faster. My head began to pound. I could barely see. I was running now, gasping, tears were pouring down my cheeks. Suddenly a car was next to me honking. It was Andy. "Hey, Annie! I was just coming over to see—Annie, what's wrong?" He stopped the car. I pulled open the passenger door and climbed in. I put my head back against the seat and covered my face with both hands. "Ohhhh…." I wailed. "I want to go home."

Andy put the car in gear and started driving. He said nothing until I suddenly said, "I'm going to throw up." He pulled off the main road and onto a path that led to the last apple orchard in town. I opened the door while the car was still moving and vomited. Andy grabbed a beach towel from the back seat and handed it to me to wipe my face. Then I laid my head back against the seat and sobbed. I felt like I was going to die.

Andy said quietly, "What happened?"

"My best girlfriend has betrayed me. She lied, Andy. I don't have a best girlfriend anymore. I'm all alone. I have no one who loves me best." I shuddered.

Andy drove me home and helped me into the house. He followed me as I pulled myself along the banister up the stairs to my room. And he watched me crumple onto my bed. I cried harder and placed my hands over my eyes. I moaned, "Oh my head. Oh my head." Andy lowered the blinds at my window and unplugged my phone. He slipped off my sandals. Then he sat in the wicker rocker and watched me. After a moment I heard him leave the room and descend the stairs. He soon returned. I opened an eye and saw him quietly place my bags from The Ladybug Shoppe on my bureau. When my mother got home from running her errands, Andy talked softly to her in the hall. Then he left and Mother came into the room. She stretched out next to me on the bed and put her arms around me. "Oh, Honey … Shhhh," she whispered. "Oh, Baby.…"

I DECIDED TO GO to the Youth Center dance that week. I knew Candy and Natalie would be there and I wanted them to see me. I couldn't bear to have them think I cared about what had happened. I asked Andy to come with me. "I have to go, Andy. I can't hide and become an object of pity among the girls. Please come with me."

"Annie, if I dance with you, you will definitely be an object of pity. I am the worst dancer in the school. I look like I'm auditioning for the Easter Seals Poster."

"Andy! Don't say things like that!"

"No, this is a job for my brother. Jeff oozes cool in these situations. I'll talk to him."

So on Friday night, Jeff was there at the Youth Center, standing by the door waiting for me. I arrived as the Orlons began to sing "Don't Hang Up." Jeff made a show of taking my hand. He bowed, "Annie, may I have this dance?" I laughed and we took to the floor. We stomped, we strolled, we Kennedy-Walked, we twisted. We even cha-cha'd. During the slow dances, Jeff leaned his cheek against mine. We were conspicuous conspirators and Candy and Natalie were taking note. Lark, Gaye and Betsy were watching, too.

At one point I ran into Gaye in the bathroom. She said, "Annie … I'm sorry about Candy. But she says you've changed. She says you're boy crazy and…."

"She's a liar. But this much is true. I'd rather have a boy as a friend than Candy any day of the week. She's prejudiced against non-Catholics. And you can tell her I said so."

At the end of the dance, Jeff made a show of asking if he could have "the privilege" of driving me home. When we got to my house, we sat in the driveway. He smiled. "Did you have fun?"

"Yeah. I did. Thanks, Jeff. It was nice of you to do this." I didn't tell him that deep inside I was still sad, that his kindness couldn't make up for losing Candy.

"Hey, it was my pleasure," Jeff said. "I think we'll be the talk of the school next week when we go back. What do you think?"

I smiled. "I don't really care what anyone thinks."

Jeff leaned in like he was going to kiss me and I put my hand up. "No. I can't."

Jeff sat back and nodded. "I'll let Andy know you did that. He'll be happy to hear it."

ON THE FIRST DAY of school, I wore my new wool Fair Isle sweater and skirt despite the fact that the temperature climbed into the 80s and I nearly expired. It was tradition to wear something new the first day— something that you bought for your back-to-school wardrobe that year. I sat next to Audrey Wexler in homeroom and we caught up on our summers. She asked if I wanted to hang out at her house on Saturday and listen to her Bob Dylan record, but I told her I would be helping my mother with Friendship Day. Audrey said, "Oh, that's right—I forgot that was this Saturday. I'll see you there."

Andy skipped his fourth period study hall to sit with me in the cafeteria during my lunch period. "I didn't want you to be an object of pity if all the girls shunned you and you had to eat alone," he said with a smile. He also offered to drive me home from school that day. I accepted. On our way we passed Candy and Natalie, walking side by side, and I fought back tears.

FRIENDSHIP DAY WAS A bit overwrought that year. Everyone in town showed up since the proceeds, in large part, would go to support the construction of a desperately needed new wing on the county hospital. Pennswalk was growing and not only was the hospital strained for space, but the school board was now proposing a new high school. The older residents, the ones who remembered the Twining farm, the Yoder farm, and the Goodnoe Dairy Farm shook their heads in disbelief that a small town could swell so quickly, and that the farmers who had held their land for centuries would suddenly in the 1960s sell their farms to developers with names like Arrigoni Development. The older residents of Pennswalk blamed the new arrivals, especially the people in Linton Hill for inciting the changes. But the biggest pressure to sell off farmland in Pennswalk had actually come from within the farm families themselves. The Yoder, Twining and Goodnoe children wanted to go to college and become lawyers and doctors rather than farm for a living like their fathers, always at the mercy of the weather and the fickle tastes of Americans who were now shunning real cream from cows for non-dairy creamer in their morning coffee. Not to mention the fact that the farmers who sold their land became millionaires overnight.

My mother, being a stickler for tradition, was dressed as she always was on Friendship Day, in her brown and black striped colonial dress with the white collar and apron and the white cap trimmed in lace. The cap was a particularly cunning touch this year as it hid Mother's inch-and-a-half dark roots. She was really beginning to look odd. TJ told her at breakfast that morning that she looked like Cruella De Vil. And Mother wasn't alone. The other blondes had all held tough through the Summer while waiting for the Zoning Commission to meet, but their resolve was being tested daily now that they had to keep their hair covered whenever they left the house. Even worse, in the evening when they removed their scarves, their husbands winced at the sight of them. Ginger told Mother that they were going to have to come up with a plan if the Zoning commission didn't make Arlene move her business out of Linton Hill. They'd either have to make peace with Arlene or go into Philadelphia to find a good colorist. After all the Pickering Manor Foundation Annual Ball was coming up in October and Ginger wasn't about to show up to the social event of the season wearing a head scarf. At least on Friendship Day, donned in colonial dresses and white caps, the blondes felt less self-conscious as they strolled through the crowd selling raffle tickets for a new gasoline powered lawn mower which had been donated by Milhous Hardware.

Liberty Avenue was blocked off from car traffic, and game and food vendors lined both sides of the street creating a narrow alley down the center. The result was that the citizens of Pennswalk, friend and foe, were pushed together having to jostle against one another as they passed. A small bandstand was set up at one end of the street. There Andy played the banjo before a happy gathering. The Friendship Day three-legged race and various relay games had been set up on the football field of the high school nearby and most of the men were there with their kids including my dad and Mr. Taylor who were referees. So I was surprised to run into Philip at a lemonade stand on Liberty Avenue. "I didn't think you'd go in for this type of thing. It's pretty corny."

Philip laughed. "Are you kidding? I can't resist a society in turmoil. So is this the day of reckoning for the blondes? Will there be a throw-down in the middle of the block? Arlene Swenson versus Beverly Hughs?"

Over Philip's shoulder I saw Arlene. She sat at a card table on which there was a sign: *Palm Readings—$1. All Proceeds Go to New Hospital Wing.* She saw me, too, and gave me a wounded look. I shook my head and shrugged, trying to wordlessly convey that I wasn't the one who told Mother. I put my hand over my heart and silently mouthed, *I'm sorry.* She looked back down at the palm she was reading. It belonged to Ellie Bobbins whose hair, I now noticed, was back to an immaculate platinum—no roots. Mother was watching them too. She and Arlene exchanged a cordial nod, then Mother moved on. Ginger joined Mother just in time to run into Laura Armitage whose hair was also freshly bleached. Another traitor. Ginger said, "Really, Laura? Have you no loyalty?" And Laura laughed and said, "No. It's stupid." Mother almost cried. "I thought we were close, Laura." Laura shrugged, "Oh, c'mon, Bev." Ginger practically hissed, "Maybe if Arlene was setting up a hair salon on your street, Laura, you'd feel differently."

"Oh, I would. But she isn't," said Laura breezily as she walked on.

Dinah Matthews and Kitty Landers walked together holding up books of raffle tickets. Suddenly they found themselves in a close press as Arlene and Ellie tried to pass them. There were murmurs of "excuse me" and some awkward jockeying until they could separate. The whole day was like that. It seemed everyone was avoiding someone. It created this strange choreography in the town square as betrayers were faced with the betrayed.

I saw Candy and Natalie playing horseshoes. Candy pretended not to see me, but her face reddened. I thought, *She's ashamed. She should be.* I stared at Natalie and while she was normally not hesitant to stare me down, I didn't flinch this time, and she looked away nervously. It affected her aim; she threw wildly and didn't win any prizes. I almost laughed.

LATE THAT AFTERNOON, I headed over to a field that was the last remaining patch of undeveloped land in Linton Hill. For two hundred years, it had been a pasture for cows on the Verhoos Family Farm. Now it was surrounded by new colonial houses, my own among them. And it too was scheduled to be divided into plots for future homes. An ancient looking tree still stood at the center; I had climbed that tree many times over the years. I'd crawl out on one of the branches, then I'd stand and survey our neighborhood. There were only three houses on the street the first time I pulled myself up into the tree—ours, the Landers, and the Taylors. But within a couple of years, we had many neighbors. The Bobbins. The Matthews. The Armitages. The Williams. Just last year I had watched Candy's house be built from the ground up.

The Verhoos family sold off their farm an acre at a time over a period of years—until all that remained was the old tree and that surrounding patch of pasture. The selloff began when old Mr. Verhoos died about twenty years ago. Then the son moved to Boston and became a dentist and the daughter went to California and married a state senator. When Mrs. Verhoos got too old to live alone in the farmhouse, she moved into Pickering Manor Nursing Home. She died there shortly after and the rest of the farm was sold by her kids. I was still in elementary school, but I attended Mrs. Verhoos' funeral with my parents. On the way home, my mother told me that Mr. and Mrs. Verhoos had been very good parents. "If you successfully raise your children to be confident, Annie, they will inevitably leave home and live far away. It's called Manifest Destiny. We Americans allow our children to be individuals—not just extensions of our egos. We let go. And our children go on and do great things for themselves and the prosperity of the nation. It's what makes Americans special." I told Mother that I never wanted to move away and I begged her not to send me off alone in the world. Mother had held me and said, "Oh, Annie, not for years. Believe me, you will be ready when the time comes to leave. In fact, you will be excited to step out on your own and invent your own life."

Now I was fifteen, wise beyond my years. Ready for the future. Ready to be a woman. I easily climbed up into the tree and realized that I had an unobstructed view of Philip's patio. I hadn't noticed that the last time I was in the tree. Candy and I had last been up there on the very day Philip moved in last Spring. We weren't there to spy. We didn't even know who he was then. We just liked to hide from everyone and daydream about meeting the Beatles. That day we had made a pact to refer to each other as Mrs. Paul McCartney and Mrs. George Harrison when we were alone—just to pretend that we were really married to them. That seemed so long ago now, but it had been in May. Just four months ago. How could so much happen in just one Summer?

I thought of the Butterfly Effect. My father had explained it to me one night over dinner.

Sometimes it's called the Chaos Theory. It asserts that a small physical change in the atmosphere—and that tiny change can actually be the result of a butterfly flapping its wings—can impact everything else in its wake. Like you can remove a grain of sand from the beach and the whole beach will feel the shift it has to make to fill in that one infinitesimal gap created when the speck of sand disappeared. Even the ocean will have to adjust. And there's no way to stop the changes once they begin. Everything on this planet is affected by everything else because everything on earth is interdependent. Especially the people. When Mother betrayed Mrs. Swenson's loyalty—or vice versa, depending on your point of view—it created an imbalance in the atmosphere of Linton Hill that led to me being betrayed by Candy. I don't even think she intended to betray me but it's a natural law. I was the innocent one. I was nice to everyone, but I became the sacrifice that was necessary to rebalance Pennswalk.

And here's the sad part—the universe doesn't care if you have a broken heart. The universe is impersonal. It can't feel and it doesn't love. It merely seeks balance. It's mathematical. Precise. So I could hate my mother and I did hate my mother, but the universe didn't notice much less care. I could hate all women and I did hate all women, but the universe just shrugged. Maybe my mother was the catalyst for change that Summer. Or maybe it was Arlene. But I would never trust girls again. All of my close friends from this moment on would be boys.

Suddenly I saw Philip emerge from the Williams house. I saw him look around furtively, then reach around the glass door and pull a woman by the hand from inside the house out onto the patio. He wrapped his arms around her and began to kiss her passionately. His hands moved all over her body, even reached between her legs. Who was this woman? She was wearing a scarf but I could see she was blonde. I could see she was slender and stylishly dressed. But I couldn't see her face. Her back was to me. She started to leave and Philip pulled her back again. She threw her head back and laughed. Then they kissed again, a long sensual kiss. Finally, she gently pushed him away and put on her sunglasses which she had been carrying all this time in her right hand. She touched Philip lightly on the chest and then walked quickly around the perimeter of the house toward the front lawn and I could no longer see her. Philip watched her go, then returned to the house, closing the patio door. And it hit me— That woman. Oh my god! *That woman was my mother!*

I slid out of the tree landing on my hands and knees. I stood up and began walking toward the patio. I was in a rage now. I began to cry. Sobbing … screaming, I broke into a run and headed for Philip's door. I pounded on the glass. He quickly appeared and seeing me, slid open the door. He looked astonished. "Leanne? Leanne! What? WHAT? Talk to me."

"KISS ME LIKE YOU KISSED MY MOTHER!!! KISS ME LIKE YOU KISSED MY MOTHER!!"

Philip took my hand and pulled me inside the dining room. I reached out to swipe all the neatly stacked typewritten pages off the table and he stopped me. He held me by the wrists and said in a controlled voice, "It wasn't your mother. It was Dinah Matthews." He released me; I closed my eyes. I moaned; my knees buckled. Slowly I dropped to the floor but before I reached bottom; Philip grabbed me by the shoulders and lifted me and then he kissed me. He pushed me against the wall and kissed me again. I kissed him back. I kissed him with my entire being. The kiss went on and on in wave after wave. He pushed his body against mine. I pushed mine against his. The kiss softened and lengthened. I put my arms around him. I felt myself opening up. There were all these secret places in me that were opening. I could actually hear a key turning in a lock as I opened more and more. Philip's hand pressed against the small of my back, holding me up, holding me closer. His kiss deepened; more doors opened. I could see inside myself. I held on to him for dear life. For my dear life.

Part Two — 1965-1970

a change is gonna come

Chapter 6

I knew my mother's face so well, I swear I could close my eyes and draw a good facsimile. And I'm not even an artist. Her face was a heart, her eyes were almond shaped and topaz-colored, the irises outlined in black. Her mouth was generous with perfect white teeth. Her nose was straight, somewhat wide at the nostrils. She said, in that last feature, she most resembled her father who died of pneumonia when she was eleven. "You would have loved him, Annie," she would say, and her eyes would fill with tears.

After her brief flirtation with blonde hair during that period that she now referred to as The Summer of Awful Arlene Swenson, Mother let her hair return to its natural brunette. She asked me one time if I thought her skin was the color of crème brûlée. We were standing over the sink eating the luscious custard right out of the bowl and I looked at my spoon and shrugged. *Sure … I guess.* Mother once told me that when I was born I looked like a Creole infant—black hair, tiny, slanted eyes and a broad nose. Ruddy skin. She said she almost cried the first time she saw me. But over the next couple months, my skin became pink, my eyes became round and blue, my nose lengthened and then turned up at the tip, and by Christmas, my hair had lightened to a honey blonde. Everyone thereafter said I had my father's coloring and Mother was relieved.

My mother was sick a lot when I was growing up. She had a recurring respiratory thing. Dr. Garner said it was simply a vulnerability to viruses, maybe aggravated by allergies. He couldn't say. Ever since I can remember though, Mother had struggled with a bout of it every Fall. It inevitably started with a cold and then, more often than not, turned into pneumonia. She would be hospitalized for a week and then come home to slowly recuperate. But Mother was indomitable and always recovered well before Christmas which was the holiday that mattered most to her. She'd set goals for herself. Usually she would plan a dinner party to be held just as soon as she was well enough to navigate the grocery store again. She'd lie on the couch in the family room during the day, propped up on bed pillows, a notebook in her lap, a pencil in her hand. I'd find her there when I came home from school, immersed in the details of her next soiree. Everything written down—the guest list, the menu, the flowers, the tablecloth, the color of the napkins, the order of the records on the hi-fi, etc. It cheered her up, gave her the will to live.

When I was still in grade school, Mother's favorite TV show was *The Millionaire*. Every week this rich man would find a deserving person and give her or him a check for a million dollars and then the story would follow how the money changed that person's life. When I was eleven, Mother was terribly sick, more so than usual, and she rallied by imagining that the Millionaire gave her the check. She propped herself up in bed with her notebook and, taking labored breaths at first, began to list how she would spend a fortune. It took her days of calculating and recalculating. First she gave her mother and two sisters, and Daddy's sister and sister-in-law a large check each. Her mother was a widow, but the sisters were all married and while Mother was fond of their husbands she felt strongly that even married women would feel more relaxed all their lives if they had money of their own. Of course, she would also give a "nice check" to Ginger Taylor and maybe to Kitty Landers next door. And to the Pickering Manor Nursing Home Foundation and the ASPCA. And a large gift to Planned Parenthood. Mother proudly displayed a bumper sticker on the fender of her Chevy station wagon that read Every Child a Wanted Child. After that, she would peel off a large block of her million to set aside for college costs for me, TJ, and John. And she'd buy Daddy a sports car of his choosing. And then she'd plan a trip to Paris with Daddy. She would set aside money to purchase some elegant new clothes for both of them in a fashionable New York store, probably Bergdorf's. I would go along and she'd treat me to some wonderful new things, too. Then she would redecorate the house completely. And then she would throw a party for fifty of her dearest friends and family and serve champagne and Lobster Newberg in puff pastry shells! Oh, and she'd get something fun for TJ and John, of course. And if anything remained of her million dollars, it would be deposited into a savings account down at the Hoover Bank under her name only. This fantasy would fuel her recovery and soon she would be up and about, dressed beautifully, and humming in the kitchen as I came down to breakfast, ready for school. "Morning, Glory," she'd sing cheerfully setting a bowl of Cheerios in front of me and I would know the crisis had passed.

When Mother got sick in the Winter of 1965, she was referred to a doctor in Philadelphia who took a long look at her lung x-rays and feared that she had tuberculosis. We were all quarantined in our house—Dad, TJ, John and me—for a week while Mother stayed at the hospital until the doctors decided that the shadows on her lungs were too slow growing for a TB diagnosis. Instead, they reasoned the shadows might just be scarring from her having pneumonia so many times. As always, Mother rallied and seemed fine by Christmas, but she was sick again in February and started seeing lung specialists at the University of Pennsylvania hospital in Philadelphia. They gave her prednisone, a steroid that made her feel so much better we all believed she might never be sick again.

THAT SUMMER OF 1965 I turned sixteen and my parents threw a birthday party for me at the famous Lavender Hall. It was a Bucks County landmark, an eighteenth-century inn that had an elegant restaurant. It was famous because it had a tree growing through the floor in the bar—a live tree. And it had a real wishing well. A song had been written about it for the Broadway musical *Pal Joey. There's a small hotel with a wishing well....* Sinatra sang it in the movie version.

Mother invited the Taylors and Landers and their kids; my grand-mothers, my aunts and uncles and cousins; and all of my friends—Lark, Betsy, Gaye, Bonnie, Audrey, (no, not Candy) and yes, Andy and his brother Jeff. Andy and I were spending an increasing amount of time together although he dated other girls because I had insisted that we keep things platonic. Andy would be leaving for Hamilton College in one year and I had already received my acceptance letter to Syracuse University even though I was only entering my junior year at high school. There had been talk among the counselors at school about me skipping my senior year and going directly to college after eleventh grade. But my mother advocated another year at home for me as she felt I was very naïve despite my high IQ.

Anyway, I picked Syracuse because, in my view, it was quite simply my destiny. First of all, Syracuse University is near Hamilton College where Andy would be going to school and I knew I wanted to be able to continue to see him. Plus I intended to major in journalism and Syr-acuse had a great program. I wrote an essay as part of my admission re-quirements. I laid out an impassioned defense of suicide as the ultimate expression of the right to autonomy in regard to one's body. I guess they thought my reasoning was stellar because I was accepted right away. Or maybe they thought I would kill myself if they didn't take me. Regard-less, that part of my future was now settled. I figured I would fashion my own degree when I got there—one that emphasized journalism, but included philosophy, art history, anthropology and biology. And maybe psychology or law. Or both. And economics. Economics is actually more interesting than it sounds. I wanted to be thought of as a Renaissance Girl. My friends all said that they assumed that I would study Creative Writing, they thought I planned to be an author and I did. But I already knew how to write—I needed things to write *about.* I needed to be ex-posed to ideas and cultures and points of view that differed from my own. You can't just write about yourself. That would be boring.

I told Andy that sex would have to wait until we were away from Pennswalk. I would, of course, need to secure birth control and I wasn't sure how Mother would respond being that I was sixteen. But more than anything, I wanted to have my first time on a bed. I thought the idea of car sex was gross. And then there was Philip. There was a part of me that still wanted to save myself for Philip. We had come so close that day last year ... so close. I fantasized about him a lot.

I did make out with a kid named Bobby Mueller that Summer. We had been in study hall together. I wasn't interested in him, but we were at a barbecue at his house and I drank a gin and tonic that Bobby sneaked out of his parents' bar and it made me horny. But I explained to Bobby on the phone the next morning that I already had a serious boyfriend. I was thinking of course of Philip, but I lied that this boyfriend was a soldier in Vietnam and that I was sorry to have pretended that Bobby's lips were those of my absent beau, but I was desperately lonely with him away. "I hope you understand, Bobby," I said. Bobby was so moved, he got all choked up and told me that his brother had enlisted in the army after graduation back in June and would be going to Vietnam soon. I was immediately sorry that I had so flippantly lied about war, so I told Bobby I would pray for his brother. And I did. That very day, I stood in the shallow end of our pool and stared at the clouds that were painted on the walls below the surface and asked the Water Creator to hear my plea that Bobby's brother be spared any harm.

As I intimated, I was still deeply in love with Philip although he had left Pennswalk soon after Friendship Day and I hadn't heard from him since. Whenever I called his apartment in New York, which I did at least once a month that year, no one answered. I wondered if Philip had given me the wrong number. Accidentally on purpose. But when Mother mailed him an invitation to my birthday party, he RSVP'd immediately.

He drove down from New York City the day of the party and presented me with a First Edition copy of *Alice in Wonderland* that he had purchased in London. He took a room at the Sycamore Inn and left the following morning. My mother was shocked that he bought me such an expensive gift. "For a teenager? You spoil her, Philip!" But I was thrilled. I love the language in that book; it's one of my favorites. I thanked Philip profusely and he said, "It's the ultimate coming of age story, Leanne. Alice has to learn to deal with the unreliable world of adults."

Philip and I had a private moment late that evening at the restaurant. We were standing by the wishing well and he reached into his pocket and pulled out two pennies. He handed one to me and said, "You go first." I closed my eyes and tossed the penny in the well. Then Philip did the same.

Philip pushed a stray hair out of my eyes and said, "Well? What did you wish for?"

I answered. "World peace."

Philip started to laugh; then realized I was serious. "I wished for a good review in the *Times*," he snorted. "I'm too shallow for you, Leanne."

"Do men love war? Did you love it?"

Philip lightly touched the gold circle pin I was wearing on my dress that evening and smiled. "Men don't make friends easily, Leanne. They aren't like women. They have to manufacture excuses to bond. So they conjure up nations. It gives them a community with a shared identity and sense of purpose. It also gives them common enemies. So they spend a lot of energy and money defending their land. And the more they do it, the more meaningful this piece of land becomes to them. Which is to say, at a certain level—yes, men do love war. They need it. It gives them a sense of belonging."

I listened carefully. Then I responded. "My mother told me about this elite Roman Legion during the height of the Roman Empire. They all had wives and children at home, but they would be deployed in these campaigns that lasted for decades. So each of them fell in love with a fellow soldier, first it was emotionally—then it became sexually. They bonded so they wouldn't be lonely. It created the fiercest fighting force Rome had ever known because these men weren't fighting for some abstract idea of flag and country. They were fighting for each other."

"Your mother told you this story?"

"She read it somewhere. Probably *Reader's Digest*."

There was a pause now. Philip and I were standing so close, I could smell his after shave. His face was serious as though he was concentrating on a puzzle. But when he finally spoke, his voice was gentle, "Are you really as wonderful as this?"

I took a step toward him. "Can I come visit you?"

He took a deep breath. "It's just not a good time for that. I've been staying in a rented house in Massachusetts. An old house, like some of the older homes in this area. Leanne, the truth is … I have fallen in love with … eighteenth-century architecture. It's so simple, balanced and reasonable.…"

I wasn't fooled. "Do you have a girlfriend, Philip?" We were both quiet for a long moment. I took another step closer to him. Now I was pressing against him. I took hold of his sleeve.

"We can't, Leanne. You're sixteen. What kind of man would I be? How could I live with myself?"

What kind of man would he be? I realized at that moment that Philip, although he was thirty-three years old and quite grown up, was wrestling with an identity crisis which is an overwhelming existential experience. I know. As it happens, I had myself gone through such a crucible many years before. When I was in kindergarten I stole a classmate's fake bunny fur jacket. I really wanted a fake bunny fur jacket of my own; they were very popular that year. One of the girls in my class had one. It was pink. And every day, my lust for this jacket grew. I became obsessed. I begged my mother to buy me one, but Mother said no, I couldn't have a bunny fur jacket. She said it wouldn't flatter me.

So one day at the end of class, I walked into the cloak room and, while Cynthia was getting a drink at the water fountain, I slipped the pink bunny fur jacket off the coat hook assigned to CYNTHIA and left the building. I was busted later that afternoon by the principal who was my Grandmother Hugh's best friend. She called my mother and then she and Mother confronted me. Neither woman could believe that I would do such a thing—actually steal another person's property. And I wasn't the least bit remorseful. I knew Cynthia's parents would replace it for her. Money wasn't an issue for any of us.

I was nevertheless forced to return it. I told my mother that I wished with all my heart that I was Cynthia and my mother's eyes became slits like a witch in a fairy tale and she said, "Really Annie? Are you sure you want to change places with that girl? You would have to *become* Cynthia, you know, and she would get to be Annie. She would have your brothers, your bedroom, your puppy, your Daddy and me. She would have vacations at the beach in Rehoboth. *And she would have your thoughts!* Could you walk away from being Annie and take the chance that being Cynthia might make you even less happy than you are right now?"

Of course, I didn't want to be Cynthia. I liked being me. I just wanted her jacket. Given the chance I would do it again. And I consider myself a very moral person. I guess I learned that you can separate what you want from who you are. And I'm certain that Philip will eventually understand that, too.

MY PARENTS BOUGHT ME a 1962 baby blue Cutlass Convertible that birthday. Mother insisted that Daddy buy me a used car to start me out until I got comfortable behind the wheel. As it turned out, I was a terrible driver from the get go. I simply couldn't concentrate—something about the forward motion, the blur of scenery in my peripheral vision. It hypnotized me and sent me into a dream-like state wherein I would lose myself in a story of my own creation. *A mysterious stranger approaches me. He has an accent. Iranian? He's a detective and he asks for my help on a case. We travel on the Orient Express to … where does that train go? Vienna? Yes … we travel to Vienna.* And then there would be the squeal of tires, the long blast of a car horn and once, I came out of my trance to find my Cutlass' front wheels up over the high curbs on Congress Street and lying in front of my severely dented grill, the 1735 cast iron gas lamp that had stood on that spot for more than 200 years. I remember a crowd gathering and Mr. Yoder, the town's only police officer whose daughter Bonnie was a friend, leaning through the window on the driver's side. "Annie, you okay, Honey? Well, whoops, huh? Come on—I'll give you a lift home and see what your dad wants to do about the car. And don't worry—we'll stand that ol' gas lamp back up. It'll be right as rain. Whew—smell that gas … listen, folks, don't anybody light a match, okay?"

After we got the car back from Hennessey's Repair Shoppe, my father insisted that Andy do all the driving in the Cutlass. Now Andy practically moved in with my family. I'd come home from a friend's house on a weekend afternoon to find Andy downstairs in the family room strumming his banjo and watching a football game with Dad. Or the two of them would be shooting hoops in the driveway with TJ and John.

So Andy drove my car when we'd go to the movies. He'd drop me off when I wanted to spend time with girlfriends and return to pick me up when I called him later. Yes, I used him like a chauffeur, but he seemed so willing. He said he wasn't wild about driving an American car, but he did appreciate that my Cutlass was more reliable than any of the half dozen cars he had parked in the long driveway of his house at the moment, among them an Alpha Romeo with a bad transmission, a Porsche that only drove in reverse, and a Volkswagen Beetle with bad brakes and some other issues. He did have one American car—a Model T that couldn't go faster than 18 miles an hour. Andy worked on his cars himself, but progress was slow. His biggest automotive triumph came when he successfully merged the Volkswagen body on top of the Porsche "guts" and somehow got the thing out of reverse. He delighted in the fact that he now had a "Bug" that could do 120 miles per hour. One day Mr. Yoder made him pull over. "Andy Wetherill! Do you know how fast you were going? I clocked you at 106!"

"Awww … c'mon, Mr. Yoder. You're kidding, right? It's a Volkswagen. There must be something wrong with your clock."

THAT CHRISTMAS OF 1965 Andy got himself into the headlines, not just in the *Pennswalk Gazette* but in the *Philadelphia Inquirer* as well. Every year on Christmas Day, a pompous buffoon by the name of Charles St. Lawrence and some other douchey businessmen from Pennswalk reenacted George Washington's famous crossing of the Delaware River at the exact spot where it originally happened on December 25, 1776. It's a Bucks County Christmas Day custom and that year, it would be attended, as usual, by many of the residents of Pennswalk and a scattering of press people and photographers. And if past was prologue, it would follow well-established tradition.

St. Lawrence and his men would wear perfect replicas of the uniforms worn by the soldiers in the famous painting by Emanuel Leutze. And they would be well rehearsed, having gathered in Mr. St. Lawrence's garage daily for an hour to practice posing exactly like the figures in the painting, beginning on the evening after Thanksgiving and continuing until Christmas Eve day. Mr. St. Lawrence would as always reenact the role of George Washington. He'd stand at the prow of the boat, his wool cape thrown back over his shoulders. Mr. Fleming, who owned the historic Sycamore Inn, would be the colonial soldier who stood behind Mr. St. Lawrence waving the Stars and Stripes. The other men, having the lesser roles, would be seated, but very animated nonetheless.

The crowd on the shore would sing "My Country 'Tis of Thee" loudly as Mr. St. Lawrence and his men boarded the rowboat and shoved off onto the river. Then everyone would cheer and say stupid things like Huzzah! When the men reached the other side of the Delaware and got out of the boat, they would wave to us. Then they would climb into a couple of station wagons and pass around thermoses of hot brandy during the drive across the bridge. They would always return to a warm reception where they would pose for photographs and talk to reporters. Mr. St. Lawrence would speak solemnly to the children gathered around him about how it did take bravery for him to cross the river in a rowboat while standing up, but "it must have been extra scary for General Washington and his men that cold day in 1776 because they had to do it in the dark." That would be quoted in the *Pennswalk Gazette*.

The river is a mere five miles from Pennswalk and my father had taken us a couple of times, but my mother couldn't stand Mr. St. Lawrence so she had never attended this event. Mother said he was cheap in spite of it being well known that he had plenty of money. He always gave a skimpy contribution to the Pickering Manor Nursing Home Foundation, and Mother took it personally because she was president of the Board. Furthermore, Mrs. St. Lawrence was overheard at Friendship Day that Fall badmouthing Linton Hill, calling the residents "a tribe of alcoholic nouveau riche Philadelphians." And Mrs. St. Lawrence would pass Mother on State Street and barely acknowledge her even though Mother was always polite, always said, "Good morning, Delores." Privately, Mother explained her courtesy to me. "I'm not going to give that woman the satisfaction of thinking I even notice her snub."

But, of course, she did. Anyone who had ever spent any time in our house would have heard these stories. Mother repeated them often, and Andy was there all the time. So Andy decided to avenge Mother's hurt feelings that Christmas of 1965. He and his friends scrounged up costumes that gave them the look of the Hessian mercenary soldiers who had been hired by the British and were stationed in Trenton, New Jersey, on that fateful morning in 1776. Andy borrowed a motorboat, and he and his friends planned to hide out on an island that was positioned about a third of the way into the river, a spot that St. Lawrence and his men would certainly have passed on their way to the opposite shore.

Andy picked me up on Christmas morning in my baby blue Cutlass which he had taken home the night before. I looked at him. "Are you really going to do this, Andy?"

"Is JFK dead?"

"Grant Fuller says President Kennedy's brain is being kept alive in the hospital in Dallas where he.... "

"Grant Fuller needs to get a hobby or adopt a dog."

I dropped Andy off about a quarter mile before the park; a crowd of spectators was gathering. He took off his coat and handed it to me.

"You're going to freeze."

"Nah." He struck a pose. "What do you think? Do I look appropriately mercenary?"

I slid behind the wheel and he opened the door and said, "Give me a kiss for luck." I kissed him affectionately and drove on to the park where I joined my fellow Pennswalkians along the shore. Soon after, General Washington arrived with his middle-aged mavericks and climbed into their boat nearly overturning it as all the men found their assigned seats. The General raised his hand, someone yelled "Godspeed, General Washington." Someone else yelled "Huzzah!" A couple of young men pushed the boat out onto the water. And the singing began. *My country 'tis of thee, sweet land of liberty....*

They were about ten yards from shore when suddenly out from behind a small isle, the dastardly Hessians appeared—led by Andy. Boldly flying a British flag, they swooped out into the open water, shaking their fists and whooping like Indians. And then one of the boys fired a toy cannon which made a loud boom and so surprised Mr. St. Lawrence that he lost his balance and fell overboard. Andy scrambled to rescue him, finally succeeding in pulling General Washington into the Hessian motorboat. Cameras flashed. People gasped, then laughed uproariously, once they saw that Mr. St. Lawrence was safe. They pointed to his hat and powdered wig which were swiftly carried downstream eventually disappearing under the current, and probably settling in the mud.

I quickly got in my car and whisked Andy away. He was shivering and I covered him with his coat and removed mine and threw it over him as well. I drove to his house where he changed into warm dry clothes while I hung out in the kitchen with the Wetherills and sipped hot cider. Andy and I returned to my house later that morning and he delivered a blow by blow retelling of the event that delighted my Dad and brothers and made Mother's eyes twinkle. "Oh, Andy," she said. "Oh, Andy, you didn't!"

In the days that followed, Mr. St. Lawrence fumed and threatened Andy with lawsuits, but the other men talked him out of it because it made them look like bad sports which wouldn't be good for their businesses. But for the next couple of Christmases, St. Lawrence hired a helicopter to fly over Andy's house and follow him if he left. And he gave the pilot one more instruction: "Shoot that kid if he gets close to the river."

For my part, I didn't care whether Mr. St. Lawrence got his comeuppance for snubbing my family. I just loved the fact that a wealthy man was humiliated by an average guy. Well, Andy was far from average, but he wasn't rich and his act struck me as inspired and instructive. A David and Goliath story for my time. So when Andy and I finally found ourselves alone that evening, I put my arms around him and kissed him on the mouth. He responded passionately. Our first kiss. "You turn me on," I said, looking directly into his eyes. Later that evening I went with Andy back to his house and while his family was watching some Christmas special on TV, Andy and I went upstairs to his room and made love for the first time. On his bed. Losing one's virginity is an ordeal not worth describing. But after that, it was common knowledge in school that I was the famous Andy Wetherill's girlfriend. Andy would openly kiss me when he saw me in the halls or at my locker and then he would yell, "I love you, Annie" as he walked backwards on to his next class. I'm not ex-troverted like Andy so I was actually relieved when he left for Hamilton College in the Fall of 1966. And I could be alone again.

I RARELY SPOKE TO Philip my last year of high school. He was always it seemed on the move. Connecticut. Chicago. London. New York. We would talk on the phone daily for three days and then I wouldn't hear from him for months. In the Spring of 1967, just a couple of weeks be-fore my high school graduation, he phoned.

"Where are you, Philip?"

"Back in New York. At the apartment."

"I want to read *Portnoy's Complaint*."

"I'm still working on it. I'll give you an autographed copy when it's published."

"Is it funny?"

"Yeah." He laughed.

"Are you going to dedicate it to me?"

"I think not." He laughed again.

"You always say I am your muse."

"And you are." Pause. "So are you all set to attend Syracuse University in the Fall?"

"Yes! I can't get out of Pennswalk fast enough."

"Well, I have news. I've accepted a guest professor position at Hamil-ton College for the next two years. Teaching American Lit. So I will be in your vicinity beginning this Fall."

My heart danced. "Do you realize, Philip, that *L-I-T* means *bed* in French?"

Pause.

"So how's Andy doing? Do you hear from him?"

"Of course."

"How has he liked his first year at Hamilton?"

"He loves it. He's studying Chinese history with a dissident."

"I don't know if he mentioned this, Leanne, but they are opening a women's college in a year. It will share the campus with Hamilton. Separate but equal."

"Yeah, Andy told me. It's going to be called Kirkland College."

"Maybe you can transfer over next year. Then you'd be close to Andy. And to me."

"Maybe when I finally get to Syracuse, I will discover that I prefer a little distance from both of you. Maybe I will want to have some adventures in which you are not involved." I was immediately sorry for saying that. There was a moment of heavy silence.

"Okay then, Miss Hughs. I'll call you next Sunday."

"I love you, Philip."

"Stop it," he said with a warm laugh.

About a week before I left for Syracuse University, I asked my mother if she would give me written permission so I could get birth control pills from our doctor. Andy was getting tired of using condoms and I was nervous that they might fail. Gaye Parsons had recently told me a story about a girl who gave birth to a baby that was actually holding a condom in its little fist.

I was packing for college and Mother was watching me. She hadn't given me an answer yet and the question hung in the air as I tried to avoid her eyes. Finally she spoke. "Annie, I have a story I want to tell you. No, please sit and face me. You can pack later. I want you to hear this." I sat on my bed and she began. "Years ago … Daddy and I were newlyweds. We were down at the beach, walking along the boardwalk one evening when we ran into an old classmate of mine. From high school. His name was Stevie Schmidt. I was wearing this darling tan jersey dress with the dark red belt that my sister Jeannie had given me for my birthday. And a pretty paisley scarf around my … oh gosh! And I was wearing the dark green alligator pumps that Great Grandmother Turner stared at the first time I met her! I always blamed myself for her stroke, but Joan said she had been sick.…"

"Mother! Jesus! I don't care what you wore!"

Mother looked at me coolly. "Oh, excuse me … I didn't realize you are in a hurry. I thought I might have some time with you before you leave for college. You're never home anymore and…."

"Fine … just…."

Mother took a deep breath and resumed. "So Stevie Schmidt was holding the hand of a lovely young woman. They stopped and he said, 'Beverly! As I live and breathe! You look wonderful.' Just like that! I almost staggered I was so shocked. You see, Stevie had the worst stutter you can imagine when he was in school. It was such a shame. He was handsome and sweet but he couldn't talk. So he had never dated, Annie. Not once and didn't even go to the prom."

"Uh huh."

"So he introduces the young woman as his wife and then he suddenly says, 'We are here celebrating. We just learned that Maryann is pregnant! We're going to be parents!' Well, Maryann blushed bright pink and said, 'Oh, Stevie … I haven't even told my mother yet!' And I thought to myself—oh my, she is such a lady. You can see that. Lovely manners. Good sense of what is appropriate. And so well groomed. And it hit me." Mother snapped her fingers. "It hit me, Annie. That's why Stevie lost his stutter."

"Mother, I'm losing the thread here…."

"She was a virgin, Annie! That's why he lost his stutter!"

"I'm totally lost."

"See he didn't have to worry about being compared to anyone else when they met. He felt secure with Maryann so he could relax and well, let Nature take its course. They fell in love, the sex was wonderful, he became confident as a man, and soon his stutter was a distant memory. And they got married. And now they were having a baby."

"Andy doesn't have a stutter."

"But you don't really love Andy, do you?" She paused and looked at me. I dropped my eyes. "Stay a virgin, Annie. Men are fragile."

The next day, Andy drove me to the Margaret Sanger Clinic at 17 W 16th Street in Greenwich Village where I was fitted for a diaphragm, which was the most embarrassing experience I had ever had. The nurse was extremely nice, but I was uncoordinated and frankly clueless about my internal anatomy. I had trouble picturing where everything was. Lying there on the examining table, I was reminded of a line from a play by British playwright Joe Orton. Philip had called me from London to recite for me part of a scene after he saw it performed in the West End. A woman is trying to seduce her young boarder. She flirts, "Until I was thirty, I knew more about the continent of Africa than I knew about my own body." Philip mimicked a perfect Cockney accent and we both laughed hysterically. I thought it was such a ridiculous observation until I tried to insert a diaphragm on my own. That was so difficult I almost committed to being celibate for the rest of my life. Almost.

Chapter 7

First semester of my freshman year at Syracuse University was pretty typical. I had my ears pierced. My parents forbade it when I was "still living under their roof as it looks very Puerto Rican." But I was no longer living under their roof. A girl with the nickname Moose who lived on my floor in Haven Hall used ice to numb my lobes to the point of frostbite, then hammered a darning needle through my flesh and into a half of a raw potato. It took days for the swelling to go down and I had two infections. But I have formidable pain tolerance, so I eventually got used to the tenderness and took to wearing a pair of cascading earrings that had been made in India and looked like miniature wind chimes. And sometimes tangled in my long hair. I smoked grass and hash. I gained ten pounds. And I got a D in Western Civilization. My mother was furious, so I sent her an index card on which I had carefully lettered a quote from *The Taming of the Shrew*:

> *I am no breeching scholar in the schools.*
> *I'll not be tied to hours nor 'pointed time.*
> *But learn my lessons as I please myself.*

My father framed it and hung it over his bar, so when any of their friends asked how's Annie doing, he could point and beam. Mother on the other hand simmered.

Andy drove us to college in my baby blue Cutlass Convertible—back and forth, to and from Pennswalk on vacations and Summer breaks. He kept my car at Hamilton where he had free parking as he had joined a fraternity last Spring and could now live at the house since he was a sophomore. It was an independent fraternity, one that had broken with the national Lambda Chi Alpha when the brothers admitted a Black student back in 1958, which was a violation of the national charter. After that it was known as Gryphon House. It was perfect for Andy. All of the boys were smart and irreverent like him. But in that way that the most rebellious boys can be—all of them were oh, so romantic. One boy, a senior, proposed to his girlfriend who was a senior at Smith, by embroidering the back of a custom-made white leather glove with gorgeous jewel-toned flowers and vines and in the palm the words, in beautiful script, *I give thee my hand.*

Andy, for his part, was learning Scottish love songs on the ukulele. He'd pluck the strings with a delicacy that gave the music a haunting almost medieval quality. Like a lute. *My love is like a red, red rose....* Two weekends a month, he would drive over to Syracuse, pick me up and take me back to Hamilton for the weekend. I'd sleep with him in his room. The Gryphon boys didn't mind. The trip took about an hour— forty-eight miles on Interstate 90, a straight shot and Andy would serenade me all the way in his beautiful, heartfelt tenor.

Twice that semester, Andy failed to get me back to my dorm by curfew on Sunday night and I was grounded for the following weekend. Which meant that I was required to check in with the Resident Advisor for our building every hour "on the hour" until curfew, which was midnight on Friday and Saturday, and 11pm on Sunday. I couldn't even just go to bed early. I had to stay completely dressed! It also meant that my parents received a phone call from the Dean of Students reporting my "unacceptable behavior." But my mother told them she wasn't "in the least upset" with her daughter since she knew who I was with and that he was "a family friend." The boys' dormitories, by the way, didn't have a curfew which I considered an example of outrageous paternalism, and I organized a protest on the front lawn of Haven Hall. One of the fraternities even sent members over to support us. Two years later, the curfews for women were finally abolished. I take some credit for that.

 from a lung specialist at the University of Philadelphia while I was away that first semester. He had studied her medical records going back years and wanted to see her in the flesh. She phoned me at school. "Maybe they want me to donate my body to science after I die," she said excitedly. "Anyhoo, I made the appointment during your Christmas break. Ginger said she would take me, but I'd like you to go with me instead, Annie. Then afterwards we can go to Bookbinders for Snapper Soup. Make it a 'girl day.' Doesn't that sound fun?"

We met Dr. Pill in his office. I kid you not. That was his name. Dr. Pill. Mother's lung x-rays were on display. He referred to them when he talked about the shadows in her lungs. "First the good news. It's not cancer. We have also ruled out TB. I have to ask you a question, Mrs..... May I call you Beverly?" Mother nodded. "Beverly, are you Black?"

I almost laughed. I looked at my mother with her creamy crème brûlée complexion. She was unruffled. "No," she said.

"Was your grandmother, great-grandmother, any of your grandfathers … anyone in your direct hereditary line—Black?" Again Mother looked him in the eye and said simply. "No."

"Did your family ever live in South Carolina?"

Mother crossed her legs and looked relaxed. She said, "Yes, as a matter of fact, my father's mother came out of Beaufort. She moved north to the eastern shore of Maryland in the late 1800s after the war. I myself was born in Philadelphia."

Dr. Pill sat on the corner edge of his big desk now and faced her. "I believe you have sarcoidosis of the lungs, Beverly. It's a progressive disease that causes inflammation in the lungs that can lead to pulmonary fibrosis. At the moment there is no cure, but it can be treated. Your form is most commonly found in people who are Black or of mixed-race backgrounds. And there is a common connection to South Carolina. We are also exploring the possibility that there is an environmental element, maybe an allergy to pine trees. They are prevalent along the coast. I think you should talk to your mother. See if she has any information. It's important that we stop guessing on your diagnosis. We need to get it right."

We skipped lunch. In the car on the way home, Mother turned the radio on and said, "Play whatever you want, Honey."

"Mother, are we Black?"

She kept her eyes on the road. After a moment, she inhaled deeply. "Yes. But you must swear to me that you will never tell anyone. And that includes Daddy and your brothers. I mean it, Annie. Tom would never forgive me for deceiving him. Your brothers' lives would be wrecked. And God, don't tell Andy. Don't tell anyone."

Later that night, after Daddy went to sleep, Mother slipped into my room and sat on my bed. She sighed. "Truth is a wonderful thing, Annie. It's just not safe in everyone's hands." She slipped a photo out of her bathrobe pocket and showed me. "This is your Gi-Gi Clara." In my family, Gi-Gi stood for Great Grandmother. I looked at the photo. Gi-Gi Clara was a petite woman, she looked more like a girl actually, and Mother said it was likely that she was only fifteen—that the photo was taken just before she was married. She had striking eyes, eyes like my mother's with that clear grey topaz, ringed in black. And a heart shaped face tilted to one side, a delighted smile on her lips. We had always been told that she was born in Spain. Now Mother presented a tale that she claimed to be *the true story of how Great Grandfather Yeo came to fall in love with and marry a light-skinned former slave named Clara.* Clara's story was elaborate, preposterous at times. Mother had learned it from her mother and now it was my turn to know the truth.

Mother said that she had kept the secret until now *not* because she bore Gi-Gi Clara any ill will but because the world is such a dangerous place. "When I was growing up, Annie, it was more dangerous to be a person of mixed race than just pure Negro. You were more apt to be lynched if you were a mulatto—especially if you married a White man which of course I did. So my mother taught us not to speak of it. Still we had to be prepared in case our baby suddenly appeared with the features of our distant African ancestors. Black thick hair, for example. That's where Clara's story about being Spanish would give us cover. Mainly Mother taught us not to tell the men. Not our husbands. Not our fathers. Not our sons. They can't keep a secret and they are fragile. This is the women's burden."

Over the next few days, I wrote a short story to capture every detail. I disguised it as fiction. And I read it every day. And every day, I got angrier and angrier. I wasn't even sure what it was that made me so mad, but I felt inauthentic, like a part of me had never been integrated into my identity. When I returned to campus after the holidays, I no longer visited Andy at Gryphon House. I told him that my homework was piling up and I was falling behind and needed to stay on campus on the weekends. He said okay but sounded hurt.

I sought out and began to attend political rallies on the Quad. In February, I met Dr. Timothy Leary. He was on campus to give a lecture on freedom in the Manley Field House. Wearing a gold-embroidered tunic of white silk, he sat on a Persian rug like a guru and advised the packed audience to "Drop Out or Cop Out!" We all knew about his recent arrest for marijuana possession, and we agreed with him that it was hypocritical of the government to criminalize weed when nicotine was so much worse for our health and yet cigarettes remained legal.

Underscoring that hypocrisy, Andy had told me that it was a fact that the big tobacco companies in America had already secured trademarks for names of marijuana cigarettes in anticipation of Congress legalizing weed which Andy said was imminent. The tobacco lobby, which had all the conservative Southern Baptist Senators in its pocket, was pressing hard for grass to be legal because there were big bucks in it and all of that money was currently going to the black market. Andy was certain that by Summer we would be able to buy packs of Acapulco Gold, Panama Red, and Maui Wowie at gas stations all over the country.

Dr. Leary continued his impassioned outreach to us, the next generation of Americans. "Get in the habit of thinking for yourselves. Question authority. Don't get trapped by the seeming ease of reality. Turn on, tune in, drop out." He was an older man. He could have been one of our fathers if our fathers were really handsome and hip with long hair. Anyway, I trusted him. So later that evening, I dropped acid for the first time with my new friends, Cool Breeze and Redhat. And I loved the experience. Colors were brighter and every word anyone said suddenly seemed to vibrate with layers of meaning. Plus Cool Breeze was smart and so funny. He did a long riff on his observations of parrot nostrils and I almost passed out laughing. One other thing. Cool Breeze was Black. I now had a Black friend.

EVERY SUNDAY NIGHT, A bunch of us on my floor of the dormitory would squeeze into Laura Hand's room to watch *Star Trek* on her little portable TV. But on Sunday night, March 31, 1968, *Star Trek* was interrupted by a special announcement by President Lyndon Johnson. We all groaned as the image of the man with the Buddha lobes hanging from his big ears appeared on the little screen. Laura hushed us—she wanted to hear what he had to say. She was a political science major and figured there would probably be a quiz in class about this. LBJ began speaking about the escalating war in Vietnam and how his efforts to bring the North Vietnamese to the table to negotiate a peace settlement had been rebuffed by the North Vietnamese leadership. I thought for a moment that he might say—*So I launched an atom bomb at them and now everyone better get in the basement.* But instead he said, "I shall not seek and I will not accept the nomination of my party for another term as your president."

There was a stunned silence in Laura's bedroom, and then Moose said, "April Fool!" But Laura said, "Wow, this is going to open up the 1968 Democratic election—now there will be choices!!"

She was right. Robert Kennedy was the first to declare his candidacy for President of the United States. A couple of the girls immediately signed up to volunteer for his campaign. But I remembered my mother saying that Bobby Kennedy almost left his wife and kids to move in with Jackie Kennedy soon after John's assassination. And I, like Mother, simply couldn't support a man with that kind of flaccid moral center. At least not for President of the United States. So I chose to volunteer for Eugene McCarthy. He was a good man and he was the Peace Candidate.

PHILIP HAD LITTLE TIME for me that first year when I was at Syracuse and he was at Hamilton. He was settling into a house that he was renting near campus in that small college town—Clinton, New York. Philip was immediately popular with the faculty as well as the students, so he didn't lack for a social life on campus. But his passion was writing. In his free time, he wrote. So it wasn't till the end of Spring semester, May 12, 1968, according to my diary, that I finally got a call from him.

"She's dead, Leanne."

"Who?"

"My wife. A car accident in Central Park. She was drunk of course."

"I'm sorry, Philip."

"I'm not. She's dead and I didn't have to kill her. I want to celebrate."

I took a morning bus from Syracuse to Hamilton and stayed with Philip until late Thursday afternoon. I didn't tell Andy I was coming, and Philip and I didn't venture outside onto the campus where I might have been recognized by one of the Gryphon House brothers. We stayed in bed the entire two days except during meals. I roasted a chicken the French way with lemons and thyme. It made the house smell wonderful. And we drank wine and ate in candlelight. And we made love repeatedly. Oh my god, I loved being touched by him. And I loved touching him in ways that made him groan. It was even better than I had imagined it would be. I thought that I had never felt so open, so responsive to another human being in my entire life. On Thursday morning still in bed, I finally shared my secret with him.

"Philip, I'm Black."

"And blue? Was I too rough?" He rolled on top of me again and nuzzled my neck.

"I'm Negro, Philip." He laughed. "I'm serious."

Philip studied me for a moment. Then he stepped out of bed and pulled on some clothes. "I'll make us coffee," he said.

I pulled on my jeans and sweater and joined him in the kitchen. "I've written a story, Philip. May I read it to you?"

The Spanish Bride by Leanne Taylor Hughs

Florence sat before her mother-in-law and kept her eyes down even though she wanted to look into Miss Clara's almond eyes. They were such an unusual color, pale topaz with a black outline; striking against her skin, the color of beach sand and smooth with not a line, not a wrinkle. Florence checked the math in her head, Miss Clara was born in 1860—yes that would make her sixty six on this day in 1926. Florence had married Miss Clara's youngest son John ten years before and they had two children with a third on the way. And yet she had never heard Miss Clara speak other than to note her whispering to her son on occasion. Florence had prodded her husband on the matter. "John, can she speak? I mean is she physically able to form language?" He would laugh and say, "Of course. She simply chooses not to." But here she was speaking perfectly clearly. It took a full minute for Florence to get past the surprise and listen to the words.

Miss Clara patted Florence's hand and said, "I wanted to talk to you privately, Dear, as what I have to say will affect you and your children forever more." Florence noticed the dulcet rhythm of the South in her accent. Perhaps she was mishearing. It was common knowledge in the County that Miss Clara was Spanish, born and bred. John Yeo had met Miss Clara through a family connection in the country of Spain many years ago and married her there in Europe, before bringing her back to the family farm in Easton, Maryland. She never returned to Spain, not even to visit her mother, not once. The family said that she rarely spoke much about Spain except how good the cocoa was. They said that within a year, she had forgotten all her Spanish words.

Miss Clara inhaled deeply and began. "I was born on a rice plantation in the Low Country of South Carolina, near the ocean. We were slaves. Florence—please sit down and sip your tea. It'll do you no good to run. You are carrying some of my blood in your womb and your other children already carry it. You need to hear what I have to say and I need to say it to you before I die." Florence felt the blood drain from her face. She sat. More precisely Florence fell back onto the cushion of the settee in Miss Clara's private parlor, the one off her bedroom.

"Yes, we were slaves, but my mother was favored by the bukruh ... that's how the Gullah people call the White master in the Carolinas. And Mama was brought into the big house when she was eleven. My mother always kept sharp count of the full moons and added them up every now and then to calculate her age. So she was for sure eleven if that's what she says she was when she became the personal slave for Mr. Hillman's wife. My mama was a pretty girl and as she grew up, she attracted the attention of many men around the plantation including a young Black slave that she married in a Christian ceremony. But the White foreman liked her, too. And there weren't much she could do to resist him. So she ended up having three children, the youngest was me and I alone came out White.

"When the war ended, President Lincoln freed the slaves but that had gone and been done a few years before when some general from the Yankee army came through the Low Country announcing that all the slaves were freed. And then just months later that got reversed and we were all slaves again. So no one trusted that it would last even when the President himself said it out loud and it was written in the newspapers. There was so much anger in the South after the war. Such a bitter defeat and White men looking everywhere for someone to blame.

"So Mama determined to send me north before it all changed again. She herself intended to stay with the Hillmans and so did her husband and my two half-sisters. They didn't know any other life and weren't sure they could start again. But Mama figured with my skin being so light, I had a chance for a different life. Perhaps, a better life. So she sent me away. I was seven years old. Mama prepared me for weeks before I left. 'You keep your eyes down, Clara, and your bonnet on and you say that your people are all dead from the war and you are looking for your mama's cousin Germaine in Easton, Maryland. Have you got that?' She practiced me saying it like a White person would—every day until I began to believe it myself. Then she put me in a wagon with several other girls and we began our journey. She called after me, 'Remember, Clara, to pray to Gawd. Gawd stick by you children.'

"I slept in the homes of strangers with no firelight after dusk. It would have been frightening for a little girl except that there were so many kind women all along the trail—colored and White—who seemed to know, unlike me, where I was headed. And then the day came when I arrived here at the Yeo Farm in Maryland. Oh, I liked the Yeos right from the start. They kept me hidden inside their big wonderful house, so I was safe from questioning eyes and they never seemed in a hurry to move me along to the next destination. I began to feel at home. Mrs. Yeo said I was a sincere helper and a good girl. The family taught me their Quaker ways and I learned to pray in silence with them. I couldn't go to the Meeting House but I didn't mind. I had a nice bed in a room that I shared with the Yeos' youngest daughter, Mary, who was my age and we would play games together in the evening after supper. I guess I assumed that I would move on eventually but years passed.

"One day—by this time I was fifteen—Mr. Yeo said to me, 'Our son Clayton is very fond of you, Clara. Are you fond of him?' I nodded my head. Clayton liked to read and I would ask him to read me stories from his book. And so he started teaching me also to read and write. He was a handsome boy then as now with a sweet smile and a gentle voice. Mr. Yeo explained on how it would be necessary to send me away for a short time and then bring me back to introduce me to the community as Clayton's wife. So a plan was made to send me to Spain on the continent of Europe. No wait, Florence … this is true. As Gawd has witnessed. Mr. Yeo's sister, Sarah, who was a teacher at the time asked to accompany me as she was very keen to see an actual part of Europe and maybe even buy a new dress there. We traveled on a large ship that set out from Baltimore. It took weeks, but when we got to Spain, we stayed with Mr. Yeo's cousin Sally who had married a successful Spanish businessman. He owned a wool factory and they had a beautiful home. Miss Sally was for sure happy to have company from Maryland so to get caught up on all the news. Oh, we lived in luxury, Florence, while we waited for Clayton to arrive with his brother Josiah. I think a couple of months went by, maybe more. I became quite fond of hot chocolate during

my time in Spain and had to buy a new dress myself since my old one soon became quite tight. I also took to doing my hair differently. When Clayton arrived, he said he almost didn't recognize me. I was alarmed but he assured me he liked the changes. In fact, he said I was beautiful.

"So we were married. And then we returned to Easton and the Yeo Farm. And Clayton presented me to the community as his Spanish bride. Which meant I was accepted now and forever more as White. I would no longer have to be hidden. But my mother-in-law attached two conditions to this freedom. I must never speak outside the house again and I must never contact my family back in Carolina. And so I never saw my mama again except in my dreams."

Here Miss Clara paused. She winced like she'd tasted something bitter. Then she continued, "I lost my first baby. And my second and I feared that Gawd had cursed me for lying about my true color. After all He tells us we are all His children and that Jesus loves us all even those of us who are colored. Perhaps Gawd thought I didn't trust His plan for me. But I prayed earnestly every morning and night. Kum ba yuh. Gawd stick by you children. And finally Josiah was born, healthy and strong, and John, your husband, followed and after twelve more years came Mary. Josiah and Mary took their fair hair and blue eyes from the Yeo family, but John had the mark of my people. A broader nose and his hair was dense and black, tight whirled along the forehead. He tanned so dark in the Summer sun that at times I would gasp when I saw him in the yard. But my dear husband Clayton just said, "John takes after the Spanish side of the family, doesn't he, Clara?" And no one in our community had ever met a Spanish person other than me so they—none of them—thought a thing about it. Including you, Florence. After all you married him.

"And so that is how you will handle it with your children. It seems your older girls have taken the fair look of the Yeos, but there will be one ... maybe the one you are carrying now. I just want you to be ready. Now, here's the thing, Florence, you must not tell your husband. John ... he doesn't know any of this. Clayton, of course

does, but when he and I pass on, the story will be only known by the women in the family. The daughters and daughters-in-law will hold this knowledge for they will carry the birth stain forward generation by generation. They must know the Spanish story in order to protect their children if questions ever arise. You see men are fragile, when it comes to such matters. They might panic and run away. Not everyone is as true in love as my dear husband Clayton has been. And I fear my son John would be distressed if he knew the truth. But you, Florence. You are strong." Miss Clara took Florence's hand and lowered her eyes in prayer. "Kum ba yuh, Lawd."

Florence walked slowly back to her house. She checked on her little daughters, Jeannie and Eleanor, and asked her neighbor friend if she would mind staying a little longer as she had a headache and planned to take a short nap before starting dinner. Then Florence climbed the long stairway to the second floor. When she got to the top step she turned and flung herself down the stairs. It didn't work; Beverly was born healthy and strong three months later. Not altogether unexpectedly, this baby had topaz eyes rimmed in black and her nostrils flared slightly. Florence nodded when people noted how beautiful she was. "Yes, she takes after John's Spanish grandmother," she'd say. The End.

I inhaled deeply. Philip was sitting motionless at the table as he had been throughout the reading, leaning on his right elbow, his right forefinger laying across his upper lip, his other fingers curled underneath. He stared at me, a curious mix of amusement and annoyance in his eyes. Finally he spoke, "Well, I guess have to think of you as a rival now."

"No, Philip, no," I said, panic rising in my throat. "I didn't do this to … I mean I couldn't anyway. You…."

"That was meant to be a compliment, Leanne. Calm down."

"It doesn't feel like a compliment and you don't seem happy."

"Of course I am. All of my writer friends are my rivals. I see them that way out of respect for their work. And I assume … I hope … they think the same of me."

"But you're not sleeping with any of them."

Philip laughed lightly. "Okay. Come here...."

"Forget it. I'm going to go back to campus." I walked to the bedroom and gathered my things.

"Come here," he cajoled, following me. "Come here," he said more insistently. He stretched out a hand and grabbed my forearm.

I pushed him away. "I'll take the bus."

He sat on the bed. "I've never seen you pull *the girl card* before."

"The girl card?"

"Yeah ... pouting, sulking...." He reached for me again.

I pushed him away again. "I'm not pouting."

"Refusing my touch? I can't touch you now?" He looked at me and waited for a response. I was silent. He continued, "I was going to say that you write well, Leanne. You remind me of Eudora Welty. I'd like to show your story to Adrienne. Remember you met her at one of your parents' parties. She's an editor with my publisher. I think she would be impressed."

"No, you can't do that. I can't show it to anyone but you. I promised my mother it would stay a secret."

"You need to show it around. Get feedback."

"I just told you! I can't! My father would find out. My brothers ... Oh my god, Mother would die."

"Leanne, when a writer is born into a family, that's the end of the family. The family does die. Metaphorically, of course. It means you can't think of them anymore or you'll paralyze yourself with editing and second-guessing."

"And I don't want Andy to find out." I took the bus schedule out of my duffel bag.

Philip snatched it away from me. "Stop it. I'll drive you to school." I sat down on the other side of the bed, my back to him. Philip sighed. "Okay ... Let me start over. Leanne, your story is well written and provocative. And very timely. The whole country is grappling with our slave legacy. The next step is to get a critique from a professional. One that you aren't sleeping with." He smiled.

"My life isn't a commodity, Philip."

He studied my face. His lips were pressed together as if he was resisting the urge to say something hurtful to me. Finally he spoke. "Why did you read this story to me?"

"Because I want *you* to know who I am. I love you, Philip."

"Okay. Who are you? How does this story tell me who you are?"

There was a long silence, during which I watched Philip's face watching me like he was an impartial professor listening to a student struggle with the answer to an academic question. Suddenly he was a stranger. I took a deep breath and said, "Never mind. It doesn't matter. I'm going to end up married to Andy anyway." I stood up and pushed the pages of the story into my duffel bag. Then I said, "I will spend the rest of my fucking life playing hostess at some foreign embassy watching my husband give speeches in a language I can't understand. I'll sit with the wives and brag about my kids' accomplishments and use too much hairspray and get drunk every night. And all the while … all the while … the men will talk about the world. I'LL NEVER BE ANYBODY."

Philip stood and grabbed my duffel bag. "Well, if you turn out to be nobody, it will have been your choice. You have talent. You have brains. You have charm. If you can't make something out of those things you don't deserve to be somebody."

I followed him out the front door and climbed into the car. We rode in silence. When we got to Syracuse, he pulled over to the curb on a side street. I watched a large group of students moving in the direction of the central quad on campus. I assumed there was another rally to protest the war in Vietnam and I thought to myself I should be with them. I should be in this fight for a better world. Philip studied me in silence. I continued to avoid his eyes. I put my hand on the door handle. He said, "What is the thing about this human stain that frightens you most?"

"My family calls it the birth stain."

"Okay, what is the part of Clara's story that scares you the most?"

I didn't even have to think about that. I knew. "That she never saw her mother again." I felt a catch in my throat. I got out of the car and walked up the steps to my dorm. The Resident Adviser met me in the lobby and advised me that since I'd failed to get permission to be off campus for the last four days, I was grounded for the next two weeks.

The following afternoon, on my way back from class, I ran into Cool Breeze and Redhat again. I hadn't seen them since February when we had all met at the Timothy Leary lecture and then later dropped acid together. They were on their way to hang out with their friend, Rain, and invited me to join them. Rain had an apartment off campus even though she was a freshman like us. She had been born and raised in Syracuse. She was what we called a "townie." We ended up ordering a pizza and getting seriously stoned. I noticed that Cool Breeze had freckles which I thought was odd for a Black person. He laughed. "I even get sunburn," he said. Then he went on this riff: "you know all humans came out of Africa and we were all Black because we needed dark skin to live near the equator … that's what it is, babe, its melanin and you got to be dark in countries where it is intensely sunny cause you'll get cancer but when humans started migrating north like to Sweden…" He stopped to take a long toke on the joint we were passing around. "… which wasn't called that then you know but they had to get out of Africa because they were probably fighting over resources like land and water you know … that shit … and food and some of them said oh fuck it and headed north you know and it started to get cold cause it was the ice age, so they had to wear like mastodon skins and shit like that and the sun shone less and less and their skin lightened up to maximize the amount of vitamin d and c that they could absorb because they needed it for their bones and teeth you know and then their eyes got lighter like blue to let in more light since the sky was like always overcast and you end up at the end of the ice age with White people but they were really just Black people who had faded."

"Yeah," I said. "I absolutely see that." Then Redhat, who was White, jumped in, "The deal about Black people is that they were denied good education. It was all a plot." Redhat bobbed her head emphatically when she was making a point. I started to laugh. Cool Breeze picked up on it and laughed, too. Redhat continued, "And like by denying them good schools and opportunities and experiences"—her head bobbed sharply—"they made the Black people seem … um, unintelligent compared to White people. Which justified their whole theory of White supremacy even though they were fucking lying! What's so funny?" She looked at

Cool Breeze and said, "I'm not talking about you, Babe. I'm not talking about you. You are, like, brilliant. But your dad's, like, a doctor."

Wow, I thought. *A Black doctor? That's so cool.* I didn't say that out loud though. I didn't want to sound provincial.

Rain said, "Yeah … yeah. Babe, I know what you're saying. We need to change the paradigm, you know." Rain looked at me now for affirmation.

Smoking dope always made me paranoid. Now I was afraid to talk because I figured I might blurt out my secret. I might tell them that I'm Black and then who knows what would happen? Like maybe these kids were my friends but maybe it was a trap to find out if I'm mulatto. Maybe they had already guessed and were trying to smoke me out. Get me to admit. But if I did, they might resent me or call me Octoroon Girl. So I said, "Black people are definitely great." And then Cool Breeze, Redhat, and Rain laughed so hard they laid down on the floor and held their stomachs. "You are the funniest chick in the world, Leanne," Cool Breeze said.

ON THURSDAY, APRIL 4, 1968, Dr. Martin Luther King, Jr. was shot to death while standing on a balcony outside his motel room in Memphis, Tennessee. I made a decision the next day to embrace my Black ancestry. It was time to be counted among my brethren. I located the house with the Black Student Union sign next to the front steps and knocked on the door. A solemn faced young man opened it and looked at me with an intensity that immediately left me tongue-tied.

"Hi. My name is … um … my name is Leanne Hughs. I came to express my condolences about … I mean I'm terribly sorry that Dr. King died, well, was … was assassinated."

He said nothing, just continued to watch me.

I stammered on. "You see, I'm … I'm Black. My … my great grandmother was a slave. I've never told anyone … you're the first. Well, actually you're the second.…"

"Look girl, I don't know what you're on, but you ain't Black."

"My mother told me that her grandmother.…"

"Look, your granny may have been Black, but your family walked away. Right? You made a choice because you could. Just so you know Black ain't blood. All blood's the same. Black is the way you are treated and you ain't Black. So go on home." He quietly shut the door.

I have to be honest—in a way, I was relieved. I had "passed" for White just as others in my family had—for three generations now. It meant I could be reasonably assured that cops wouldn't sic their dogs on me or aim fire hoses at my face. I could stay in any hotel I wanted to and never be lynched for looking at a Black man. But I felt sick with shame. Survivor's guilt is what they call it.

My father once told us—TJ, John, and me—a story about a man he knew a number of years back. This man had boarded an airplane one day and as he was taking his seat, he suddenly heard a voice in his head telling him to get off the plane immediately. So he did. He stood in the terminal and watched the plane take off and climb higher and higher then abruptly nosedive into the ground and explode. Everyone on board perished. The man told people afterwards that an angel had whispered in his ear. That he had been literally saved by divine intervention. And he knew that his life going forward must justify that rescue. He tried and tried to think of a way he could help all of mankind. But nothing ever came to mind. He was just an ordinary guy with an ordinary imagination. It made him crazy and he ended up drinking himself to death. Daddy said the moral of the story was that sometimes you get lucky. Don't overthink it. Just be grateful.

ANDY DROVE US HOME at the end of the semester. The car radio played bouncy pop tunes that evoked hot vacation days on the beach. *Summertime … Summertime … sum … sum … Summertime….* But Andy and I were subdued. As we got close to Pennswalk, he said, "Annie, I think we should take a break from each other. See other people."

"Okay." I agreed, but I was surprised to hear him suggest it.

He cleared his throat. "I'm seeing a girl now who attends Kirkland. We had a couple of classes together. She lives in Buckingham. I told her I'd call her this Summer. You know. Ask her out. Her name is Patti.

With an 'i.'" He rolled his eyes and snorted. I remembered that when Kirkland College for Women officially opened its doors back in September and began to share the campus with Hamilton College for Men, the official Hamilton school newspaper had run a front page editorial with the headline "Go Somewhere and Giggle." I thought it was a disgraceful way to welcome the girls. Andy had chided me, "It's funny, Annie. Don't be such a wet blanket."

We rode in silence for another couple of miles. My heart was pounding. Andy was dumping me. Why? What did he know? Did he know I was Black? Did he know about Philip?

"Aren't you going to say something?" Andy said finally.

"Actually, Andy, I ... I think it's for the best. We're too young to be so exclusive. I mean we need to experience other people as well. You know so we're ... well-rounded." *Well-rounded? Jesus, I sound like a guidance counselor.*

When we pulled up in front of Andy's house, I moved behind the wheel of the Cutlass. Andy removed his stuff from the trunk. Then he leaned in my window and said, "Can I stop by and see your family some time?"

"Of course! This isn't the end. We love each other. We're just having growing pains." I saw his mother waving from the kitchen window. I waved back. She had taken to painting pure abstracts this past year. I'd seen some of them at Christmas. Large kaleidoscopes of intensely colored rectangles and triangles, with messy borders. She told me they more aptly reflected her world view than the precision of her former still-lifes. "Everything is transitory, Annie. We're all just passing through time," she said. Andy remained in the yard, watching me drive away. Once he was no longer in my rear-view mirror, I began to feel as though I was shedding leg irons. I felt buoyant. Lighter than air.

Chapter 8

I got a Summer job immediately—my first job—selling magazines door to door in the Ivy League community of Princeton, New Jersey. Affluent neighborhoods where the wives of Princeton University faculty answered the door wearing khaki shorts and white polo shirts or tennis outfits. I showed them my pamphlet and told them I was working my way through Syracuse University. Of course, that was a lie, but it made me seem unspoiled. They often invited me in and always bought something from my list. "I represent a cornucopia of reading tastes from *Ladies' Home Journal* and *McCall's* to *Atlantic Monthly* and *Ramparts* to *Sports Illustrated* and *Field and Stream*. There's something for everyone," I would say politely and hand them a pamphlet. It was easy to talk to these women. They were like my mother and her friends. But what I loved most about my Summer job were my teammates.

We were arranged into small crews of three girls by the company that hired us. A crew leader—her name was Myra—drove us from neighborhood to neighborhood, canvassing the district that we had been assigned. And she would remain in the car and check on us if we didn't return in fifteen minutes to make sure we didn't get stuck with someone too chatty or weird. Myra was cool. A drop out from New York University Film School, she was spending the Summer "getting her head together" which for Myra involved smoking a lot of grass and dating a super cute guy named Jagr Ziska, a Czech graduate student at Princeton University who was getting a master's degree in Western Philosophy. He was also a poet. He and a couple of friends, international students, were renting the upstairs apartment in a house on campus and Myra would take us there after work and we'd get stoned and listen to records and talk.

The other teammate was to become my best friend. Her name was Mimi Moreau. She had been born and raised in Princeton, New Jersey and lived there still with her parents when she wasn't pursuing adventure elsewhere. She had studied ballet and jazz for years as a kid and had been accepted at the prestigious Joffrey Ballet School in New York City while still in high school but developed a love of pantomime her senior year and, at graduation, announced to her parents that she wanted to go to Paris and study with Marcel Marceau. So that's what she did. She returned this past Spring—a French mime in America. Unfortunately, no one was hiring French mimes in America except for Ed Sullivan and he always picked Marcel Marceau, so Mimi, ever resilient, simply changed direction. She decided to go for *the college experience* and to that end, she enrolled at Syracuse University and would enter in the Fall with a double major in French and Drama. She squealed when I told her I would be returning there for my sophomore year. We immediately made plans to live together when we got to school.

For someone who practiced The Art of Silence, Mimi rarely shut up. She was always talking or singing. She sang constantly in the car. Her voice was lovely but she couldn't carry a tune if you put it in a paper bag and handed it to her. Myra and I didn't find it annoying though. She just sounded like she was harmonizing with someone only she could hear. Mainly Mimi was beautiful. A fabulous body, of course, but her face was the real draw. Her skin was clear and porcelain white. Her hair, blue-black and shoulder length. Her violet eyes, rimmed in thick dark lashes, rivaled Elizabeth Taylor's, and her smile was so genuine that even though my initial reaction was to be insecure around such a beauty, I couldn't help wanting to spend every moment I could with her. By the end of the first day, we were finishing each other's sentences. And we would only get closer as the Summer days passed.

Mimi confided in me that during her year in Paris she had decided to transform into a French woman. She said she had "grown weary of being an American;" America was "intellectually lazy." In America, everything was "trivialized" because everything was "too available" including "freedom," which no two Americans seemed to be able to define, let alone value, in the same way. Mimi said it was just easier to get her arms around French culture. For one thing, the country was smaller. Plus France was older; there was less "national identity angst" in Mimi's view. And there was a formality about the French people that Mimi appreciated. Privacy was respected. None of that American penchant for forced intimacy just because you happen to sit next to one another on the train. None of that cloying hail-fellow-well-met crap so superficial and yet so essential to American relationships. In Paris, strangers were politely ignored; smiles were reserved for friends and children; and "oh, Leanne, the food! The food is superb!"

Mimi began her transformation by changing her name from Jennifer Kenyon to Mimi Moreau. She stood on the Pont Neuf one early morning that Winter and spoke her new name into the River Seine. She swore that after what had been days of tepid sunlight leaking out of a dirty sky, the clouds parted, and a wide beam of brilliant white light christened everything below including the newly minted Mimi Moreau—indicating to her that the universe was very much on board with her decision to reinvent herself. The new name felt immediately natural to her, and her parents weren't troubled by it in the least. As it turned out, they had also reinvented themselves in their youth. This was at long last the opportunity they had been waiting for to tell their daughter *their* story.

In 1939, during the Nazi invasion of Poland, Mimi's parents had been rescued from the fiery remains of their neighborhood in Warsaw by Catholic relief workers who shuttled the ten-year-olds through an underground network of safe houses to an orphanage outside of London where they remained for the next six years. At first it was assumed that the boy and girl were brother and sister, and that they were Jews. But the former was not true and the latter, if it had ever been true, no longer mattered. If they ever had, they would never again believe in God. Their families were gone, leaving not so much as a photo behind so they were free to re-imagine their past, and, with the help of the Mother Superior at the orphanage, they began to fashion a future. They took the names Robert Kenyon and Marion Beckett. Official papers were drawn up and the children were educated and treated with kindness but at sixteen, Robert and Marion ran away together. They had a plan. They lied about their ages, married, and hopped a ship that crossed the Atlantic and, on a Spring day in 1945, arrived in New York City. And then Mr. and Mrs. Kenyon began their transition into becoming Americans.

They were immensely attractive people each with a gift for seducing influential individuals who encouraged them to attend universities, even offering them generous scholarships. Doors opened for them and the Kenyons proved to be as intelligent as they were ambitious. By the time, Mimi was born four years later, and given the name Jennifer Kenyon, each of her parents was finishing an undergraduate degree—Robert in Marketing and Marion in Chemistry. Robert landed a job as a copywriter at the Warner Elkins Advertising Agency on Madison Avenue, and Marion immediately began working at Rohm & Haas Company in Philadelphia creating specialty chemicals for household products. They purchased a Cape Cod style home in Princeton, New Jersey—a geographical halfway point between their offices—and settled into the comfortable life of the upwardly mobile middle-class.

Mr. and Mrs. Kenyon loved everything about America—its style and pace, the fashion and music, and especially American holidays. Fourth of July was the most sacred, celebrated with friends and fireworks, and hamburgers served on the patio. Thanksgiving was also a special day in the Kenyon house, kicked off with an elaborate breakfast in front of the TV and mandatory viewing of the Macy's Day Parade followed later that afternoon by a lavish traditional feast of turkey, cranberries, stuffing, and mincemeat pie which, of course, they shared with friends. They celebrated Christmas but only because Mrs. Kenyon regarded it as an utterly secular holiday, and besides, Mr. Kenyon was in the business of persuading Americans to buy stuff and Christmas was definitely his biggest season.

But the hands-down family favorite when it came to holidays was The Miss America Pageant which occurred every September. That day, they celebrated privately as a family—just the three of them.

On the evening of the pageant, Mimi and her parents would dress up in their finest clothes and gather before the television in the living room. Mr. and Mrs. Kenyon would drink cocktails and, until Mimi was sixteen and old enough in the view of her parents to drink wine, she was given a special punch made with orange sherbet and 7-Up. Mrs. Kenyon would lay out an elaborate variety of finger foods for the three of them—shrimp with cocktail sauce, tomato tarts, cheese balls with assorted crudités and chicken salad tea sandwiches. And Mr. Kenyon would distribute the scoring materials and a freshly sharpened pencil to each of them.

He had long ago invested in professionally printed cards that listed six critical categories whereby the family would judge each Miss America pageant contestant. He said it allowed them to feel that they were seated among the judges in the front row of the Convention Center in Atlantic City. The Kenyons could award up to ten points per each of the following categories:

a) Poise
b) Intelligence (as demonstrated during the extemporaneous response to the question posed by the host Bert Parks.)
c) Bathing Suit
d) Evening gown
e) Talent
f) Overall Personality

During the program, the family would thoughtfully evaluate each girl, sometimes arguing among themselves about the sincerity of a girl's smile or whether Miss Alabama's comedy ventriloquism routine was actually more difficult than Miss New Hampshire's immaculate flute solo. During the final commercial, the family would tally up their scores, write the name of their proposed winner on a small index card and place it face down at the center of the coffee table. When the winner was announced, they would flip over their cards and see if any of them matched the judges' decision. Invariably, Mr. Kenyon would become so overwhelmed with patriotic feelings watching the new Miss America begin her teary stroll down the runway—accompanied by the syrupy crooning of Master of Ceremonies Bert Parks—that when she looked into the camera and blew a kiss to the country over which she would reign for the next twelve months, Robert Kenyon would quietly bow his head and weep with gratitude for the gift of being an American himself.

"You're making this up," I said to Mimi.

"Who would make this story up?" Mimi exclaimed. "I'm telling you, Leanne, my dad is a savant!"

Mimi said it was uncanny how often her father picked the winner. He had a real understanding of what qualities defined the ideal American. For that reason, the commercials he created resonated with families across the country who aspired to be like the mothers and fathers and children they saw in these ads and slavishly followed their example when it came to purchasing breakfast cereal, shampoo, and automobiles. Mr. Kenyon understood the power he wielded and was therefore discriminating about the brands he represented. He told Mimi that being an advertising executive was a job of enormous responsibility: "I reach Americans right in their homes, on their couches, in their living rooms or propped up in their beds. I have intimate access to Americans, Mimi. And that requires me to always project the very finest image of our nation. First and always, I want to make Americans proud to be Americans."

A week after Mimi and I met for the first time, I was invited to dinner at the Kenyon house. I found her parents to be lively conversationalists, especially Mr. Kenyon, who told stories about the naughty underbelly of advertising influence. My favorite concerned an unscrupulous ad man during the early sixties who, unbeknownst to everyone, spliced a single film frame or cell as it is called in the industry, into the reel of a Hollywood movie. It was a simple blue background printed with white letters: *Buy Popcorn. Drink Coca Cola.* Viewers didn't consciously "see" the cell—it went by too fast—but it registered in their subconscious, a claim supported by the fact that there was an 18 percent jump in sales of popcorn and Coca Cola at movie theaters when this film was shown. Fortunately, the ad man was caught and interviewed by the FBI. I think

Mr. Kenyon said there was even a Congressional investigation. Mr. Kenyon said that the ploy had dangerous implications for Americans who went to the movies. Studies had proven that Americans were most susceptible to propaganda when they were laughing or eating or both. The problem here was that the influence was covert; viewers were being influenced without any opportunity to critique. Mr. Kenyon now looked at me and said, "Imagine, Leanne, what would have happened if this was done by an enemy of the United States. Our nation is only as strong as our people and our people are only strong when they are free of malevolent influences."

"I completely see your point, Mr. Kenyon," I said.

Mr. Kenyon said the solution was to take a straightforward approach to advertising on the big screen. He called it "product placement." He said there was nothing wrong with having Paul Newman drink a Coca Cola right out of the bottle while he was playing a fictitious character in one of his fine films. "Frankly, it enhances the feeling that we are watching real life." He added, "After all, that's the goal of movies—to look like life."

"That's so true, Mr. Kenyon."

"Of course, it also provides a tacit testimonial for the product. The viewer assumes that Paul Newman drinks Coca-Cola off screen as well. It's just a great way to market everything. And it's completely legal," he said and smiled warmly at me.

"That's so clever, Mr. Kenyon," I responded and smiled warmly back at him.

Mr. Kenyon had immediately set up a new department in the Warner Elkins Agency to be the liaison between advertising clients and the movie producers. Lots of money changed hands. And Mr. Kenyon was given all the credit. By the time he was thirty-six, he was Vice President of Creative at Warner Elkins Advertising on Madison Avenue in New York City, a top shelf agency whose clients included Ivory Soap, Halo Shampoo, Chevrolet, Crest Toothpaste and Coca Cola.

One day a couple of weeks later, Mimi and I were on our lunch break. I don't know where Myra was that day, but Mimi brought up her father again. She said that Mr. Kenyon had cultivated a keen eye for the

All-American Girl. Mimi said he often asserted that the All-American Girl was an international phenomenon. Raised on a steady diet of freedom, healthy food, and love, as well as material comforts, she stood out among all the teenagers in the world. He said that she was more than just the sum of her features; she had a combination of innocence and confidence, a cheeky sweetness at the heart of her appeal. I bit into a peach and listened intently. Mimi then added, "I think my dad has a crush on you, Leanne. He named his new boat—*Leanne's Smile*," Mimi said. "So be careful around him, okay? He means well, but he gets carried away."

I often slept over during that Summer of 1968 because Mimi's house was so much closer to our Summer job than mine in Pennswalk. She lived right in Princeton where we worked. That saved me a forty minute drive in the morning. And her parents didn't mind. Sometimes we'd all play Monopoly in the evening and the game would be competitive and go on so late that I was grateful for the invitation to sleep in the guest bedroom. Plus Mr. and Mrs. Kenyon were nice people, funny, smart, and frankly, very attractive. Especially Mr. Kenyon. He had a broad face with perfectly balanced large features. His warm brown eyes looked at me with flattering interest. His smile was wide and there were deep dimples, like parentheses, that framed his beautiful mouth. He had a solid body with powerful arms and a protruding belly that struck me as very masculine. I have to admit, sometimes when I was with him, my mind would wander and I would imagine making love to him. I caught him looking at me during one of those times and he smiled, a very intimate smile, as though he knew what I was thinking. I think he was having the same fantasy about me. I turned red and he laughed.

The Kenyons, like their daughter and me, were liberal Democrats. That made them easy for me to talk to. My own parents, as Republicans, were more apt to challenge everything I said now. It drove me crazy. And Mother would be so patronizing. "It's easy to criticize America, Annie, but keep in mind that we are a young country. Goodness, we're not even two hundred years old yet. Our country is simply going through its adolescence now. One must be patient with its growing pains. As I have always been patient with you."

It was hard to be patient. There had been 159 separate riots in American cities reported in 1967 alone and then in April of 1968, while college campuses erupted in demonstrations against the Vietnam War, Dr. King was assassinated and that set off more inner-city riots. Some close to home. Trenton, New Jersey was nearly leveled by the violence that Summer and never fully recovered. The country felt more divided by race and politics than it had since the Civil War. Then in June, Robert Kennedy was assassinated.

I had planned to sleep overnight at Mimi's so that we could watch the California Democratic Primary together. We were crushed when Eugene McCarthy didn't win-as we had planned to volunteer for his campaign when we got to school in the Fall—so we were already in tears and about to turn off the TV when we saw Bobby Kennedy walk out of the ballroom and head toward the reporters to announce his victory. Suddenly there were shots and Bobby dropped to the floor. His eyes remained open, looking around, confused. There were screams and Mimi and I stopped crying for McCarthy and watched in disbelief as another Kennedy died in full view of an American television audience in the millions. Mr. Kenyon had joined us by this time and held us as we silently watched the Special Report on the news that followed. Then Mr. Kenyon turned off the TV and walked me to the guest room and kissed me goodnight on the corner of my mouth as though he had intended to kiss my cheek and somehow slipped.

I undressed and got into bed. I found myself thinking about Jacqueline Kennedy and how Bobby had wanted to leave his wife to marry her—at least that's what my mother had read. And a part of me now felt bad that he and Jackie were never able to consummate their love. Life is so precarious. It can end in the blink of an eye. Love should never be delayed. Just because a person is married is no reason to shut out another's heart. Even if you don't die young, old age would only be even more miserable if you have regrets.

MIMI, MYRA, AND I had fallen into a fun pattern. We'd sell magazines every weekday until late afternoon. Then we'd head over to the apartment where her boyfriend Jagr and his roommates lived. One afternoon, we were all smoking marijuana when the apartment below us was loudly raided by the police. Terrified, Jagr began distributing handfuls of the weed from a large communal bowl that sat on the floor. "Eat it. Swallow it!" he said. "Quickly, every bit."

"Flush it down the toilet, Jagr!" Myra said.

"No—the cops will hear the flush. Please. I will be deported."

So we stuffed the herbal grass in our mouths and then everyone hid. Jagr pulled me into a closet and we sat on the floor and I felt like my insides were expanding beyond my outsides. It was the freakiest feeling I've ever had. Even weirder than an acid trip. I saw myself as molecules and there was no distinction between me and the clothes hanging behind my head, no distinction between me and the floor and the air, me and Jagr Ziska. I was one with everything. At first I was scared and Jagr, who was apparently experiencing the same thing, whispered, "You're okay. We're okay. It's just the dope."

We sat in the closet for hours. We were silent the entire time. It felt like a year passed. I think we slept a bit. When we finally emerged from the closet, it was dark outside and everyone had gone home. Even Jagr's roommates had left the apartment. We drank several glasses of water each and Jagr said, "I can't drive you home right now. I'm still too stoned. You can stay here till morning if you want. You will be okay. I won't try to fuck you."

Chapter 9

Philip called me late on a Thursday evening in early July. We hadn't spoken since those days we had spent together at Hamilton, back in May. It was the way Philip was—he'd come and go. I was getting used to it.

"Hi," he said, his voice soft and sexy.

"Hi," I said, matching his tone.

"You sound happy."

"I am. I have a Summer job, Philip."

"Mazel tov. Doing what?"

"Selling magazines. Door to door. In Princeton."

"And you are enjoying it?"

"I love the women on my crew. Myra and Mimi."

"Myra and Mimi. Sounds like a sitcom."

"Mimi's a mime."

"Now I know you're making this up."

I laughed. "And I met this really interesting guy, Philip. He's a grad student at Princeton."

"Oh?"

"No, it's not like that. He's Myra's boyfriend. He's Czech. His father is a playwright. He lives in Prague. His work is … like … satiric and experimental. Absurdist, I guess they call it. And so provocative that the Soviets are watching him like a hawk. So he's trying to get his work over here … you know … to someone in the States to be protected and … you know … maybe published in English? Jagr's going to try to find me one of his plays that has already been … you know … translated so I can read it." There was a pause. "Philip? Are you still there?"

"Yeah. Yeah. I'm just thinking. I have a friend who regularly corresponds with some writers in Prague. Maybe he can help. What is the last name of this playwright?"

"Jagr's last name is Ziska. But I don't know if his father uses that name. I'll ask him."

"Yeah, do."

"Thank you, Philip. I'm anticipating that he's … like … really good. You know? He's famous in Czechoslovakia. A lot of great writing seems to come out of the most repressed countries … like … look at Solzhenitsyn's *One Day in the Life of Ivan Denisovich*. I just finished reading that. So powerful!"

"Don't romanticize repression, Leanne. There's nothing inspirational in living under tyranny. And please stop the 'you knows' and the 'likes.' It drives me crazy listening to you when you do that. Say what you want to say with precision. Commit to your words."

Philip had never criticized me before and I struggled with a reaction other than my immediate urge to tell him to go fuck himself. He must have sensed my annoyance. He spoke again, this time his tone was caressing. "Listen, Darling, I'm in New York for the weekend. I wondered if you'd care to visit for a couple of days."

I didn't respond to his invitation. Instead I continued with my news. Speaking with precision. "Jagr's sister is a dancer, Philip. The whole family is artistic. Even the mother—she's a painter. There is increasing pressure on them to join the Communist Party but they have resisted that so far, on principle. Still, Jagr is worried that something bad is coming. There have been a number of reforms enacted in the past several months. The Czechs have experienced more freedom of press and freedom of speech than any of the surrounding satellite countries, and the Kremlin is getting nervous."

"Uh huh."

"I'm actually thinking of changing my major again to Literature, Philip. The literature of Eastern Europe."

"You'd better pick up some Eastern European languages then."

"Ugh. I'm terrible with foreign languages."

"You have to apply yourself."

"Thank you, Professor. I wouldn't have thought of that on my own."

Another pause.

I heard Philip inhale and exhale. Then he said, "Leanne, did you hear me? I'm back in New York now. I'm taking a mini vacation from writing. I'd love to be with you."

I continued as if he hadn't spoken. "I just want to add that you'd like Mimi. She's really smart and she's going to Syracuse next Fall...."

He raised his voice. "LEANNE, DID YOU HEAR WHAT I SAID?"

I raised mine. "YES, PHILIP. DID YOU HEAR WHAT I SAID? I HAVE A JOB!"

His voice softened. "Hey, come on. Come tomorrow. Take the train. I'll meet you at the station."

"Myra is counting on me, Philip. I can't just...."

"Oh, Honey.... Please. Hearing your voice makes me so horny."

I took the train to Penn Station the next morning. I had called Myra the night before and told her I needed to see my friend in New York. She was cool. Then I called Mimi and she said, "Hurry back. I'll miss you." And I realized I would miss her, too. We had become inseparable. I hadn't had a friend like her since Candy.

Philip met me at the station. He was always easy to discern even in a crowd. Tall and lean, darkly handsome. He kissed me chastely and said, "Let's go back to my place and fuck all day." Philip's apartment was in Greenwich Village. Since this was my first visit, I took careful note of the details. A three-floor walk-up. It was Summer and hot as Hades in the hallway. Inside his apartment, the air was cool and damp; the window air conditioning unit huffed like it was breathing hard. Standing at the center of the living room was a large oak dining table, which served as

Philip's desk. Stacks of typewritten pages were neatly arranged and next to his typewriter, leaning against a brass lamp, was an index card with a quote by Flaubert in Philip's handwriting. *Be orderly and regular in your life like a bourgeois, so that you may be wild and original in your work.*

"Is that your mantra?" I asked.

"Yes. I stole it from Bill Styron. Do you know his work?"

I nodded. "*Confessions of Nat Turner.*"

"Have you read it?"

"Yes."

"Tough read, huh?"

"Heartbreaking. It's especially agonizing to read about slavery now knowing that I'm Black. And you didn't steal that quote from Styron, Philip. You and he borrowed it from Flaubert."

Philip smiled at me. "Maybe we'll drive up to Connecticut someday and you can meet him. You would probably get along well with Bill. He's a good Liberal Episcopalian like you."

I snorted. "I don't believe in God."

Philip made a face. "You're an atheist?"

"More than just an atheist, I'm stridently anti-religion. I think religion is the cause of most of the world's misery. And it seems the most religious people are the cruelest."

Philip's eyebrows seemed to leap. "My god, Leanne, we *are* made for each other. Frankly, I don't know why that still surprises me." We kissed deeply. Then Philip said, "Anyway, Styron is strongly antiwar and he was a marine. Saw action in Korea. He's signed a pledge to not pay federal taxes until we get out of Vietnam. It's circulating among the writers I know."

"Did you sign it?

"No."

"Why not?"

Philip sighed. "Because I'm not a fan of impotent gestures. Besides I don't want to be distracted from my work."

I unzipped his fly slowly. He watched me; a smile played across his lips. "I hope this won't distract you, Philip," I said and dropped to my knees.

We eventually ended up in the bedroom. I would have described it as retro-Puritan. A double bed with a white cotton chenille spread. A straight-backed chair in the corner. A simple chest of drawers, dark wooden floors that were clean albeit scarred from years of shuffling shoes. I imagined the lives that had played out in these old apartment buildings. Many of them were a first home for newly arrived immigrants. Poles and Czechs and Lithuanians who had left absolutely everything behind in the old country to become Americans. They had imprinted these walls with their spirits. I could sense them. Their loneliness, exhaustion, and grief, but underlying it all, the hope. Always that conviction that a better day would dawn. Because … America. They were in America now.

Maybe my spirit would someday haunt this very apartment as well. And maybe it would confront the spirits of those generations of refugees who lived in these rooms so long ago. Maybe I would be the iconoclastic ghost who pointed out that the American experiment was built on a Founding Lie. At the very moment the Founding Fathers were signing their names to a document that declared all men to be created equal, several among them owned slaves. Maybe that declaration was aspirational? Or maybe it was all part of a cynical advertising campaign to make the world believe in America's exceptionalism so they would send us their best, their brightest, their hardest working people to forge a national prosperity the world had never known before. But now, in 1968, America was falling apart. Because it is a fact that Americans have never seen each other as equals. We see each other as rivals. It's tearing our communities apart.

Philip, like me, was highly critical of the government, but I noticed that he still stubbornly held on to a fantasy about America as the Superman of the planet, always swooping in to rescue the little guy. I think that had something to do with his age. He was born in 1933 and experienced the decisive victory at the end of World War Two. The Nazis and the Japanese surrendered, and America gorged itself on national pride.

But that war introduced the atom bomb. My generation was born under the mushroom cloud of mutually assured destruction. We've grown up with endless war, which is now a game of chicken that no one ever wins. Armies battle to a standoff. Then they retreat to recalculate their plan and inevitably move the battle to a new field in a new country. But regardless of where we fight now—Korea, Eastern Europe, Vietnam—regardless of what we name those wars now—The Vietnam War, The Korean War—it's still the US and the Soviet Union facing off against each other. Again and again.

There will be no more glorious victories. No V-days. No ticker-tape parades when my generation's soldiers come home. Just death and destruction, suspicion and hate—the futility and waste of never-ending wars of attrition. Because if one side starts to win, the other side will threaten to blow up the planet. That's the equivalent of taking your ball and going home in the post-Hiroshima age. I don't think my parents' generation has thought this through, and they are in charge of the country. I'm not even sure Philip fully accepts the trap we are in. It's up to my generation. We have to push our elders aside if we are ever to have peace. I looked down at the top of his head between my thighs and thought to myself, "Philip, you're getting bald."

Chapter 10

August 29, 1968

Dear Diary-

I've decided not *to share this information with Philip, so I'm hiding it here in my journal. I love Philip and I don't want him to stop loving me. But men tend to be possessive when it comes to sex. Even Philip. He seems to bristle when I bring up other boys. Yet I know he has other women. Many of them. Although I suspect there is one in particular now. If I confronted him and accused him of embracing a double-standard, he would probably just shrug and say, "Yes, I do. So what?" I should be more like that. But even Philip seems fragile to me at times. I wouldn't hurt him for the world. So I am better off just not sharing anything about Jagr.*

Oh ... where do I start? Jagr. Jagr. I can't stop thinking about Jagr Ziska. I tell him his grey eyes are beautiful. He tells me they are the color of the Winter sky over Prague, of the water in the Vltava River on a January day, but that my eyes are the color of an azure sky on a Summer afternoon and that my smile radiates warmth like a thousand suns. I tell him he has beautiful shoulders, elegantly muscular without being brutish. I tell him that his body excites me. He says that I rock his boat. That he gets hard when he looks at my photograph.

Oh, I wish I didn't have to go back to school, but Jagr says he will be at Princeton for another year and he will drive up to stay with me at Syracuse as often as he can. Mimi and I are trying to get permission from the university to live in an apartment off campus. Then he and I can be together all day and all night when he visits.

So I am nineteen years old now and I have had three lovers in my lifetime to date. Andy was the first. He would watch my face the entire time we were making love. It always unsettled me— made me feel self-conscious. And he always did everything exces-sively, past the point of pleasure. Too much fingering. Too much sucking. I know he thought I liked it. And I didn't want to hurt his feelings by telling him I didn't so I'd squirm hoping he would stop, but then he would misread that and continue even more intensely until I'd actually dry up and intercourse would be painful. But I didn't know how to tell him. So he continued to watch my face and I'd continue to pretend I enjoyed sex with him. I'm kind of relieved that we are no longer lovers. The only part I miss is that he would whisper I love you, Annie. Again and again. And I know he did love me. He loved me more than anyone ever has. Probably still does.

Philip, on the other hand, is exciting and I am always ready for anything with him. He's very dominant—sort of a teacher in bed—which as it turns out, turns me on. I call him the Professor of Desire. He explores my body with such confidence and mastery. He's very sexually experienced and he's taught me to vocalize what I like and don't, to not be shy about asking him to do things, to act out fantasies. I blush now thinking about some of them. The first time he put his "mouth on me" and his tongue inside me … well, I was so shocked. But he smiled at me to let me know it was okay and I ended up loving it. Oh, I really love it. And I love to put his cock in my mouth because I know how much he loves that. That's really the key. Making each other happy. I think I'm a good lover now because of Philip. He's a very good teacher. Of course, I'm an excellent student—at least when it's something I want to learn. Anyway—with Philip—it's always an adventure. I actually get a rash on my chest just from the rush of heat that I feel when I see him naked because I always anticipate being thrilled. Philip calls it my Scarlet Letter. Oh, we laugh a lot, even during lovemaking. He can be so playful. And then in the midst of a silly moment between us, he will suddenly turn serious and hold me so tightly against him and urgently whisper that he adores me. And, in those moments, I feel overwhelmed with love for him. Oh, I don't want to ever lose Philip.

But Jagr.

Jagr moves like water, enveloping me so silently. So utterly that at times I am certain that we levitate when he enters me. I feel us lift off the bed and float softly around the room like lovers in a Chagall painting. Jagr's passion is intense, but he takes his time. He whispers poetry in my ear. He sings phrases from songs we both love, all the time rubbing my stomach, stroking my hair, my cheek. Kissing my ankles. He says he likes me to come many times and the secret is to take our time. To make the time we are together last and last.

Jagr tells me that Russian tanks invaded Prague this week and the first thing they did was to kidnap the Czech leader; his name is Dubček and he is a decent guy. He has been democratizing the country, allowing more freedom of the press, even allowing the people to express dissent. The Kremlin sees him as a threat and is afraid that other countries in the Warsaw Pact will get the same idea. So tanks rolled into Prague, people have been killed, and Dubček has been "invited" to Moscow. Everyone assumes that he will be executed there. One thing is certain, there will be no more reforms. The "Prague Spring" is over.

Jagr has asked me to fly to Prague with him next Summer. He says he needs to be with his family but he can't bear to leave me. His father is in jail now awaiting trial for treason. His crime?

He writes plays that ridicule the communists. Jagr says that a half million people have been stripped of their jobs—most of them were teachers and artists and journalists. On a bizarre note, Jagr's sister, a celebrated ballerina, has been forbidden to perform with the state ballet company anymore because she still refuses to join the Communist Party. To shame her, the authorities have given her a job in the National Library in the room where banned foreign newspapers and magazines are kept—it's called "the dirty room." Jagr laughs, albeit bitterly, when he relays this story to me. "Communists are too dull-witted to realize that this is a gift to someone like my worldly, literate sister," he says. "She is in heaven! She gets to read the New York Times *cover to cover every day! The library has a subscription! She gets to read about the major dance companies in the USA! But she can't dance. She can't dance and she cries every night."*

I told Philip that Jagr says all the menial jobs are now given to artists. Major writers are working as floor cleaners. I said, "Philip, imagine your beloved Bernard Malamud cleaning the restrooms in a bus station. That is what's happening in Prague. The Kremlin leaders disdain art as much as they disdain freedom." Philip replied, "That's the point, Leanne. Art is freedom. You suppress one; you suppress the other."

I asked Jagr if he would like to stay in America, become a citizen. I told him I would marry him if he wants to seek asylum although neither of us is the marrying type. Jagr said no, he wants to always remain Czech. His nationality is his identity. His biggest fear is that the Soviets will completely absorb each of the satellite countries into their empire, erase their languages along with their borders. Make them all Russian! Jagr says it is the cruelest form of genocide when they destroy your language because it destroys your stories and your memories. It's a living death. Jagr says, "Look at your American Indians. Look what the invaders did to them. First they lost their land. Then they were sent to English speaking schools and were forbidden to speak their mother tongue ever again. And that is how they lost their identity."

But this is a strange fact—in spite of all the efforts to suppress the ethnic differences in America, we are increasingly a multicultural country, we are a "melting pot." You can hear it in our language. American English is always absorbing a new word from a foreign place. Boudoir ... silhouette ... angst ... mirage ... macho ... incommunicado ... papoose. I personally go out of my way to include these foreign words in my vocabulary. I like the way they sound. Very chic. Andy told me that there is a Portuguese word that describes the feeling that is evoked when one is running one's fingers through another's hair. I wish I could remember now what it is; I'd definitely use that word. Andy says that every country names what they value and that we should notice what isn't named because that tells us what the culture is trying to suppress. Anyway, I see myself as a citizen of the world now. Therefore I could live in Czechoslovakia. I could live anywhere.

Except here. I am definitely ready to get out of America. It seems to get more fucked up with each passing day. Last week I watched the Democratic Convention in Chicago on TV with my brothers. Armies of cops and National Guard soldiers beat peaceful students who were protesting the war. They beat these kids bloody at the direction of the city's mayor. And he's a Democrat!! Inside the convention center, the Democratic Party was nominating that lame Hubert Humphrey while on the streets, young people were facing bayonets. In America! That's no different than what the Soviets are doing in the streets of Prague. Our fucking government is using violence to shut down dissent!

My poor little brothers sat next to me watching all of this bloodshed on TV. John kept saying, "Annie, is this a movie?" He was white as a sheet. So was TJ. They are teenagers now. "No," I said. "It's really happening. This is our government." I am certain of this—I won't let my brothers go to Vietnam. They are not dying to preserve this shit. I will take them to Canada myself before I let that happen. Fuck America.

Chapter 11

I returned to Syracuse in late August. Mimi and I had petitioned the university for permission to move into a university-owned apartment so we could be closer to the theater department which was a couple of miles from the center of campus. While we waited for an answer, we stayed in Shaw dormitory, sharing a room. Mimi had immediately declared her major in Drama and was quickly fitting in with the others in the theater program. I had initially signed up as a Journalism major but changed to Buddhism and then Biology over the course of my freshman year. But I really wanted to be a writer so at the start of this year, my sophomore year, I changed back to Journalism. My immediate goal was to write something that would be accepted by the Syracuse University student newspaper—*The Daily Orange*.

I saw potential for a story in the daily eruptions of "political street theater" in and around campus, so I started hanging out near these spontaneous performances. They usually took one of two forms. There were "die-ins"—which involved students throwing themselves on the ground and rolling and moaning in agony as another student read a report of the most recent horrific statistics from the war in Vietnam. There were also "freak-outs," usually in response to a riot somewhere, a city burned to ash, or the mistreatment of Black people by the cops. In a "freak out," students typically ran around madly tearing at their clothes and screaming in the faces of bystanders. Sometimes a "freak-out" was followed by a "die-in" but not always. While some of the street theater performances were planned, most were spontaneous which led me to become a participant. I BECAME A street actor. And that led to my involvement in bigger and bigger political demonstrations.

I joined the Students for a Democratic Society. Mark Rudd, who had become famous as the face of the student occupation of the Dean's office at Columbia University last April, and had been arrested and actually gone to jail, came to our campus to recruit new members. He was traveling around the country now, going from college to college setting up SDS chapters. He spoke passionately on all the issues that were of most concern to me— Poverty, Imperialism, Racism, Feminism, and War—and he showed how they were linked to one another, how they actually fueled each other. He asserted that the source of society's pain was a corrupt and failed government that was no longer responsive to "the people," so it needed to be torn down and rebuilt. Mark advocated widespread disruption on college campuses as a first step. "Democratic channels of government will not change anything," he said. "It's going to require an escalation in the confrontation. Our campuses will provide the base for organizing our generation of patriots."

Mimi refused to join the SDS. "It's too obvious, too American. I am a French woman after all," she said. "But of course, my sweet Leanne, I will support you. You are my sister now and forever more. And even though I think all of these protests are stupid, I will support you until death." So the following day, I got Mimi to join me at The March for Peace led by students in the theater program. We wore white robes and chanted Stop the War. We gathered on the quad and then moved in one large mass, a sea of white— like a prayer made visible solemnly floating through the city streets. We arrived at the front door of the Syracuse University Experimental Theater and there the crowd parted, and the upper-class drama students stepped forward and performed an almost ecclesiastical presentation about poverty and oppression that was largely unscripted and, to my mind, one of the most moving performances I had ever attended.

So I switched my major again to Drama and tried out for a play with the incredible title—*The Persecution and Assassination of Jean-Paul-Marat as Performed by the Inmates of the Asylum of Charenton under the Direction of the Marquis de Sade*. Or *Marat-Sade* for short. It was about the French Revolution and took place in a mental institution. It had a huge cast, so Mimi and I both got parts.

Mimi got a plummy role. She would be one of the severely disturbed mental patients who formed the ensemble of characters in the play. She would get to invent her own malady, so she immediately set about trying on various grotesqueries. She'd stagger around our dorm room wearing a twisted expression on her face, dragging a lame leg, emitting a creepy cackle. I was cast as the privileged daughter of the man who ran the insane asylum. I guess that is what's called type casting. My role was simply to sit primly on a dais at the side of the stage and observe the mayhem along with the audience. There was a moment in the play when I am attacked by one of the inmates and get to scream but that was my only "line." Frankly, I didn't care what role I had; I was just excited to have the opportunity to watch the play go from page to stage. I got hold of the script immediately and read it cover to cover. Then I wrote a summary for the school newspaper. I hoped the editor might print it. It would be great publicity for the production.

Syracuse University Theater Department Announces Spring Play

Marat-Sade is a play within a play written by Peter Weiss. It is set in an insane asylum, Charenton, outside of Paris in the year 1808. The French Revolution had ended in 1799. For all its blood and fury, it had failed to sustain its populist goals and the people are now in despair. Many are turning against their revolutionary leaders. Napoleon now claims the title Emperor. The central despair of the play is that the revolutionary leaders sold out the people and, in the end, the people turn on them. Chaos ensues and the people eventually welcome the ascendance of a dictator to finally restore order. The play runs from March....

The newspaper editor rejected the story because he said it was confusing, but he said he was intrigued nevertheless and would attend opening night.

Jagr arrived on the following Wednesday. He said even though Thanksgiving was coming up in a couple of weeks and I would soon be home in Pennswalk and he would see me there, he couldn't stay away from me any longer. He drove up from Princeton and rented a motel room where we spent a passionate twenty-four hours. It started romantically. Then, while we were still in bed, I told Jagr I was going to be in a play. I was thrilled to learn that he was actually very familiar with *Marat-Sade*, having seen a great production with his family in Berlin in 1964.

We were drinking wine; Jagr was drinking quickly. He refilled his glass and continued, "The playwright is a Marxist, Leanne. Peter Weiss is a very serious man like all true artists. His play is a warning. People grow exhausted by the fight for freedom. And, in the end, the people welcome a strong man who will take control so they don't have to think anymore. So they can go home and live their simple lives. People are basically lazy, you see. I don't know why I bother to care anymore."

Before I could respond, Jagr began to pace the room. His face contorted and he spoke bitterly. "The Enlightenment was bullshit, Leanne. That's where it all began! All that emphasis on the individual. Oh my god, the dignity of the individual." He pranced foppishly flapping his arms.

I laughed in spite of myself. "You look like the suitor in a Fragonard painting!"

He stared at me. "I'm serious, Leanne! This is not funny! All that emphasis on the Rights of Man has stripped away our sense of the common good! The common welfare has been replaced with the almighty Me ... Me ... Me.... Every man for himself. It is the INDIVIDUAL'S RIGHT to be rich at the expense of everyone else. Nay—it's his duty! The right to own property is sacred. Every citizen will in fact be judged NOT by the content of his soul, but by the content of his wallet! That is the brilliance of Peter Weiss' play! He understands this." Jagr kissed me. Then he added, "All those Revolutions —in the seventeenth and eighteenth centuries, the twentieth century even—they all have this in common— after all the upheaval, all the bloodshed to overthrow the King—in the end, the people WELCOMED a new tyrant. Napoleon followed Marie Antoinette. Stalin followed Tsar Nicholas."

"Well, it won't happen here in America, Jagr. Our generation is not materialistic like our parents. We will be content to live on the land, we will set up communes and share everything with our brothers and sisters. We will be color blind. We will challenge the status quo."

Jagr finished the bottle of wine and opened another. I was still working on my first glass. He was on his fifth or sixth? He grabbed me by the shoulders. He forced me to kneel. Then he knelt before me. We were both naked. His cool grey eyes locked on mine. "It's all hopeless. Leanne. Every revolution ends in tyranny."

"That doesn't have to happen...."

"There is no point in resisting, my darling. I might as well join the oppressors at the outset. Why should we die for a lost cause? Patriotism is lunacy. Eat or be eaten!"

"Jagr, I don't understand what you're talking about. You wouldn't abandon your family. You would never abandon your father. I know you, Jagr. You'd never join the enemy." I gently slid my fingers over his beautiful face.

Jagr shook me roughly by my shoulders. Then he kissed me hard on the lips. Still kneeling before each other as though we were supplicants in some sort of church, he began to cry, "I can't feel anything anymore, Leanne. You see. I have been anesthetized by the selfishness of the modern world. I'm afraid I have been corrupted. Save me, my darling Leanne. Help me feel again, my dearest. And I will help you. I shall go first." Jagr then offered his naked back to me, still kneeling, and said, "Whip me with your hair, Leanne."

I went along with whatever Jagr asked me to do that night. I was frightened at times, but I must confess that I was also excited. I know this sounds awful, but I think revolution is a turn on.

ON FRIDAY AFTERNOON THAT week, I took the bus to Hamilton. I was spending most of my weekends that Fall with Philip at his rented house near the Hamilton campus. We no longer hid our relationship. We even went out for dinner together. Once we ran into Andy at a chamber music concert in the Hamilton Chapel. He was with a girl, so I didn't feel too bad, but I think he was shocked that I was holding Philip's hand.

I would take the bus on Friday afternoons so that I would arrive just as Philip was wrapping up his final class or appointment for the week. He'd pick me up at the station and then we'd head back to his house and fall into bed. He was incredibly voracious considering he was thirty-five years old now. They say men peak sexually in their twenties, but I think he was still peaking. Women by the way peak in their thirties, so I hoped he wouldn't wear out before I got to my peak.

On Saturday mornings Philip and I would stay in bed long after we were awake. We'd drink coffee and talk and take turns reading the Times to one another. Sometimes we'd just lie next to each other listening to the sound of silence. On this particular morning Philip was awake but pretending to be asleep. He was lying on his side, his back to me. I kept talking anyway, trying to get a reaction from him. "Guess what, Philip? Mimi and I finally got permission from the administration to live in an apartment near campus rather than in one of the dormitories. Our parents wrote letters to the Chancellor attesting to our maturity and fine moral caliber." I looked at Philip's back waiting for him to make a smart-alecky remark. He didn't stir but I could sense his amusement; an almost imperceptible shiver scurried along his spine as though he was being tickled. I continued, "We're moving in right after Thanksgiving. It's a great place. Two bedrooms, big living room. Our friends Cool Breeze, Redhat, Pookie and Rain have the apartment across the hall. We're going to have a housewarming party in January after the Christmas break. Wanna come?" He said nothing, I went on. "Oh, Philip, did I tell you? I changed my major again, this time to Drama. Well, what is it they say? Fifth time's the charm?" I paused for a reaction; I could tell he was dying to respond, but he continued to pretend to sleep; he released a fake-sounding snore. "By the way, I've been going out with a football player. And I must say, I'm learning a lot. All that strategy! All that ball handling!" Now Philip laughed—loud guffaws. I leaned across him and kissed his shoulder and whispered, "I knew you were awake." He rolled over and grinned at me, his dark eyes looked rested and content; his dark brows danced.

"Mimi insisted I change my major to drama because she thinks I'm a natural actress. I got cast in the Winter production at the theater. We both did. But to be honest, I think I'm too intellectual to be an actress."

Philip laughed again and threw his arms around me and squeezed me so tight I squealed. Then he loosened his grip and said, "How did you get the bruises on your bottom?"

I shrugged. "It was just a game."

Philip said, "Would you like me to spank you, too?"

"No." There was an awkward pause. I was still feeling unsettled about my night with Jagr. I looked at Philip and said, "Do you love me?"

"Of course, I do."

"Are you in love with me?"

"From time to time."

"Are you in love with me now—at this time?"

"Yes, I believe I am." He wrapped an arm around me and pulled me close. Both of our heads rested on his pillow now.

"Why do people get married, Philip?"

"I'm surprised you would ask that. You're such a romantic."

I shrugged. "Why did you get married?"

Philip's face darkened. "I was tricked. She lied that she was pregnant."

I suspected that was the reason but we had never talked about it. I said, "So love had nothing to do with it?"

"Oh, I suppose I had feelings for her at one time."

"I always assumed when I was a kid that I would one day marry for love."

Philip's voice softened. He stroked my cheek. "I suspect that you will, Honey."

"But I don't know if I can be faithful, Philip. I don't think one person can provide everything."

"I'm afraid I can't offer any advice on that." Philip rubbed his eyes. "I've got to pee." He rolled out of bed and crossed to the adjacent bathroom. He left the door open, so I continued talking—a bit louder—over his stream.

"Will you come and see me in my play? It's next March."

I heard the toilet flush, and Philip appeared in the doorway. I flopped back against the pillow and stretched my arms over my head. "It's important to me."

"I can't promise but I will make every effort." He smiled and blew me a kiss. "I'm going to make us coffee."

"You have a cute behind, Philip Roth," I said as he left the bedroom. He laughed. He eventually returned carrying two mugs of steaming black coffee and handed one to me. He was naked as was I, but I was still in bed covered with a sheet. He was standing, very much on display, which I thoroughly enjoyed.

"Mimi says that men's penises look like turkey necks," I said and blew into my cup all the while keeping my eyes on his face to see his reaction. He looked down at himself and feigned despair. I laughed. "But not yours, Philip. You have a handsome penis."

"I suppose I'm now expected to wax poetic over your pussy."

I grinned. "Mimi just likes to be provocative. Besides she stole that line from *The Bell Jar*. Sylvia Plath said her husband's privates looked like a turkey neck and gizzards."

Philip winced. "Let's change the subject why don't we?" He climbed into bed next to me and leaned back against the headboard. He sipped his coffee. I cuddled against him.

"Mimi told me she's gay."

"Do you think that's true?"

"Well, certainly, Philip. Why would she lie?"

"Will that make it difficult to share an apartment with her?"

"Not at all. We had a frank talk. I told her that I love her from the tip of her toes to the crown of her head. But there's no sexual attraction. She said she loves me like that too. And we agree that even if we found ourselves attracted suddenly, even if we got drunk … well, we would never risk losing our best girlfriend ever by screwing her. We consider our sisterhood sacred."

"Have you ever had a sexual experience with a woman, Leanne?"

"As a matter of fact, there was a woman I met at a party at Jagr's last Summer. I found her very attractive, and I think had she been inclined to move on me...." I shrugged. "But she didn't. I mean the notion doesn't disgust me. I think sexuality is very fluid. You know there are animals that can switch gender when conditions demand it. Like if there is a shortage of males, some of the females become males and vice versa. Nature doesn't make a big deal out of sex. It's in the business of life." I sipped my coffee. "So—what about you, Professor? Same question. Have you?"

Philip sighed deeply and intoned, "Yes, Leanne. I have had a sexual experience with a woman." He gave me a deadpan look. I laughed and gave him a playful shove. He added, "Honey, I'm strictly hetero. But I don't mind homosexuality in others. Especially women. I really admire it in women." He grinned lasciviously. "So let me know if you and Mimi ever want to have a ménage à trois. I'm very open-minded."

"You're a dirty old man...."

"Hey, I'm only thirty-five! I'm a dirty *young* man!"

"Depends on your perspective, Professor. I'm nineteen, remember?" We sat in silence drinking our coffee. Sunshine poured in through the blinds of the single window throwing a coverlet of white Winter light across the bed. Philip took my coffee mug and placed it on the nightstand next to his own. Then he slipped under the sheet and pressed himself against me. I closed my eyes and allowed myself to feel completely happy. He murmured something in my ear. I thought for a moment he was saying *I can't live without you. I love you, Leanne. Marry me.* But I may have been imagining that.

Chapter 12

Thanksgiving Day was wonderful. My aunts and cousins came to our house along with the Taylors and at one point all of the women, me included, were in the kitchen. The conversation bubbled like Asti Spumante. At one point my dad showed up in the doorway and said, "Who's listening?" That made everyone laugh harder.

I missed Mimi though. After having spent the Summer together selling magazines door to door and then being nearly inseparable at school, well, except for weekends when I was with Philip, it was actually a shock for Mimi and me to be apart on that Thanksgiving Day. So the next morning, I got in my car and drove to Princeton to be with Mimi only to find that she and her mother were gone for the day—a trip to New York City to see the elaborately decorated Christmas windows on Fifth Avenue and do some holiday shopping. That left Mr. Kenyon alone in the house. I knocked and called out, "Anybody home?"

"The door's unlocked, Leanne. I'm in here!"

I found Mr. Kenyon sitting on the floor in the living room surrounded by strings of Christmas lights that he was testing by plugging each by turn into a wall socket and checking for "dead" bulbs. He looked up as I entered. Then he sprung to his feet and wrapped me in his powerful hug. "Happy, happy Thanksgiving, Leanne!" At the sight of his generous face, I had the urge to cry. I buried my head in his chest so that he couldn't see my eyes. I had betrayed him just two months prior at the beginning of the semester, on Saturday, September 7, when I joined the march in Atlantic City to protest the Miss America Pageant. It was my first real protest march and now seeing him and remembering how much that pageant meant to him, and how he thought of me as a daughter ... well, maybe not exactly a daughter ... But in spite of knowing all that, I had carried a sign that day that said *Shame on You Miss America* and now, wrapped in Mr. Kenyon's warm hug, I was sick with guilt.

But what happened was this: Red Hat knew one of the protest organizers from her high school on Long Island. So as soon as we were back at school, Redhat began enlisting girls to join the upcoming protest on the boardwalk, just two weeks away. When she came to me, I didn't hesitate to say yes. I was frankly appalled, as an American woman, to find myself a second-class citizen in the year 1968. The list of grievances was long— unequal opportunities in the workplace. Unequal pay. Violence in our homes as well as everywhere else. We were denied autonomy over our own bodies and privacy regarding our own reproductive health. Every semester, there were stories of desperate co-eds who ended up at the emergency room after trying to abort a fetus with a coat hanger. And women were considered to be inferior to men intellectually. I think that's the issue that pushed me over the top. The Miss America Pageant epitomized all of the regressive attitudes about women that the country continued to foster. The main message to girls in America could be summed up in three words—Just be pretty. So I signed up to march in Atlantic City.

Our contingent from Syracuse consisted of four girls—Pookie, Rain, Redhat and me. And Redhat's boyfriend, Cool Breeze, who offered to drive us to Atlantic City. We left on Friday after lunch. Since it would be a long drive and since his parents lived in New Jersey, Cool Breeze made arrangements for us to spend the night before the pageant at their house. They lived in an integrated housing development in Willingboro, New Jersey, an eighteenth-century community that was expanding wildly as farms gave way to new housing developments in the early 1960s, much like my own home town. Except Black people could buy a house in Willingboro.

I don't know what I was expecting but staying overnight in a Black family's house was pretty much like bringing friends to stay overnight in my own home. Cool Breeze's father was a doctor and his mother, a former nurse, who now spent her days gardening and planning dinner parties. Mrs. Bridges asked us about school and our plans after graduation while Dr. Bridges grilled hamburgers on the patio and addressed the issue of the Miss America protest. "Oh, I understand," he said solemnly, "that it seems to objectify young women based on their looks alone and that is offensive. I see that. But it does provide a college scholarship to the winning girl and that can change a young woman's trajectory in life." Red Hat pushed back. "But Dr. Bridges, they send Miss America to Vietnam to entertain the troops. So the Miss America Pageant, in addition to insulting smart young women with its emphasis on how one looks in a bathing suit —is also supporting an immoral war."

Dr. Bridges nodded and said in his level voice, "I was a soldier in World War II. And regardless of my feelings about the merits of that war, the GI Bill gave me the opportunity to go to college and ultimately realize my dream of being a family doctor. I am the first member of my family to go to college let alone become a physician. It may be hard to stomach at times, but we all have to negotiate with power in our lifetimes. Even privileged young ladies like yourselves."

Redhat didn't pursue the argument further. None of us did. We were all polite girls from polite families. We thanked Dr. and Mrs. Bridges for the dinner and for the Rice Krispies bars before bedtime, the fresh towels for a shower in the morning, and the freshly made beds in the two guest rooms. And then we said goodnight. I lay awake and suppressed the urge to slip downstairs and find Dr. Bridges, who I suspected was still in the family room; I could hear the mumbled drone of the TV. I wanted to press him to expand on his comment about his feelings about "the merits" of World War Two.

My father had served in the Navy during that war but he rarely mentioned it. Mother had told me that the Navy had tried to get him to sign up for submarine duty. Daddy had passed all the psychology tests with flaming colors because he was so stoic and stable. But then they found out that he was almost pathologically claustrophobic. Mother had said, "You'd think that would have been the first question they asked." But Mother said Daddy distinguished himself on his ship in the Pacific. He saved several guys—actually pulled them out of a fire on a day when their ship was hit by a kamikaze. Of course, he never told me that story. I'd ask and he'd say I didn't need to know. All that mattered was that we were all safe now. Daddy never said a thing about the merits of World War Two either. And when one of my older cousins joined the marines and was killed two weeks after arriving in Vietnam—I was in high school— my father drove all night to upstate New York to talk his brothers, my father's nephews, out of enlisting for revenge.

Early the next morning, we piled into Cool Breeze's car, thanked the Bridges again, and within a couple of hours, joined hundreds of young people—mostly women—on the boardwalk in Atlantic City. There we took our place in the slow procession to the Convention Center. We sang WE SHALL OVERCOME. At one point, we passed the Freedom Trash Can and I removed my bra and tossed it into the large barrel. Other girls had already contributed their underwear, dust mops, lipsticks, issues of *Playboy* magazine and cans of hairspray. Someone had even stuffed a pink chiffon prom dress in the barrel. We never set fire to it—the newspapers lied about that part. But I heard that somewhere in the crowd some of the women crowned a young sheep as the new Miss America. I didn't see that myself, and frankly I don't approve of using an innocent animal as a prop in a protest. I'm sure that poor sheep was scared to death. That was cruel.

The speakers were powerful though. One older woman noted that females have been deliberately kept isolated from one another, stuck in their houses cleaning and raising children, completely dependent on their husbands. "We have been made to believe that other women are our rivals. It has weakened us and made us dependent on men. That cannot continue! We are sisters! We are a sisterhood. One for all and all for one! We must join forces if we are to change society. The revolution begins first in our minds!"

In the end I was glad I went. The feeling of common cause between all of us was inspiring. And I got to know Redhat, Pookie and Rain better and liked them a lot. And I really loved Cool Breeze. I learned that he was named David Bridges, Jr. I told him he was a lot like his dad. And he laughed and said, "Yeah. I guess that's inevitable." Best of all, the protest was covered on national TV news that night. And even though there was a lot of pontificating from old men-politicians and preachers, mainly— who called us sluts and women's libbers—our own parents were support- ive. Even mine. I called my mother when we were back in Syracuse and told her every breathless detail. She told me she was proud of me. And I was surprised to realize how much her approval meant to me.

BUT WHEN I SAW Mr. Kenyon just a couple of months later, on that day after Thanksgiving, and I thought of the stories Mimi had told me about the annual custom in the Kenyon family of celebrating the Miss America Pageant as a national holiday. And how Mimi's father who had escaped the Nazis as a child seemed at times to conflate Miss America with Lady Liberty in the New York Harbor—like America was some sort of magical kingdom. And at that moment I felt an overwhelming urge to protect Mr. Kenyon from my generation and the changes we would force on this country. No matter that they were for the good. That they would change the balance of power between the races and between men and women, that they would finally uncover the true history of working people and slavery. That America would look less like a fairy tale and more like a work in progress. And ultimately we would be better off as a nation. But I knew these changes would distress him and threaten his serenity for a while, and I suddenly wanted to comfort him. So I took his handsome face in my hands, and I kissed him deeply on the mouth. Then I looked into his animated eyes and gave him an assuring smile. And the next thing I knew we were naked in the guest bedroom and I was on top.

Christmas Day 1968

Dear Diary,

The astronauts on Apollo 8 are circling the moon as I write this. They wished everyone a Merry Christmas and read from Genesis. "And God created the heavens and the earth." Mother was so excited that at the last minute, she had us all go to St. James this morning for the service. Our minister said, "The whole world is united, watching these men and praying for their safe return. And by the way, Jesus had to leave the Earth to save mankind so maybe these astronauts have done the same thing. In any case, it's a miracle. The people of the world have come together this Christmas. There is peace if only for this day."

Chapter 13

In January, Mimi and I decided to throw a party for our friend Burton. He was a fellow drama student and he was turning twenty-one. We decided to make it a combined birthday party-housewarming for our new apartment. We spread the word and then realized we would be hosting about forty people if everyone showed up. We decided to serve Salad Niçoise. Mimi had made it for dinner one night during the Summer when I was staying over at her parents' house, and I thought it was the most scrumptious thing I had ever ingested. In fact, it was all I wanted to eat from that day on. So Mimi made it for me often. She had discovered the recipe in Nice during her year in France. The essential ingredients are flaked tuna, Niçoise olives, blanched green beans, boiled potato wedges, and hard-boiled eggs. We could get all the ingredients in Syracuse except the Niçoise olives but we found Greek olives at a small deli and they tasted similar. Very salty. Yum! So we gathered twenty-five cans of tuna, fifteen pounds of potatoes, twelve pounds of green beans, quarts of olives and I boiled dozens of eggs. Then we realized that we didn't own any serving bowls large enough to accommodate that many people, so we used the bathtub. *Dear Reader, don't freak out!* I of course cleaned it! I mean I CLEANED it! I scrubbed and bleached and sterilized it with boiling water. By the time I was finished, that tub was so clean it squeaked when you ran your finger across the porcelain.

Mimi invited everyone in the drama school including a girl she had recently started dating named Olivia who was our age, a tall quiet girl from Omaha. She had hazel eyes and freckles. And a ponytail that swung back and forth when she walked. She wanted to be a stage manager and was in the directing program with Mimi. The attraction between Mimi and Olivia was immediate and as it turned out, would be lifelong. I sensed that even at the start. Just seeing them together, you felt the deep trust. I confess I was jealous. I loved Mimi. Certainly not in the same way that Olivia did. But I loved her. So I struggled at first to be happy for them. Mimi seemed to understand intuitively and went out of her way to keep me in their circle of love.

About an hour before the party started, we put the salad ingredients into the tub and Mimi tossed them with her (very clean) hands. She then whipped up the most exquisite olive oil, garlic, and vinegar dressing and mixed that in too. We sampled the result. It was scrumptious. The final grace note—we set mason jars on the broad rim of the tub at either end and placed a thick candle in each. Voila! Our bathroom was transformed into an elegant buffet. I hope it goes without saying that we didn't let anybody pee, etc. in there during the party. We directed everyone across the hall to the apartment that Redhat, Pookie, Rain and Cool Breeze shared.

Olivia arranged stacks of pretty paper plates and plastic forks and napkins on a wooden picnic table that we had secured from a friend for the evening—along with several baskets of saltine crackers. And wine. Gallons of wine. Redhat had dropped by earlier with a lavish bouquet of red and orange mums to use as a centerpiece. The apartment looked Left Bank chic. Even my mother would have approved. Mimi wore a black leotard covered with a long paisley skirt. I wore my new mini dress, a Mary Quant knock-off—a straight shift in a bold red and black plaid with a white collar and cuffs. I don't remember what Olivia wore. Probably her favorite blue sweater and jeans. She was from Nebraska.

People began arriving at seven and soon the apartment was wall to wall college kids. Everyone in the building was invited, too, so no one complained about the loud music. We gave Burton a pack of Trojan condoms as a birthday gift. He had played Hector, "the noblest Trojan of them all" in a production of Shakespeare's *Troilus and Cressida* last semester, so we couldn't resist. Burton loved his present; he laughed, and then laughed even harder when I told him what Mimi went through to get them.

I had accompanied Mimi to the Pharmacy to purchase the Trojans a day before the party, but I told her that she had to do the talking. You had to ask the pharmacist for them; they were kept "in the back." Mimi, of course, had no qualms. She stepped up to the counter and faced the pharmacist—a stocky bald man who looked more like a carnival barker than a white-collar drug dealer. Mimi said, "I'd like a pack of Trojans, please."

The pharmacist eyed us both and exhaled with disdain. "What size? Three, Six, Twelve?"

Mimi said, "I don't know what size he is. We're just friends."

The pharmacist replied, "I meant the number is in the package. One size fits all." He smirked.

Mimi eyed him boldly and said, "In that case—make it a dozen. It's his birthday."

To be fair to Mimi, I didn't even know that condoms were one size fits all, and Andy had used Trojans for months before I was finally able to secure The Pill. Speaking of Andy, I was shocked to see him walk through the door about a half hour into the party. He grinned and pointed to Mimi and said, "Your better half invited me. Is that okay?"

"Of course!" I kissed him affectionately and took his coat to my bedroom to toss on the bed with the others. He followed me.

"I've decided that I'm going to teach you how to tell a joke tonight."

I laughed. "Good luck with that. I'm hopeless."

"I'm committed to saving you. It's part of your education. Everyone needs a good joke in their repertoire for those occasions when they need to break the ice with old people. Old people love jokes. That's what they do at cocktail parties, you know. They tell jokes."

"Okay—first you have to try some of Mimi's Salad Niçoise before it's gone."

Andy got a plate and we found an unoccupied corner in the living room and sat on the floor. "What are you doing this Summer?" he asked.

"I'm going to live with my parents and be an intern at the Bucks County Playhouse in New Hope."

"Ditch that and come with me."

"Where are you going to be?"

"I have a three-month internship with our embassy in Tokyo. It's a way to meet State Department types. Our ambassador is sponsoring me."

"What would I do in Tokyo?"

"Tell jokes and break the ice with old diplomats at cocktail parties. You'll be my secret weapon, Annie. Everybody falls in love with you."

"I can't, Andy. I have to start thinking about my own resume. I'm going to be an actress."

"Seriously, Annie? You're going to work at The Bucks County Playhouse in New Hope? That place is Witchcraft Central."

He was right.

NEW HOPE, PENNSYLVANIA IS this very cool old village on the Delaware River full of silversmiths and trendy art galleries and custom furniture workshops like that of the internationally renowned George Nakashima. And as I already noted, it is the home of the Bucks County Playhouse, the premier Summer playhouse in the country. It had been created out of an eighteenth-century grist mill and opened in the late 1930s as a theater. From the start it was a destination for New York producers, playwrights and actors who came to rehearse and "try out" brand new Broadway-bound shows.

My parents often attended the Playhouse in the Summer, hoping to run into celebrities after the show. One night at a late dinner at Chez Odette—a fancy restaurant that overlooked the river—Lucille Ball walked right by my parents' table. Daddy called to her "Hi, Lucy." And she turned and gave him a sultry smile. "Well, hi handsome," she said. My father called everyone he knew the next morning and relayed that story. He was always star struck. So he was thrilled that I would be interning there for the Summer. Mother wasn't as keen on the idea.

Because here was another side to New Hope that wasn't known to the Summer tourists and the actors who trod the boards at the Playhouse. But everyone who lived in the area was well aware of it. New Hope was the longtime home to a very large coven of witches who, following the practice of their forebears, continued to manifest magic along the Delaware River. Some of them practiced white magic which is gentle and well-meaning; some of them were healers who traded in herbal medicines and miraculous oils. But there were those who went in for the black arts and from time to time there were gruesome stories of ritual murders on late Summer nights along the river. The police never solved a single case. And the stories were quickly muted so as not to impact property values. But it was tradition for farmers in the area to paint Hex signs on their barns. The word HEX comes from the German word meaning *witches' foot*. The Hex patterns were varied but all were recognized as protection from evil.

My mother worried about me being in New Hope. "You always attract a lot of attention, Annie. I don't believe in that black magic, but there are witches who do. And if they use you in one of their spells, it won't matter that *you* don't believe in what they're doing. They might hurt you."

In spite of Mother's general wariness about witchcraft, as a playful taunt to the sisterhood in New Hope, she had named her favorite cat—a coal-black beauty with a devilish temperament—Satan. I remember Satan scared the shit out of some young Jehovah's Witness Evangelists-in-Training who visited my dad every Saturday one Summer. Daddy was Episcopalian, but he would always listen patiently to the plain young girl in the plain cotton dress who would sit by our pool and enjoy the lemonade my father offered and bring him pamphlets and go on and on about how Jesus is not part of a Trinity. Sometimes she would bring other Witnesses-in-Training along. And Daddy would bring out more glasses of lemonade. I guess he made them feel welcome in an otherwise rather hostile WASP neighborhood. Those visits ended abruptly one day when Mother came to the back door and called for Satan to come into the house for her ear-infection drops. "Satan, Satan … come to Mother." And Satan walked languidly past the stunned Witnesses purring seductively as she approached my mother. I was weeding by the fence gate, so I saw the whole thing. The young people leaped out of their chairs and literally ran backwards out of our yard and down the street. It was the freakiest thing I've ever seen. They never came back. I think Daddy felt bad about that. But Mother said, "Oh, c'mon, Tom. They don't even exchange Christmas presents. What a boring religion."

ANDY FINISHED HIS FIRST plate and helped himself to a second. He returned and sat next to me again. "Are you still seeing Philip Roth?" I nodded. "He's too old for you, Annie. When you're 90, he'll be 106. You do realize that, right?"

I started to laugh, but Andy looked serious. Cool Breeze and Redhat joined us on the floor now, and I introduced Andy. "He's going to teach me a joke," I said. "So I can entertain old people at parties someday."

Cool Breeze stretched out on the floor. "Far out. I dig jokes."

The Joke (as told by Andy)

A man walks into a bar. He is nice-looking, probably in his mid-thirties. Well dressed, clean shaven. He scans the room and then takes a seat next to a beautiful blonde who is sitting alone at the bar. He orders himself a drink and after a moment, he turns to her and casually says, "Tickle your ass with a feather?"

The woman looks at him in shock. "What did you say?"

The man looks back at her, innocent and confused. "I said 'unusual weather we're having.'"

Her face softens, she half laughs. "Oh, I thought you said … well, it doesn't matter. Yes, you're right. It's been unusually cool, hasn't it?"

And with that, the two start chatting. He orders her another drink. They laugh and within the hour, they kiss. Soon after, they leave the bar arm in arm.

A drunk at the end of the bar has watched this little drama play out with great interest. The next night, when the nice-looking man appears again, the drunk is in place to watch. As before, the nice-looking man takes a seat next to a beautiful woman who is sitting alone. He orders a drink. Takes a sip and says, casually, "Tickle your ass with a feather?"

Her head snaps around and she glares at him. "What did you say?"

He looks at her with wide-eyed innocence. "I said, unusual weather we're having...."

She immediately giggles. "Oh, my gosh ... I thought ... well, never mind. Yes, it's been surprisingly cool...."

They begin to talk and laugh. The man orders another round. Eventually they kiss and soon after, leave the bar arm in arm. Now the drunk realizes this is a foolproof way to pick up a woman and he returns the next night ready to take his shot. He's so excited he loses count of the martinis he's imbibing, but it's safe to say that he is even more drunk than usual when the nice-looking man appears and takes a seat next to a beautiful woman at the bar. It all plays out exactly as it has before.

"Tickle your ass with a feather?"

"What did you say?"

"Unusual weather we're having."

"Oh, yes ... oh, yes. It's been so cool...."

Drinks. Kisses. They leave the bar.

Now the drunk feels ready to try it on his own. He sees a beautiful woman sitting by herself at the other end of the bar. He slides off his stool, nearly collapsing to the floor but somehow stays upright and pulls himself along the bar. When he is next to her he struggles to get onto the stool. The woman tries to ignore him. Once finally seated, he takes a deep breath, turns to her and screams in her face, "SHOVE A FEATHER UP YOUR ASS?" She recoils in shock, "What did you say?" The drunk gives her a seductive wink and replies, "Fuckin' cold out, ain't it?"

Andy stayed overnight and slept in my bed with me. We kept our clothes on and simply wrapped our arms around each other until Andy fell asleep. I loved lying next to him; it had been over a year since we had been intimate. "Hey, Andy, you wouldn't really want me to say 'fuck' to an ambassador, would you?" I said as he was dozing off.

His eyes remained shut, but he grinned and said, "Probably not. But it would be fucking hysterical if you did. You just don't look like someone who would ever use that word. And he would immediately think it was cute coming from you."

Andy left about mid-morning and I called Philip and told him the joke. Of course I got laughing about two-thirds of the way in and Philip was laughing too and saying, "Leanne! Leanne! I can't understand a word you're saying!"

When I finished, Philip said, "Don't quit your day job."

I laughed again and said, "I'll write it down. I'll bring it to you next weekend."

There was a pause. Then Philip said, "I'm not going to be here, Honey. *Portnoy's Complaint* is being published next week on January 12...."

"OH, Philip, that's wonderful!"

"My agent is setting up some interviews in New York. With the Times and Esquire ... It's expected to be what they call a 'splashy debut.'"

"Oh, wow—when do I get my copy?"

"I'll pop one in the mail."

"In the mail? Philip, I want to see you. I want to celebrate with you...."

"Leanne, I'm leaving Hamilton this Saturday. I'm moving back to New York."

"When did you decide this? I ... I can take a bus to New York...."

"I'm going to London later in the Spring. I was going to call you...."

"I can come with you...."

"Leanne, I'm going to be tied up for a while."

PORTNOY'S COMPLAINT WAS AN instant bestseller. The praise from major newspapers and magazines was pretty much unanimous. Critics hailed Philip's brilliant conceit of using a monologue delivered by a neurotic young man to his psychoanalyst-as a means of exposing the anxiety of the Jewish male during the liberated 1960s. I grabbed a copy immediately at the local bookstore and read it cover to cover in one night. The novel is about fucking in every way imaginable and when not fucking, thinking about fucking—in every way imaginable. It's about being Jewish and guilt-ridden because you are obsessed with screwing Protestant Blondes. Philip used sex as a means to talk about everything—history, politics, culture, and religion—even identity. It was outrageous and hilarious and flat-out brilliant. But for me, it was also unsettling. When I came across this passage, I stopped laughing:

"What I'm saying, Doctor, is that I don't seem to stick my dick up these girls, as much as I stick it up their backgrounds—as though through fucking I will discover America."

Chapter 14

In May, Andy left for Tokyo, Philip left for London, and Jagr went to Prague. Mimi stayed at Syracuse for the Summer to pick up credits in Summer school. She had started a year behind me, but wanted us to graduate together, so she was taking classes in the Summer to catch up. Olivia stayed with her in our apartment and got a Summer job off campus. I interned at the Bucks County Playhouse in New Hope as planned and lived at home.

Dear Reader, I suppose I should have mentioned this earlier, but I wanted you to get to know me, hopefully even like me, before I told you that I am a drug addict.

It started the Winter of 1964 when I was fourteen. I had gotten my period for the first time in January and my body was changing. You may remember that I mentioned that my breasts had gotten big quite suddenly. And Mother worried that I was getting fat. She spoke privately to Laura Armitage who directed Mother to a friend of hers who had a daughter who had also gotten her period that year and was seeing a famous diet doctor in Philadelphia who had given her a prescription for a drug that was slimming her down. Weirdly enough, that daughter was my close friend, Gaye Parsons, who had never mentioned a word of this to me. But of course, she wouldn't—we simply didn't speak about such things in those days. Amphetamines were considered to be the purview of inner-city junkies and Judy Garland. Not nice suburban teenaged girls.

Dr. Lawrence wasn't what I expected. He was a short middle-aged man. Loose skin hung from his cheeks and his arms, like he had once been very overweight himself and had gotten rid of the fat but his skin had been stretched too far to snap back. It was kind of creepy; I found it hard to look at him. I frankly wondered why he wore short sleeves, but maybe he was proud of his weight loss and felt his loose epidermis was the best advertisement for the effectiveness of his methods. Personally, I think he would have looked much better if he had just stayed fat. Anyway, I don't remember much about that first visit, except that Mother was with me in his office. He at one point asked me if I had ever been "internally examined," I said, "I don't know" and turned to Mother. "Have I, Mother?" And Mother looked at him confused and he restated his question. "I'm talking about sexual intercourse. Have you ever had sexual intercourse, Annie?"

Mother gasped, "She's fourteen, Doctor!"

I added, "No. I haven't."

I remember he asked me if I was a good student and before I could answer, Mother replied, "She's a straight A student, Doctor. Top of her class. Well liked. Involved in extracurricular activities...."

Dr. Lawrence pointedly ignored her and said to me, "Well, Annie, you are going to be an even more exceptional student on this drug that I'm about to prescribe for you. You won't need to sleep but a couple hours a night. Think of all you will accomplish!"

He started me out on four pills every day—two in the morning, two before dinner. They were square tablets, the color of baby aspirin—that light orange. And he was right. I felt peppy right from the start, peppier than I had ever felt. So peppy that I couldn't sleep at night even though I was always tired now. I'd lie on my bed, awake, listening to the sounds of the house creaking, my father's snore down the hall, the furnace coming on, a feral cat in heat somewhere in the woods— every sound was exaggerated, sudden and sharp, creating phantasmagoric images in the darkness. I started keeping a light on all night, but it didn't help. I was afraid of my own imagination.

My father bought me a radio alarm clock for my nightstand. "Just rest, Honey," he'd say. "Listen to music and let your body rest even if you can't sleep." I listened to classical music for hours and became quite enamored of anything by Schubert. So dramatic, so moody. It would be the soundtrack for elaborate mystery dramas that I would create in my mind. I also discovered a good radio station in Boston—WBZ. While I could never pick it up in our little town in Pennsylvania during the day, at night—after midnight—it came in clearly and kept me company until the sun rose and my family started to stir. The DJ often played recorded interviews with the Beatles and I could sometimes nod off for an hour or so, listening to Paul McCartney's gentle voice.

Food. I had always eaten at my mother's table—which meant I ate a balanced diet of fresh fruit and vegetables in season, and meat and poultry and fish. We did not eat "junk" in my house. And we never had casseroles unless Coquilles Saint-Jacques was considered a casserole. But Mother made that only once a year on my birthday at my request. I had a sophisticated palate and grew up never craving anything, but now my stomach burned all the time and I ate anything that was quick and handy to soothe it. When I didn't lose any weight during the first month, Dr. Lawrence upped the dose to six tablets a day and scolded me. "Do you ever want to have a boyfriend, Annie?"

I started writing poetry at night. I read books. I read, I read, I read. And I thought big thoughts about history and science and religion. I'd lie in bed and my mind would do cartwheels. During the day, I had to fight the impulse to interrupt my friends because they all seemed to speak so slowly. At times it would make me feel almost hysterical inside. But I got used to the anxiety and the pills soon became just my way of being. I never questioned my "medicine" and my parents never questioned it either. And I certainly didn't tell anyone outside of my parents—not even Candy or Lark. And as I said, Gaye and I never discussed it. I guess she, like me, was ashamed of the fact that she was seeing a diet doctor. And taking drugs.

By the way, the night of the luau, that June night in the Summer of 1964—the night I first met Philip—I accidentally learned that Arlene Giampaoletti Swenson was also one of Dr. Lawrence's patients, and she, too, was on the "medicine." It was about one in the morning, and the party was still going strong down by the pool. I had just watched Philip return to his rented house across the street. I went down to the kitchen to get a drink of iced tea and found Arlene alone hanging over the sink. She sounded like she was throwing up. She gasped when she saw me, "Get my bag, Annie. Please. Quickly. It's outside. I left it on a chaise. I forgot to take my pills before dinner." I ran quickly and found her white leather clutch tossed on the grass. Mr. Taylor called drunkenly from the pool. "Annie! C'mere. Come swim with me." But I shook my head. "I have to give Mrs. Swenson her pocketbook." Arlene was sitting at the table, holding a glass of water when I returned. Her hands shook as she retrieved the prescription bottle and opened it. She dumped a half dozen orange tablets into her hand and began to swallow them two at a time. Then she closed her eyes. I watched her. Within minutes her grimace relaxed into a tired smile. "Thanks, Babycakes," she said and shrugged as if to acknowledge an embarrassing slip.

SO AT THE START of my Summer at Bucks County Playhouse in 1969, I had just completed my sophomore year at Syracuse, I was nineteen years old and I had been an addict for five years. I now swallowed twelve tablets a day. My first morning as an intern, I entered the empty, barnlike theater, and found two boys swatting tennis rackets at a flying brown bat. They greeted me and one of them said, "We're going to capture this one alive and sell it to a witch over on Mechanic Street. She came by this morning and offered us fifty bucks for one with a beating heart!"

I grabbed the racket that the other boy was swinging. "You should be ashamed!" The boys put down their rackets and watched me for a long moment as I struggled to get my trembling under control. Then one of them extended his hand and said gently, "My name is Noah Barton Alexander. What's yours?"

The other boy was Jimmy Green-Green. No lie! His mother had been married to a Mr. Green, who was Jimmy's father, and divorced him and then married a different Mr. Green. Jimmy delighted in using both names thereafter. Anyway, Noah and Jimmy were interns for that Summer as well and after the incident with the bat—which they never repeated—we became good friends. Actually, I liked all the interns. There were twelve of us. Six boys and six girls. We were all college students and came from different parts of the country. I immediately befriended a girl from California named Christine. Pretty with thick blonde hair that fell naturally into long ringlets. She had small, marine-blue eyes, and a deep S curve in her side that gave her posture a slouchy indifference and made her seem very cool. She liked me, too. We spent the morning dragging large flats out of the scenery workshop and laying them on the blacktop of the back parking lot. There, under the supervision of the tech director, a man named Bert Heckel, we painted them and stenciled patterns to look like a wallpaper border. These flats would be the "walls" of the set for the first show of the season.

At one point, Bert came over and spoke very directly to me as though he wasn't aware of the other interns being privy to the conversation. "What is your name?"

"Leanne Hughs."

"I see all sorts of astrological symbols—the moon and planets—around your head, Leanne Hughs."

"Oh, that's interesting. I used to see a moon in my bedroom every night when I was a kid ... like when I was five. It would just float near my bed."

"Were you afraid?"

"At first. But it wasn't the real moon, of course. It was just ... It was just...." I half-laughed. "A spirit?" I shrugged. "I was the only one who could see it."

"What did it do?"

"It just watched me. My mother put black-out shades on the windows but it didn't keep it out. So I just learned to live with it." *Why did I bring this up??*

Bert closed his eyes. Then opened them. "Please come to my office when you arrive tomorrow morning. I have a project for you. I'll explain then."

I noticed that the other interns were watching me now somewhat warily. But when we broke for lunch, we all headed together to a small outdoor café on Main Street. Christine and I walked side by side at the front of our little herd. I learned that she was a sophomore at UCLA. Her parents were divorced and she lived with her mother but she worshipped her father who was a professional theater stage manager and currently on the road with the national Broadway tour of the play *Rosencrantz and Guildenstern Are Dead*. The tour was scheduled to come to the Playhouse at the end of the Summer and Christine could talk of little else. She promised to introduce me to her dad and said he would take us backstage to meet the actors.

Noah, Jimmy, and another of the boys, Bernie, walked directly behind us on the way to lunch. I was intensely aware of Noah's propinquity. As we approached the café, he called to me. "Leanne. You and Christine can walk with us." I looked at him over my shoulder. "And why would we want to go backwards?" Christine laughed. I winked at Noah to let him know I was teasing. He nodded and stuffed his hands in his pockets; then with an exaggerated step landed next to me. He grinned broadly. "May I sit next to you at lunch?" I laughed. "Of course, Noah. Let's not be so formal. We're going to be spending the whole Summer together."

Over lunch, I learned that the theater owned a house about a mile away, in which the interns were living for the Summer. All except Christine and me. I, of course, lived at home in Pennswalk, a thirty-minute drive from New Hope. And Christine's dad had rented a furnished apartment for her, for the Summer. It was right on Main Street in walking distance of the Playhouse. It would of course become Party Central for the interns that Summer. And I would often sleep over. At least until Noah and I became "an item."

Noah looked like a young David Niven. Nice-looking, patrician. Intelligent eyes. Short dark hair. He wore a leather cap, identical to one that John Lennon always wore. Noah appeared aloof and arrogant at first glance. I think that was due to his good manners. He seemed to be of another age. But he was gentle and sensitive and once he felt comfortable with the rest of us which didn't really take all that long, he became genuinely interested in everyone's story—asking questions and listening carefully as each of us shared details about our lives. On our walk back to the Playhouse, Noah and I separated from the others. He whispered to me, "We are the alpha couple here, you know. The others are already deferring to us, Leanne. That means it's up to us to keep an eye on these kids, make sure they stay safe this Summer. For some of them, it's their first time away from home. We have to be like their parents."

On Saturday nights, after the show, the interns would gather at Christine's apartment. We'd ask one of the actors to purchase wine and beer for us. You had to be twenty-one to buy alcohol at that time and none of us was older than twenty. One Saturday night a few weeks later, we were all at Christine's of course. Noah was trying to tell me a story about the Roman Emperor Augustus, but I could barely hear him over the music. So he suggested we take a walk along the river. Noah was obsessed with Greek and Roman history. So much so that he had purchased a replica of the cape worn by the Roman Praetorian Guard. It was a rich brown color with a grey satin lining, and he had it draped over his shoulders that night despite the heat. When we arrived at the river, Noah gallantly spread the cape over the grass. He then asked me to lie on it. I did and he joined me. We kissed. Just as things were heating up, I began helplessly sliding over the satin lining of the cape, down the incline of the river bank, and before either of us could react, my feet were submerged in the mud and murky water along the shore. After an astonished moment, Noah helped me up. I removed my sandals and moaned, "They're ruined!" I threw them in the river and he said, "I think we had better do this on my bed."

I walked barefoot with Noah back to Christine's apartment where I used her phone to call my mother. I lied that I was staying overnight with Christine and gave Mother Christine's number in case she needed to get a hold of me. I advised Christine that she was my cover for the night.

Then I hopped in Noah's car, and we headed to the Company House where he was lucky enough to have a private room.

A remarkable thing happened that first night with Noah. I slept. Like a rock. We had sex, of course, which I likened to a trip down the river in a speed boat, exhilarating and over quickly. But after the sex, he surprised me by simply cupping himself around me—we were in a twin bed—and then, as he reached over and turned off the lamp on his bed stand, he said, "We're sleeping left to right, tonight." And with that I instantly fell asleep. The next time I opened my eyes, it was dawn, seven hours later. Seven hours of deep, uninterrupted sleep. I couldn't remember the last time I had experienced that. It was bliss. I couldn't wait to have sex with him again. And fall asleep for another seven hours.

June 29, 1969

Dear Diary,

Philip says my generation—the Baby Boomers—is the first generation of Americans to take the separation of sex and procreation for granted. Certainly, the widespread availability of The Pill has liberated us to explore sex for other than reproductive purposes. But I think there is an angle to this new age of sexual freedom that wasn't anticipated and could turn out to be very beneficial to the country. Promiscuous sex is opening channels of communication between men and women in ways that no one would have predicted. At the start, the idea of "free love" generated images of horny teenagers banging their genitals against one another. But what the older generations failed to anticipate is that my generation has a hunger for spiritual bonding. And through sex, we are becoming deeply soulfully knowledgeable about one another. We are communicating with our bodies. Lovemaking has become a form of asomatous conversation for my generation. And it is transforming the relationships between men and women. Creating a new society of respect and trust.

For example, Noah told me tonight that he meditates every day. On sacred symbols from ancient Greece. He said he's nev-

er told anyone about that except me. I told him I felt honored to know something that private about him. I wanted to share something personal about me but I couldn't think of anything I wanted to reveal. But I'll come up with something.

Chapter 15

The next morning, I arrived at the theater and went directly to Bert's office, a cramped little room on the second floor with a wide window that overlooked the stage. His desk was covered with blueprints and set design drawings. "Have a seat, Leanne." I sat and tried not to stare at him. He was probably in his forties. Bald, but I could tell that he shaved his head; a dark shadow of regrowth was apparent over his dome. His eyes were colorless and he wore an insincere smile at all times. His nose was so long and thin that I wondered how he managed to breathe through it. He was very tall although his torso was unnaturally short so all of his height was in his legs. He looked like Rumpelstiltskin on stilts.

I sat and we faced each other across the desk. "Leanne, do you dream in color?" "Yes. When I sleep … I don't sleep a lot … Well, I'm sleeping better now actually.… "

He cut me off with a wave of his hand. "You see I'm a professor of psychology during the Winter months. At NYU."

"My father is a professor at Penn."

"Yes, I heard that. I am working on a project, Leanne … analyzing dreams. I imagine your father has research projects from time to time. You are probably familiar with the methods." I shrugged. Bert continued, "I wonder if you might be willing to participate in this study. I can assure you, your name would remain confidential. I am just interested in the details of what you dream."

I shrugged again. "Sure. I'll tell you what I remember.…"

"I'd like you to come to my office every morning when you arrive for work. I'll have coffee. Tea?"

"I love coffee in the morning."

"Then I will have coffee."

"Thank you."

"You will simply sit with me for about a half hour and tell me anything you remember. I sense that you have vivid dreams."

"I guess."

Bert paused then, for an unusually long time, but he kept his eyes on my eyes. I was so uncomfortable that I dropped mine and stared at a bracelet I was wearing. I began to twist it round and round my wrist. Finally, Bert stood up. "We'll start tomorrow then." He walked me out of the office and down the steps. He said, "Sweet dreams, Leanne," gave me one of his forced smiles, and we parted.

AT DINNER THAT NIGHT, Mother handed me a letter that had arrived that day. A blue, air-mail envelope posted from Czechoslovakia. It was a letter from Jagr, his first communication with me since the semester ended last month and he returned to Prague. I opened it at the table and read silently. It was uncharacteristically restrained.

> *Dear Leanne,*
>
> *How are you? I am fine. My father received a very fair trial but has been declared guilty and is being sent to Russia to serve his sentence. 5 and 1 /2 years in prison. My sister has married her long-time French beau and was given an opportunity to leave the country which proves that the Communist Government is treating us well and is not as authoritarian as the Western*

I stared at the letter and said, "Holy Shit!"

Mother was startled. "Annie!"

"It's my friend Jagr. He's joined the Communist Party."

I called Mimi that night and read her Jagr's letter. She responded, "Oh, my god, Leanne—he sounds like he's got a gun pointed at his head."

"Exactly. That's how it sounds to me, too."

Mimi and I talked for an hour. She told me that she and Olivia and a boy named Wolf had started a theater. Mimi and Olivia had attended a performance by a troupe of Chinese puppeteers who were touring in the United States. They employed an ancient style of storytelling that was done by creating shadows on a screen with paper puppets on sticks. Mimi decided on the spot to embrace the methodology but with a twist—Mimi would incorporate her extraordinary mime gifts into the show. Instead of puppets there would be shadow-bodies performing the story—hers and Wolf's. The theme for the upcoming season would be *Saving the Earth*. Mimi and Wolf had already written the first show and were rehearsing every evening. Olivia was directing. "See Leanne," she said happily, "It's all coming together for me. My art is now serving a profound mission. My art is now in service to the earth." She added that Wolf had moved into our apartment. "He sleeps on the couch. You'll like him, Leanne. He's nice."

Mimi said that she would be home when the Summer session ended in mid-August and we would be able to hang out until we returned to school where we would of course hang out even more. "Oh, by the way, Leanne—my parents have been asking about you. You should stop by and see them some evening. They adore you. Mon Père wants to take you out in his boat. On second thought, maybe you better wait until I'm home to do that so I can chaperone. I think he has a crush on you." She laughed.

THERE WERE NO PERFORMANCES at the Playhouse on Mondays so that was our day off. On the first Monday, I told my parents I was meeting my college friend Redhat in New York, but that was a lie. I met Mr. Kenyon in the city. We hadn't spoken since our first "encounter" the day after Thanksgiving and I was truly surprised to get a call from him one evening, about a week after my conversation with Mimi. He asked me about school, my final grades for the semester, my plans for the Summer. I told him about my internship at the Playhouse and then he asked if he could treat me to lunch on the following Monday, at Maxwell's Plum, a snazzy restaurant on First Avenue, not far from the Warner Elkin's Agency on Madison.

I met him at his office and he gave me a tour, introducing me as his daughter's best friend. I was so nervous I barely made eye contact with him on the walk to the restaurant, but my shyness quickly thawed over French Onion Soup and Maxwell's famous apple cake, which we shared, taking turns feeding each other forkfuls of the buttery confection. Then when he finally leaned in and kissed me, I kissed him back. A long kiss. We walked to a nearby hotel where he had reserved a room for the afternoon. We did the same thing the next Monday. And while I had to drag a wagon full of guilt behind me all week because I worried continuously that Mimi might find out—Mr. Kenyon assured me that his daughter would never know. So we did the same the next Monday, too, and the next. Oh, I was crazy about him.

Finally, in July, he managed to get a whole Monday off work, the whole day. He wanted to take me out on his boat so I drove to the Kenyon house in Princeton early that morning and found him standing in the garage arranging the beach towels, a blanket, and a picnic basket in the trunk of his car. He turned and smiled as I entered the garage. He kind of reminded me of Mr. Clean, the genie in the TV commercials. Tall—he told me that he was six feet one. Powerful—he always stood with his legs slightly apart as if to balance his broad chest. A big man with a big personality. He could be intimidating I suppose, but his eyes were those of a child. Dark brown flecked with starlight, full of wonder. Certainly the most optimistic person I had ever met, and considering his sad childhood, I found that intriguing. It made him seem tender and vulnerable to me despite his overt masculinity. His voice boomed when he saw me, "Leanne!' As I got closer I felt his eyes traveling boldly over every inch of me. He said, "You're even tanner than you were last week! I thought you'd be pale as skim milk this Summer spending all your days backstage."

He started to kiss me and I pulled away, warily backing into a shadowy corner of the garage. He smiled indulgently, "We're alone, Honey. It's Monday, remember? My wife is at work. Mimi's at school. It's just us." I ran back to him and we kissed wildly.

Mr. Kenyon kept his boat in the little seaside town of Toms River on the New Jersey coastline. He had a friend at work who gave him the keys to his pied-à-terre, a pretty little cottage with its own private beach, and he let Mr. Kenyon dock the *Leanne's Smile* there all Summer long. The owner was never there. He had discovered soon after he bought the place that he hated sand between his toes and the sound of the waves repeatedly smacking the dock made him nauseous. He offered to sell the cottage and dock to Mr. Kenyon who considered it for a time. It would provide a convenient and comfortable hideaway for us. But of course, it was hard to say how long our affair would last. My mother had told me years ago about a cousin of hers named Edith who was in an affair with a married man for over a dozen years and they kept it a secret the whole time. But I had trouble seeing that play out for Mr. Kenyon and me. And if Mimi found out about this affair, she would never trust me again. I figured we'd last the Summer and that would be that.

On the ride down to Toms River, Mr. Kenyon talked happily about work. "I think you should join the Warner Elkins agency when you graduate, Leanne. You would be good at advertising. You're very alert to the culture."

I said, "Honestly, I think I would be distracted working with you."

He clutched his heart and laughed. "Oh, you sexy girl. You say the kindest things."

We were in Toms River within an hour and soon aboard the *Leanne's Smile.* As we pushed off into the bay, Mr. Kenyon patted his knee. "Come sit on my lap. I'll teach you to drive the boat."

I shook my head. "I'm not a confident driver, Robert. Not on land, let alone sea."

"I'll teach you. And I will hold you tight until you are ready to take off on your own."

I sat on his knee but it was like sitting on a wooden plank. I returned to the cushioned seat beside him. "I don't see any point in being uncomfortable, Robert," I said. He stuck his lower lip out in a fake pout and I laughed. Gulls called to one another overhead. The water slapped the sides of the boat noisily, the bay exhaled its briny breath into our faces as we leaped over the waves. When we got to open water, Mr. Kenyon cut the engine and allowed us to drift. I felt a familiar sensation. "I love being on the ocean," I said. "It always feels like it notices when I'm here. Like it remembers me."

Mr. Kenyon nodded. "It feels like a cradle today, doesn't it? Rocking … us … to … sleep." Mr. Kenyon suddenly fell forward, face down, onto the steering wheel. I jumped up. "Robert!!!"

He opened his eyes and turned his face to me and grinned. I shook my head. "You Dope! You remind me of my brothers!"

The houses along the shoreline retreated and the water of the bay darkened as we met the deep Atlantic Ocean. Robert engaged the motor again to retake control of the boat and keep us from being pulled out further into the open sea.

"Did it bother Mrs. Kenyon when you named the boat after me?"

"Marion and I are best friends, Leanne."

"But does she know about us?"

"Yes, she does."

I gasped. "You actually told her?"

He smiled. "Marion isn't troubled the way some wives would be. We have lived together every day of our lives since we were kids and taken out of Warsaw together after the bombing. We are more than husband and wife. She is my only family." He smiled and pointed to a school of dolphins in the distance. "Over there! Would you look at that!"

"Do sharks ever come into this bay?"

"You seem nervous today, Honey. What's going on?"

I shrugged.

"Come. Sit on my lap. I want to smell your suntan lotion."

At lunchtime, Mr. Kenyon docked the boat and grabbed the picnic basket. He had packed some of my favorites. We headed to the private beach and spread out a blanket. Mr. Kenyon handed me half of a large sandwich. Pastrami. The best in New York. And he placed a coconut macaroon on my naked thigh. He leaned down and took a bite out of it. I smiled at him. Then he started talking again. He always talked. Even when we were making love, he would suddenly tell me a story.

"Marian's father was a traveling salesman before the war. Very successful guy. Sold textiles. Dry goods, they called them then. Dress fabric and fabric for men's suits. His sales territory extended far beyond our city so he traveled almost all the time. He always offered to take his wife along, but she wanted to stay at home with her daughter—Marion. I guess she was something of a recluse."

I interrupted to remind him. "You promised that Mimi won't find out about us. Please tell Mrs. Kenyon not to tell her either. Mimi would hate me if she knew. And I would be heart broken."

Robert nodded. "No. Marian won't say anything." He kissed me. "And Mimi would never hate you. No one could ever hate you, Leanne."

He resumed the story about his wife's dad. "Marian said whenever her father returned from a trip, all three of them would sit in the kitchen and he would tell these elaborate tales about exotic places and beautiful women dressed in jewels and feathers and tiny iridescent shoes. And waitresses in smoky bars with dark red lips who swung their hips, brushing his elbow, as they passed him. Marion said her mother would listen like a kid with a radio. And it would go on all night, long after Marion was tucked into bed. She'd hear them talking downstairs in the kitchen. All that night—Marian's father would tell his wife story after story. Some of them ribald, Marion thinks. In fact, Marion believes that he had affairs and shared the details with his wife and she didn't mind!" Robert's large eyes grew even larger. "Maybe it turned her on, Leanne. Who knows? Nobody's business but their own, right?"

Mr. Kenyon put down his sandwich and laid back on the blanket. He took my hand and pulled me to his side. We kissed. "So my Marian, like her mother, stays inside her world where she feels safe, and I go out and gather the stories to bring home to delight her. She's happy, Leanne. She trusts me. She knows I will never leave her. And that is the way our marriage works."

"So Marian has turned into her mother?"

"Yeah. I suppose every girl does. That's how wisdom is carried from one generation to the next."

We were both quiet now. We laid side by side, looking up at the sky. The clouds were scant like blown feathers, remarkably white on a field of cornflower blue. After a while, I rolled toward Robert and traced the deep dimples on either side of his mouth with the tips of my forefingers. I said, "You should write fairy tales."

"Oh, I do, Leanne. That's my job. I create stories of beauty and safety and convenience where all the people are attractive."

I WAS SITTING WITH Bert Heckel a few mornings later, inventing a dream for his research project. I hadn't yet shared one of my actual dreams and we had been doing this daily now for weeks. Frankly, I didn't want to tell him my real dreams because they were incoherent, something I hadn't realized when Bert enlisted me as a subject in his research. But now that I was sleeping more, thanks to Noah, I was aware of just how strange my dreams were. Janky images—the side of a house, a dog walking backwards. My mother laughing maniacally. Someone talking to me in a language that I didn't recognize. Philip making coffee in a toaster … and on and on. All these quick scenes that had no relationship to one another. Sometimes I would dream of lights flickering. Once I saw steam coming off a bathing cap and I actually smelled chlorine. It woke me up. If I told Bert these dreams, it would reveal something too intimate about my brain; like the possibility that it was damaged. I worried about that all the time now. I wondered if the amphetamines had done real damage.

I glanced at Bert and cleared my throat. "Well … there's a giant and he sits on my grandmother's house and almost crushes it, but I get my

Nana and cousins out and tell them to all hold hands and I pull them in a line up to a cloud because I can fly...."

Bert makes no attempt to hide his boredom. He doodles on his notebook. Then suddenly, with no warning, everything goes black. When I open my eyes again; it seems like only minutes have passed. "Wow, Bert. Sorry—I must have nodded off. Sorry about that...."

He looks at me unsmiling. "No, you didn't nod off."

I look at my watch. Two hours have passed. My heart pounds. It's two fucking hours later. I pretend I don't notice. I'm afraid of Bert now. I try to steady my breathing and act like I didn't notice that there was anything amiss. "Well ... um ... where were we?" I say casually.

Bert gives me an icy stare. "You were talking about the bees."

I feel cold. "I haven't had any dream about bees."

"I'm not interested in playing games, Leanne. Now finish the dream about the bees."

"I don't know what you're talking about."

Bert sits back and folds his hands in his lap. The pupils in his colorless irises shrink to inky dots. The corners of his mouth pull down. He glares at me. "That's it for today. We'll try again tomorrow." He stands and waves me off.

I stand up shakily and walk out of his office and down the stairs. I walk quickly out into the lot and stop to stare at my shadow on the ground. It doesn't look like it's attached to me. I see Noah and run to him and wrap my arms around his waist. Noah smiles down at me and says, "You're amorous today."

Chapter 16

On Saturday night—it was a strike night—we were *striking* or taking down the set of the show that had closed that night so that the new set could be loaded in the following week. I was working in the barn, sorting props that needed to be put away. Some were too heavy for me to lift by myself so Christine and Noah had joined me. Bert came up to me and handed me the keys to the Playhouse van and said, "Go fill it up at the station on Lower York Road. He's still open." I looked at my watch. It was after ten. I was surprised that anything in this sleepy little river town was still open.

Noah stepped forward and said, "I'll do it, Bert."

And Bert said, "No, I assigned it to Leanne. You continue to do what you are doing."

I squeezed Noah's hand and said, "It's okay. I'll be back quickly."

There was no one on Lower York Road and only a few street lights. I pulled into the station and the man who was working came out and said, "You just made it. I was about to lock up."

He inserted the gas nozzle in the tank of the van and grabbed a squee-gee from a bucket of window cleaner. We chatted as he washed the front window. "Are you an actress?" "No—just an intern this Summer. But someday maybe." "You're cute." "Thank you." When the tank was full, I heard the gas pump click. The man removed the nozzle and came to my side of the car and opened the door. "That'll be five dollars and forty cents."

I turned to my purse that was on the seat next to me but as I reached in for my wallet, the man was suddenly on top of me. I was now laying on my back cross the two seats, pinned by his body. My feet dangled through the open door and the man was pulling my shirt open and fum-bling with my bra with one hand and my shorts with the other. With great effort I slid my right leg under the man and pulled my foot onto the gas pedal. With my one free hand, I turned the key that was still in the ignition. I moved the automatic shifter to D and arching my back, pushed down the gas pedal as hard as I could; we lurched forward. The man held onto me. His hand was now inside my underpants, his mouth on top of mine. I stomped harder on the gas pedal and we blindly took off. The van rumbled over a curb and bounced onto the street; the man let go of me and fell through the open door. I pulled my legs in and sat up. I grabbed the steering wheel and yanked the door shut as I floored the gas pedal and sped off down the empty road without looking back.

I returned to the Playhouse, parked and turned off the engine. I took several deep breaths and straightened my clothes before I got out of the van. Bert was standing in the doorway of the scene shop. Looking at him from this distance, I had a sudden sick intuition that Bert might actually be pleased to hear that I was attacked. I didn't understand his animus and it frightened me. But I was determined not to give him the satisfaction of knowing my thoughts let alone what I had just been through. "You're back already?" he said coolly. "Yes," I said pleasantly. "You were right, we were low, almost empty. That will be five dollars and forty cents, sir." I kept my eyes on his eyes and extended my hand. Bert dug in his pocket and handed me a five-dollar bill and change. I hadn't paid for the gas, but I pocketed Bert's money anyway. For my trouble. Then I rejoined Noah and Christine. I decided not to tell them that I had nearly been raped. I decided to just forget the whole thing.

THE NEXT SHOW WAS *Scuba Duba,* a comedy about a man who is an advocate for civil rights but, when his wife leaves him for a Black scuba diver while they are vacationing on the French Riviera, he becomes a lot less open minded about race. The play was funny and provocative. The cast included Ron Liebman and his wife Linda Lavin as the White Couple. They were both great in the roles but pretty wound up during the run of the play. I never tried to chat with them. One night I was standing in the wings ready to hand Mr. Liebman a prop when he came offstage and whipped off the windbreaker he was wearing and snapped it at me. I caught it but not before the zipper made a shallow cut over my cheek. He didn't even notice that he'd done it, he was so focused on his next entrance.

There was another actor in the company—I think his name was Gary. He had a fairly small role as the Gendarme in the play and I wondered how he even got that part. He was one of those hammy actors who tries too hard to make his lines funny. Frankly I would cringe when he entered a scene. And I sensed that the other actors in the company didn't think much of this guy either. So he hung around with the interns most of the time. He would come down to the costume shop and sprawl on a couch there and watch me sort the laundry every week. And make small talk. Sometimes the other kids would be there as well and we'd all shoot the breeze about theater and New York. He would try to impress us with the names of famous actors with whom he'd worked.

One morning, on a break, all of us were gathered in the shop listening to Gary who was sitting on the couch holding court. At one point, he insisted that I sit next to him. I obliged despite the fact that he made me uncomfortable. He turned to me and said, "So which of these fine studs are you balling, Leanne?" He grinned and surveyed the interns. I turned red and everyone half laughed to cover our collective embarrassment. Noah stepped forward. "Hey, Gary. That's enough."

Gary laughed. "Aha! I think we have a winner." Then he smirked at me. "Is he good, Honey? Does he get you wet?"

Noah again interceded. "Knock it off, Gary."

I stood up and Gary pulled me down next to him again. He started to sing to me, a song from the Broadway show *Hair: Sodomy. Fellatio. Cunnilingus. Pederasty....* He moved his hand over my thigh and slid it between my legs. I jumped up.

Noah moved towards him. "I said Knock It Off!" Noah took my hand.

Gary grabbed my other hand. "Sit down," he commanded. "Sit down." Now Jimmy Green-Green moved towards him. Gary grinned. "Oh, look at this. We got a pair of White Knights here. Gonna save the maiden's virtue."

Noah said, "Okay, everybody, let's get back to work." The interns silently filed out of the costume shop. And Noah and Jimmy flanked me as we, too, exited. Gary remained on the couch, grinning like a devil.

The next day was Sunday. There was a matinee performance that afternoon. I was working backstage as a dresser for the older actress who played the Landlady in the show. When she came off from her first scene, she asked me to get her a glass of water. I tiptoed through the darkness of backstage and through an exit onto a landing where we kept a pitcher of water and a stack of paper cups. I poured the water and was returning to her when Gary appeared out of the blackness and silently grabbed me and started kissing me hard on the lips. He startled me and I lost my grip on the cup and accidentally dumped the water down the front of his dark pants. Over his crotch. He looked at me in horror but had no time to change. We heard his cue and he had to go on stage looking as though he had just peed himself in the wings. There was murmured laughter in the audience. The other actors looked likewise amused. When he came offstage he went immediately to his dressing room. Noah was working the curtain. He whispered, "What happened?" I told him and Noah said, "Good. He deserved it. Now maybe he'll leave you alone."

After the show, the theater quickly emptied. Some interns scattered to straighten dressing rooms. Others reset the props on stage. I gathered dirty laundry and headed for the costume shop to throw a load in the washing machine. I was alone when Gary entered. His eyes looked at me with cold fury. I thought he might hit me. He locked the door. I said, "Gary, I apologize. It was an accident. But you startled me." He grabbed me by the shoulders and threw me to the floor. My head banged on the cold tile and for a minute I thought I was going to black out. Then he raped me. I didn't resist but he tried to make it hurt as much as possible. When he was finished he got up and left. He never said a word.

I sat on the floor for the longest time. My legs trembled and then my entire body shook. I didn't cry. I felt mad with fear and fury. Eventually Christine came in. She looked at my expression with alarm. "What happened to you?" She sat on the floor beside me. I told her. And then I started to cry. She gasped. "I'll get Bert. Gary should be arrested."

"No, don't tell Bert! Don't … he won't do anything. He'll just blame me."

Christine didn't argue. She put her arms around me and said, "Let me take you to the hospital."

I shook my head. "No … no. And don't tell Noah. Don't tell anyone." Christine whispered okay and just sat with me for the longest time.

I cried again on my way home in the car but pulled myself together when I got to Linton Hill Drive. I didn't go into work the following week. I told Bert I had tonsillitis. I told Mother I wanted to spend my birthday week at home with the family. Mother was pleased by that and planned a couple of "girl's days" for us. One with Mrs. Taylor. It actually felt good to be with the women who loved me most.

Noah called the next afternoon. "Bert says you're sick?"

"Yeah … I have this … sore throat. I'm on antibiotics. I'm supposed to lay low for several days."

"Can I come visit you? We don't have to do anything. I bought you a birthday present."

"Oh, Noah. That's so nice of you."

"You know, Leanne, the season is ending in a couple of weeks and well … we haven't talked about what happens next for us."

"Oh … well, I suppose you go back to Boston U. I go back to Syracuse. We can stay in touch if you like.…"

There was a long pause. I realized how cold that sounded. I continued. "Noah, there is someone … I am involved with someone. He's been out of the country this Summer, but he's returning. See I didn't expect to fall in love with someone else … I really didn't, but you are so…."

"You're in love with me?" He sounded amazed and happy to hear this.

Of course, I wasn't in love with Noah, but I couldn't bring myself to be *that* honest. Instead I said, "I don't know … I don't know … I'm confused. It's been a whirlwind, hasn't it?" *Oh, god, I sound like the dopey girl in a romance novel.*

"What's his name?"

"His name?" I took a deep breath. "Um, Philip … Andy."

"Philip Andy?"

"Yes. I call him PA."

"Like the state?"

Noah came over that afternoon. I tried to look like a person with tonsillitis so he wouldn't know that I had lied about it. We sat by the pool alone for over an hour and, in his gentle company, I relaxed and confessed something I had been unable to tell anyone else.

"I think Bert is a warlock." I tried to laugh, tried to sound normal.

Noah studied my face. "Why do you say that?"

I swallowed hard. "I think he's trying to hurt me."

"In what way?"

"He … he hypnotized me."

"What?" Noah took my hand. "When did this happen?"

'Oh, um … last week. Um … before *Scuba Duba* opened."

We were silent for a long moment. Noah grew pale. Finally he said, "So what did he do while you were hypnotized?"

"I don't know … I was hypnotized." My heart was pounding now.

"Did you tell him something … something personal?"

"I was telling him about a dream. You know for the project. I told you about that. But I was making it up."

"The dream? Why were you making it up?"

"Because I don't trust him. It's his eyes … I don't think he's a professor."

"Shhhh … don't cry…."

"When he hypnotized me … I didn't even feel myself going to sleep—it was like I blinked. And then my eyes were open again and I realized two hours had gone by, Noah. TWO HOURS!" I started to shake.

"I'm here, Leanne. I'm here…."

"It was so scary. He acted like we had been talking the whole time. Like nothing unusual had happened. Like he hadn't even noticed that I was … gone. Like I'd just paused mid-sentence. I thought I had nodded off for a minute and then I was actually embarrassed for doing it. Like it was rude." I gasped. "He said I was telling him a dream about bees. And I said—I didn't have any dream about bees and then I happened to look down at my watch and I almost screamed. TWO HOURS!!!!"

"Shhh … Leanne, your mother will hear you…."

I whispered, "What did he do to me, Noah? Two hours I was unconscious with that man! How did he do it? Why did he do it? What did he do to me?"

Noah wrapped his arms around me and squeezed. I continued talking into his shoulder. "Did he implant me with some evil? Am I a Manchurian Candidate now? Will I suddenly do something that … ?"

"Why didn't you just tell him you changed your mind about participating… ?"

I sobbed harder. "You are so rational, Noah. You don't understand. Things happen … things that aren't rational. You don't always have control."

I sat back and looked at Noah and, in a terrifying epiphany, I thought—Oh, my god—Noah is part of this plot. I stood up and stepped back. I composed myself. He reached for me again and I backed up more. "You know what?" I said. "I think maybe I just have a fever from my tonsillitis. Um … just forget what I said." I made myself laugh. "I'm probably just hallucinating."

Noah looked at me earnestly and said, "I know someone who can protect you."

"No, that's okay," I said, growing more terrified.

He reached into his pocket and pulled out a small blue envelope, one of those air mail envelopes like the one that contained the letter that

Jagr had sent me from Prague. Noah pointed to the return address. *Oric Bovar. Firenze, Italie.*

"This man has power, Leanne. Spiritual power. He is a leader. He is gathering artists who will produce a new Renaissance of beauty and harmony in the world. He only works with true artists because their molecular structure is malleable. He is changing our actual biology through meditation. But it takes discipline to be one of his disciples. He's been slowly building this confederation for years. He started with dancers in New York. Because they are the most disciplined artists. They repeatedly punish their bodies for art. Next he selected opera singers and finally actors and all other artists. I was contacted this past Winter at school. He can pick up your vibration in the atmosphere—even over there in Italy. He's amazing, Leanne. He's going to change the world."

Noah told me that Oric was an American man living in Florence. He had grown up traveling around Europe and the Middle East because his father was an expert on ancient mystical artifacts, particularly those of the Mediterranean and Egypt. He even ran the national museum in Cairo for ten years when Oric was a child. And one of the popes in the late forties gave him access to the Vatican Library and there he found the original mystical writings of Plato. Dozens of symbols that can alter the physical world."

Noah continued with complete sincerity. "When Oric was thirty, his father gave him the symbols and told him to use them for the good of mankind. And that is what Oric has devoted his life to, Leanne. He's a very wealthy man. He doesn't have to do this. And there's no cost at all to the disciples. If you are picked by Oric to be a part of the Renaissance, he gives you the symbols for free."

"Would he be open to including me?" I murmured.

Noah took a deep breath. "I suppose I really shouldn't be telling you all of this. He will have to select you himself. But I'm going to call him this afternoon. He lets us call him in Florence, Italy. I will tell him that you are in immediate danger. And that I believe every word you say. He understands that there are forces of evil. He is trying to counter them every day. I'm fairly certain he will reach out to you."

I looked deeply into Noah's eyes and knew, without a doubt, I could trust him. He took my hands and said, "Do I have your permission to contact him on your behalf?'

"Yes," I said.

A FREAKY THING HAPPENED the next day. Mother and I were sitting on the back porch silently folding clothes; Daddy was cutting the grass in the back yard. The familiar steady roar of the mower, the chatter of birds in the trees were suddenly interrupted by a piercing scream. We ran out onto the patio and watched my father below in the yard, running like a man on fire, waving his hands above his head, engulfed by a dark cloud of hornets that were being reinforced by a steady stream of their comrades pouring out of a nearby nest in the ground. Apparently my father had run over it with the mower and these creatures were in a vengeful rage. Dad ran toward the pool and Mother shouted, "NO, TOM—DON'T GO IN THE WATER! THEY WON'T LET YOU UP FOR AIR—THEY'LL HOVER OVER THE WATER. YOU'LL DROWN!!!" Then she added, "TAKE YOUR SHIRT OFF! THROW IT AWAY FROM YOU! THEY'LL FOLLOW THE SWEAT!! COME IN BY THE GARAGE!" Dad pulled his t-shirt off and tossed it as far as he could. It worked; they aimed for the shirt. The hornets were diverted, at least momentarily. It gave Dad a bit of a head start. He ran through the gate and toward the laundry room door next to the garage. Mother and I were already there, holding the door open. Dad ran for his life as he heard the loud buzz of the hornets return. They were closing in as Dad managed to slip inside and Mother slammed the door. We all watched through the window in the upper half of the laundry room door, mesmerized, as wave after wave of hornets attacked the thick glass. Like tiny kamikaze pilots, each of them gave their life to the battle, falling to the threshold of the door. Their wings twitched as they died.

Dad had at least a dozen stings. Probably more. None on his face though—he had protected it with his forearms; they bore the brunt of the attack. Mother handed Dad an aspirin and a glass of water. Then she quickly made a paste of brown Fels-Naptha soap and applied it to the welts. It was her go-to remedy when dealing with wasp stings, mosquito bites, and poison ivy blisters. She kept a bar of it handy in the laundry room. Some ingredient in it—lye, perhaps—seemed to cool the burn and draw out the venom, reducing the shock. Mother kissed Daddy's red face and said, "Come sit down, Honey. I'll get you a glass of iced tea."

We regathered upstairs on the porch and looked out through the screens. Hornets continued to fly out of the ground nest below in the yard, providing replacements for the already dead and dying. They formed a high, black column in the air and then at some silent signal, they deftly divided into two armies. One headed for the laundry room door where they continued the attack on the window, determined to find an access point; they knew the enemy was within and they were determined to reach him. But one by one they, too, expired, dropping onto a funeral pyre forming at the base of the door. The other swarm continued to dive-bomb the empty t-shirt lying in the freshly mowed grass, a futile frenzy that led them to the same fate as their brothers at the laundry room. Twenty-four hours later there was still a muted, but ferocious, buzzing coming from the separate sites. It wasn't until Thursday that we felt safe to approach the dead hornets. We raked up mounds of carcasses in each location; they filled two empty grocery bags to the rim. Every single hornet in the nest had sacrificed itself to the cause. And that nest must have extended from the middle of our yard to the creek.

That night at dinner, Mother said, "I read in *Reader's Digest* about a man who drowned in his pool when this happened to him. He jumped in to get away from them and they hovered above the water, watching him, knowing that he would eventually have to come up for air." Mother took a deep breath and coughed. Then she continued, "Well, when he did come up, gasping for air, they attacked and attacked and attacked. They stung him like a thousand times on his face alone! And he screamed and screamed—"

TJ threw down his fork. "Jeez, Mother! We're trying to eat here."

Mother continued breathlessly, "So that's why, Tom ... I'm so glad I was here ... oh, my God ... Otherwise you might have ... I want you kids to learn from me. There's still so much I have to teach you. I won't always be around. You need to pay attention to me."

LATER THAT NIGHT I stood in the middle of my room, trembling. I kept replaying in my mind the attack on Daddy. How terrified he was. How frightened I was. Thank god my mother was there. I wouldn't have known what to do, but she did. I swear she could be a general in the army. So decisive and confident. She never hesitates in a crisis. But that's the way you have to be to survive in this world. You have to be strong. You have to be fearless. You have to outsmart your enemies.

Suddenly Bert Heckel's voice was in my ear. *"Finish the dream about the bees, Leanne."* Bees? I wasn't talking about bees! What made him say that? Suddenly it was clear. He had indeed hypnotized me. To somehow implant this awful plan in me. He is a warlock! He manifested his mean fantasy to hurt me, knowing how dearly I love my father. Bert hates me. But why does he hate me? Because I'm popular. He's jealous. Yes, that's it. He's jealous of me. He has probably never been popular in his life. So he wants to destroy me.

I remembered his colorless eyes. The way he looked at me with barely disguised disgust. It had to be Bert causing the violence around me this Summer. The gas station attack. The rape. Now he is threatening my family! Things like this had never happened to me before. It all made sense now. He had told me he saw the moon and the planets around my head. I'm sure that scared him. That's surely a sign that I have power, too. I must have magic. But I'm a good witch. I would never be like him. So it's my job now to destroy Bert Heckel. Or at least emasculate him and neutralize his power. For the sake of all the interns. For the sake of the world!

I spent the rest of the night rehearsing a plan of attack. The next morning at seven, I left the house, telling Mother I had a quick meeting with my supervisor at the Playhouse but that I'd return as soon as I could. Mother had made plans for us and Mrs. Taylor to go to Philadelphia that afternoon to see *Goodbye, Columbus*. Philip's book had been turned into a movie.

I raced my baby blue convertible along River Road into New Hope. Bert was sitting alone in his office when I came through the door. He looked up surprised. "Back so soon?" he said, coolly. I came around the desk and leaned over him, baring my teeth. "I know what you are, Bert

Heckel." I hissed menacingly. "But I am here to tell you that I TOO AM A WITCH. AND I AM FAR MORE POWERFUL THAN ANYTHING YOU HAVE EVER ENCOUNTERED BEFORE IN YOUR LIFE!! YOU ARE IMPOTENT NEXT TO ME! I WAS BORN HERE IN BUCKS COUNTY AFTER ALL! I AM TO THE MANNER BORN!!"

I wasn't sure what that actually meant, but it sounded scary. And it seemed to register with him. He looked nervous. I smiled menacingly and continued, "But you already know all of that, don't you, Bert? You know all sorts of things about me, don't you? You hypnotized me, you bastard!" He looked at me curiously. I hummed an eerie tune that I composed on the spot and took a seat on his desk facing him. I shoved all of his paperwork onto the floor. He didn't protest; he sat there as if frozen in place. Now I took his hand, he tried to pull away. "LOOK AT ME," I demanded. I lifted his face with two fingers under his trembling chin. "I SAID LOOK AT ME!" He obeyed. His clear eyes now looked actually frightened, his pupils enlarged. I studied his eyes for a long moment, relishing his fear. Then I spoke again, spitting the words out in careful measure so that each would hit its mark.

"If one more thing happens to me, Bert … or to my family … or to anyone I love … ever again … I will come for you. I will find you. You won't escape me no matter where you hide. No Hex symbol will protect you. I will leak like a shadow under locked doors. And when I find you, I will unleash HELLFIRE on you, a fury so terrifying that you will spend the rest of your pathetic life cowering under your bed begging for mercy. I swear to you—as Satan is my witness—I will make you suffer. DO YOU UNDERSTAND???"

Bert nodded. He was ashen. I added, "SO DON'T FUCK WITH ME, BERT." I turned to leave. Then I gathered myself and turned to face him one last time. "I will be back on Saturday for the *Scuba Duba* strike. You stay out of my way. And next time, you get the fucking gas."

I walked out of the office and out of the shop. I looked around the empty lot. The interns wouldn't be arriving until nine. I got into my baby blue convertible, turned on the radio, and slipped on my sunglasses. The classical station was playing Schubert's String Quartet in G Major. I drove along the River Road back to Pennswalk, swept along by the thrilling music, my hair whipping my face. Savoring my macabre triumph, I thought to myself, *maybe I should be an actress after all.*

When I got home, I ran into the woods and puked.

I RECEIVED A PHONE call the next morning. I took it in my bedroom.

"Hi Beautiful. Happy Birthday."

"Who's this?" I asked. I knew it was Philip but thought I'd pretend that I didn't. There was a pause.

"Leanne … It's Philip." He sounded wounded.

"Oh," I said. Another pause.

Philip exhaled audibly. "I guess I deserve that."

"Oh, I don't know. Six months without a phone call? Frankly, I don't think about you anymore." I forced myself to laugh nonchalantly. "Are you still in London?"

Philip was subdued now. "No, I'm back. I'm in New York."

"I won't even ask how long you've been back. I don't care." *I could feel myself trembling. I hadn't taken my orange pills yet this morning. I always felt sick in the morning until I got my first dose. And I especially needed fortification now—talking to Philip. My heart ached. Why did he think he could abandon me for months and then return like it meant nothing?*

He sensed my annoyance and pivoted to lighten the mood. "I thought maybe we could spend the weekend here in the City...."

"I'm not available, Philip. I'm interning at the Bucks County Playhouse and we load in a new show next week. They need me."

"I miss you, Leanne."

"I don't care."

Pause.

"I want you, Leanne. I need you."

I wanted to cry. I wanted to say—where the fuck have you been, Philip? I've needed YOU. Instead I said, "I read somewhere that in Elizabethan times, girls put a peeled apple in their armpit and locked it in place with their upper arm. And held it there for a week and then they would send it to their lover as a token of intimacy. He could then smell her when he got lonely. Wouldn't that be more convenient for you, Philip? I'll get started on it right away."

"What do you want me to do, Leanne? This is the way we operate."

"I've got to go, Philip."

"We have lives that keep us apart from time to time. You know that. It's always been that way and we have always made it work."

"No, Philip, this is the way *you* operate. I've never been given a choice. You have always controlled this relationship and, as a result, you've always controlled me. You determine when we see each other. You determine when we talk. I've put up with it because I was afraid you'd walk away if I pushed back, and I'd never see you again. But I guess I have to accept that you will eventually leave me for good anyway, so I might as well be the one to say goodbye first if only for the sake of my pride."

"Why didn't you say something? I thought we were on the same page...."

"Why did I have to say something, Philip? Are you that dense? Or is it just because you don't think of anyone else?" I struggled not to cry.

Pause.

"I'm sorry, Honey. Truly. I apologize. I know I've been remote. It's the notoriety I guess. It caught me off guard. All the analysis of *Portnoy*." He sounded anxious and genuinely contrite. He continued. "Part of this—you understand—is my concern about you and how your family would respond to the news that we are lovers. Do you think your mother is aware of our relationship?"

"No, and she would never even suspect.... Not in a million years."

"Why not?"

"Because she doesn't think I'm attractive."

"Oh, come on...."

"Never mind. It's girl stuff. "

"I don't think you're reading her right, Leanne...."

"Don't change the subject, Philip. We are talking about you." *Now my hands are shaking. I hate confrontation. I need to get off the phone and get my meds.*

"Okay. Okay. You are right. I have kept you hidden—that's true. I worry what people would ... I mean you're a teenager, Leanne."

"No longer. I'm twenty today."

"You're still very young compared to me. And frankly, I'm not sure how my family would handle our relationship."

"You've never introduced me. You've never given me the chance to.... "

"Or my friends. Or my readers. Or, oh Christ, the critics. The fucking critics. Can you see the literary types at the Times calling gossip columnists all over town, whispering behind their ink-stained fingers, "Psst, Roth is fucking a child. Pass it on...."

"I'm not a child. I've never been a child."

"I'm trying to protect you, Leanne. These critics can be vicious."

"The critics adore you. They called you morally brave and hilarious."

"Oh, yeah ... that from the 'literary critic' at *Newsweek* ... ha!"

"*The Times* also gave you a rave...."

"Yes, they love my writing, yes, so now they're looking for a reason to hate me personally. As a man."

"Why are you so paranoid?"

"Americans with their Puritan plasma, clenching their collective sphincters whenever they encounter a dirty joke, can you imagine what they really think of *Portnoy*?"

"Who cares what Americans think?"

"Imagine the unseemly pleasure Americans are finding in my books."

"I no longer see myself as an American, Philip. I'm considering moving to Canada."

"And they can find my book—right there on a shelf at Bookmasters."

"A *New York Times* Bestseller, Philip! It's amazing!"

"They don't even have to ask for someone to get it out of the backroom, wrapped in brown paper. It's like a *National Geographic* with all its naked images of exotic women in exotic places. Completely available to the masses. Only my book is about Jews. The goy can read up on the dirty habits of their Jewish suburban neighbors and co-workers. Rude and lewd sex scenes. The goys read it under the sheets with a flashlight, you know. And they want more! So they have to hate me as a person to relieve their consciences for looking! They wag their forefingers at me and say, 'Philip Roth, you bastard you! You are funny, you are brilliant, but you are an alphabet of perversions. What you must have done in your life so far to know this stuff, to write this stuff!"

"No, they don't, Philip. Nobody's saying that. It's all in your head."

"Because I'm a Jew. Let us not forget that. I'm a Jewish Jew."

"Philip … stop it."

"And a bad JEW! A Jew who makes all other Jews look bad. Rabbis all over New Jersey, and New York are plotzing and clutching their tzitzit and oy gevalting into each other's astonished faces. He's a Masturbator! they cry. This Philip Roth—he spilt his seed all over Summit Avenue, behind the bleachers at the playground, even at Summer camp! He extracted semen in vain all over Newark! And he wrote about it —every detail— in *Portnoy's Complaint*. Like he was proud. Let me tell you—as a teenager boy, he—Please get the children and the women out of the room—they must not hear this. As a teenager boy, this Philip Roth Masturbator, in the bathroom of his mother's home, he is shtupping a piece of raw liver AND his sister's training bra, AND a cored apple—all at the same time. I can give you the page number from the book. In his mother's home! While she's listening to Arthur Godfrey on the radio!! Can you believe this Shvantz?? Has there ever been a bigger putz than Philip Roth? Doing the Devil's dance, buttering a biscuit, AND NOW WE FIND OUT— WITH A TEENAGE GIRL! AND A SHIKSA, NO LESS!"

"Is this a rehearsal? Are you going on *The Tonight Show*?"

"One thing is certain—you shouldn't be anywhere near me, Leanne, because PHILIP ROTH is also a MISOGYNIST. Yes, A WOMAN HATER. They say I treat my women characters like shit."

Long pause.

"What crime have I committed, Leanne? I write books. I create real people out of my imagination. But I didn't invent sex. Real people masturbate and have anal sex and fight and argue and lie. So do my characters. What is my crime? That I wrote about it? That I made it funny? I committed a crime against propriety? For that they label me a misogynist? A woman hater? And a self-loathing Jew who hates his mother? Do you know what this is doing to my family? I'm a pariah in my hometown, Leanne. The rabbis give long lectures about me at synagogue every week. They say I am an example of a traitor Jew. They say I will only intensify

the antisemitism in the country because I've given the Jew-haters ammu-
nition. They can now point to my book and say ... see, we told you ...
these filthy Jews ... they are not real Americans!"

"Philip, you need to go back to therapy."

"They are going to ban my books, Leanne. You watch."

"No, they're not."

"My poor parents are on the defense even with old friends now. All
because of my books. No one in this fucking country can read a fucking
book and understand that it is an act of imagination. And you wonder
why I'm not trotting you out in front of the world as my girlfriend? Because I love you, Leanne. You are precious to me."

Pause.

"Talk to me, Leanne. C'mon ... please, Honey, talk to me." *I heard
his voice crack and my heart cracked with it.*

"I don't know what to say...."

"Anything. Just ... just talk. Let me listen to your voice."

Pause.

I took a deep breath and said, "The other day I watched my father get
attacked by bees."

"My god! Is he okay now?"

"Yeah. He and Mother have saturated the backyard with gallons of
insecticide now. I figure the birds will be dropping out of the trees any
time. Eventually the trees themselves will keel over. Probably next Earth
Day. Mimi's going to have a stroke." Philip laughed. A laugh of relief.
I continued. "On a bright note though, my brothers have a new puppy.
We named him Philip."

"Oh, shit. I really am in the dog house with you, aren't I?"

I laughed. "Nah. He's much loved. Like you."

"Leanne, if it's any consolation, I am being punished for my perceived
sins. So you don't have to punish me."

"I'm not punishing you, Philip."

He was crying now. "It's been a tough Summer for me, Honey. I'm
afraid to keep writing but I have to. It's my work. It's my compulsion.
It's my life."

"I've had a terrible Summer too, Philip."

"What? What happened?"

I sighed. Then tears rolled down my face. I swallowed hard and made myself say, "Look. I think I need a break from you."

"Please don't.…"

"Not forever. Just a.…"

"How long a break?"

"I'll call you. I promise."

"I need you, Leanne. I need you right now."

"I know. But I'm only twenty. I can't fix everybody."

I RETURNED TO THE Playhouse on Saturday to the news that Bert Heckel had quit that week and left town. Didn't even say goodbye. Noah told me that he felt responsible. I studied his face. "*You* feel responsible? What did *you* do?"

"He made a pass at me, Leanne. More than once this Summer. I finally had to tell him there was no chance; I wasn't wired that way. Besides, I told him, I'm in love with you."

Noah and I climbed up a ladder to a loft in the workshop where we could talk uninterrupted. "I spoke to Oric," he whispered.

"Well … will he help me?"

"Yes. He said he knows Bert Heckel. He says he *is* the head of the New York Coven. He says he's the most powerful warlock in New York, maybe in the country. So your intuition was right, Leanne. Oric says you are probably a medium."

"What is a medium?"

"You are a channel for energies. People are attracted to you even though they may not know why." Noah paused and looked at me curiously like it was suddenly occurring to him that he wasn't sure what he actually saw in me. Then he continued, "That makes you very susceptible to people who want to use you to manifest their agendas."

"Oh, God! I am a Manchurian Candidate?"

"Shhhh, Leanne! You are protected now. Oric has already set things up. You have to go into the city … New York … and pick up your first meditation assignment from his assistant. I'll take you on Monday."

I CANCELED MY STANDING date with Mr. Kenyon and Noah drove us into New York. To a large apartment building on the upper West Side. The Dakota. I would be meeting with a man who was the assistant to the conductor of the New York Philharmonic. His apartment was on the fourth floor. I had the number. "He is also on The Work, Leanne. Many musicians are on The Work." Noah smiled encouragingly. "He will hand you an envelope and give you brief instructions and that will be it. Don't engage in any conversation with him. We are all supposed to be strangers to one another. I'll circle the block until you come back down." Noah kissed me and I got out of the car.

The assistant conductor, a slender, dark-haired man in his thirties, opened the door with an aggrieved expression on his face that suggested that he was tired of being the one who gave new recruits their papers. I wondered how many of us there were. I started to step into his spacious apartment and he said, "No—stay out there." He closed the door leaving me standing in the empty hallway. A few minutes later, he returned and handed me a standard white envelope. It was sealed. Then he recited the following in an emphatic tone as though he was already expecting me to defy the rules and fall out of Oric's grace. "There are three symbols in this envelope. Meditate on each five minutes a day. Do them consecutively. If you ever fail to complete The Work within a twenty-four-hour period, you will be dropped by Oric. No exceptions—no appeal. You will be getting a personal letter from Oric within the week. These symbols are your meditation for the next six months—then Oric will send the next assignment. Do not tell anyone you are on The Work. That is between you and Oric from this point on. Understood?" I nodded. He didn't wish me luck or even say goodbye. He just closed the door and I returned to the street. A minute later, Noah came around the corner and I hopped into the car. I was trembling but I felt better.

Noah dropped me off at my house and left so I could be alone with The Work. I went to my room and locked the door. I unsealed the envelope and shook the contents out on my bed. There were three square-inch pieces of plain white paper and on each a symbol was drawn in pencil. One was a circle with a dot in it. One was a simple equilateral triangle. And the last one was two short lines of equal length, intersecting at the midpoint. A cross.

I sat on the floor and placed the three symbols in front of me. I closed my eyes and pictured the first—the circle with the dot. I was to concentrate on it for five minutes and then immediately move on to the next for five minutes and then the last for five minutes. But after one minute, my attention had already wandered. I started again. The same thing happened. My fifteen-minute meditation took over an hour. But I wasn't frustrated. I actually found it relaxing.

August 15, 1969

Dear Diary,

My letter from Oric arrived today. Three pages. He types on that onion-skin paper. His writing is meticulous but conversational, a style midway between formal and informal. But it felt personal; somehow he already knows me. He talked a lot about drugs. He said "even in the little villages of Tuscany, there is drug abuse by the young people and with it, all the attendant behaviors. Sex without commitment. Vulgarity in language and manner. This is not the world we want, is it, Leanne?" He went on to say that he understood that I had captured the attention of the dark forces but that so long as I faithfully did the meditation daily, I was protected from that. So I should "not give those forces further influence by lending them your thoughts. Even your worries. Be aloof." He told me the most powerful color combination for me was green and blue. "A plaid of those colors in a pretty skirt would wrap you in immunity to evil." I didn't have anything like that in my wardrobe but I figured I could check out The Ladybug Shoppe that week. Finally, he ended the letter by saying that he would contact me again in six months with a different set of symbols. In the meantime I was to do the meditation daily. And he added this-"Your mind will wander. Don't be discouraged. Remember, Leanne, the true benefit of The Work is in the act of setting your intention and gently pulling yourself back to focus if you drift.

Each time you bring yourself back, you are performing an act of mental and spiritual discipline. That is what will make you strong." He ended with *"Good luck, dear Leanne. I am with you now. You are safe."*

THE NEW SHOW—*Rosencrantz and Guildenstern Are Dead*—moved in and I met Christine's father. He didn't seem like a dad. He was nice, but so distracted, like he was nervous all the time. I don't think he spent even five minutes alone with Christine. And it broke my heart to see her sad face. She had been waiting all Summer to be with him. The cast for that show stayed at a motel on Route 532 just outside of New Hope. There was a pool and Christinc's dad invited the two of us to the opening night party that week which was held at the motel. It went late. Finally, it was just two of the actors and Christine and me remaining by the pool. We took our clothes off and swam nude under a moonless sky. One of the actors was Black and he began to kiss me. I told him that he was beautiful. I wanted him to know that his Black skin was just as beautiful as my white skin. I had recently begun reading Eldridge Cleaver's *Soul on Ice.* Cleaver's rage at what White people had done to the Black culture was now consuming me.

The Black actor kissed me again and I said, "Do you date Black girls, too?" He pulled back and looked at me suspiciously. I continued, "Because Black women are beautiful, you know. Black is beautiful."

"What are doing, girl? What's this about?"

"I'm just saying you are justified if you hate White people because.... "

"Who the fuck do you think you are? I'm justified-"

"I'm just saying that *Soul on Ice....* I'm reading it ... and it has expanded my understanding of...."

"You understand nothing.... "

"It enrages me that Black men have been taught to think only White women...."

"You're enraged? You're enraged?"

"See I also feel pressure from this culture to be beautiful on THEIR terms. You see.... "

"I don't need a sociology lecture from a spoiled White princess."

"I just want you to know that I understand. More than you can imagine...."

"FUCK YOU DO."

"I want to be your ally. Actually more than an ally...." I touched his face. "I want to be your friend...."

"SHUT UP!" He grabbed my wrists and shook me. "Okay, little girl, you want to know why I am hitting on you? It ain't because I think you're beautiful. I don't think you're beautiful. It's because you White college girls are so easy. Yeah. Much easier than the Black sisters. Cause you're a whore. And I just wanted a whore for the night."

He released my wrists and I swam away from him and climbed out of the pool. I got dressed and left the motel. Christine ran after me. "I'm okay, Christine. I'm okay. I'll call you in the morning...." I got in my car and drove to the Intern House. I knocked on Noah's bedroom door. He opened it, surprised. It was one o'clock in the morning. I put my arms around him and he wrapped me in his, laying his cheek against mine. He said, "Marry me, Leanne. I love you." And I said, "Okay."

Chapter 17

I returned to Syracuse in late August, a junior. I was relieved that the Summer of 1969 was over although there were hanging threads that still had to be dealt with. Andy was back from Japan. And driving us—me and Mimi—to school again. In my baby blue Cutlass. He assumed that we were a couple again now that the Summer was over but neither of us had addressed that. I did resume spending occasional weekends with him at Gryphon House. Andy was a senior now. He planned to attend Georgetown University in Washington, DC immediately after his graduation from Hamilton in the Spring. He would be getting a master's degree in international affairs. He seemed different to me now—more grounded. He still had his wonderfully irreverent sense of humor, and his eclectic curiosity, both of which made him the most entertaining company alive, but now he seemed more confident, less needy. Increasingly his focus seemed to be centered on me.

He attended each of my opening nights at school and once he came backstage and said, "I would have paid to see you in that. That's how good you are, Annie." It was a wonderful play, directed by Mimi, in which I played a young girl who lived with her schizophrenic mother and mentally damaged older sister. This girl discovers her self-worth when she learns from her science teacher that a part of her "came from the sun." It was such a sad but powerful and moving play that I considered switching my major to Astronomy. Andy bragged about me in front of his friends now. And he often mused about the possibility of his finding a job with a diplomatic Think Tank in Washington, DC after grad school. "Think about it, Annie. There are wonderful professional theaters in that city. We could make a life together there." I hadn't yet mentioned the fact that I was now engaged to Noah.

Noah, for his part, was back at Boston University. He had agreed to keep our engagement a secret out of respect for the fact that I needed time to let my old boyfriend—"PA"—down gently. Noah called one evening and suggested that we plan on spending Christmas with his family at their Winter home in Palm Beach, Florida. And there we could announce our engagement officially. Noah said my parents and brothers would, of course, be invited as well. There was plenty of room. He asked if his mother could reach out to my mother. Apparently she wanted to know my family. I said, "Oh, not yet. Not yet. I haven't told my parents yet." Noah said, "What? You haven't told your mother that we're engaged?" I struggled to come up with a plausible rationale. The best I could do was this—"Well, see ... my father was attacked by bees ... my parents are still in shock."

"Oh, God. That's terrible. Are you doing The Work?"

"Yes, yes."

"Every day?"

"Yes. But my parents ... uh ... I just don't want to excite them right now."

Noah phoned more often after that, a couple nights a week at least. But now that we were away from the Bucks County Playhouse, I strained to find common ground even for a phone conversation. We had The Work in common, but that was it. And we weren't supposed to talk about it.

"Leanne, did you get a letter from Oric this week?"

"No. Why?"

"Well, he doesn't want us to eat peanuts anymore."

"Okay."

"Their molecular structure is counter-clockwise."

"I don't think we're supposed to talk about The Work with each other, Noah."

"Oh, that's right."

One night he asked me my preference when it came to diamond engagement rings and I freaked out. "NO! NO DIAMONDS!! For heaven's sake, Noah, read the history of diamond mining in South Africa! The White colonialists stripped the native population of their own land. The Whites took everything from them! The native people became SLAVES in their own country! Diamonds are blood money, Noah."

"Shhhh ... Leanne ... shhh. I'm sorry ... I won't buy a diamond," Noah cooed. "I'll buy you a sapphire instead."

Speaking of South Africa, I learned that week at a meeting of our chapter of the SDS that the Syracuse University Board of Trustees had invested in stock that financed South African silver mining. Syracuse University was enabling Apartheid with student tuition money! I went up on campus the very next day and found my way to the open microphone that was now standing most afternoons at the center of the quad. It was sponsored by the Student Union. Students would take the opportunity to espouse on anything that they felt strongly about. Most of the impromptu speeches were about the escalating war in Vietnam and the upcoming Draft Lottery. But I wanted to talk about racism.

I don't remember exactly what I said into the microphone that afternoon on the Quad, but I drew the attention of some of the SDS leaders, seniors who were administering the agenda for our university chapter that year. And I soon was involved in the planning for the occupation of the Administration building tentatively scheduled for the following Spring. One of our objectives was to force the Trustees to unload the South African silver stock and put a few students on the Board of Trustees which at the time consisted entirely of rich, old men.

That Fall, Dow Chemical Company announced that it would be on campus to recruit and interview and ultimately hire chemistry and biology students who would be graduating in the Spring. Our SDS members quickly planned a Freak-Out to protest the Dow visit. Dow Chemical had created and supplied the U.S. Military with Napalm, a sticky gel like fuel that created a firebomb on impact and burned slow and long on anything it attached to. Dumped from planes, there was no way to target anything specifically so it hit livestock and live people. Civilians. Even children. It burned flesh at 8000 degrees and could even burn underwater. It wasn't just a weapon of war. It was pure terrorism.

On the day of the Dow Freak Out, I stood at the microphone at the center of the Quad and spoke passionately about all of this. Protesting students rolled on the ground and screamed in simulated agony. Dow left campus after the first hour. It was a victory for our side; but the campus increasingly felt like a war zone to me. Protest demonstrations popped up spontaneously every other day. The sounds of sirens and angry voices, even screams created a soundtrack for that Fall of '69. Tear gas was now used liberally by the cops to bust up the more rambunctious demonstrations. One windy afternoon, I was walking down a quiet street toward campus on my way to class. I could hear the familiar sounds of protest off in the distance. Then suddenly my face was burning, my eyes stung. I was engulfed. Tear gas is invisible which makes it hard to escape. You don't know where it ends. I ran with my eyes closed, coughing and choking and was nearly hit by a car.

Redhat's apartment was searched by the cops one morning when we were all at class. She, Cool Breeze, Pookie, and Rain came home that afternoon to find their front door open and all of their clothes pulled out of the bureaus and tossed around the living room. At first they thought they had been robbed, but one of the girls downstairs said she heard the cops come in and saw them on the stairs heading to our floor. If the cops were looking for weed, they didn't find it. Cool Breeze's stash was still securely taped to the underside of one of the fire escape steps. That had been Pookie's idea. Even if the cops found it, she had explained, they couldn't make a definitive case that it belonged to Cool Breeze or anyone else. Pookie was pre-law. She was our go-to for anything that involved the cops. Anyway, I guess the cops were pretty frustrated when they left. They hung the girls' panties on the closet doorknobs throughout the apartment and took their birth control pills just to be mean.

A couple of days later, I was arrested. Cool Breeze and I were on the sidewalk, heading to the anthropology class we took together. Cool Breeze was telling me that he was thinking now he might go into medicine like his dad. A girl named Robyn, who was in my art history class, stopped to chat with me about the semester term paper that had recently been assigned and the next thing we knew, two cops were shoving all three of us into a car and advising us of our rights. Our offense was that "we were inciting a riot." Gathering in numbers greater than two was now forbidden, because someone—the Governor?—had just declared Martial Law. Or that's what the young cops told us. We spent three hours in a jail cell and were eventually released, without charges, and without an apology, when a lawyer from the ACLU showed up. Robyn and I were released first. Cool Breeze was in the cell an hour longer because he was Black and they wanted to fuck with him.

I decided to write a Letter to the Editor of *The Daily Orange* about the obvious and outrageous racism in the Syracuse police force. It was published and I met the Chief of Police, Tom Sardino, when he came to an anti-war rally later that week. He was there not to address the students— but to join us. Turned out that he was taking classes himself and, as a fellow student, wanted to demonstrate his support for peaceful assembly and protest. I told him about the bogus arrest and he said he would look into it. He never got back to me but I suppose he had a lot on his plate those days. Dealing with all the demonstrations, and rogue cops plus having to do homework every night.

I was now speaking at the Quad once a week. My focus was increasingly on Civil Rights. I avoided talking about the Vietnam War because, frankly, I wasn't against every war. I was conflicted because Czechoslovakia was still under siege by the Soviets. I'd written Jagr right after I received his letter back in July, but he hadn't written back and I worried that he might be dead or in a Soviet prison himself. I figured his father was probably in Siberia by now. I tried to make the case at an anti-war rally that week that there are times when war is justified. Like in self-defense. We each must decide what is worth fighting for. But my speech wasn't well received; I was booed. I tried to explain that fighting Communism in Europe, for example, is a battle for human rights. I raised my voice, "Vietnam is different—that's a civil war that has become a proxy war between the imperialistic Soviet Union and the U.S. But the Czechs were invaded and the Czechs need our tanks for self-defense."

Mimi and Olivia were always supportive of my efforts but tried to get me to speak about environmental degradation, specifically about eliminating pesticides. They thought it was a more upbeat message and a break from the never-ending talk of war and riots. They were using their shadow theater shows to spread a message of reverence for Mother Earth and they were actually drawing a decent sized crowd now whenever they performed. It was like the whole campus had been divided into two entirely separate worlds. One world was loud and violent and always on the verge of a nervous breakdown and the other world was one in which everyone sang Joni Mitchell songs and made the peace sign with their fingers when they ran into one another.

Both Mimi and Olivia wore flowing skirts and blouses now. They insisted that all their clothing be constructed of natural fibers. They stopped shaving their armpits and their legs. And they frequently painted flowers on their faces. I felt they were being a bit Pollyanna-ish. Not that I didn't believe in saving the earth; I did. But imperialism and escalating war—that just felt more urgent to me. For one thing, if either of the superpowers ended up setting off a nuke, pesticides would be the least of our problems.

Wolf moved out of our apartment in October and in with his girlfriend, an art student named Jane. She designed and distributed dramatic weekly flyers that announced date, time, and which corner of the campus an interested audience would find the little wooden theater that week. Wolf was performing now in every show and had a personal following, mostly girls. He had even written a theme song that his most avid followers learned and sang loudly while waiting for the show to begin. It became an overture of sorts. I had yet to become involved, but I always tried to attend their performances.

Mimi was also spending a lot of her time designing a future beyond Syracuse for Olivia, me and herself—and Wolf and Jane if they were inclined to hang with us after graduation the next year. Mimi's plans were all about going "back to the land." To that end, she wanted to find "an acre with a view," as she put it—somewhere in the southwest—where we could build a solar-powered house big enough to accommodate all of us. She spent hours making lists and designing aluminum-foil-lined curtains that would reflect heat away from the house during the day but insulate the house during cold evenings in the desert. She had visions of all of us farming a large garden of organic fruits and vegetables. Olivia was obsessively developing recipes that would give us balanced nourishment while still "eating clean." She made glorious soups and started baking bread every weekend. She grew fresh herbs on our kitchen windowsill. Our apartment smelled like the Garden of Eden.

Olivia convinced Mimi that we should eventually open a small café. A French café in the desert—somewhere near Taos, New Mexico. With a view of mountains in the background. The specifics changed every day, but Mimi and Olivia smiled all the time now. They looked half-stoned, but neither of them did drugs anymore, not even weed. "We're high on life, Leanne," Mimi would say. "I want you to live with us forever, ma cherie. You and Andy.... Maybe you will have a baby and we can all raise her together."

I SHOULD MENTION THAT Mr. Kenyon and I had agreed to suspend our affair at the end of Summer so that I could concentrate on school and live with Mimi without fear of discovery. A week before I returned to Syracuse, he surprised me by reserving a room at the Plaza Hotel for our last night together, a suite with a large bathtub and room service on demand. Even champagne! We had never spent a whole night together. And he told me he wanted it to be special so that we would feel sustained by the memory until we could be together again. For me it was a dream come true.

When I was a kid, I read the books about Eloise, the six-year-old girl, a true free spirit, who lived at the Plaza with her mother. I envied her so much I ached. So whenever Mother and I went into New York City which we did at least once a year beginning when I was around six, we would make a pilgrimage to the Plaza in honor of Eloise. There at the corner of 59th and Fifth Avenue, Mother and I would spend a full minute in reverent silence ending with some quasi-religious gesture like crossing our hearts. And then I would blow a kiss to the upper floors and make a wish that I would someday get to spend the whole night in one of the elegant pink bedrooms.

As I got older my fascination with the Plaza only increased. On November 28, 1966, Truman Capote hosted a ball at the Plaza in honor of Katherine Graham, the publisher of the *Washington Post*. Katherine's husband had committed suicide just a few years before. Truman wanted to cheer her up. So, he rented the Grand Terrace Ballroom and invited 540 of his closest friends. I knew every detail by heart. Mother, Mrs. Taylor, and I had poured over the story and photos of the gala in *Life* magazine. It was called the Black and White Masquerade Ball. *Life* magazine called it the Party of the Century.

Everyone who was anyone was there and they were instructed to wear black and/or white only. And a mask. Truman announced each guest as they entered the ballroom. Lots of Hollywood showed up. The Old Guard. Like Tallulah Bankhead but she had to *beg* for an invitation! *Can you imagine?* Lauren Bacall was there. And Frank Sinatra came with his new wife, Mia Farrow, who had recently had her hair cut very short by Vidal Sassoon for the movie *Rosemary's Baby*. Frank hated it! Henry Fonda came with his *fifth* wife, Shirlee Mae Adams. *Fifth Wife!* There were world-class fashion designers, and famous novelists; Norman Mailer and Dominic Dunne showed up. As did princesses and contessas and Jacqueline Kennedy's sister, Lee Radziwell, the American socialite who was one of Truman's closest friends. And artists! Andy Warhol arrived and was the only guest not wearing a mask. Everyone danced to the music of the Peter Duchin Orchestra and sipped champagne and nibbled delicacies. They say this ball relaunched Katherine Graham's social life!

I relayed every detail I could remember of the Black and White Ball to Mr. Kenyon. "I know it makes me sound superficial, Robert, but this is the life I really want. I want to dress beautifully and travel and have fascinating friends." And Robert said, "Then that is the life that you create for yourself. You make it happen." And I said, "But I'm torn. All of my true friends would abandon me. They would think I was shallow." And Robert said, "Your new life would come with new friends. It would all balance out." And I said, "No, I don't think I would be happy if my true friends weren't still with me. I love them." And Robert said, "Then don't change."

EVERY TWENTY-FOUR HOURS, I did The Work; I never missed. I was getting regular postcards from Oric now. "Don't eat tomatoes." "Don't drink coffee." And I loved the meditation. It wasn't work for me. I looked forward to feeling serene for fifteen minutes every twenty-four hours. Regardless of my shaky mornings waiting for my first dose of amphetamines to kick in, regardless of the chaos I might face on campus during the day, The Work provided a quiet space in which I could retreat from the world and recharge. I was grateful to Noah for putting me in touch with Oric. Nevertheless, during Thanksgiving break, I called Noah and broke off our engagement. I told him I was gay, that I was ready to come out of the closet, and live an authentic sexual life. That, of course, was a lie, but it was kinder than telling him the truth which was—I can't marry you, Noah, because you bore me to tears. He was silent for a long time. But he gently accepted it. I knew he would. Noah was an incredibly decent human being. "It's probably The Work," he said quietly. "It's clarifying you. That's a good thing, but...." He started to cry. I felt sick. I almost relented. But finally he said, "This is part of the Aquarian Age, you know. We are all becoming who we are meant to be." I agreed. Noah assured me that he would always hold me in the highest esteem in his heart. He didn't, however, offer to stay in touch.

Chapter 18

In January, at an SDS meeting, I met a young man—with a very closely shaved head. "I'm not a Republican," he said when I queried him. "I'm not a Democrat either. I'm non-aligned."

"Why are you at an SDS meeting?" I asked.

"You never learn anything new just hanging around with people who agree with you all the time."

"That's true," I said and extended my hand. "I'm Leanne."

"Finn," he said. "You have time for a cup of coffee?"

"Sure."

He told me that he had just returned from Vietnam. He had been a soldier. Front line. I had never spoken to a soldier before. At least not one in my own generation. I was immediately intrigued, but I approached him carefully. I didn't ask him what it was like in Vietnam. I had enough of an idea given all the reporting on the nightly news and in the papers. And to be honest, I was afraid to hear the details. I already had trouble sleeping, especially with Noah gone. Instead I said, "So what is life like for you back here in the good ol' USA?" He stared at me. I said, "I'm being facetious, Finn. I'm sorry. I meant to say how are you doing?"

He rubbed his closely shaved chin. "I have a sense of direction now," he said. "And a purpose for my life." He had a soft voice with a slight Southern drawl. I learned that he was twenty-six years old and had joined the Peace Corps right out of high school. He wanted to honor President Kennedy's commitment to a peaceable world. I found my attention drifting now. There was a rumor that had circulated when I was still in high school, that President Kennedy had been assassinated by our own government, and that LBJ and the CIA were involved in the plot. Some of the boys in my homeroom asserted that you can't trust our government. And I was coming around to that point of view now.

I refocused my attention. "I'm sorry, Finn.... I missed the last thing you said. Can you repeat… ?"

He leaned in and whispered, "I said I'm going to bomb the bank on Marshal Street."

I FELT SORRY FOR Finn. He had a family in Mississippi, but his relationship with them had deteriorated over the years to the point where he basically described himself as homeless. Oh, he had money, a job, and an apartment—I think he had an apartment. I never learned where he actually lived and he was always alone when I saw him. He wasn't a mad man though—quite the opposite. He was hyper-rational. He said that money was the route of all evil. And if we were to ever have a chance of creating a world that is peaceful and prosperous for all, we have to attack inequality. I certainly agreed with that. He then told me about a secret cabal of obscenely wealthy men. "No one outside this nefarious men's club knows who they are but it is fairly well known that they control every lever of power on earth. They pick the kings and queens, the dictators, even the elected officials—even here in the U.S. They hold no political principle. Their only agenda is to keep generating indescribable mountains of wealth for themselves. To that end, they keep the world eternally at war because war makes them money."

Finn offered to treat me to lunch and we entered a fast food place on Marshal Street. We stood in line and he continued to talk. "They own all the weapons of war, Leanne. They control the manufacturers, the materials, even the distributors. They own the military-industrial complex … Boeing, Dow Chemical, Lockheed Martin, Northrup are all in their pockets. And they control the armies of every nation because they own the leaders of every nation. War is their business and they generate an endless demand for their war munitions by stirring up hate in every corner of the globe. They pit us against one another and then they sit back and watch human nature do its predictable worst. And they never care who wins because they can't lose so long as we continue to hate one another."

When we got up to the counter, a tired looking young woman took our order. Finn was gallant with her, asking her how she balanced a job and school and yet still managed to look so radiant. She leaned in and whispered, "For being so nice, I'll throw in the fries for free."

Finn wasn't what I'd call handsome, but he was definitely charismatic. And persuasive. Our food arrived and as we headed to an empty table, Finn said, "Did you ever wonder, Leanne, why Switzerland, right there in the midst of Europe, is never involved in any war? Is always neutral? It's because that's where these monsters live. They call themselves the Illuminati."

A strung-out kid approached our table. "Hey, man," he said eyeing our burgers.

Finn smiled at him. "Hey, man. What's up?"

The kid staggered a bit. "Listen, man … can you borrow me a dollar? I left my wallet at … you know … um … you know … the bookstore."

Finn reached into his pocket. He pulled out his wallet and handed the kid a five. "What's your name?"

"Thanks, man. Kenneth. I'm Kenneth." He didn't look at the bill in his hand. Like that would be too gauche a gesture, make him look too anxious and uncool. He just tucked it casually in his pocket to savor later.

"You're eating, man?" Finn said gently.

"Oh, yeah, man." Kenneth pulled up his shirt and patted his concave stomach. His ribs protruded. "I'm eatin'. Definitely."

Finn continued, "You have people, man? Someone to talk to?"

The kid said, "Oh, I got people." He waved his arm in a circle, encompassing the other diners. He laughed.

Finn nodded. "Okay, Kenneth. Well, I'm on a date with this young lady so you need to move along now."

Kenneth nodded his head and drifted on. Finn and I watched him leave the restaurant in silence. Then Finn said, "He was in Vietnam."

"Oh, do you know him?"

"No. I can just tell. He's been through trauma. He's self-medicating with drugs."

We finished lunch and Finn walked me back to my apartment. He was still talking. "The only way to disrupt their power is to disrupt the flow of money. And one way to do that is to get people to stop using banks and start hiding their money under their mattresses. A cash economy. And barter. Pure and simple. That's step one. And step two-we have to start turning our hate away from each other and towards the rich."

The more Finn spoke, the more sense he made. "We'll start small," Finn said. "Make it look random. A little bank here. A little bank there. We will target college campuses because the kids will freak out but their parents will freak out even more. And demand that banks be more and more fortified until no one uses them anymore. This won't be accomplished in a week or a decade. It's a long-term project. It's going to take commitment. But in the end, no one will trust the banks anymore."

I invited Finn to come in and meet my roommates but he declined. "So can I count on you, Leanne? To join my team? I promise you no one will be hurt."

"Your team?"

"There are a few of us—Patriots who have joined the mission. You don't need to know all of our names. We will all have a role to play. We're going to bomb a bank this Spring. I'm serious. So are you in?"

I said yes. But I told no one about Finn. I didn't want to burden Mimi and Olivia with worry about my involvement. And Finn had promised that no one would be hurt.

MY MOTHER PHONED THAT week and said, "Guess what. Annie? We have a brand new color TV."

"Why? Daddy just bought one last year."

"Well, Daddy was driving home from a conference two Sundays ago. It was about nine o'clockish at night. And it was pouring. And Daddy said there was hardly a soul on the turnpike but there was this one car on the side of the road. So Daddy pulled over to see what he could do. Well, it was a man traveling alone—going home himself and he had a flat. So Daddy helped him change it. In the pouring rain. And the man was so grateful, he said he wanted to send Daddy a gift and he asked him to write down his address. And Daddy, of course, said, that wasn't necessary. But the man insisted and Daddy wanted to get out of the rain so he gave the man his name and address. Well, yesterday, a big furniture van pulled into our driveway and the delivery men lifted out a beautiful console RCA color TV and brought it into the house. When Daddy got home he opened the card that was addressed to him. It read: *Thank you, Tom! You make me proud to be an American.* And it was signed Perry Como!"

"Wow."

"We're going to give our other color TV to the Black family in town. We have a Black family, Leanne! Did I tell you? I met the wife. She's lovely."

"Mother, don't give them our TV. That's embarrassing."

"Why? It's practically new. It works great."

"You're making assumptions."

"My god, Annie, I thought you would be pleased that I'm reaching out to this family. Making them feel welcome."

"It will make them feel like charity cases."

"Oh, for heaven's sake, Annie!"

"Just give it to the Goodwill. And invite the woman to join the Historical Society."

"Oh, Annie. I can't win with you."

ANDY CAME OVER TO see me in a play that Mimi directed. It was part of a one-act festival that was staged in the small studio theater upstairs. The play was *Birdbath* by Leonard Melfi and had two characters. I played a waitress and a guy in our class named Frank played the cook. The play was well received by the audience. And on our walk back to my apartment, Andy said, "I'm really proud of you, Annie."

We stopped for a moment. The snow on either side of the sidewalk was thigh high on me, but the night was calm. He leaned down and kissed me. Then he looked at me and said gently, "Marry me."

I shook my head. "I can't."

"Why are you so reluctant to marry me, Annie? Tell me the truth. Maybe I can allay your concerns if I know what they are."

I took a deep breath. "I'm not neat enough for you, Andy."

He half-laughed. "What? Are you being facetious?"

"I know you could do better than me. I have … I have problems. I can't tell you about them … but I want you to marry someone wonderful, much better than me. You deserve the best."

"Annie? Annie … You have my whole heart. I gave it to you years ago. I have nothing left to give anyone else. And I don't want anyone else. I want to be with you."

"You have to make yourself look around, Andy. I mean it. For your own happiness. I'm not good enough for you. Trust me … I'm fucked up, Andy."

Andy looked at me, horrified. "You're serious? Let me help you."

"You can't."

"I'll do anything. Give me a chance."

"No."

When we got back to the apartment, Andy grabbed his things and without a goodbye, drove off. I immediately called Philip. He answered, "Hello?"

"Hi, it's me."

"Leanne! Oh, Leanne … I'm so glad to hear your voice."

"Am I interrupting?"

"No … no. I just finished dinner."

"Are you by yourself?"

"Yes."

"Is everything okay, Honey?"

"Yeah, Philip. I just felt like talking to you."

"I was thinking about you, too. I can come get you, bring you back to the city for a few days. I could be there in a couple of hours. It's been a long time since we held each other."

"I have midterms this week, Philip."

"Okay, let's just talk then. It feels so wonderful to hear your voice."

"So what are you writing now?"

"A skewering of that son-of-a-bitch Nixon and his hitmen. I couldn't resist."

"I'm sure it's wonderful."

"Thank you. I was just thinking this morning … you will be done in one more year. It went fast, didn't it?"

"I guess.… "

"What's the matter, Honey? You don't sound like yourself."

"Andy is mad at me."

"Why?"

"He asked me to marry him … Third time. And I said no."

"Good for you. You're too young to marry, Leanne. And too smart to get trapped. Hey, skip class this week. I'll come get you … throw some things in a suitcase and toss it out the window. Then jump—I'll catch you."

I laughed. "Are you asking me to elope?"

"No. But we'll hide out at my place. Get away from everyone. I don't have to be the reputed sex maniac with you. You don't have to be the reputed Belle of Linton Hill with me. We can just be ourselves. Wouldn't that be nice?"

"That actually sounds wonderful, Philip. I wish I could. But I have exams."

"Okay. Okay. When's Spring break?"

"In two weeks."

"I'll come get you in Pennswalk during Spring break. I love you, Leanne."

"I love you, Philip."

I WENT HOME FOR Spring Break. Dr. Lawrence called me there and asked me to meet with him in his office. "Listen," he said. "I can't renew your prescription. The Federal government has placed amphetamines on a list of illegal drugs. They have determined that they are addicting." He shrugged. "It happens with pharmaceuticals from time to time. Anyway, … you'll adjust. Now going forward—watch your calories. Drink a lot of water. Get plenty of exercise. You're never going to be thin, but you have a normal body. Try to be positive."

I could hardly breathe. I knew that I was in for a rough ride. Once at school when my mother didn't send my prescription renewal to me as fast as I needed it, I went through almost a week without my pills. I was immediately plunged into a physical nightmare of tremors and sweats that was only relieved when the pills finally arrived along with a chatty note from my mother. *Dear Annie, Sorry, I didn't get this to the post office sooner, but Daddy and I had tickets to a show at the Bucks County Playhouse last night and I thought I'd wait until after we had seen the play so I could tell you all about it. Oh, Honey, it was terrific….*

I told Mother that evening that I didn't have to take my meds anymore, that Dr. Lawrence said they were illegal now. Mother didn't look at me. Instead she wiped some invisible dust off the buffet in the dining room and said with forced cheeriness, "Well, that's good." My withdrawal began the next day. I told Mother I apparently had the Flu, It was going around school. I stayed in my room, mostly in bed. I shook constantly. I vomited. I ached. I had severe leg cramps and arm cramps. My jaw hurt. I couldn't sleep and didn't want to—I hallucinated when I was awake but at least I had some rational sense of what I was seeing. If I slept, my nightmares overwhelmed me.

Philip called mid-week, and Mother answered the phone. She told him I had Hong Kong flu. "But I'll tell Annie you called, Philip. So nice to hear from you. Annie will be tickled to know you remember her."

By the time I returned to school, a week later, most of the symptoms were easing. I still vomited most mornings though and I had trouble concentrating on my classes, but the aching had stopped. Mainly I was just exhausted. I couldn't eat. I had no appetite. I slept fitfully. By the end of the month, I had lost almost thirty pounds. Mimi kept asking me what was wrong and finally, I told her and Olivia the whole sorry tale of the last seven years. Mimi kept rubbing my back in a manic attempt to … what?—revive me? I cried, they cried, too. Then Mimi announced, "You will be well again." She repeated it even more emphatically. Then she wrote it on the mirror in the bathroom: YOU WILL BE WELL! Olivia marched immediately into the kitchen and made a soup with chicken and broth and fresh herbs. And starting the next morning, either Mimi or Olivia walked me to most of my classes to make sure I didn't miss any of them. I reminded myself daily that I was strong, but I was so grateful to Mimi and Olivia. I don't think I would have been that strong if it wasn't for them.

FINN CALLED ME THE last week of April. I hadn't seen him since before Spring Break. He was ready to set the date for our first bank bombing. We met on the quad. A large peace rally was in progress and a student was speaking about Gandhi and Dr. King and nonviolent resistance. "Don't look at me," he said as he sidled up beside me. "We don't know each other." My body stiffened. He whispered, "Monday, May 4th. We will do it on Monday, May 4. Early. We will meet at five in the morning behind the bank. Then you will go to the front door and lure the security officer out of the bank just as we planned." I didn't reply. He lit a cigarette and nonchalantly scanned the crowd. "You will talk through the window to the security guard. Say your car broke down. I will have parked a car across the street. The keys will be under the visor. Point to it and say it's your mom's car and she doesn't know you took it. And you are going to be in trouble. Beg him to look at it, see if he can get it started for you. He will believe you if you cry. He's young. Still in school. It's his weekend job. You can do this, Leanne. You're an actress. Once he's outside, I will detonate a bomb. No one will be hurt. And we won't steal anything."

May 4, 1970

I didn't show up at the bank that morning. I couldn't do it. I'm a coward. I'm a fraud. I think I'm changing the world. But I'm a big nothing. I'm going nowhere in this life. I would have sent

*Finn a note or called the day before to tell him I wouldn't be there,
but I never knew how to reach him. He was the one who always
found me. I knew without me to get the guard out of the bank,
Finn would be forced to postpone the whole thing. Maybe cancel
it altogether. I knew he would hate me. But so what? Get in line,
Finn. I've disappointed better men than you.*

I got dressed and called Philip at his apartment in New York. He
answered the phone.

"It's me," I said hoarsely.

"How are you? You still sound like you have the flu."

"I need you to come and get me."

"Why? What's wrong?"

"I need to be with you, Philip."

"Leanne...."

"I will make you happy. I promise."

"Leanne, I have to tell you something."

"What?"

"I am in a relationship with a woman. I've known her for some time
now.... It's become quite serious in the past couple weeks. I will always
love you, but...."

I hung up. He called back. I ignored it. He called again. I ignored it. I
left the receiver off the cradle so he couldn't call again. I climbed into bed
and pretended I was reading in case Mimi came in to talk

That afternoon Mimi and Olivia left the apartment together and
headed to the theater for a stagecraft class; it was required for directing
majors so I knew they would be gone for at least two hours. I was still
lying on my bed, fully dressed, staring at my book when they left. I sat up
and did my meditation, but it was by rote. I felt numb. Finally I stood up
and left my room. I crossed to the bathroom. I entered and ran a warm
bath. Then I grabbed a straight edged razor that Wolfe had left behind
in the medicine chest when he moved in with Jane. I removed the safety
cover and when the water was about five inches deep, I climbed into the
tub. I didn't bother to undress. I sank into the soft water and then in one

quick, deep swipe, I slashed my left wrist. I avoided looking at the blood; I closed my eyes and told myself it would all be over soon.

The last thing I heard was Mimi screaming from the living room, like a dream. "Leanne? Are you still here? There's been a bombing on Marshal Street! Two people are dead! One's a kid … He was a student here at Syracuse, a freshman! And in Ohio, Leanne! Oh, Fuck … In Ohio—the National Guard is killing the university students there!!! The war has started, Leanne!! They're coming for all of us!! We have to leave school right now! You have to call Andy! The government is coming after us!!! Leanne, where are you?" Her voice was closer now. "Leanne, we have to … LEANNE! OH MY FUCKIN' GOD—WHAT HAVE YOU DONE? LEEEEAAAANNE!!!!"

The End

Intermission

"So that's it? That's how you're going to end it?"

"Yes, Philip."

"I don't get it. You write all these pages and now you quit? Because why? Because I chose another woman?"

"That's part of it."

"This is your fantasy, Leanne. Rewrite that part if you don't like it."

"You say yourself, Philip, that there is a knowledge that writing produces that is not your own. I stopped outlining after Chapter 6. I didn't need to anymore. I really know you now."

"That's good. It means you're writing authentically."

"Always the professor."

"I thought you liked my instruction. I thought that's why you summoned me back across the veil."

"Oh, come on, Philip. I didn't bring you back to mentor me. I was lonely."

"Well, you can't have Leanne die by suicide. She's too strong. The readers won't accept it."

"This novel had all the elements of an epic love story. It could easily have gone that way. Lovers divided by faith, by social class, by age ... even by death—"

"Oy, rub it in, why don't you?"

"—*set against the backdrop of war. And it was working, Philip. I believed you loved me. But you wrecked it, because when the chips were down, you wouldn't commit to me. Even in my own fantasy. How do you think that makes me feel? Now I'm left wondering what to remember of our affair—the love or the anxiety.*"

"*Your project was much more ambitious than a love story, Leanne. You wanted to discover America.*"

"*Oh, I believe I know America now.*"

"*I'm listening....*"

"*I discovered that America is a chimera. It is insubstantial, just a reflection of the people who are within its borders at any given time.*"

"*That could be said of most nations.*"

"*No, other nations seem to stay consistent in their sense of identity. We Americans constantly adapt to every new group of refugees who hits our shores.*"

"*But that is part of our identity, Leanne. We reach out to the world and welcome the huddled masses. They become Americans. We are all renewed by their idealism.*"

"*But that idealism doesn't last. They soon become like the rest of us—materialistic, individualistic, smug, and self-interested. Generation by generation, we are tearing this country apart.*"

"*Nevertheless, Leanne, I am an American because I have a recognition of home.*"

"*What does that mean?*"

"*At first it was my mother's face in the apartment where we live. But as I grew up, my sense of home expanded to include my neighborhood and then my city and my state and then New Jersey, Pennsylvania and Illinois ... I began to travel abroad in my twenties—I left America—and always, when I returned, it would quietly register that I was home. I came to recognize that the whole country was my home. And sometimes it would make me happy to come home. And sometimes it would feel like a burden to be home. Sometimes I'd look around and the view would be familiar like my old neighborhood. But sometimes no two people would seem to have anything in common and everybody would be a stranger and yet I still recognized that I was home. If it was a choice to be American, I must have made that choice when I wasn't* looking because I don't remember ever considering any alternatives. I just always knew that I'm American because America is my home. Being American is subtle. It's the way the water tastes. It's the way the air smells. Being American doesn't make you happy or sad. Or smart or dumb. Or scared or safe. Or even proud. If you are American it's simply because you recognize that America is your home."

"I wish I had been born in your generation, Philip. Maybe I would have been happier."

"You would have hated the Fifties."

Pause.

"Just for the record, I want you to know that I was faithful to you, Philip."

"You are what is called an unreliable narrator, Leanne. Not that it matters, but you were never faithful to me. In fact, you covered this topic at length in Chapter 10. Remember?"

"YOU READ MY DIARY? How dare you violate my American sense of privacy!"

"You slept with Jagr and Andy and Cool Breeze and ..."

"Not Cool Breeze ... I didn't need to sleep with Cool Breeze ... I could always talk to him."

"So how many more were there? How many men?"

"Why do you care? You set the tone for our affair, Philip. You were never monogamous. But we could have had a really good marriage, you know. A happy ending."

"You really are conventional, aren't you?"

"Yes. And so are you."

"Well, the sex has been wonderful, Leanne. Thank you for that."

"Thank you. You certainly held up your end."

"Hey, I have an idea. How about I write the next chapter? It's been awhile, but I like to think I'm rested rather than rusty. I'll get us back on track, Leanne. Your story is by no means finished."

"You're going to write as a woman? As me? Now that's hilarious."

"No, no—I'll write from my perspective. Wouldn't you like to see yourself from my point of view?"

"I don't need your pity, Philip. I've gotten over other crushes."

"But isn't the little narcissist inside you already aquiver with anticipation at what I might have to say? I have been paying attention to your story, you know. I know what you want. You want to be a hero."

"My life has actually turned out fine. I have my health."

"Don't be glib. Listen to me—you want romance? I can do that. You want more sex? You want openness? YOU WANT TO MAKE A DIFFERENCE? Come on, Leanne, gimme the reigns."

"You could always make me laugh, Philip."

"Gimme the reigns."

"Ha ha."

"Gimme the reigns."

"Okay … Fine. Write the next chapter. See if I care."

"Now vee may perhaps to begin."

Chapter 20

as told by Philip Roth

I have to park three blocks from her apartment building, but it's a fine day to walk; the first day of Fall Semester 1970. I pass kids who are moving into fraternity houses and apartment buildings, schlepping boxes from cars double-parked on the avenue; and there rising in the distance, the dormitories before which anxious parents unload heavily laden station wagons while their freshman children search the incoming class for a potential best friend. The atmosphere is one of a jolly county fair, music pours out of open windows and doors—the Rolling Stones, the Beatles, Big Brother and the Holding Company—are among those I recognize. The anti-war protests that climaxed with the killing of the Kent State students—shot dead by the Ohio National Guardsmen last Spring—that shut down universities across the country including Syracuse one month before the official end of the semester and sent Leanne to the Emergency Room, seem to have taken an extended intermission. Everywhere I look I see carefree teenagers in skimpy shorts and t-shirts. I am no longer teaching. The publication of *Portnoy's Complaint* last year—number one on the *Times'* bestseller list for a total of seventeen weeks, banned in Australia, talked about everywhere—has made me an international celebrity or pariah, depending on one's point of view, and wealthy beyond the dreams of my Eastern European forefathers. I won't teach again; I will write full time from hereon. But I feel nostalgic for the classroom already at the sight of all these co-eds.

I approach her building and see her face in the open window on the third floor just as I saw her for the first time six years ago at her mother's belated celebration of Hawaii's statehood. Then she was a bright fourteen-year-old in blue eyeshadow, clutching her diary to her chest, scanning her parents' backyard in search of me. Twice we made fleeting eye contact, and moments later I found her upstairs in the hallway outside her bedroom. She boldly locked eyes with me, her willful chin upturned, heavenward, daring me to kiss her; barely five foot two wearing a pink sleeveless dress that emphasized her flourishing bosom. Barefoot that night and so it has been nearly every time we are together since; she kicks shoes and boots off with abandon regardless of the season; she says she likes the feel of freshly mown grass beneath her naked toes; she says she gets "a rush" from standing barefoot in the snow. She simply can't bear restraint in any form. The first time we made love I explored her tanned and supple skin sliding my fingers slowly down her legs. Reaching her feet, I took one of them in my hands and delicately kissed each toe. She watched, delighted. I said, "You have triangular shaped feet, Leanne." She responded without hesitation, "I know. Triangular shaped feet are a sign of royalty." Where did you hear that? "From one of my father's friends. Mr. Matthews, I think." And so I am reminded that I am dealing with the Lolita of Linton Hill. Wise beyond her years, she tells me. And a sexual precocity to match.

I approach the building and see a Volkswagen parked sideways blocking the entrance. It has been driven or shoved up onto the concrete steps that lead to the front door of this prewar edifice. The front door itself stands open, but the only access to it now is across the front seats of the Beetle. The car's doors have been accommodatingly left open and kids are sliding in and out of the building, across the seats, squealing with laughter as they negotiate the stick shift in the middle of their path. I

have a dirty thought! Then I hear Leanne calling to me. I look up and
see her waving from the third-floor window. "Philip! Come around to
the back door. I'll let you in." I haven't seen her since her birthday last
month. I treated her to a Broadway show—"Company"—and dinner at
Sardi's. And a night in my new bed in the ritzy apartment I have recently
rented on West 86th. As always, she managed to be genuinely grateful
for my generosity while at the same time accepting any demonstration of
my adoration as her due.

I arrive at the back door of the building just as she throws it open and
flies into my arms. We kiss and she laughs. "Cool Breeze drove his car up
the steps out front, so he could unpack some equipment. He's building
a motorcycle across the hall in his living room." She giggles. Her voice
is bright and ladylike. She sounds like her mother when she laughs. And
she has inherited her mother's resilience; that's obvious. After months of
deep sadness, she has rebounded. She is happy again and I'm relieved.

Her apartment is large and very clean. She says she does all the cleaning herself because—and here she adopts the pose and metallic bright-
ness of a TV housewife extolling the latest miracle product—"I adore
Comet cleanser. It's so restorative. And I am obsessed with Clorox. You
wouldn't believe how begrimed these wooden floors were. Philip. I had
to change the water in the bucket six times. But look at them now!"

"Honey, I think you stripped the varnish off the wood."

"Oh?" She innocently scans the floor. "Well, it's better like this. Trust
me. And the best part is I now have a skill. I could be a cleaning lady if
my acting career doesn't pan out."

She leads me to her bedroom; she pulls back the thin, red and gold
paisley coverlet on her single bed. She locks the door, turns on her record
player and the Doors groan, "I'm a back door man…." Leanne walks to
me, wraps her arms around my torso and buries her head in my chest.
We stand silently holding one another and I remember why I love her.
There is a sweetness about this girl, born of her complete empathy with
and trust of everyone she meets. She reaches up and unbuttons my shirt.
She pulls her t-shirt over her head. She's not wearing a bra. She slips off
her jeans, she's not wearing underpants, and lays back on the bed. "What
was the very first book you ever read, Philip?"

I unzip my trousers. "I don't remember. Probably something about baseball. Babe Ruth...."

"Mine was *Black Beauty*. It introduced me to the disparity between the classes. The cruelty of poverty. It made me thoughtful."

I drape my slacks over a chair and climb in beside her. I take her face in my hands. "Let's not worry about the poor people today, okay?"

She sighs and smiles at me. "I'm so glad you're here."

Later we walk together, holding hands, toward the campus drama department and theater. They occupy a building about eight or nine blocks from Leanne's apartment. Leanne wants me to see the main stage and the rehearsal hall. She has been cast in a major role in the Fall production. She, as a senior, is the hot commodity this year although strangely she talks very little about acting. Her attention is always on playwrights and the text. "I think I prefer rehearsing to performing," she says.

"Maybe you *are* too intellectual to be an actress," I say and she grins. We stop for a quick lunch at a fast food place on the way.

"Philip, do you masturbate when you think of me? When we're apart?"

"Miss Hughs! What a thing to ask!" We are now standing in a long line.

She shrugs. "I'm curious. Do you?"

I lean in and lower my voice. "Of course I do. Don't you masturbate when you think of me?"

She shakes her head. "I don't masturbate at all."

I laugh. "You're lying."

"No, Philip. I wish I could, but masturbation leaves me cold. I have to have sex with a man or I don't feel anything. It's definitely a conundrum. Because you're in New York all of the time now and I'm too busy to visit you there."

"Maybe it would be in my interest to teach you to masturbate effectively by way of keeping you faithful to me?" I grin at her.

She shrugs. "I suppose there's no harm in trying." Then she flashes her radiant smile.

MY PATTERN WITH LOVERS is two years. My sexual relationships rarely sustain beyond two years. I usually find at the end of two years I have worn out my welcome or my lover has worn out hers. It isn't that I'm incapable of feeling something other than lust for a woman— I am; I have wonderful relationships with women, some going back to grade school. I keep in touch. I value friendship. But when it comes to lovers, I find my attention drifting when the sex becomes familiar. Leanne and I have been lovers for two years now. Two years and five months, if anyone is keeping track. I don't feel that we are heading for the exit anytime soon. If anything I am finding her more enticing. I attribute the anomaly in part to the fact that we don't see each other often enough for anything about her to become predictable. Frankly I find myself in strange terrain—addicted to a young woman with bedroom eyes and an incautious approach to life. The plain truth is this—I find it hard to look away from her.

We carry our trays to a table by the window. I'm taking my first bite when Leanne nonchalantly mentions that "a guy pulled a knife on me in this place one night last Winter. It was after rehearsal. We were doing *Much Ado about Nothing* and I stopped in for some cocoa to break up the walk back to the apartment. I was sitting by myself over there, and this guy sits down next to me. Big Black guy—not a student. He says, 'Hey you're a friend of Kevin, right?' And I say no and he says, 'Oh, so you're saying you don't know Kevin now? That isn't what my acquaintance has led me to believe.' And he points to this White guy—really strung-out type—standing by the door. I realized right away that I had met him once. Finn gave him money."

Leanne stares at her French fries paralyzed by memory. Just as I am about to say something, she rallies. "So I say, 'I'm sorry I don't know him' and then this Black guy puts a knife to the inside of my wrist. 'Well, you're going to get to know us now. You have something that belongs to us.' Holding my hand and keeping the point of the blade pressed against the inside of my wrist, against my vein but out of view of the other customers in the place, he begins to press. The tip of the knife slips below the surface of my skin. A tiny ruby bubble erupts at the point of the blade. It doesn't hurt after the initial prick."

"Stop, Leanne." I pull at her hand. "Look at me. Leanne, look at me."

She smiles wistfully. "I'm okay."

"Are you still seeing Dr. Fine?"

"Yes." She leans toward me. "Dr. Fine has made me fine." She takes a sip of her Coke and resumes. "So the Black guy says, 'stand up—you're going with me now-we're going to take a ride.' So I stand up and we're walking toward the door and I'm looking around for an escape and I see a table of guys—big guys—all jocks I'm sure … and I swing away from the Black guy and yell "BILLY!!! HOW DID YOU DO ON THE EXAM?" And I swoop towards these guys and sit in an empty chair at their table, and I say under my breath 'Please play along. That guy over there is trying to kidnap me.' And the three jocks look at me like they're going to laugh and I show them my wrist and the blood trickling down my arm; then one of them says, 'shit I think she means it,' and they all turn and look at the big Black guy who stands frozen at the door. He glares at me and leaves. The strung-out White guy follows. And the boys give me a lift back to my apartment. Weird, huh?"

"And you still eat here?"

"Sure. I haven't seen him since. He's just a dealer. He just confused me with someone else, I'm sure he's figured it out by now. I mean it's not like Kenneth was a reliable witness." She snorts dismissively.

"Aren't you afraid of anything, Leanne?"

"Of course, I am … I'm afraid of nuclear war."

WE ARRIVE AT THE theater. Leanne enters with the confidence of an upperclassman. She is a woman now, twenty-one years old. A serious scholar. A generous friend. Students turn and smile as she passes. She knows everyone by name and greets them warmly. I have never heard Leanne criticize a soul. Other than LBJ, Nixon and Humphrey. But Leanne would argue that they don't have souls so they don't count. Even her old boyfriend Andy, in spite of the fact that they ended their affair, is spoken of with affection and complete respect, and he reciprocates with the most enthusiastic support of her interests even though he is now in D.C., attending Georgetown grad school; they talk on the phone at least once a week. And Andy has seen each of her shows whereas I have been unable to coordinate with her schedule of performances, so I have yet to see her on stage. Okay, frankly, I dread it. I'm nervous that Leanne in the guise of anyone other than her grand and authentic self would appear embarrassingly artificial, stunted even. I can't imagine any role that could contain her. But Andy called me last Winter and urged me to make time to see her. "She's really good, Philip," he said. In some ways Leanne and Andy are closer now than ever. I'm enamored of their success at transitioning from lovers to friends.

In the rehearsal hall, Mimi and Wolf are pushing a wooden stage out of a storage closet. They will be setting up outside the Hall of Languages at the center of the campus later this afternoon and once the sun dips below the horizon, the show will be performed under a canvas canopy, with light provided by Mimi's girlfriend, Olivia, who will be lying on the ground behind the stage wielding two industrial-size flashlights to create shadow silhouettes of the magical fingers of Wolf and of Mimi's glorious body. They will be projected onto a bed sheet that is stretched between two poles that provide the screen.

The Incorrigible Victory of Truth
Shadow and Mime Extravaganza

is now in the third year of its sporadic run on the Syracuse University campus and, according to Leanne, they have amassed a genuine following of fans who at times become part of the show by standing on cue to sing a song that Wolf wrote the first year which has been incorporated into every new production since, becoming the vehicle for kids to assert their membership in this strange little cult.

Mimi emerges from the closet now with a small box of props and greets me effusively. Seeing Mimi in the flesh after a hiatus of months produces the same effect on me as coming out of a dark building into a Summer day. It takes a moment for my eyes to adjust. Mimi is a stunning young woman with startling violet eyes and a tiny curvy figure. She's a raven-haired Tinker Bell; I always half expect her to take wing. But then she laughs, a telluric laugh, robust and dirty, and she no longer seems out of reach for a man like me. Except that she isn't interested in a man like me. Or any man. Leanne watches my reaction to Mimi with the utter conviction that Mimi, despite her beauty, is no rival for my love because of that fact. But frankly I am preoccupied with the worry that Mimi is *my* rival for Leanne's love; Leanne clearly adores her and asserts that *Mimi is the sister I always wanted* so often that I have grown suspicious. I observe Mimi looking at Leanne with fierce tenderness, if tenderness can ever be fierce.

It was Mimi who found Leanne last Spring, the day of the Kent State killings, lying in the bathtub, her clothed body surrounded by water marbled by threads of crimson; her eyes shut, her lips parted. Still breathing. It was Mimi who called the ambulance, Leanne's parents, and me. And Mimi was the one who spoke to the cop who reported the suicide attempt to the Administration and returned to the apartment to ask if Leanne knew a young man named Finn. He had died in a bank bombing that morning along with the on-duty security guard. Leanne of course did know him but Mimi at that point was unaware of the relationship. She told the cop, "If Leanne had known this guy Finn, it was only in passing for if he had been a real friend of hers, I assure you Leanne would have introduced him to me. I'm her best friend. I know everything. And I have never met him!" Mimi said this with the full force of her French accent and the cop was quiet for a long moment. He seemed intimidated by the authority in her voice. Or maybe he was just momentarily stunned by Mimi's ravishing good looks. But eventually he regained his footing and pressed on. "Here's a photo of Leanne talking to Finn at a rally." Mimi brushed it aside dismissively. "Big deal. She was a popular speaker at the rallies. Hundreds of students surrounded her." The cop said, "Leanne is political though, isn't she?" Mimi grunted, "So's Nixon. What's your point?" The cop said, "I guess I'm wondering why a popular girl would suddenly want to end her life. Was she remorseful about something?" Mimi snapped, "Look at this fucking country, man! Who isn't remorseful about what a hell hole America has turned into?" Mimi insisted one last time that Leanne was responding to the death of the kids at Kent State that day, not the deaths of Finn and a bank security guard who died coincidentally on the same date. And the cop finally left.

 Truth—Shadow and Mime Extravaganza performs that afternoon before a small crowd. I count maybe thirty heads in front of me inside the tent at the center of the quad; we all sit on the grass, me in the back row with Leanne at my side. I am unexpectedly captured by the vitality and artistry of Mimi's and Wolf's performances. Wolff's shadow fingers are mesmerizing as they emerge as a sapling and slowly grow into a full oak in Summer—the thick trunk of his combined forearms, the leafy canopy of his curling fingers extending in all directions. The "tree" shivers in Winter and undulates happily in the warmth of Summer breezes. Then Mimi arrives and mimics the tree's movements; stretching her amazing body in sympathy with the tree trunk. The branches seem amused. They tremble with excitement. There is a playful interlude where Mimi and the tree trunk make out. Then Mimi appears to evolve into a murderer. Now I have to work to stay with the story whereas others in the audience seem to follow along with seamless comprehension and pleasure. I can report the following events although I am at a loss to interpret them, much less enjoy them. Mimi tries to chop the (shadow) tree down with a (shadow) axe. The tree becomes agitated and whips her with its branches; then traps her underneath its trunk, then things get sexual. Then the tree caresses Mimi's face. Leanne had advised me earlier in the day that this particular play is a celebration of Mother Earth. If you're stoned, I guess you might interpret it that way. But I wasn't stoned and—I haven't a fucking clue what the fuck it was about. And I don't care. But I congratulate them afterwards and shake Wolf's hand. His fingers don't seem human to me, they feel sticky and boneless.

After the show, I help take down the theater again and watch as young college age girls gather around Wolf, flirting openly. This nerdy puppeteer is an actual sex symbol on campus. His girlfriend Jane runs interference, getting us all to the car where we pack up the stage and props once again and head back to the theater. Yeah, this Wolf kid has a girlfriend now which means he finally moved off the couch in Leanne's and Mimi's apartment. One of the many bonuses of being a member of the Free Love generation is that apparently anyone can get laid.

In the theater lobby, I meet Gary Howland, the dean of the School of Speech and Drama. A very fit looking, fifty-year-old wearing jeans and a sports coat. He is talking to a heavyset man and a slender dark-haired woman. They look familiar. Dean Howland calls to Leanne to join them. She brings me along and Howland introduces his guests. They are the actress Claire Bloom and her actor-husband Rod Steiger in town for a film festival. Claire is an old friend of the dean and has offered to teach an impromptu acting class the next day. Leanne introduces me. Claire and Rod seem extremely pleased to meet me. They admit they have yet to read *Portnoy*, but say that they have heard "great things" and they both loved *Goodbye, Columbus*. Claire says, "Philip, I should have played the mother in the film version of that book. I understand that woman." Claire's eyes meet mine and I have to turn my attention to Steiger in order to master my furious blushing.

I am a fan of Steiger's work. Films like *On the Waterfront*, *The Pawnbroker* and, more recently, *In the Heat of the Night* are among my favorites; Steiger stands out regardless of what role he takes. He is that rare breed, a serious intellectual on the American screen. Now I turn to Claire and my knees feel weak. I tell her that I was her devotee from the first time I saw her on screen. I tell her that I saw *Limelight* five times when I was in my late teens, that even then I found her performance intelligent as well as sensual. Oh, god, I am a schoolboy again standing before her, struggling to keep my voice level, to not stammer and embarrass myself in front of the adults. She must be close to forty now, at the height of her womanly power, sexually alluring, in full command of her considerable charms—the lilt of her London accent, her quicksilver intelligence borne of her complete command of the great writing of the English-speaking stage. She still carries her body like a dancer, and I am even more entranced by her genuine kindness as evidenced in her exchanges with Leanne. I hear her say, "Our daughter Anna is ten and already she has plans to sing opera. It's a great life, performing … How old were you, Leanne, when you first felt the bug?" Leanne answers honestly that she feels that she is perhaps better suited to being a playwright. Mr. Steiger says to her, "Yes. You love the text. Then I suspect you will achieve great things, Leanne. You are living during an interesting era. If you can capture the zeitgeist…." Now Dean Howland interrupts and insists that Leanne is a gifted actress, that she will be Masha in this Fall's production of *Three Sis-*

ters, and Claire lights up. "Oh, what a wonderful part, Leanne. All three of the sisters are so interesting in that play. Do you have any sisters?"

Leanne says, "Just brothers."

Claire nods, "I have a brother, but, like you, no sister. Well, then I guess you will have to *act.*" She grins and winks at her husband, who laughs and says, "My wife is a critic of The Method. Like most British trained actors, she is suspicious of anyone who tries to *inhabit* a role. She thinks that's cheating, don't you, my darling? She believes that acting is an art that requires discipline and craft—not transmogrification."

Claire laughs easily and turns to me. "Philip, how do you and Leanne know each other?" Before Leanne can reveal that we are lovers, I say, "We're longtime friends. I used to live across the street from her family." Leanne says nothing but I can sense her annoyance. Claire notices it as well, and, in that way that women are able to communicate wordlessly, she seems to intuit the specific cause of Leanne's pique. Claire looks back at me, a sly look, almost amused, and then, taking Leanne's hand, she announces, "I think we should all have dinner together. That would be fun, huh?" She turns back to the dean. "Well. Gary, where should we all go? Someplace jolly. This will be Rod's treat."

Late that night, Leanne and I lie silently side by side on the large bed in my hotel room. She has been sulking all evening but I refuse to indulge her silly jealousy. "Claire Bloom is wonderful, isn't she?" I say.

"Yes, I think you should marry her." Leanne remains dressed while I lie naked beside her. She refuses to look at me.

"Are you going to sit in on her class tomorrow?" I ask.

"I told her I would."

"So you are playing Masha in *Three Sisters*? You didn't tell me that. I know the play quite well. Chekhov, as you know, is one of my favorite writers. I intend to come opening night."

Leanne shrugs. "I'll believe it when I see it."

"Fair enough."

I tuck closer to Leanne's side. I press my thigh against her knee. She doesn't react; she continues to steadfastly stare at the ceiling. I say, "Masha is the sister who takes a lover outside her marriage."

Leanne looks at me now and says in a level tone, "I don't think it will be so hard for me to imagine that I could lose interest in a man I once loved passionately."

Suddenly I extend my arms out in front of me and begin to wiggle and stretch my fingers—like the branches of a tree. I make the sound of wind blowing and sway my torso awkwardly, rolling left and right. I see Leanne's mouth twitch in amusement. "You make a lousy tree, Philip. You're more of an elephant trunk."

I roll over on top of her and my fingers still extended and twitching, graze her face and move down her throat to the buttons on her shirt, to the waistband of her skirt. My fingers move more rapidly now, undressing her. She doesn't help but makes no attempt to stop me. I make the wind blow harder. I add bird calls, a couple of owls, even a rooster. I'm pulling out the stops now. I add a dog bark. I begin to tickle her. Leanne squeals and screams "Stop it, Philip!!" I suddenly wrap my arms around her and look in her eyes. "I'm crazy about you," I say. "I can't live without you. I love you, Leanne. Marry me."

Part Three — 1971-1973

petit à petit l'oiseau fait son nid

Chapter 21

"Philip, I've decided that if I ever write a memoir about working at the Warner Elkins Advertising agency, I will call it *My Life as a Man*."

I waited for Philip to respond, but he was deeply involved in the examination of a milkweed plant, slowly turning over the macerated leaves, looking for the stripy caterpillars that would metamorphose into monarch butterflies later in the Summer. I was spending the weekend with him at the eighteenth-century house in Warren, Connecticut that he had purchased the year before. I visited every weekend that Summer of 1973, leaving our New York City apartment early on Friday afternoons and driving alone the two hours it took to arrive in bucolic Litchfield County at the foothills of the Berkshire Mountains. Regardless of the hour of my arrival, Philip maintained the discipline of a medieval monastic scribe, writing daily, six days a week, from 8:30 in the morning until five in the afternoon or later, soldiering on—word by word, sentence by sentence—creating books "by the pound," as he put it.

He had produced three novels in the past four years since *Portnoy's Complaint* rocked the literary world. One was a political satire starring none other than that master of deceit—Tricky Dick Nixon. The next book, also a satire, followed a homeless professional baseball team during World War Two and featured a character named Aunt Jemima as the wealthy owner of the Negro League. The third book was the flabbergasting tale of a college professor who inexplicably turns into a female breast. I considered the possibility that I was partial inspiration for the latter because I had shared with Philip the story of my sudden development of large breasts in ninth grade. But then Philip and I traveled to Czechoslovakia together two years ago—his graduation gift to me was a trip to Paris and there was a last-minute side trip to Prague—and there I came face to face (well, face to spirit) with Philip's man-crush, the writer Franz Kafka. And I became convinced that *The Breast* was actually homage to the great Czech absurdist. But Philip flatly denied both premises, saying instead that the book was simply his response to his literary reputation, in the wake of *Portnoy*, as a sexual freak or as he put it "a crazed penis." Nevertheless, he said the simple-hearted satisfactions of the life he now led in rural Connecticut supported the excesses in his writing, allowing him to live Flaubert's dictum to the letter: *Be orderly and regular in your life like a bourgeois, so that you may be wild and original in your work.* No doubt Flaubert would be incredulous to discover how wild this conventional man would allow himself to be. At least on paper.

I searched Philip's face as he exited his writing workshop, a charming cottage separated from the main house by a large garden. I had put down my book and scanned his face for signs of his mood. Exultant or depressed? Everything depended on how the writing had gone that day. He laughed warmly when he saw me. Relieved, I quickly crossed the yard and wrapped my arms around his torso. He kissed me repeatedly. "I made good time," I said. Not that it mattered. That just meant more hours for me to fill waiting, waiting for him to emerge. "You've become quite the motorist, Mrs. Roth," he said. I took his hand and we set off on our walk.

Philip exercised every afternoon—usually it took the form of a bracing stroll around his forty-acre property. Sometimes we would swim in a nearby lake, but today we traveled a well-worn path along dusty, old roads that crisscrossed a large expanse of meadow, framing perfect separate vistas like paintings in an open-air museum. Tall spears of grass danced across the horizon, providing a backdrop for the profusion of wildflowers that graced the landscape. In Spring, petals were gossamer, seeming to float above their slender stems like delicate bubbles in the breeze, iridescent, in shades of lavender and palest pink. Now in mid-July, the sturdier plants were taking over, their colors rich and lusty. Shaggy bouquets of cobalt blue flax, tall purple bottlebrush, and my favorite, flame colored ruffles on thick stalks—I could never remember the name of that one—all held their own against the strong wind and rain of the Connecticut Summer mistrals. But no sign of storms today, not even a breeze. The heat that afternoon felt like a warm hand on my back, the air was spongy, so humid I imagined that if I clapped my hands together, I would release a stream of dew.

I repeated my statement. "My Life as a Man. That will be the name of my memoir about working in the ad agency." Again I waited for Philip's response. Finally, he stopped walking and gently fingered a dainty parasol of Queen Anne's lace that curtsied along an old stone wall.

"It's a great title," he said, "However, other than being provocative, I don't see its relevance to you."

"None of the women like me at Warner Elkins Advertising, Philip. I've told you this before. I haven't made a single girlfriend there in the past six months. My only friends are men. So much for feminism in 1973. I feel the sisterhood is shunning me, punishing me for being the only female copywriter in the department."

"Because your college roommate's father gave you the job?"

"I suppose that's part of it."

"I'd say that's most of it."

"Well, someone had to be first! Why not me?"

Eventually we came to the intersection of the dirt road with a newly paved state highway. Cars rushed by and at that point, Philip and I turned around and headed back, away from the turmoil of the twentieth century, back to the eighteenth-century house where he now lived as a country gentleman. Back to the serenity of quiet meals and early bedtimes. Back to our intense lovemaking and relaxed Sunday mornings spent in bed, talking. We never ran out of topics. Our affaire de coeur had lasted nine years now and we had recently embarked on a new journey together. That of husband and wife. We were making up the rules as we went along, to see if we could define the terms of our marriage outside the constraints of convention. It wasn't easy.

Philip said, "Maybe you should look for a different job." Then he casually added, "Or maybe it's time to come live with me."

"And how will I spend my days? Weaving macramé plant hangers to sell at the county fair?"

"You could write."

"I tend to be too overwhelmed by the current historical moment to write about it. I'll write when I'm old. Emotional things remembered in tranquility. At this point in my life I'm more useful to a novel as a character than as a writer."

Philip watched me with amusement. He looked as though he was about to speak and then didn't. We stood still facing each other; he pulled me close and rubbed the small of my back. We kissed and I put my arms around his neck, "Oh, Philip, when I'm with you I think I love you to excess."

Philip kissed me again and said, "And what about when you're not with me?"

I could ask the same of him. I knew that his prodigious sexual appetite was being fed by at least two women in the area, one married to a writer of prominence but lesser talent than Philip. She was what Mimi and I always called a star-fucker, a woman who gained status by screwing powerful men. I was given this report by the woman's rival, another local housewife who hosted noisy dinner parties on weekends so that I could attend. She invariably found a private moment during those evenings to sidle up to me and funnel gossip directly into my ear, always in a hoarse whisper, usually over after-dinner drinks. She avowed that the star fucker visited Philip during his lunch break "every Wednesday at one." I came close to saying *and which day have you reserved for yourself, Madam?* But I simply grinned at her. I already knew of Philip's trysts and accepted them. It was part of our arrangement.

Philip asked, "So are you still sleeping with "Mr." Kenyon?"

I shook my head. "No. I told you. We're done."

MR. KENDALL AND I had ended our relationship months before what I would forever-after call the Ivory Snow Detergent Porn Scandal of 1973. I had been working at the Warner Elkins Agency less than six months at that point when Marilyn Chambers, a young model whose pretty face was gracing the cover of millions of boxes of Ivory Snow Detergent as the All-American Young Mother—hand-selected by none other than Robert Kenyon, the connoisseur of All-American females—made a pornographic film. And she became famous for it. This wasn't just nudity. This was hard core explicit sex. It might have gone unnoticed by the housewives of America, but for the fact that the triple-X-rated movie called *Behind the Green Door* moved out of the subterranean world of peep shows and into the prestigious Cannes Film Festival that Spring. It was the first time anything so overtly pornographic had been recognized by the mainstream movie industry. I guess it was a sign of the times. We were becoming shock-proof as a nation. A shameless Marilyn Chambers and cast attended the premiere in the south of France. They did interviews; they smiled for photos. Of course, a preliminary scan of Marilyn's resume revealed her former life as a model and it didn't take but half a day to link the exhibitionist to the adoring young mother on the Ivory Snow box. Ivory Snow? 99 and 44/100ths percent pure? Late night comics had a field day. The client had a meltdown. And when an interview with Miss Chambers appeared in the *New York Times* that morning early in May of 1973, well, that was the final straw.

Marilyn Chambers, whose smiling face adorns millions of boxes of the "safest possible soap for diapers and baby clothes"—Ivory Snow—is winning new fans as the star of a pornographic film. The 21-year-old actress-model from Connecticut, who deplores simulated sex on the screen as "dishonest," is appearing in the hard-core sex film Behind the Green Door *in the role of a young woman abducted and ravaged at a secret sex club. As for her old role as the Ivory Snow girl snuggling a baby, she said her latest role should help "sell a lot more soap."*

I COULD HEAR MR. KENYON'S howls all the way down the long hallway and around the corner to the break room where I was pouring myself a cup of coffee. "THAT CUNT!" I ran to his office. His secretary sat red faced at her desk outside his door.

I knocked. "Mr. Kenyon, it's me—Leanne. Let me in."

"FUCK!!!"

"Mr. Kenyon, please. Open the door. You can be heard the entire length of the floor. There are people from Heinz Ketchup meeting with...."

He opened the door. "THAT FUCKING CUNT! DID YOU READ THIS?"

"Shhhh … Robert!" I closed the door.

He held up the Times. "The top brass at Proctor and Gamble have called me three times in the last hour. They want to sue her, sue the agency, and sue me personally for choosing her!" He looked at the paper again. "THAT CUNT!"

"Stop it, Robert! That word is an insult to—"

"I'm not in the mood for your precious Love Child shit right now, Leanne."

Within days, boxes had been pulled from grocery store shelves across the country. Auditions were set up for a new Ivory Snow girl. And it was made very clear to the models who showed up that the winner would have to sign all sorts of iron clad agreements, promising to refrain from—among other things—fornication with two men and a woman all at the same time. On film.

Of course, a new baby was needed as well. The last baby was now two years old. The audition for a new All American Ivory Snow Cherub was held on the sixth floor of Warner Elkins—the whole sixth floor. Eight-month-old babies were brought in by mothers and agents and placed on the floor to see how they would behave around strangers. We—the secretarial staff and copywriters—were the strangers. And we were told to gently interact with the babies for the next two hours. Some of the children cried at some point for their mothers; those babies were disqualified and immediately removed from the audition. The others, the ones remaining in contention, had the run of the place. Some of the secretaries got on their knees and sang or played patty cake. One of the men was on the floor playing peek-a-boo. I sat inside an office doorway and jiggled my keys to see which baby would be curious and approach me. Soon enough, one slapped her way merrily towards me, crawled to my side and sat up, one plump little leg curled under her. The other leg extended; the fat little toes pink and round like rosy peas. And suddenly without warning, without any preparation, I found myself overwhelmed by a hormonal tsunami. I fell in love as I had never fallen in love before. For the next two hours I pretended this baby was mine. Everything around me receded. I forgot where I was. I saw only her. I pulled her onto my lap and hugged her and kissed her plump cheeks. She squealed with delight. I squealed with delight. I let her tug on my shirt and pull my hair. She spit up on me. "Whoops," I said. Whoops!" My baby studied my mouth and made an attempt to approximate that sound. Oh, my baby was so intelligent. I repeated it again softly, "Whoops." And then my baby looked in my eyes and cooed. I cooed back at her. She watched me keenly as though she now understood that we were communicating. I fell so madly in love with my baby that when the audition ended and the mothers returned to take the babies away, my mind searched desperately for a way not to give her back. Afterwards, after I watched my baby leave on the shoulder of a stranger, I went into a stall in the ladies' room and sobbed. "I want a baby," I whispered over and over to myself, shuddering with the intensity and immediacy of my sudden desire.

PHILIP AND I FINISHED our walk and returned to the house. It was now six o'clock but the Summer sun was still high in the western sky. "How long are you staying this time?" he said.

"I'll go back after dinner on Sunday night as usual." Philip nodded solemnly and I changed the subject. "You're still receiving mail at the apartment. I brought it with me. It's on the breakfront."

I entered the kitchen and unwrapped a small pork loin and seasoned it with fresh thyme and rosemary that I had just pulled from our garden. I placed the roast in the oven and set a timer on the counter. I then stood at the sink and sorted through a bag of freshly picked green beans that I had purchased at a farm stand that morning on my drive into Warren. Philip entered the kitchen with a letter in his hand. He read silently, then said, "We're invited to a birthday party for Saul Bellows. Next week. July 10. It's going to be in the city. I'll come in and spend a few days at the apartment with you. Think you can get some time off?"

"Sure."

Philip opened a bottle of wine and carried a glass to me. There was a long silence. I stared out the window. Philip came up behind me. A drink in one hand, he slipped the other under my waist band and began to massage my bottom. I sighed contentedly. "What are you thinking about?" he asked and nuzzled my neck.

"I'm thinking about Jagr Ziska."

"Why?" Philip pulled away.

"No … I'm over him. God, I'm so over him."

"I would hope so."

"I'm thinking of the choices Jagr made when he returned to Czechoslovakia. I guess I'm trying to imagine the circumstances. He was a poet-philosopher when I knew him back in school. Very romantic. Now he's an enforcer for the Soviets in Prague."

Philip looked at me sympathetically. "How did you meet Jagr? You never said."

"He was Myra's crush that Summer Mimi and I were selling magazines. Myra used to take us to Jagr's apartment after work. We'd get stoned and talk."

"So you stole a friend's boyfriend?" Philip raised an eyebrow in mock disdain.

"No, I didn't. He told me the first night we were together that he wasn't interested in Myra. I made sure before I … I don't think Myra really liked me even before that happened."

"You do have problems with women, don't you?" Philip was enjoying my defensiveness.

"I'm trying to get along with the women at the Warner Elkins Advertising Agency, Philip! I would love to be invited to one of the secretarial pool's birthday parties. You think I like being shunned?"

Philip leaned on the counter and grinned at me. "I think as long as there is a man around, you will never be lonely."

"Oh, stop it, Philip."

Philip laughed out loud now. "Okay. So Jagr was a poet. I didn't know that."

"Well, he wasn't a good poet. Let's just say he was *poetical*. He was so idealistic at one point."

"Well, you don't practice idealism unless you believe you can effect change. Obviously he lost hope at some point. Or he's leading a double life. Maybe it was a question of survival, Leanne. He had people depending on him. Didn't you say he had kids?"

"Yes. Two. Maybe more by now. Do you think I'll ever hear from him again? I mean he did this one good thing. But he hasn't made any attempt to contact me again."

Philip shook his head. "People are contradictory, Leanne. You know that. I have friends who are public atheists, who loudly disdain religion, and yet earnestly embrace the role of godparents to the children of close friends who are Catholic. Take them to Church and catechism classes … It isn't hypocrisy; they remain upfront about the fact that they don't believe in god."

"Boy, I think that says more about those Catholic parents."

"People are complex. And the smarter they are, the more obtuse their doctrines become. Because belief systems aren't necessarily rational. All sorts of things weigh in—not the least of which is love."

"Well, I'm no longer an ideologue. I'm not sure what I believe anymore."

Philip left the kitchen now and I followed him into the living room. He put a record on the hi-fi and I joined him on the couch. He draped an arm over my shoulders and said, "For what it's worth, I'm not an ideologue either. I don't think you can be an ideologue if you want to write fiction. Otherwise you would always write characters who simply validate your point of view."

We sat quietly and listened to the music. I snuggled against him. Finally I spoke, "Am I complex?"

"Oh, yes." He kissed me.

"Am I difficult to understand?"

"Absolutely."

"Does that turn you on?"

"It's why I married you." We kissed. "You are my muse, Leanne. You engage with the world. Then I write about it."

"I notice that you always fall for a maiden in distress, Philip."

"Are you a maiden in distress?" he laughed indulgently.

"I have been."

He nodded. "That's true." He sipped his wine.

"It's the nice Jewish boy in you. You always want to save the girl. I see the women who catch your eye. It isn't their bodies although you may think that sex is the driving force for you. No, your good heart is a divining rod. It seeks out the troubled ones. Of course, if you can't fix them, you end up resenting them. Even hating them. Like your first wife." Philip started to protest. I talked over him. "Nevertheless. NEVER THE LESS. You recognize vulnerability and your immediate impulse is to protect. It's a good thing, Philip. A very good thing. It's why I love you so much."

Philip's eyes flooded. "Thank you, Darling. You have a good heart, too."

"You will be a dear and wonderful father to our children, Philip."

He was silent. I knew he struggled with the thought of being a parent but I had made it clear that I wanted children. That was a condition of our marriage. We were still working out the timing. My mind was drifting now. I closed my eyes. After a moment, Philip nudged me, "You still awake?"

I nodded but kept my eyes closed. "Now I'm remembering our trip to Prague."

Chapter 22

The trip to Prague was the idea of Jason Epstein, Philip's editor at Random House. In September of 1971, with our planned trip to Paris just one month away—Philip, Jason, Jason's wife Barbara, and I met for dinner in New York with Ivan Laska, a Czech writer, who had recently escaped his communist homeland. Early in 1970, Philip had put together a network of his writer friends and each of them had adopted a dissident writer still living in Prague, to whom they sent envelopes of money—small amounts to avoid detection by the authorities, but frequent enough to keep these men and their families alive. Ivan wept when he met Philip that evening in New York. "You are an icon in my community, Mr. Roth," he stammered as he took his seat at our table. And Philip took his hands and shed tears himself.

Czechoslovakia was one of the eight satellite countries of the Soviet Union. Each of the satellites had their own government, but they were expected to mirror the policies of the Kremlin. In the Spring of 1968, the leader in Czechoslovakia, a man named Alexander Dubček, began adopting reforms to "liberalize communism." Most dramatic of the changes was an increased freedom of speech that tolerated dissent. The Soviet Union moved swiftly to crush the Prague Spring, as it was called, lest the other satellite countries follow the Czech example. Mr. Dubček was removed from office and replaced by a hardliner. Following the ferocious violence in the streets of Prague that August, artists who resisted joining the Communist Party were isolated and punished. Writers were especially targeted. They could no longer have their writing published. Their existing books were banned outright, even burned in public displays of cultural cleansing. They could not teach. They could not travel or drive. And their children could not attend the academic high schools.

Every artist was given a choice—join the Party and write/paint/sing/act/dance per the Party line or starve. The country's best minds and talents were forced into demeaning jobs that paid poorly. Many lost their homes and were shoved into shabby apartments in what would be called slums in the United States. Even in the grip of their rage and despair, some still managed to resist. Writers kept writing and painters kept painting in their small dark rooms. Dancers danced in the alleys. Actors recited Shakespeare on the fire escapes. All in defiance of the not-so-secret police.

Philip had spent the past year familiarizing himself with the work of these dissident writers still living in Prague. He located translated pieces—novels, stories and plays—still in circulation in Paris and London and championed the best of them with his own publisher in New York. That evening Ivan handed Philip a story he had written, one that he had managed to smuggle out of Prague during his escape to the West. Philip promised to read it and share it with his friends at *The New Yorker*. I immediately thought of Jagr's desire to get his father's last play out of Prague before the authorities found it and had it destroyed. I asked Ivan how he had managed it. He replied, "In my suitcase. Sometimes you are lucky."

Several times during the evening, Ivan stopped eating, laid down his fork and said, "I am in America! Somebody pinch me!" And then he would cry again.

"Oh, please don't glorify America, Mr. Laska," I said. "American students were mowed down by National Guard soldiers for protesting the Vietnam War just two years ago right here in America. Young people were savagely beaten when they demanded a voice at the Democratic Convention. That was August of 1968, the same month your country was invaded by the Russians. And now the U.S. government is moving against Philip's books."

It was true. Philip's writing had always been popular in Czechoslovakia. His first two books—*Goodbye Columbus* and *Letting Go*—had been translated, published, and sold in book stores throughout that country in the mid—sixties, soon after their debut in the United States. *Portnoy's Complaint* had been likewise readied for the Czech literary market in 1969 immediately following its debut in the West. But its publication had been stalled by the Soviet invasion. And now Odeon Publishing in Prague was telling Philip that the book would not be published in Czechoslovakia at all; that it was deemed by the authorities to be "too kinky" for general release. But more alarming was the news that the American authorities in Washington, D.C. agreed with the Czech Government's assessment of the book and not only did they not push back, they took this opportunity to remove Philip's books from the American Library in the U.S. Embassy in Prague. Philip's books were actually being banned by our government in an American tax-payer financed facility. Philip was outraged. "Where does this lead?" he demanded to know.

Jason suggested that a goodwill trip to Prague might ameliorate the situation with the local authorities and the Embassy. And since we were already planning to be in Paris in October—my graduation gift from Philip—perhaps we could add a slight detour en route and spend several days in Prague. Philip's New York publisher would make arrangements for us to meet with the Czech publisher who would, in turn, set up interviews with the appropriate government authorities. And Philip could drop by the U.S. Embassy and have an informal chat with our ambassador.

I suggested that Jagr Ziska also be contacted. I told Jason and Ivan that he was a friend from my school days. Philip watched me warily, remembering that Jagr and I had been lovers. But it was Jagr who introduced me to the plight of Czech writers in that country. And I, in turn, had relayed the crisis to Philip. I said, "Jagr is now in an official position with the Committee for Decency and Standards in Prague. He might have some influence with his fellow authorities. I can't imagine that he wouldn't sympathize with Philip's situation. He loves literature. His own father is a playwright and has been imprisoned as part of the crackdown." Ivan added that he had known Jagr's father years before. "He was good writer. Very funny. Too funny. They made an example of him. I'm afraid I don't know the son."

JAGR WAS STILL AT Princeton and I was a sophomore at Syracuse that August of 1968 when Prague was invaded. He and I talked nightly on the phone, as new lovers do. Jagr was increasingly beside himself with fear for his family. Especially his father whom he adored. The Soviet tanks had rolled onto the cobblestone streets of Wenceslas Square at the heart of the capitol city and aimed their guns at innocent men and women, many of them Jagr's neighbors. The Soviets quickly overwhelmed the citizen brigades who took to the streets with bottles and kitchen knives and any organized political resistance was soon reduced to random acts of martyrdom.

On January 16, 1969, barely six months after the invasion, a twenty-year-old university student positioned himself in front of the famous King Wenceslas statue at the center of the square and set himself on fire. A few days later he died of his horrific burns. His name was Jan Palach. On the day of Palach's funeral, thousands of students gathered in Wenceslas Square and then defiantly marched to Olšany Cemetery carrying Czech flags and photos of the young man. Many held cardboard signs that read *Věrni Zůstaneme. We will remain faithful.* In the following months two more young Czechs committed suicide by self-immolation and the mounds of flowers around the base of Good King Wenceslas spread across the Plaza. The authorities routinely cleared the area, but still the flowers appeared daily, delivered now by older housewives who quietly wept as they placed them at the King's feet.

Jagr had followed this news with rising hysteria. Then just before Thanksgiving he had driven to Syracuse. We spent a highly charged night together and when he left I was worried that he intended to return to Prague to martyr himself as an act of Resistance. His father had been imprisoned while he waited for his trial on seditious slander. He had refused to bow, insisting that it was a basic human right to think and speak one's truth. So in May of

1969, Jagr returned to Prague. I had heard from him only once since then. I learned that he had capitulated and joined the Communist Party. Still, I didn't believe that the Jagr I loved could so easily abandon his principles. Philip said that in a censorship culture, everybody leads a double life of lies and deception. It's why literature is so necessary. "Literature is truth's only voice when tyrants take over," he said.

NOW AT OUR TABLE, the waitress cleared the dishes and brought coffee. Ivan lit a cigarette off the end of the one in his mouth. "Soviet communism is an unpopular ideology that can only be enforced by guns and tanks. And lies. Get this—the soldiers who attacked us? They were told that they were being sent on a mission to save the Czech people and that they would be welcomed by the citizens. We've been through this before. It can take decades, a century even, but Czechoslovakia will always emerge intact. Every Czech understands this. It's why we hold on."

Ivan then described what he called "the last token of the Resistance, at least for the time being"—Jan Palach's simple grave in Olšany Cemetery. "The Communists removed the headstone but everyone knows where it is. It is said even now, two years later, that the grave is visited seven times every twenty minutes. Two hundred pots are needed to hold the daily offerings of flowers. And the site of Jan's sacrifice—the statue of the King in Wenceslas Square—it is now fenced off. But they can't stop people from remembering. You see. That is the ultimate weapon we retain. Memory is survival. Memory is resistance."

Philip and I agreed to adjust our trip to Paris. We would go first to Prague. I was going to see Jagr Ziska again.

Saturday, October 9, 1971

Dear Diary,

Our flight arrived in Prague this morning. It circled the airport twice before landing. There were other planes arriving as well so we had to wait our turn. Tourism seems to be flourishing after two years of very few visitors. Philip and I find that surprising, but then we remember what Ivan said, "Those who don't resist the communists seem to be better off than they were before."

Philip held my hand as we de-boarded and didn't let go as we passed through two sets of passport inspections. Then our luggage was opened and the contents carefully examined. I was so nervous that I held my breath for what seemed like twenty minutes. Philip and I are wearing gold bands on our left ring fingers. We aren't married yet, but Philip is concerned that his reputation as a libertine will generate excessive attention. We have been told that the country is under 'morals patrol.' So we are sharing our hotel room as Mr. and Mrs. Roth for the duration of our stay. We were met at the airport by a chauffeur-driven state vehicle provided by the government Art Council. The driver, a weary-looking, older man, was holding up a sign—PHILIP ROTH and Party. "I guess I'm the party," I whispered to Philip. He whispered back, "Remember, Leanne. Caution is the name of the game. These people don't have a sense of humor."

Last year at this time, there had been rumors of another Soviet invasion to mark the second anniversary of their brutal reconquest of this country. But it was just a scare. The famous statue of King Wenceslas now oversees a plaza alive with food vendors and well-fed families. The air is redolent with the smell of savory sausages and sauerkraut. The blood stains in the cobblestones have all but faded completely. It would seem that the Czechoslovakian people have turned away from politics altogether now to concentrate on weekend leisure. But there are still indications that the Resistance is alive. As we approached our hotel, I leaned across the front seat and spoke to the driver. "So many roses and chrysanthemums around the statue of King Wenceslas. Is it a holiday today?" "No. He is patron saint of the Czech people. Very important to our history. Beloved by every citizen." "Why is he fenced off?" "To keep the people from vandalizing him."

I expected Philip to be in a rage, the entire time we were in the city, in anticipation of his meeting with the Odeon editorial board, but instead he was like a schoolboy on a pilgrimage to visit the shrine to his idol. That first afternoon, after dropping off our baggage at the hotel, Philip and I walked to the house where Franz Kafka, the ground-breaking twentieth-century surrealist had lived with his parents, writing tales of spiritual disorientation and despair until he was forty. He then married Dora, a woman half his age who devoted herself to him, and they moved to Germany, escaping—for the first time in his life—his overbearing and abusive father, and the passive mother who never understood him or his extraordinary writing. He had resisted marriage throughout his twenties and thirties despite multiple engagements because, as he wrote in the famous forty-seven-page letter to his father, "Marriage is your domain."

Being with Philip since I was fourteen had had a profound effect on my reading tastes over the years. I often read to please him. As a consequence I had gone through a lengthy Kafka period. I read *Metamorphosis* and *The Trial* more than once. I read them as commentary on the political environment of that time because that's how I read everything when I was in high school and college. Kafka was Jewish and Eastern European. Although he died before the Nazis could eliminate him, I figured he had suffered antisemitism and that had made him write an absurd and fantastical story about turning into a bug. But as I came to know more about Kafka's life, it was easy to now assume that his stories were a response to his oedipal struggle with his parents. Philip would have burst into flames if I even suggested that *Portnoy's Complaint* contained a whiff of autobiography but I was genuinely curious—how can a writer separate his writing from his own experience? I retooled my question. "Philip, do you think a happy personal life is an obstacle to becoming a great writer? Must a writer always be so tortured?"

"Tolstoy seemed fairly content, up to a point. Of course, like many writers, his relationship with women had its complications."

"Complications? Tolstoy was notoriously unfaithful to his wife and mistresses."

"Well, to be fair, he said he wanted 'to do them good but they wouldn't hold still for that.'" Philip laughed.

"I swear you are all misogynists," I said, and he laughed again. I faced him. "Are you happy, Philip?"

"I'm happy with you if that's what you mean."

We moved to another room in the house. More sad photos of Kafka. I said, "Maybe I will rewrite the great cannon of Western literature and give every tortured character a happy ending so they can finally rest in peace."

"Actually that might be funny."

"Like I'll make Anna Karenina my best friend in high school. I'll make her the class valedictorian. And a cheerleader. An All-American girl."

"There has to be some conflict, Leanne. Readers expect conflict."

"Okay. She gets hooked on diet pills."

Now we were silent. Philip took my hand and said quietly, "Sometimes I marvel at how strong you are."

The next morning, after ten hours of jetlag sleep—the kind that makes you feel like you blacked out—I woke up ravenous. I had been too tired the night before to eat dinner. Philip and I had a wonderful breakfast in the hotel dining room. "Oh, this is so good," I said, biting down into a piece of chewy white bread on which I had piled ham and slices of hard cheese. "I am becoming so carnivorous, Philip. Have you noticed? I never cared about meat before. I could sustain on salads alone. But now I want beef and pork. Ham for breakfast every day. Have you noticed a difference in me during our love making? Am I more vigorous?"

"Leanne, there are probably microphones under the tablecloth."

"You know sex is the only freedom these people can still enjoy without government interference, Philip. I imagine it gets quite wild after dark in the bedrooms across this city." Philip laughed and I leaned towards him and whispered, "Velcome to Prague, Darlink! Velcome to the orgy!"

A waiter came to the table now and refilled our coffee cups. He grinned at me and then retreated to the kitchen. Philip arched his brows. "You see. He heard every word."

I shrugged. "I gave the waiter something to smile about. So what? I'm sure he appreciates that. These people could probably use a laugh."

After breakfast, two guides provided by our Embassy met us in the lobby. One was taking Philip on a tour of a dense corner of the city which was the Jewish community prior to it being razed by the Nazis. Hitler had preserved the synagogues with the intention of turning them into museums to commemorate his destruction of Jewry. One of them, the Pincus Synagogue, now stood to honor the memory of the Czech Jews who were sent to the concentration camp in Terezín, about thirty miles north of Prague. Philip spent hours quietly taking in the modest shrine where a collection of children's toys, woman's toiletries, men's overshoes, books and photographs bore witness to ordinary lives. An elegy and a warning. This can and will happen again and it might just as easily be you next time. After all, even in America, during the Second World War, Japanese Americans, law-abiding citizens of the United States, were rounded up by the government, stripped of their property and shoved into detention camps surrounded by barbed wire. One hundred and twenty thousand American citizens of Japanese descent were prisoners of the American government from 1942 until 1946. I was born three years later.

I know this was true because Mr. Yamamoto who sold tomatoes, strawberries, and melons at a fruit and vegetable stand in Pennswalk had been interred during the war and his family lost their construction business. When I was in seventh grade, our civics teacher invited him to come to our class and tell about that experience. But a group of "concerned parents" took umbrage. They said it would sully our young minds, give us the wrong impression of how great America is. So he was uninvited. But Mother told me, TJ, and John the story anyway.

MY EMBASSY GUIDE HAD arranged an official meeting with Jagr Ziska. Jagr had offered to give me a tour of the Royal Garden which was part of the Prague castle, the imposing ancient site of royalty that faced the river. It now housed the administrative offices of the Czech government and the Czech Communist Party. Jagr was waiting for me at the public entrance to the garden. He stood at attention as our eyes met. Seeing him so suddenly after two and a half years made my heart lurch. He seemed much older now. His compact body was softer, doughier. Twenty-eight years old and he already had a middle age bulge circling his once taut abdomen. It strained the buttons on his suit jacket. He had the dorky haircut of all the other young communist bureaucrats I'd seen since our arrival. Closely trimmed at the sides, longish sideburns and poorly shaped flop of hair at the crown of his head. The only feature unchanged from the last time we were together—his eyes. Still cool grey, still seductive with a fathomless intensity. What was he feeling now as he looked at me? Sadness? Regret? Lust? Resentment? I approached him and leaned in to kiss his cheek, but he took my hands and held them, keeping me firmly in place about six inches from him. I flushed, embarrassed by his rejection. "I am married, Leanne," he said, gently. "A friend from my days in primary school. We reunited when I returned. We have a son and another child on the way."

I struggled with a momentary attack of jealousy but finally managed to smile and say, "I'm happy for you, Jagr."

He relaxed. We began to walk. My guide from the Embassy dropped back about thirty feet but continued to follow us. A man in a tan trench coat emerged from behind a fountain and conspicuously paced us from a distance on the right as well. "Who is that man, Jagr?"

"He is assigned to spy on me."

"I thought you were one of them."

"I am." He laughed. "That guy is being followed too. We are all in the business of surveillance now."

"Do you hear from your father?"

"No."

"I'm so sorry."

He shrugged. "He made his choices. He knew the consequences. Does that make him brave or stupid? What do you think?"

"I think he's brave."

"Being brave and dead or in prison means you are no longer in the game. You're useless."

"Unless you're a martyr. Martyrs inspire others after they are gone."

"Inspire them to what? To leave flowers?" Jagr shook his head. "You never change, Leanne. Always the cockeyed optimist. You Americans feel so entitled to happiness that you even codified it in your national doctrine."

"We embrace the *pursuit* of happiness, Jagr. Nothing is guaranteed. We understand that. Happiness for us is aspirational."

He stopped walking and looked at me. "So are you happy, dear Leanne?"

"Some days."

"You are married now to Roth?"

"Yes. And before you ask, I will answer. Yes, Jagr, I love him."

He studied my face a bit longer. "So what brings you to Prague? You could never be a spy. I know that. You'd be lousy at subterfuge. You are far too memorable."

I slipped my left hand into his right now, a gesture of affection that he didn't resist. I said, "Thank you, Jagr, for seeing me. I've missed you. It would break my heart if our friendship was over."

He lifted my hand to his lips and gave it a gallant kiss. "Okay, Leanne. We are friends forever." We resumed our walk.

I explained our visit. "Philip is upset. His new book is not allowed to be published here in Prague."

"Yes, I understand it is over the top. Quite vulgar."

"It's for adults, Jagr. My god. And it's satiric and funny."

"Language matters, Leanne. Do you have children?"

"No. Not yet."

"Well, when you do, you will be sensitive to the coarseness of contemporary culture. You will see the impact of casual vulgarity. It leads to valueless lives. And promiscuity."

I stopped walking. "Do you regret now that we...."

"Yes, I do. Not because I didn't love you. I did. But to waste sperm is a sin, Leanne. I should have married you."

I was incredulous. "You are Catholic now?"

"I am."

"Wow. You just said you thought martyrdom was pointless."

He frowned. "It depends on the martyr."

We walked for the better part of the next hour. He told me the detailed histories of certain of the roses in this grand garden. *This bed was established by Queen Whatshername*—that sort of travelogue stuff. I barely listened. Apart from the fact that he didn't offer to help Philip, he now seemed condescending. At one point, he said, "Do you still tell your little dirty joke at parties, Leanne?"

"What are you talking about?"

"The one with the drunk. Tickle your ass with a feather?"

I thought of the night Andy had taught me the joke to break the ice at parties. He wanted me to accompany him to Japan. Instead I interned at the Bucks County Playhouse.

I laughed now and said to Jagr. "Oh, that one! Well, I haven't told it in quite a while."

"But you remember it?"

"Yes. Apparently, you do too. What's your point?"

He shrugged and we walked on. Finally, we were back at the entrance to the garden where we had first met. He said, "I hope you have enjoyed the tour. It has been a pleasure to see you again, Leanne. Please give my regards to your husband."

"I will. I wish you—you and your family—all the best, Jagr." All so formal again. Back where we started. I felt like I should curtsy.

Jagr snapped his fingers. "Oh, I almost forgot—I will see you and Philip tonight. My office has arranged tickets for a play this evening. You will be my guests. In fact, I believe we are seated together. So I guess that means that we don't have to say goodbye just yet."

IT WAS OPENING NIGHT of the new season at the National Theatre, a hulking brown building that faced the murky water of the Vltava River. We had been advised by Ivan back in New York that censorship was applied so rigorously now even to the plays of Chekhov and Shakespeare that producers no longer risked offending the authorities by including them in the theater repertoire. Instead new plays were created by aspiring communist bureaucrats. Their offerings were little more than turgid Russian propaganda. But even they were subjected to rigorous censorship. The standard practice was that there were always two premieres before the official opening. The first was a private performance in front of the authorities who scrutinized the play and the performance of it for any potential double meanings. Afterwards there was a serious conference with the cast, the director, and the crew to review any offenses. Corrections were made and the following evening, the authorities returned to watch a second premiere. If all was deemed satisfactory, the play opened officially the next evening before an audience of state dignitaries, high ranking Party members and their families, and visiting V.I.P. guests.

I dressed carefully, modestly. I had been warned by my Embassy guide not to draw attention to myself. I wore a modest black velvet dress, sleek and floor length. High neck, long sleeves. The only adornment, a rhinestone pin. In the crowded lobby, Philip and I stood to one side and watched a trundling parade of women wearing frumpy gowns in muddy shades of grey and mauve heading through sets of double doors to take their seats in the enormous mezzanine. The men wore tuxedos as did Philip. But Philip looked handsome whereas the rest of the men in their awful haircuts, looked pinched and miserable. No one smiled. The Manager of the National Theater approached us and his eyes fell on my pin. "A gift from my departed grandmother," I said softly, demurely covering the sparkle with my hand. "I wanted to have her memory close on this special night." "Ahhh," he said and nodded. "Family is eternal." Philip squeezed my hand. In truth, I had bought the pin at Bloomingdale's for a Christmas party the year before.

Jagr Ziska emerged from the crowd and approached Philip and me. I introduced him to Philip and then a bell rang and it was time to take our seats. About thirty minutes into the performance, which was wretched on too many levels to count, Jagr slipped a small piece of paper into my hand. I looked at him and he whispered a barely audible "Shhhh...." At intermission I found the restroom and went into a stall. I unfolded the clandestine note and read: *Tell the joke tonight at the party with the dissident filmmaker.*

I read it twice; then flushed it down the toilet. I didn't understand why Jagr was asking me to tell the joke that he had earlier disdained. But I trusted him. I would do it.

Chapter 23

Philip and I had been invited to the home of a film writer and director named Martin Czerniak, known throughout Europe for his depictions of life in the Eastern Bloc. It was hoped that he might offer Philip some strategies for dealing with the authorities who had banned *Portnoy's Complaint*. Communist censorship had not impeded Martin Czerniak's work in the least. He had continued to create his avant-garde films and they were always smuggled out of the country in a timely manner with assistance from Communist Party ministers who appreciated the bribes. After introductions, Martin led us to a makeshift bar. The furniture in the apartment looked new, whereas the chairs in our "fancy" hotel room, by contrast, were actually threadbare in places.

"This whiskey is not bad," Martin said. "I get it brought in from Poland. I think they get it from Albania which has it smuggled in from Ireland. Of course, that all takes time. So it is aged to perfection!" He poured us each a generous glass; then grinned impishly and asked, "So how do you like the play tonight?" Before we could answer, he began to laugh. A rich chortle. I figured he was older than Philip but not by much.

Maybe late forties. He had dark hair and lots of it. Nice eyes. Warm and curious. His shirtsleeves were rolled up to his elbows revealing beautifully sculpted forearms and muscular wrists. And he was tan. I don't know why I was noticing such things. I pulled my attention back to his face.

Philip said, "Is it safe for me to be candid?"

"Oh, yes," said Martin. "The authorities have my place bugged, of course, but that is simply for their own entertainment. If my guests were to stop being provocative, the police would be bored and move on. I see my parties as a public service, Philip. The cops leave the petty thieves alone for the night and those fellows get to ply their trade unsurveiled as the cops remain in their van out front of my building, huddled around the receiver, listening to my apartment like a play on the radio. We do our best to keep them enthralled."

There was scattered laughter among the guests in the room. One man raised his glass. "Here. Here!"

A tall woman, dressed in silky pajamas like a 1930's movie star, now approached us, crossing the room with authority and loudly proclaiming, "GOD KNOWS THERE IS NOTHING INTELLIGENT TO SEE ON THE STAGE ANYMORE!"

Martin laughed. "Ahhh, here we go. May I present the premier stage actress of Czechoslovakia … beloved for her Desdemona, unmatched for her Masha…. "

"TRACTOR OPERAS—I CALL THEM SHIT! NOTHING BUT SHIT BEING PRODUCED NOW ON THE STAGE!" She leaned confidentially towards me and winked. She seemed intoxicated. "Don't you agree? Who wants to watch blocky farmers and their sturdy wives singing about the fucking harvest? Every single time … every fucking month a new variation of that same moronic paean to fucking Mother Russia!"

"Ladies and Gentlemen, my beautiful wife. The ever-eloquent Otka."

She leaned towards me again and grinned. "My friends in the West call me Lucky."

"Really?" I said. "That sounds like a good story. I'm all ears."

She flashed a magnificent smile. It transformed her rather plain face, made her beautiful. "Thank you, Sweetheart. You must be Leanne Roth."

"Yes. It's nice of you to invite us." I extended my hand. She took it. Then she turned to Philip.

"And this magnificent man—this is the famous Philip." She looked at him so lasciviously that I reflexively took his hand.

We gathered in the seating area with the other guests. Philip asked Martin why he moved to Prague. "I understand you were living in London, Martin. You actually *chose* the austere life of an artist living under Communist censorship. I'm genuinely interested in hearing you talk about that."

"First of all, Philip, I am Czech. I was born in Austria but my parents are native to Prague. We spoke Czech in my home growing up. I have always dreamed in Czech. So that's where my ideas come. My imagination speaks in Czech, Okay? You understand? I came here as sort of a native son. Or a refugee."

We heard a toilet flush. A man joined us in the living room. He did a quick jig and said, "It makes you agile being a refugee. Right? Like a turtle with his house on his back? I guess not … poor analogy. Please excuse me." He plopped down next to me on the couch.

Martin continued, "Frankly, I don't fear the repression here. The bureaucrats are so easily corrupted that I can get my films distributed outside the country, in England and in France, no problem. But the real reason I stay is that I find that I work best in these tight conditions. I need repression to focus my attention. To actually stimulate my senses. You see. Otherwise I don't have no discipline. And my work rambles … gets sloppy."

The man next to me now offered his hand. "Kozel Folta."

"Leanne Roth." *The sound of my new "married" name makes me giddy. Or is it the whiskey?*

"I am a film actor. And you?"

"I just graduated last Spring from an American university drama program. I have yet to really test the waters."

"Ah. You probably married too soon then." He shrugged and turned away from me.

Martin resumed his monologue. "It is sensual living here in Prague—knowing that one misstep could lead to prison. You must be so aware of every word, every glance. Every sensation carries information. You understand? So my senses are always alert, Philip. It is for me like being tied up and blindfolded and then slowly touched everywhere by a naked woman. Your imagination is set on fire. Life here is erotic, Philip."

Otka laughed and rolled her eyes. "Oh, my god.... By the way, Philip. We read your book. *Portnoy* is available on the Black Market." She made a thumbs up gesture.

Martin continued, "Just eating a meal here can give you hard on."

There was a loud whoop from several of the guests.

Martin looked at them innocently, "No ... I make my point, please." He turned back to Philip. "We notice everything because everything is scarce. We savor what we have. You see? Whereas you in the West are always full—uncomfortably full—because everything is available to you, you notice nothing and you are bored by tea time every day. But here in Czechoslovakia nothing goes and everything matters. You understand? I'm telling you the sex in our country is the best you will ever have, Philip. Even with your own wife!" He winked at me. "Because you know you are being watched."

I was really feeling drunk now. The whiskey had stopped burning my throat. It now slid down too easily. I had finished one sizable portion and my glass was being refilled by an actress friend of the Czerniaks. Her name was Alzbeta. "What was the last movie you saw in America that you were impressed by?" she said, taking a seat next to me.

"*Women in Love*," I said without hesitation.

"I don't know this movie. What made it so special?"

Otka crossed to us and sat on the floor in front of me. "I know this book. By D.H. Lawrence, yes? You can't purchase it anymore in Prague. Too dirty."

Alzbeta looked at me, her eyes sparkling. "It's a dirty movie?"

"No ... no. It's beautiful. Lots of nudity, but it is beautiful. There is this sequence ... A young couple they are in love. Besotted with love. Sick in love." I crossed my legs. It made me sway and almost topple over on the couch pillows. *Fuck, I'm really drunk.* But I straightened myself again and kept talking. "So they go swimming naked in a lake—this couple—during the party. They take their clothes off—and they enter the water. And they're kissing and so happy. But then the woman disappears under the water and her lover is screaming for help and dives under to find her and he doesn't come up again either. They drain the lake the next day and find them. The girl is holding the boy like she pulled him down on top of her and wouldn't let go. The girl's brother says to everyone, 'She killed him.' I really can't get that image out of my mind."

Otka snorted. "Typical of Lawrence, I think. He hated women."

Alzbeta says, "But to literally die in your lovers' arms. That is powerful. I want to see this movie."

"Love can be so dangerous when it is obsessive," said Otka. "Take me for instance. I killed my first lover."

I gasped, "Oh my god!" Alzbeta had her hand over her mouth. "Otka!"

After another long moment, Otka laughed explosively. "Oh, you two. You would believe anything!"

Alzbeta put a hand on my knee. "I think you are drunk, Leanne. I think I am, too."

Otka stood up. "I'll make us coffee."

Martin had turned his attention to our conversation. "Your American writer Saul Bellows … do you know what he says about women, Mrs. Roth? He says 'women eat green salad and drink blood.'" He laughed.

I looked at Philip. He had his best poker face on that night. I couldn't tell what he was thinking, but I sensed that he didn't like Martin. Otka called from the little galley kitchen. "Ah, Bellows misunderstands women. We just want to be adored. Right, Ladies?" She returned with the coffee, and handed me a cup. I took a sip, then stood unsteadily, and said, "Speaking of misunderstandings between men and women, that makes me think of a joke."

Otka clapped her hands. "Everybody! Your attention. Our dear Leanne is going to perform for us an American joke." The room quieted. Philip looked at me incredulously. I took a deep breath and began. "So a man walks into a bar and sees an attractive woman sitting by herself on a stool and he takes the seat next to her and he orders a drink. When it comes he takes a sip, then turns to the woman and says, 'Tickle your ass with a feather?'" The laughter built throughout my telling, slowly at first like a car idling then ramping up slipping into higher gears, and when

I nailed the punchline—'Fuckin' cold out, ain't it?' the guests roared. Even Philip laughed. He said, "She's been practicing that joke for three years."

At two in the morning, Martin called us a cab to take us back to the hotel. We said goodnight and left. "Did you have a good time, Philip?" I said when we arrived on the street. Philip hissed, "He's a fraud. He's a fucking collaborator." Before I could respond, two men in military uniforms approached us and insisted we get into their black van. "We are Americans," Philip said. "May I ask where you are taking us?"

"Your wife is under suspicion of making derogatory remarks about the Party. She will be interrogated at Police Headquarters."

"I demand to call the Embassy. I want a lawyer."

"We aren't talking to you, Mr. Roth. Your wife is the subject of the interrogation."

Philip continued to argue, but I was sleepy and still feeling the effects of the whiskey even though it had been three hours since my last sip. My ears buzzed with a sound like static. My heart raced. At the station, Philip and I were separated. He remained in an enclosed waiting room, and I was taken to a smaller room—windowless with a table, a lamp, and two straight-backed chairs. I was left there alone for hours; at some point I finally dozed, sitting in a chair, with my head cradled in my folded arms on the table. I awakened at the sound of the door opening. Jagr entered the room accompanied by one of the uniformed military police.

Before I could express my relief, he looked at me with disgust. "You are being sent away from here immediately and you must never return. Is that understood? You are being put on a plane this morning."

"What did I do?"

"You told a joke, Mrs. Roth. A vulgar joke about our beloved country. You made our people seem ridiculous."

"That's not what the joke was about. And you know it."

He cut me off. "You are no longer welcome in my country."

"I'm an American. I don't speak in metaphors. I don't have to. It was just a joke." I started to cry. "Where am I being sent?"

"To Paris, of course," he said with slight surprise. "You and your husband should not have come here. You should have stayed with your original itinerary."

"So Philip is coming with me?"

"Of course. He is not welcome here either."

"But our clothes are still at the hotel."

"I sent my assistant to pack your bags. He has personally put them on the plane. There will be no part of you left here. Do you understand me?"

I nodded. "May I have a drink of water, Jagr? And I'd like to wash my face, brush my—"

"No, you may not. You are lucky, Mrs. Roth, that I am in a position to interject some word of support for you. I told the authorities that you were an American school girl, naïve and silly, not ill meaning. But even I am appalled at your behavior tonight. Now follow me. And don't speak."

Philip and I sat silently in the black van on the way to the airport. We climbed the steps to the plane in silence. There were about forty other people on board, all heading to Paris. I wondered if they were also being thrown out of the country. Philip sat stiffly next to me. I took his hand and whispered, "I'm so sorry."

"Don't say anything, Leanne."

I was unsure if we were really being flown to Paris right up until the moment we touched down. We gathered our luggage, and moved through Customs aware of the stares from the people around us. Me, still in my long black velvet dress. Philip in his tuxedo. We grabbed a cab to our hotel and headed to our room. I said, "May I take the first shower? I can't stand myself any longer. Even my rhinestone brooch has B.O."

Philip rubbed his neck. "What possessed you to tell that joke? You knew the place was bugged. You knew the authorities think humor is subversive."

"Because he told me to!"

"Who?"

"Jagr! He passed me a note at the theater. It was written by him—*tell the joke tonight at the party with the dissident filmmaker*. So I did. I don't understand why he got so upset."

Philip shook his head. "That's curious. Maybe you misunderstood something."

Philip lifted my suitcase onto the bed. I opened it and there on top of the hastily folded clothes was a large, thick grey envelope. "What's this?" I said and Philip came to my side and watched as I opened it. I began removing pages and pages of a typewritten script. "Oh my god," I said. "Look! Oh my god, Philip! I think this is a play! Yes! It's Jagr's father's play! Look at the name!!"

Philip began examining the pages. The language was Czech but the format was that of a script. And the name on the first page, the only thing I could read in Czech, was Ziska. "He got the play out of Prague, Philip."

"He used you, Leanne."

"No, he trusted me. He trusted me and I didn't let him down."

Chapter 24

It was to Paris that the American literary giants of the 1920s escaped when the spasms of censorship threatened to ban their books in their home country. And now in 1972, Paris had welcomed America's latest pariah, Philip Roth. *Portnoy's Complaint* looked out from shelves in bookstores all over the City of Lights. "Look at you, Philip, in the company of Fitzgerald and Hemingway, Henry Miller and Gertrude Stein. You would have been a lively addition to their onanistic confederacy."

One evening a week or so later, we were taking an after dinner walk through the Latin Quarter when we came upon a movie theater, a small one that offered mostly foreign films, and a Czech movie was showing. *Nepopírat.* Translation: *Do Not Deny.* The filmmaker was Martin Czerniak. I wanted to see it and after a short argument, Philip and I walked in just as the eight o'clock show was beginning. There were subtitles and, even with our limited French, we were able to piece together what was happening because there was so little dialog. Just images. It was avant-garde in style—jerky camera work, an improvised script, but it was a sweet and bittersweet story about a group of young artists in the mid-nineteenth century in Paris who are trying to have their work displayed at a government sponsored art exhibition. They refuse to follow the Academy's rules which require that they paint religious scenes and so they are turned away. We left the theater and walked back to our hotel in silence. Philip was in a dark mood.

As we were crossing the Pont de Neuf, we stopped to look at the beautiful Seine River below. The water was inky black that night but sprinkled with starlight. I finally spoke. "I actually liked that movie, Philip."

"Czerniak is a fraud, Leanne."

"I'm not talking about Czerniak. I'm talking about the film."

"I've learned a few things about our friend Martin since we left Prague. He's quite wealthy, Leanne. It's all family money that he received upon the death of his parents. He was the sole heir. He keeps the money in a Swiss account so it is completely untouchable by any authorities. And then he plays the bohemian rebel in Prague."

"Have you ever heard of the Illuminati? They are based in Switzerland."

"That's a conspiracy theory, Leanne."

"No, Philip. I don't think it is. I had a friend who...." Philip put his hand up. "Not now, Leanne." We were quiet for several minutes. Then Philip returned to the subject of Martin Czerniak. "What gags me is his audacity at suggesting that artists thrive in oppressive societies. Because he gets an erotic tickle out of being told *no*. Even though he doesn't accept no for an answer from anyone. And he can afford to slip around and through the authorities. In the meantime, as you know, his fellow artists in Czechoslovakia are suffering. Those who continue to write do so often at a terrible price. And then Martin does a film like this that suggests that he is on the side of angels. I may start a campaign to protest this bastard. I think this film should be banned."

"Are you hearing yourself, Philip? Advocating for censorship? You?"

"No, I am advocating for him to be exposed."

"If we vilify every artist who is a vile human in his private life, what will that leave? We'd have to start off by eliminating Nabokov, Tolstoy, Cheever, Hemingway, Fitzgerald, Faulkner, Flaubert...."

"No ... no ... this is different."

"And what about your buddies, Styron and Bellows? And Mailer! Jesus, if a pure private life is the standard, all of these men should see their writing burned in the public square. You, of all people, Philip, should know the risk if you don't separate the art from the artist."

"Czerniak's a collaborator. That's different, Leanne. This is not a simple failure of judgment in one's personal life. This impacts entire countries. I regret that I spent the money to see this film."

"My mother was so devastated when someone told her that Coco Chanel was a Nazi sympathizer, that she stopped wearing Chanel No. 5. That was in 1954. But guess what? I love Chanel No. 5 so I wear it now. I manage to enjoy it and still hate Nazis all at the same time. If we can't allow ourselves to love the art of monsters, we won't have any beauty left. I don't believe in litmus tests."

Philip nodded. "I admit. It's become personal for me. But I know the names of the writers who are suffering, who face prison every day. Czerniak could use his influence to at least get them out of the country. He has an international audience and influence with the Czech authorities. He could try to get Jagr's father out of prison."

"You know I wonder why Jagr set us up to meet Martin. It must have been Jagr—he knew we were going to that party before we did. Why do you suppose he would want us to meet Martin Czerniak?"

"Because they are both collaborators."

"Or maybe, like Jagr, Martin is leading a double life. Maybe Jagr and Martin planned for me to be arrested so they could plant the play in my suitcase and rush you and me out of the country before the authorities would have time to discover it. Maybe Czerniak is actually working behind the scenes. On the side of angels."

Philip smiled at me. "You always try to find the best in people, don't you?"

"Why not? I have to live in this world."

A FEW DAYS LATER, having soaked up a sunny autumn afternoon in Luxembourg Gardens, Philip and I bought an ice cream cone and sat in view of a statue of the founding saint of Paris. Genevieve, who in the year 451, led the embattled people in a marathon prayer vigil that repelled Attila the Hun and saved the city. I said, "Boy, it must be great to have that kind of faith. That kind of conviction that you can will away evil."

Philip suddenly said, "I want you to live with me, Leanne." He then announced that he intended to buy a house when we returned to the states. Something old—perhaps in Connecticut. Not too far from New York but outside the urban-suburban loop. A place in the countryside with room to walk and daydream. A haven away from the wagging fingers. Philip took my hands. "I need a real home, Leanne. I'm a great sucker for domesticity."

So when we returned to New York, Philip enlisted a realtor to scan the New England countryside and find him a home. A month after that, he and I stepped into a grey two-story clapboard farmhouse, built in 1799, standing with quiet dignity beside a small grove of maple and ash trees that obscured it from the main road. Acres of wildflowers were furrowed with old walking paths. And there was a private lake to the west. And a large garden in the side yard. The Stone Room on the main floor featured high beamed ceilings, the original stone floor, and a large stone fireplace. Built-in bookcases flanked the entrance to a smaller living room which like the dining room retained the original chestnut and oak plank floors. There were beautifully paneled cupboards and doors and French windows throughout the house. And the original spindle staircase led to a second floor with four bedrooms. Two out-buildings stood on the property—the original barn and a small cottage, built in the last century, which would provide a separate writing space for Philip. A carport had been added ten years ago. For Philip, it was love at first sight. He said, "This is a place where I can work."

And so that March, we moved in. Philip began writing immediately in the cottage and I spent my days visiting local antique shops, ubiquitous along the main road. I began to fill the house with beauty and comfort. An elegant eighteenth-century breakfront. A glorious dining table surrounded by American Windsor chairs. Lamps, occasional tables. Soft couches and wool upholstered armchairs. Beautiful Oriental rugs. And a pair of lovely needlepoint pillows that reminded me of Paris. I gathered a comfortable and sturdy mix of pieces, old and new. Philip approved of everything I selected. He kissed me often and said, *"Petit à petit l'oiseau fait son nid."* Little by little the bird builds its nest.

I equipped a proper French kitchen. Copper pots soon hung from black iron hooks, a large cast iron roaster sat on a side table, too big to fit on the painted, pale-yellow shelves. I found a complete set of beautiful dinnerware that reportedly had been used in a local French restaurant. It had closed in the early sixties when the owner and his wife were killed in an automobile accident. I felt like I was, in some way, helping their spirits find peace by giving these dishes purpose again.

I arranged for Philip's massive collection of books to be moved from his New York City apartment to "the farm," soon after we arrived. We spent an entire week of evenings arranging the books per his directions. And then I spent the month of May uncovering the old garden. I planted roses in shades of yellow, ivory and pale pink—the old-fashioned ones with large petals that open fully revealing their golden hearts; the ones that emit an alluring perfume. I added borders of foxglove and delphinium. And watched with delight as a bed of lavender, planted by a former occupant of the house, began to bud. Finally, I carved out a space for herbs. Rosemary and thyme, basil and mint. Philip disappeared every morning into his writing cottage. After breakfast, I seldom saw him again until dinner.

One evening—Philip was grilling a steak for us and I was resting in a lawn chair nearby. He called to me. "Let's invite Bill Styron and his wife to dinner this weekend. They live right in this vicinity. We can have Jason and Barbara up from New York, too, and do a nice dinner for the six of us. Show off the place."

I stood up and crossed to him. "Philip, am I ever going to officially meet your parents?" I had met Mr. and Mrs. Roth briefly a couple of years before at the Weequahic High School in Newark, Philip's alma mater. Philip had addressed the graduating seniors and introduced me to his parents in the lobby afterwards. Then rushed me out of the building and back to his apartment lest the press get a glimpse of me.

Philip looked somewhat sheepish. "My parents do know about you, Honey. I've told them about you. But yes, you're right. It's time we get everyone together. My brother and his wife, too. Invite your parents and TJ and John. We'll do the whole thing. An engagement party."

"Are we engaged, Philip?"

"Well, I thought we were. Aren't we? What are you doing tomorrow? Let's get you a ring."

The next day, we went to one of the local shops that specialized in antique jewelry and Philip told me to pick out whatever I wanted. I spent an hour trying on rings and then selected a simple eighteen-carat gold band embedded with an oval, blood-red garnet. The proprietor said that it had belonged to an actress in the late nineteenth century. Philip pocketed the ring before I could put it back on. Then, taking my hand, he pulled me outside the shop where he dropped to one knee, right there on the sidewalk, in the full light of day, and said, "Will you marry me?" Pedestrians smiled as they walked around us. Some stood at a distance and watched. But all I could see now was Philip's earnest face. I kept my eyes on his and answered with one of the most beautiful monologues of all time, one I had committed to memory soon after I met Philip Roth that Summer when I was fourteen. Molly Bloom from James Joyce's *Ulysses*.

> *I was a Flower of the mountain yes when I put the rose in my hair like the Andalusian girls used or shall I wear a red yes and how he kissed me under the Moorish Wall and I thought well as well him as another and then I asked him with my eyes to ask again yes and then he asked me would I yes to say yes my mountain flower and first I put my arms around him yes and drew him down to me so he could feel my breasts all perfume yes and his heart was going like mad and yes I said yes I will Yes.*

Philip slipped the ring on my finger. He stood up and put his arms around me and kissed me rapturously in full view of the town of Warren, Connecticut. And yes, we went home to our home yes, yes we fucked on the new rug in the Stone Room. And yes, Philip said, "yes we will fuck in every room in this house fuck in every room in *our* house, even the pantry, mark this house mark it like a cat so it will always be of us and yes I love you Leanne, yes."

PHILIP CALLED HIS FAMILY the next morning and invited them to celebrate our engagement here at the Farm. He picked the last Saturday in June, four weeks away. I, however, hesitated to invite my family. My mother and I never failed to talk on the phone Saturday mornings, but I had revealed next to nothing to her about Philip, about my relationship with Philip over the past eight years. At this point Mother still regarded Philip as the handsome celebrity, who spent a Summer in our neighborhood and, out of the goodness of his heart, took an interest in her aspiring-writer daughter. She had no idea that I had been sleeping with Philip since I was nineteen. Nor did she know that we were in love. She would never have imagined that I was now engaged to marry him. I can keep a secret.

But there was another blind spot in our relationship. Mimi had asked me several months ago if I had ever shared with my mother how sick I had been when I went through withdrawal after seven years of taking diet drugs. The question made me defensive. I shrugged and said, "No—it's water over the dam, Mimi. I've moved on." But I hadn't moved on. I deeply resented my mother. I was put on a regimen of amphetamines at the age of fourteen. I spent my fourteenth birthday in the University of Pennsylvania hospital where I was put on a two-week supervised fast— no food. Dr. Lawrence wanted to get "a baseline reading" of my metabolism. I stubbornly managed to lose less weight than he anticipated. So in the years that followed, Dr. Lawrence increased my drugs annually at my once a year checkup; ultimately to punishing levels just to stay ahead of the increasing demands of my addiction. Just to keep me from having public tremors.

In the meantime, my parents continued to pay for the drugs and pick them up every month at the Hoover Pharmacy. Drugs that kept me from sleeping, maybe stunted my growth. Drugs that were only stopped when the U.S. government determined them to be dangerous and prohibited their sale seven years later. And that fucking doctor never followed up with me to see if I survived withdrawal. Not so much as a phone call.

But I blamed my mother more than anyone. She knew they were high risk long before they were outlawed. There were articles in women's magazines and in *Reader's Digest* all through the sixties, warning about diet pill addiction. It was the scourge of the upper-middle class. I can't imagine that Mother and Ginger Taylor hadn't discussed my "prescription." They shared every secret. And Mrs. Taylor had been a nurse. Surely, she must have had concerns. But my mother chose to ignore all the warnings.

It isn't that I ever believed that Mother didn't love me. I knew she loved me. She wanted the best for me. In everything. The best friends, the best clothes, the best schools. And the best beau. But she didn't think I was pretty enough to attract these things on my own. Because I wasn't thin. How would I ever attract the best in life without help? That's all this was. Just like the Rolling Stones song. The pills were Mother's Little Helper, but, in this case, Mother wasn't using them herself—she was giving them to her daughter. Now Mother would say that the end always justifies the means and it was true—Andy fell in love with me. And boy, he was "a catch!" Mother probably congratulated herself for being proactive.

But Mother knew the pills were making me sick. She knew when I was still living at home, during high school, she knew that I didn't sleep night after night. She knew that I was so exhausted I quit the swim team and spent entire Saturdays lying on the couch. She knew when the pills were finally taken away from me, seven years later, that it wasn't the Hong Kong Flu that made me lose thirty pounds in a month. I waited for her to raise the issue so we could finally make amends. I wanted her to say she was sorry so I could say I forgive you. And then we could be close again like we were before. But she never did. The elephant in the corner of the room kept growing and my relationship with my mother was being squeezed into a hard knot. I stopped sharing anything personal with her. My phone calls were small talk, superficial as chatter with strangers on a bus.

But I finally called my mother and told her I was engaged. Mother squealed, "You and Andy … at last!" And I said, "No Mother, not Andy. I'm marrying Philip." And she said, "Who's Philip?" And I said, "Philip Roth." And she said, "*The* Philip Roth?" And I said, "Yes." And she said, "*The* Philip Roth, *the* writer?" And I said, "Yes." And she said. "How do you know him?" And I said, "Mother! He lived across the street when I was fourteen. He came to my sixteenth birthday party! We have been lovers since I was nineteen. And now we are getting married." And Mother said, "Philip Roth is going to be my son-in-law? Gosh, Annie, people are going to think I'm a lot older than I am." And then she said, "Well, Honey, if he makes you happy and you make him happy—that's all that matters. I'm thrilled for you."

Chapter 25

Over the next few days, Philip sent out close to a hundred invitations to our engagement party. What had begun as an intimate family affair was now going to bring together every one of Philip's friends from childhood through the present. He invited his best buddies from the old neighborhood, Marty and Bob. He invited his favorite high school teacher, Dr. Bob Lowenstein, a brilliant man who had suffered the many mortifications of the American blacklisting during Senator McCarthy's reign of terror back in the Fifties. Dr. Lowenstein had warned Philip and his classmates that "tyranny is always better organized than freedom," a warning so profound that Philip had printed it out on a small piece of cardstock and kept it propped on his dresser so that he read it every morning and every night..

Philip invited another of his teachers, a woman who had encouraged his writing during his undergraduate days at Bucknell. He invited colleagues from his teaching days at the University of Chicago, Princeton, the University of Pennsylvania, and Hamilton. He invited his publisher, his agent, secretaries and editors with whom he had worked. He invited fellow writers—friendly rivals like John Updike and mentors like Saul Bellows, and his idol, Bernard Malamud who had written a novel about baseball called *The Natural* that Philip especially loved. He invited artists and theater people he knew in New York. The playwright Arthur Miller, a man that Philip had disparaged to me in private, was coming. Philip said, "I want to start our married life with an abundance of goodwill, Leanne."

He invited all of our current neighbors, including numerous married women who flirted with him quite openly during weekend dinner parties. He even invited the mailman. Guests who had spouses were told to bring them. Even dogs were welcome. Bill Styron and his wife were neighbors of ours; he was also a literary rival so he accidentally ended up on two lists and received two invitations. Styron phoned Philip and said, "Do you mind if I sell one of my invitations to Mailer?"

"Oh, shit," said Philip. "An oversight. I swear. I'll call Norman and make it right." Yes, the news of our party had traveled from the Farm in Connecticut to every borough of New York City.

My own guest list was modest. My family, of course, and Mimi and Olivia. Mr. and Mrs. Kenyon were coming. Mr. Kenyon and I were still "involved"—I was trying to find a graceful way to end our affair. One that would leave us with happy memories and an ongoing friendship. Like I had with Andy now. Andy was in Japan again, teaching at the University of Tokyo. I called him and told him I was engaged.

Andy said, "When you are 100, Philip will be 116." I said, "He will probably die then and I will be free to marry you." Andy said, "In that case I will wait for you." And then we ended our call as we always did. I said, "I love you, Andy Wetherill." And Andy said, "I love you, Annie Hughs."

I invited Cool Breeze and Redhat who now went by their given names, David and Melissa. David was in med school at Columbia in New York and Melissa was teaching gifted kids in Brooklyn. They had recently gotten engaged, too.

I invited a friend from my days at the Bucks County Playhouse. I had lost track of Noah, but Jimmy Green-Green was living in New York now and I had run into him at Bloomingdale's one Saturday last Spring on a shopping trip to the city. I invited Gay Parsons from Pennswalk and her new boyfriend, Alfie. And my Syracuse friends Pookie and Rain. Pookie was in law school now at NYU and said she'd be at the party. Rain sent regrets—she had moved to Canada after graduation and was attending med school at the University of Ottawa. My mother invited my aunts and uncles and cousins, and, of course, the Taylors.

Now I was panicking. Suddenly my self-assurance was collapsing. I needed Mother's steady hand to plan and pull off this party. So at my invitation Mother moved in like an English nanny and took over. She calmly located a caterer in a nearby village after talking to a woman at the local bookstore. "She was wearing a pair of khaki shorts and a wrinkled white polo shirt, Annie. So I knew right away that she was wealthy. They are the only women who can afford to dress so thoughtlessly. She even had dirty hair. I knew she would know a fabulous caterer so I struck up a conversation."

Two days later we met with the delightful young owner of A Moveable Feast Catering, and quickly agreed to make the party menu an upscale picnic of finger-foods. There would be four grills set up in the yard. The meaty aromas of seasoned beef, pork, and chicken would greet and grab our guests by the nostrils and lead them to our backyard from the dirt road where they would be required to park 100 feet away. The menu would include spicy Indian chicken skewers, savory steak kabobs, mini blue cheese hamburgers, and shredded pork drenched in a sweet vinegar sauce and stuffed into dumplings—those would be steamed in bamboo baskets. There would be stations of vegetables and fruit. Platters of boiled shrimp. Platters of deviled eggs. Lots of good bread and a tray of cheeses. And a great tureen of cold potato and chive soup surrounded by fried squash blossom cups. For dessert—mini cherry cupcakes filled with chocolate mousse. And pistachio ice cream on mini waffle cones—my favorite. Of course, there would also be an open bar. Three bartenders. Mother requested extra staffing by the caterer to keep the platters filled and trash cleared. And a large tent to protect the food area in the event of rain.

I had prepared for the party by reading something by each of the writers who would be attending. It was important to me that I be seen by these men as a serious thinker, a careful reader, and one who was well-versed in the literary canon of the day. Someone who could and should be included in their lively debates involving literature, art, history, and the current state of the world. I never doubted Philip's love and admiration for me, but I suspected that the fact that I was just shy of twenty-three years old raised more than eyebrows among these lusty men. They didn't care if I had a mind. So the party was the opportunity for me to introduce myself—my real self. Leanne the Brainiac. So while Mother handled the flower arrangements, and the rental of 100 lawn chairs, I rehearsed imaginary conversations with these powerful men.

> *Arthur Miller! I am overwhelmed to meet you given that ... now this is the truth ... I have spent the past eight years—ever since I read* Death of a Salesman *for the first time in tenth grade—preparing to play the role of Linda. The wife of Willy Loman. Yes, I know I'm young for it. Yes, I know she's forty —five. Oh, is she fifty? Well, I am an old soul, Arthur. I can do it. That speech you wrote for Linda? May I do it for you?*

> "He's not the finest character that ever lived. But he's a human being and a terrible thing is happening to him. So attention must be paid. He's not allowed to fall into his grave like an old dog. Attention, attention must be paid to such a person."

> *Thank you, Arthur. Well, they are your words. As an actress, all I can do is honor the text —first and always. And in that short speech, Arthur, you nail it. The man lost his job and his life is over. This is capitalism at its most heinous. Your writing serves notice to all Americans. Attention must be paid! Yes, let's stay in touch. Definitely. Here's my number. Please call any time. We have so much in common, Arthur. You see, like you, I'm a Marxist.*

> *Bill Styron ... So good to see you again. Thank you ... you look very nice, too. I'm so anxious to talk to you about your novel—*The Confessions of Nat Turner. *I have to tell you, it was only a few years ago that I learned that my own great grand-*

mother was the child of slaves so I probably read this book with heightened anguish. Really? Do you think there is a chance that you might be Black as well? See, that's my point. Well, there was so much mixing of the races—who could keep track? Exactly. And you are a Southern man ... Well, your empathy with the horrifying life of a slave.... Nat Turner.... I mean you took this historic figure and you made him flesh. You made slavery visceral. All I had known of slavery when I was growing up was Mammy and Prissy in Gone with the Wind. *Isn't that disgraceful? Slavery was the holocaust on our own soil and too many Americans are still pretending that slave owners were benevolent. Oh my god, the willful ignorance in this country ... Don't get me started. I just want to say thank you for writing this book. Excuse me. I see Saul Bellow ...*

THE TEMPERATURE CLIMBED INTO the eighties that afternoon of the party, but there was a cooling breeze out of the nearby Berkshire Mountains that continuously fanned the crowd. The sky was clear and the bright sunshine seemed to outline everyone's face like a halo, giving their features startling clarity. I wore a red-orange halter dress with a ballet length hem that Mother had picked out for me in Lord and Taylors on one of our day trips to New York. "Very Grace Kelly. Don't you think, Annie?" she had said as we stood side by side in the dressing room studying the dress on me in the full length mirror. "The length, I mean. It's ladylike. And the neckline is low and yet not immodest. But that color is heart-stopping."

"Do you think the color is too bold, Mother? Grace Kelly always wore white, didn't she?"

"Yes, but she met a prince, Annie, and had to turn into a virgin, and pronto, if she wanted to marry him. You, darling, are marrying Philip Roth. You just want to look sexy and brilliant."

NORMAN MAILER WAS ONE of the first of our guests to arrive. Philip and I were still standing side by side at that point, greeting our guests as in a reception line, smiling and shaking hands. Mailer entered the yard looking edgy, but when I took his hand, he seemed suddenly fragile. He had the eyes of someone who struggled with ordinary life. Those eyes traveled continuously in their sockets, looking to the left, then to the right, up and down—searching, it seemed, for something solid and secure, to which he could tether his attention for the evening. His pugnacious history with other writers was well documented in the newspapers. He was always in a rhetorical battle with some public figure. But Mailer could be violent. He had actually spent seventeen months on a psych ward for stabbing his second wife with scissors because she had the audacity to tell him during one night of heavy drinking that he was a lesser genius than the writer Dostoevsky. And he had recently stabbed his fourth wife as well. Or tried to. So that night, the night of our engagement party, he was breaking in a fifth wife. I was worried when Philip told me he had no choice but to invite Norman Mailer. Philip had said, "Believe me, Leanne, he'd never get over the snub if we didn't. And we don't want this guy on our bad side."

So I dreaded meeting him but by luck or design, he was immediately corralled by my father and Herman Roth, Philip's dad, shortly after he arrived, both of whom approached him and expressed genuine admiration for *The Naked and the Dead*, Mailer's astonishing first novel about the war in the Pacific. Incredibly the three men stayed together for the entire evening sitting in lawn chairs talking about the war first, then moving on to Muhammad Ali. Making frequent trips to the food tables for the steak and chicken and the ice cream cones; but always returning to their little corner of the yard where Mailer would launch into another story that would hold their rapt attention for yet another hour.

Soon everyone was paired up with someone. I saw Robert Kenyon in conversation with Philip's older brother, Sandy, who also worked in advertising in New York. I caught Mimi's eye and she joined me briefly. She said she had already had a wonderful conversation with Arthur Miller about the 1968 Democratic convention in Chicago, the one that turned into a street riot. "Arthur was a McCarthy delegate from Connecticut, Leanne! Did you know that? No, neither did I. So was Paul Newman! Maybe you can be a delegate next time."

In the kitchen I gathered with my mother, Philip's mother and my soon to be sister-in—law, Trudy, and Mrs. Taylor. Mrs. Roth presented a gift to me. "Leanne, I saw this in an antique shop and thought you would appreciate it." She handed me a heavy rectangle, elegantly wrapped. I opened it to find a walnut case and inside, secured side by side in felted slots, were five antique serving spoons. Pewter. I gasped. "Oh my, these are beautiful, Mrs. Roth!"

She smiled and said, "Call me Bess."

My mother echoed, "What a lovely gift, Bess!" And Mrs. Taylor said, "Are they monogrammed?"

Bess said, "The dealer told me they came from an old Connecticut family. They are dated 1838. Look on the stems, Honey. They are engraved with the letter L. I just couldn't resist. They belong in this house with you, Leanne." I kissed her and thanked her. And she beamed.

I returned to the party and lifted a glass of wine off the tray of a circulating waiter. I waved to Mr. Taylor who was happily visiting with Robert Brustein, a theater critic whom Philip had gotten to know in the last year. Then my eyes fell on Philip. He was joking and laughing with his best friends from high school. I marveled at how Philip maintained relationships. He never let go of people he loved. I noted that my brothers were right next to him as well, watching him with all the adoration of two teenagers in the company of a handsome, witty favorite uncle. Every now and then Philip threw an arm around one or the other of them in that easy affectionate way he had with other men as well as women.

Philip suddenly caught my eye and I smiled, flirtatiously, at him. He left his admirers and crossed the yard to me. "It's surprising to see a pretty girl here without a date. Is there something wrong with you?"

"Well, I have a lousy personality."

"Yeah, that's what all the fellas said. But I notice you have big breasts."

"I do."

"Well, as it happens, I'm one of those guys who likes big breasts."

"Do you? You're not just saying that to be nice?"

We stood there grinning at one another. Philip's smile seemed to bubble over, past the edges of his face. He was so happy. And it made me so happy to see him so happy. He bobbed and weaved a bit, continuing to play the awkward suitor. Then he said, "Do you think there's a chance you might be willing to have sex with me at some point?" I laughed and said, "I don't know. You're not really my type." Then he stepped toward me and put one arm around my waist and took my hand in the other hand. The music had stopped so we swayed back and forth and leaned into one another and he quietly sang, *Fly me to the moon and let me play among the stars....*

My father now approached us, smiling his silly head off. He put a hand on each of our shoulders and squeezed. "This is a great party," he said.

Philip said, "You are doing yeoman's duty, Tom, keeping Mailer happy."

My father laughed. "You know he's had quite a life. Jeez, one story after another. No wonder he's a writer. Of course I understand that some of your fictional novels contain stories that the author actually made up." Daddy winked at me.

Philip laughed, "Decent of you to notice that, Tom."

Daddy moved on to the food table. And Philip gave me another kiss and returned to his friends. I scanned the party. Bill Styron had arrived late, already drunk, and I could see that he was proceeding to get drunker. I approached him. "Hi, Bill. Glad you could make it. Let me get you something to eat." But before I could continue, he jumped me, knocking me into the lilac bushes. He began kissing me and pawing my dress. I was so shocked I could barely register what was happening. A couple of guests pulled him off and helped me to my feet. Bill blamed it on my dress. "Your fault, Leanne. I'm just an old bull. I see red and charge...."

"Fuck you, Bill," I said and walked into the house, through the kitchen door. There was a powder room on the first floor and I stood in front of the mirror and assessed the damage. The dress survived, but from what I could see of my back, it was covered in tiny scratches from the bare lilac branches that grew low on the tree. I began to shake uncontrollably. I remembered the rape. That wasn't so long ago. Four years? Time telescoped and I had the helpless feeling that still haunted my dreams some nights. That terrifying paralysis.

"You okay?"

I turned and recognized John Updike standing in the open doorway. He smiled at me politely.

"I saw the incident. I'm glad you refused his apology."

He picked a small leaf off the back of my skirt and held it up. "Final remnant. You look wonderful again."

You wouldn't describe him as handsome. His face had a corvine quality—small bright eyes, a huge beak. His mouth seemed to hold too many teeth, but his voice was soft and measured and there was an essential kindness in his cordial manner. "Mary went to locate your fiancé. I don't think he saw what happened or I'm sure he would have been here by now. It's quite a crowd out there."

"Mary?"

"Mary is my wife. Well, for the time being."

I nodded but said nothing.

"Congratulations by the way. At the risk of sounding trite, I think Philip is a lucky guy."

And then Philip was suddenly pushing his way into the powder room. John backed out and Philip pulled me close. "I told Bill to leave. He's gone." He kissed me. "I'm so sorry, Honey. What can I get you? Come stand by me. I want you to meet Dr. Lowenstein."

"I'm going to change, Philip.

"No, don't. You look so beautiful. Don't let him ruin...."

"I'll find you later." I kissed him softly on the mouth. I went upstairs to my room, removed the dress, and laid down on the bed. I laid there for two minutes and then I thought, "Oh heck, Leanne, you've survived worse than that." And I got up and put my dress back on and returned to the party. I looked for John Updike and found him standing alone surveying the scene.

I walked up to him and smiled, "It is said that we are moving into the Age of Aquarius. And in this bumpy time of transition out of the Age of Pisces, we can expect to experience increased confrontation between the old and the new; the traditional and the future."

He grinned and said, "Is that what we are experiencing?" I continued, "I imagine you feel caught in a vortex of powerful currents yourself during these times. Philip tells me you support the Vietnam War.

I imagine that makes you feel isolated, especially in this crowd." John's eyes became wary now, but before he could respond, I said, "John, I have deep respect for people who have principles and a moral compass, regardless of whether they are my principles or my moral compass. I want to always surround myself with people of integrity. I'm interested in what you have to say."

John smiled warmly at me and said, "Let me get you a drink, Leanne, and we'll take a walk. I'd be honored to be your friend."

THE PARTY ENDED WITH a touch-football game. I changed into khaki shorts and a white polo shirt. My nineteen-year-old twin brothers begged to be on Philip's team and so he bumped his own brother, Sandy, to the opposing team's side. So, in the spirit of intrafamily sportsmanship, I joined Sandy's team. Towards the end, Sandy sacked Philip, who was of course playing quarterback, and Philip moaned as he went down, "My back!" He had to sleep on the floor in the Stone Room that night. I created a thick bed of soft blankets on top of the hard floor and joined him there. We didn't have sex for the next three weeks while he recovered. But he returned to his writing room the next day and rigged up a desk at which he could stand and type. His work simply couldn't be delayed. I fetched for him, cooked for him, and gently massaged his neck and shoulders every evening. When he was feeling whole again, I moved into our apartment on West 86th Street in New York. I told Philip I was going to get a job. I needed a life of my own.

Chapter 26

Philip and I were still engaged and very much in love, but I frankly was increasingly concerned that my relationship with him was erasing my identity a smudge at a time. King Lear asks, "Will no one tell me who I am?" I didn't want to get to old age and still find myself unable to answer that question. So my agenda for the next six months would be an existential examination of my potential. I would find my bliss.

First I needed to deal with my conscience. I had been seeing Dr. Fine, a psychiatrist whose office was on West 58th Street, since I slit my wrists back in May of 1970, two years before. He had helped me compartmentalize my guilt over the young security guard—the one I was supposed to lure out to the street before Finn set off the bomb, the one who died that day at the bank on Marshal Street. My sadness about that was recurring and at times, the guilt was overwhelming.

Dr. Fine argued that it was most likely an accident since Finn had made it clear that this was just the first of many banks that he intended to disrupt. Dr. Fine said, "While you bear some of the responsibility,

Leanne—after all, you did sign on to be an accomplice—the fact is that you exercised your free will to change your mind in the end. That wasn't cowardice; that was a choice based on your central moral principles. And that gave Finn the ultimate choice—whether to continue with the plan. The fact that he did and that it resulted in Finn's own death, well … Do you believe in God, Leanne?"

"No, I don't."

"Oh. Well, forgive yourself. It's over."

I wondered what a young person in my situation would do if he or she didn't have parents who could afford to enlist an expensive shrink to explain to them how blameless they really were. Regardless, it didn't work. I didn't feel absolved. Mimi always said if you need a really good therapist, talk to an actor. An actor can empathize like no others since that is what they do for a living. An actor can literally put himself or herself in another person's shoes. So when I moved to New York City after the engagement party, the first person I contacted was Jimmy Green-Green, one of the interns from my Summer at the Bucks County Playhouse. We had spoken briefly at the party. He was now a working actor in New York.

Jimmy was appearing in an off-off Broadway theater production of a new anti-war play called *Sorry for You, Pamela*. He got me tickets for opening night. I went by myself to the East Village. The play wasn't what I would call stellar, but it had some decent scenes and Jimmy was terrific as a blind Vietnam veteran who was angry at the world and cruel to everyone especially his sister who was trying to care for him. He accidentally stabs her in the end and makes her blind, too. The interesting thing about the play for me though was how convincing Jimmy was as a blind person.

Jimmy and I went to a deli after the show, and I ordered matzo ball soup and he ordered a sandwich. I learned that Jimmy, like me, had gone on The Work when we were at the Playhouse that Summer of 1969. He had been feeling hopeless about his future at the time, and Noah, being the self-appointed caretaker of all the interns, hooked him up with Oric. Jimmy drove into New York, got his envelope from the Assistant Conductor of the Philharmonic, just as I had, and started meditating on the three symbols immediately. He noticed that The Work gave him self-discipline so when he got to the city after graduation, he joined The New York Health Club and started working out every day. He looked fantastic now and was starting to get acting jobs.

"Jimmy, did you get that last letter from Oric?"

"Yeah … the one about sex?"

"Yeah."

"Frankly, Leanne, I think Oric is losing it."

Oric was sending his letters more frequently now. They always started with an affectionate greeting and then he'd launch into some bit of news from the village next to his own in Tuscany, Italy where some kid had gotten high on drugs and raped and pillaged an entire neighborhood. Oric would inevitably end his letters with some admonition to stop something. It began when he told his disciples that we must stop recreational drugs. I did. Then he turned to food. He said to stop eating peanuts. I did. Then it was tomatoes, coffee, peaches, bouillon … the list of things we weren't supposed to eat grew. These foods had "a counter clockwise cellular structure" according to Oric, and that was bad for our auras. I continued to drink coffee anyway—although I felt guilty about that. And sometimes I'd eat spaghetti. I felt bad about it. But the latest letter wasn't about food. This one was about sex. Oric was now saying we mustn't engage in sex.

"Jimmy, are you being celibate now?"

Jimmy shrugged. "Sort of."

"Well, I'm engaged, so this is a big problem for me."

"It's a big problem for me too, Leanne."

"Do you have any sense of a timeframe? Did your letter indicate whether this would be for a week or a month or...?"

Jimmy shook his head.

"So, Jimmy, do you think Oric means forever? Like we have to be celibate for life?"

Jimmy looked at me and said, "I'm thinking of getting off The Work."

"You know what, Jimmy? I'm getting off it, too."

We shook hands and then we ordered peanut sundaes and coffee. And then we went back to his place and had sex. Just for fun. But true to my thesis that sex opens the door to communication, Jimmy and I did end up having a deep conversation. I told Jimmy about the bank bombing and how I was haunted by it. And Jimmy said, "Oh, Leanne, I'm so sorry that has been such a burden for you. I myself am becoming a Buddhist. Enlightenment shows us that all human life is suffering. So you aren't the only one going through shit. But Buddhism teaches us that we will get another shot at doing things better in our next life. That way—no matter what you did—you still have a shot at becoming a good human being eventually." I said I would look into it.

I went back to see *Sorry for You, Pamela* again two nights later. It was closing after a three-performance run. I wanted to wish everyone in the cast well and exchange phone numbers with the playwright who was a young woman my age. I told her I'd love to workshop anything she wrote and she was thrilled by my interest. I especially wanted to study Jimmy's performance one last time. I needed to learn how he had managed to act blind so convincingly because I had need of protection now that I had gone off The Work and had forfeited Oric Bovar's protection. And I had an idea.

There was a huge Mafia War going on that Summer and every day the headlines were about another Mafia Boss being shot in the face while he ate clams at a family restaurant in Little Italy. Then one of the Mafia bosses was shot in the face eating a piece of Black Forest cake at an up-scale café on the Upper West Side, not that far from Philip's apartment, and I freaked out. My biggest fear now was that I would inadvertently witness a Mafia shooting and would never be safe again. I pictured men wearing white suits, black shirts, white neckties and fedoras tracking me down like an animal, unloading their tommy guns into me. Just like the old movies. Rat-a-tat-tat. Me staggering backwards, trying to get away, then dropping in the middle of the street where a yellow taxicab would run over me and finish me off. There would be a horrific photo of my splattered corpse on the front page of the *Daily News* the next day, bloody beyond recognition. Mimi would volunteer to identify my body to spare Philip and my parents the agony. "Yes, officer, it is her. It is Ma Cherie Leanne. I recognize the shoes."

So I adopted a ruse that would protect me if I saw any men in white suits, black shirts, and fedoras on the street. I pretended I was blind. I began to carry my umbrella every day, rain or shine. I'd tap it along the street, affecting an unseeing stare. I figured that way, when some Mafia Hit Men rubbed out some guy standing next to me at a street corner waiting for the light to change, one of the killers would say to the other killer—"Nah, leave the girl alone. Can't you see she's blind? She ain't going to witness against us. Are ya, Honey?" And then I would pretend I was also deaf. And the killer would say, "Oh, Jesus! She's a mute, too. Poor kid!"

Speaking of deaf, Mimi was now acting with the National Theater of the Deaf. She had been hired while we were still at Syracuse and went to work right after graduation. The company was based in Waterford, Connecticut but had recently embarked on a national tour. Olivia got a job with the touring company as well. She was hired as the assistant to the Stage Manager. So Olivia and Mimi remained inseparable. As usual I had to struggle with my jealousy. But Mimi called me at every stop of the tour to check in. And each call would end with her exhorting me to go to auditions so that someday we could all be together again working in a theater.

I had read an old *Newsweek* magazine that I found in the waiting room of Dr. Fine's office when I was there for my last appointment soon after I arrived in the city. There was an article about the slaughter of baby seals in Newfoundland by Canadian fisherman who sold their silky skins to fur traders. It made me sick and I was seriously toying with the idea of moving there to join the protesters and interrupt the hunt. I had even looked into hotels in that area—there weren't many. But before I booked a flight—just to appease Mimi—I picked up a copy of *Backstage*, a weekly newspaper that listed acting auditions in the city. It not only described the roles being cast, but noted which auditions were for non-union performers like me. Actors Equity was the actors' union but you had to be offered a contract at a professional theater to be able to join the union and go to the Equity auditions which included auditions for Broadway. I was a beginner. Most of the non-union auditions were for showcases and other non-paying performances. But one non-union audition caught my attention. It was for the New York City Shakespeare Company. No this wasn't a fancy company like the New York Shakespeare Festival or Shakespeare in the Park. This was a small touring operation that mostly played local high schools. They paid a small stipend though. That made it almost professional. And the auditions were the following day.

I dressed carefully the next morning. I wore a black turtleneck and black slacks thinking that would minimize my curves and make me look serious and artistic. They wanted a prepared monologue from one of Shakespeare's plays. I chose *Hamlet*, the role of Gertrude, his mother. Looking back perhaps I should have gone for something younger. I had just turned twenty-three. Five foot two inches tall with long straight blonde hair. And big boobs. Probably not what most casting directors had in mind when they cast the role of Hamlet's mother, but in for a penny, as they say. I was ready for my first audition in New York.

I stood in line for hours. Hundreds of young actors had shown up that morning. But the line kept moving. And finally my moment came. I was escorted into the audition room and stunned to see a real TV star, the actor who had played Grandpa on *The Munsters*. I'd watched that show every week with my brothers when I was in high school. There he was in the flesh, sitting at a table with two other men. Grandpa Munster introduced himself and we shook hands. He said he would be directing the production. He introduced the stage manager and the costume designer and he asked me where I had gone to school and then he motioned for me to stand on a taped X on the floor in front of the table. He took his seat and said, "Whenever you're ready, Leanne."

I stepped into place, closed my eyes and took a deep breath to "center" myself in fifteenth-century Denmark; and then just as I was about to begin, Grandpa Munster said, "Wow. You're really stacked for a little girl." And in that instant, I forgot my audition piece. Completely. It was like swallowing gum. The words just slipped down the back of my throat. I had only a few seconds to consider my options. 1) Run out of the room, crying. 2) Get angry and scold Grandpa Munster for sabotaging my audition. 3) Make something up.

I chose Door 3. Yes, I made up a Shakespeare soliloquy. In front of Grandpa Munster and the artistic staff of the Shakespeare Theater

Company. I weaved together lines from *Comedy of Errors*, *King Lear*, and from the poem *The Love Song of J. Alfred Prufrock*. I also threw in a few Laura Nyro lyrics. Anything that came to mind under the duress of the moment. My delivery was hyper-emotional. When I finished, there was shocked silence. Then Grandpa Munster said, "What the hell was that?" "*Violanus*. Act Two … scene … seven," I said. "Next," he said.

Normally having fucked up that big and in public would have sent me into hiding, but it had the opposite effect. I was finally liberated. I realized that no one was looking at me. And even if they noticed me, it was in passing. In this city, this swirling mass of humanity, you were anonymous so it was easy to reinvent yourself—and keep reinventing yourself until you got it right.

The very next day, I showed up for an audition at the back door of a warehouse in the East Village. There were only two other girls there so it was a short wait. This audition was for an independent production being staged by a start-up company called The Phoenix Also Rises which turned out to be two guys who recently graduated from Penn State. Their premiere effort was *The Maids* by Jean Genet. It's a play about power struggles between two young maids and their mistress and the destructive shame of poverty. I didn't have to prepare anything, just be ready to read from the script. I was ready. I knew this play well. My friend Daria had been in a production at Syracuse and I had watched it twice. She had been sensational. All I had to do was channel her performance.

When my turn came, a young woman who identified herself as the stage manager took my hand and led me into a pitch-black building. She pulled me along a dark hallway through a doorway into an even darker space that was illuminated by a single hanging light bulb. It looked like a Nazi Interrogation room in a movie about World War Two. Even scarier than the room I sat in at the Prague Police Station. But almost immediately, two young men—who I couldn't see—called out happily from the surrounding void. "Hey! Hi! Thanks for coming. Stand under the bulb." Then the young woman handed me some pages of the script and disappeared back into the darkness. One of the men called out "Read the part of Claire." I took a deep breath and began to read and immediately heard the same guy say, "Thank you. That's enough. You can go."

Before I could move, I heard the other guy say, "What the hell, Dave! I want to hear her read more than that."

And Dave said, "No, she's wrong."

And the other guy said, "Well, I like her."

And Dave said, "Are you crazy? She's terrible. Her voice is so annoying."

And then I called into the blackness, "Listen, I'm happy to wait outside if that would be better. If someone could help me find my way outside again."

And the other guy said, "I want you to continue reading. I think you're very special, Barbara."

"My name's Leanne."

And Dave said, "We're doing art, Matthew. Not running a dating club. Put it back in your pants."

And Matthew said, "Fuck you, David. I quit."

And with that, Matthew who had just quit, stepped out of the black void and into the circle of the light of the hanging light bulb and took my hand and pulled me through the darkness and finally out the door onto the street where we stood squinting, trying to adjust to the blinding Summer afternoon light. When he was able to focus, he looked at me and said, "Listen … I'm sorry about that. You're a fine actress. I'm going to start a different theater company. Wanna have dinner with me some evening? I'll tell you my plans."

And I said, "Actually, I'm sort of planning to go to Canada and save baby seals."

And Matthew said, "Oh, very cool." And then he handed me a business card and said, "I work here. Come on down tonight and I'll buy you a farewell drink."

Max's Kansas City was a popular night club on 18th Street and South Park Avenue where lots of musicians and artists hung out. Mick Jagger and Keith Richards were always there when they were in town. And David Bowie and Bob Dylan. And Andy Warhol. Warhol controlled the back room when he was at the club. You had to be invited into the back room. But anyone could walk right into Max's—there were no doormen to keep anyone out. I found my way to the bar and there was Matthew.

He was the Assistant to the Bar Manager. He gave me a drink on the house and told me he got off at midnight and that there was a party at The Factory, Andy Warhol's place, and he would take me. So I spent the evening watching the music. And drifting from conversation to conversation with other young people, many of them teenagers, too young to be served so they were drinking Cokes.

Then at midnight, Matthew and I walked to Warhol's place. It was packed. Lots of actors and artists. I met the nicest girl who turned out to be a guy. She told me that she was going to appear in a movie that Warhol was writing. She then told me her life story which was terribly sad. And then on my way to the bathroom, I saw a drugged young woman burning her face with the lit end of a cigarette. Sitting on the floor in front of Warhol like he was some king, and he was watching her with an amused look on his face, like he was entertained, and I went over to her and pulled the cig out of her hand and tried to take her to the bathroom to wash her burns and she started screaming for me to leave her alone. I looked at Warhol and he half laughed, and I left that party. But from that moment on, I despised Andy Warhol. Oh, and I think his art is stupid.

AT THE END OF September, I found myself making out with Mr. Kenyon on the *Leanne's Smile*. It was a beautiful day on the Delaware River. I had barely spoken to him at the engagement party back in June, but we had had a few minutes alone when he had first arrived and had agreed to get in a final trip to Toms River before he put the boat up for the Winter. It would be our final communion as lovers. I was tired of lying.

But oh my god, I would miss his wonderful kiss. We stripped and made love as soon as we got to our beach. And afterwards, he offered me a job as a junior copywriter at Warner Elkins. I told Mr. Kenyon that I would accept the job, but I told him that I would have to start on January 3, 1973.

He looked at me surprised. "That's three months away."

"Yes. I had my palm read last week. I was told that I would be offered a job, but I must start it on Monday, January 3. I don't want to defy karma."

Mr. Kenyon laughed. I straddled his hips and kissed him. Then I looked him in the eye and said, "So, do you think you could wait for me? I'm a hard worker, Robert. I learn fast. I promise you I will make you proud."

He laughed. "Yeah, Sweetheart. I will wait for you."

THE PALM READER WAS the grandmother of a girl I met at another audition. It was a cattle call for an off-off Broadway production of a new play about a returning Vietnam veteran who was paralyzed, and lived with his blind sister, and their dead mother. I figured I was a shoo-in for the blind sister part as I had the unseeing stare down by this time. But the line of actors was so long, and that late August day was so hot, that when the girl standing in front of me turned to me and said, "This is a waste of time," I agreed. Then she said, "Let's get a snow cone at least." I said sure and we walked away from the line.

Her name was Janice. She was twenty-eight, five years older than me, which seemed like a lot, but I think it was part of the attraction for me. She was a real grownup. Everything about her seemed solid and grounded. She was perfectly round, but firm. Her body was a perfect apple. Her arms were round. Her thighs were round. Her calves were round. Her feet were round. Her toes were round. She had a round face with round eyes that were a deep Caribbean blue and crinkled at the edges when she looked at me. She wore her dark brown hair in a short bob that cupped her round chin. She even had "bee-stung" lips. She was simply adorable.

She was born and raised in Manhattan, one of the few people I met in the city who could say that. Most people in Manhattan came from somewhere else. And many of the people who were in fact born in New York City seemed to have left for the spacious suburbs of Pennsylvania, New Jersey and Connecticut first chance they got. But Janice's family was still in the city on the same block in the same apartment building where they had landed after emigrating from Italy in 1943. Janice had attended a secretarial school right after high school graduation and immediately found work in an import-export company that was owned by her mother's brother-in-law. But she wanted to be an actress. "I think I'm too intellectual to be a secretary," she said.

Janice Trussardi had that real Manhattan accent. Not Queens. Not Bronx or Brooklyn. It was lighter than that. Sophisticated. She sounded like a graduate of a fancy finishing school. I noted that she referred to Cuba, the country, as *Cuber*—like President Kennedy used to say it. But he was from Boston. Anyway, whenever the topic of Castro came up, which with Janice was often, she would fixate on the Cuban Missile Crisis that had occurred in 1962 on President Kennedy's watch. Janice was eighteen years old at the time and feared that Manhattan would be obliterated by a bomb. She immediately became a Republican and still was. For some reason she thought that would deter the Russians. I thought of John Updike. He was also a Republican. But he wasn't Italian. This was my first time talking with a Republican who was ethnic.

Sometime that afternoon, Janice invited me to dinner at her "house" which was a two-bedroom apartment on East 76th Street right off First Avenue which she shared with her parents and an older sister. Her mother was making her *famous* sausage-and-mushroom ravioli, which, according to Janice, was "to die for." She stopped at a public telephone and made a quick call. She emerged from the booth, smiling. "Ma can't wait to meet you."

We hopped a bus and rode uptown. Janice talked the entire way and I listened. The closer we got to her parents' apartment, the more I noticed a change in Janice. She became more animated. She seemed to chew every word. "My Grandmother lives on the 2nd floor, right below us? Her husband died in the war? 1939? She's still in mourning? It never stops? She still wears black up to here?" She pointed to her throat. "She has always eaten dinner with my family. Every night. So she'll be there. And she's a bitch, Leanne. Forgive me but it's true. My mom's younger sister—my Aunt Connie and her husband, Uncle Jo-Jo? They are great. They live upstairs on the fourth floor. Connie works at Bloomingdale's in lingerie and gets me a discount on underwear. They have one son, Allen. He graduated from Penn State last year and works at a marketing firm on Park. He's stinking spoiled and arrogant. That's all I will say." She rolled her eyes as punctuation. "My mom's older sister Anna lives with her husband Richard in Washington Heights. They used to live in the building, but they are snobs. And that's not just me talking. Aunt Connie says it and she loves Anna. No one can believe they gave up their apartment though. All the units in our building are rent-controlled. I swear Anna and Richard will rue the day. Finally my sister Maria. She still lives at home. She's thirty-one, unmarried, and dating a Mafia hit man. Yes, my mother's ready to take the gas pipe."

I thought to myself, *Jesus, these mafia—they've infiltrated everywhere....*

Janice continued. "Maria brings him home to my parents' table for dinner several nights a week. He'll probably be there tonight. Don't make eye contact with him! Yes, my family is Italian. But we are not Sicilian!" She threw her hands up in the air and shrugged. "We are from the north! Sicily is the south! Bad blood, Leanne. You don't want to know." She shook her head and then continued, "Oh, one other thing, my family is very patriotic. So don't badmouth Nixon in front of my dad. And don't bring up Kent State. There was a big riot in the city last year and all these hippies were protesting and then eight hundred construction workers showed up—among them my dad. Oh, he got into it. Jesus, it was a brawl. The fire department had to help the police break it up and they hate each other. Anyway, it's just lucky my father didn't end up in the slammer. My mother still gets the agita.... So don't get into politics, okay? We'll just eat and talk and enjoy our evening."

Janice's father was sitting in his recliner watching *Password* on TV when we entered the apartment. He didn't look at me when I was introduced, even when I said, "Mr. Trussardi, I have a friend who won ten thousand dollars on *Password* last year. With Sandy Duncan. So they have stayed friends. He's an actor. They talk on the phone all the time." He continued to silently stare at the TV. I said, "Actors are the nicest people. Really. That's how I met your daughter."

Janice's sister, Maria, came out of the bedroom now and shook my hand. She was Janice's polar opposite: slender, athletic looking, dark hair cut in a choppy shag. The doorbell rang and Maria said, "That's Mickey." She buzzed him in. I clutched my umbrella. Janice's mother came out of the kitchen wiping her hands on her apron. "Welcome, Leanne," she said pleasantly. Over her shoulder, I saw an old woman, dressed in black, sitting at the dining table with her back to the living room. She didn't stir. I assumed that was Gramma.

Kitchen towels were draped over the backs of several of the dining room chairs. On top of them flour dusted sheets of fresh pasta lay drying. Janice saw them, too, and said, "Ma, you haven't made the Raviolis yet?" And her mother said, "I thought Leanne would like to see how it's done." She turned to me and said, "You're not Italian, are you, dear?"

I followed Mrs. Trussardi into the kitchen and she gave me expert instructions. Soon there was a small pile of stuffed pillows made by me which she added to the massive quantity of ravioli that she had already prepared. She sliced the remaining sheets of pasta into narrow strips. "I'm making noodles and gravy for the side," she said.

At dinner, Janice's father sat at one end of the table. Janice's grandmother remained at the other. Silent bookends, both glaring into space. I sat next to Gramma who seemed to take an instant dislike to me. Janice was on my other side and whispered in my ear, "Gramma gives the stink eye to everyone when she first meets them. Ignore her." Across from me was Mickey, the mafia hit man. A dark eyed, sinewy kid in his twenties who kept nodding his head and saying to no one in particular, "How's it going?" Next to him sat Maria who queried her mother about the sausage. "You got this from Tito? Really? It tastes different."

We had just started eating when Aunt Connie and Uncle Jo-Jo arrived. "Oh, Clara," said Connie to Janice's mother. "You have company." She looked at me. "We're intruding."

Mrs. Trussardi who had just sat down, stood up and said, "Please. I made enough for an army. Sit. I'll get more plates."

Aunt Connie kissed Gramma on the cheek and Gramma grimaced and turned to me and said, "I have no food for three days. Just a piece of bread. My children don't come to see me. No water...."

Connie laughed, "Stop it, Ma. You are visited more than the shrine at Lourdes." Connie winked at me and added, "I brought her breakfast this morning. Jo-Jo stopped by at lunch with a cold cuts hoagie from his sales call in Trenton. Which she devoured while he watched. And now she's here at Clara's eating again.... What are we having? Ravioli?? Oh, dear Lord, I should remove my girdle first."

Janice announced, "This is Leanne. She's an actress like me."

"Unemployed," mumbled Mr. Trussardi.

Jo-Jo reached across the table and took my hand. "Hi. Honey. Call me Jo-Jo."

I instantly liked him and I loved Connie. She was a very pretty woman, vivacious and affectionate. She shoved a chair between Gramma and me and said, "So Leanne, talk to me."

Mickey looked at Gramma and said, "How's it going, Gramma?" Gramma flipped the fingers of her right hand off her double chin and growled, "F'Naples." It almost sounded like she said Fuck Naples. And from everyone's reaction, I soon understood that I had heard her correctly.

Maria said, "C'mon, Gramma! That's not nice" and Mickey laughed.

The food was scrumptious and every now and then Mrs. Trussardi would call down the table, "Is Leanne eating?" And I would reply, "Oh yes, Mrs. Trussardi. Everything's delicious. Thank you so much for having me." But she'd ask again minutes later. The third time she did it, Janice stood up and screamed, "SHE'S EATING, MA! FOR CHRIST'S SAKE, SHE'S EATING!"

Janice and Connie delighted in making off-color remarks about Tito, the butcher, and his first-rate sausage. Janice's mother pursed her lips and said, "Really? You two! When we have a lady here? Leanne, you must think we're awful."

And I said, "Not at all. I'm having a wonderful time. Again, thank you for inviting me." And I meant it. It was wonderful to be in a real home. Crazy and loving. A real home.

Uncle Jo-Jo called down to me, "So what do you weigh, Leanne?

"Um...."

"A buck twenty-five?"

"Yeah," I said. "Something like that...."

Then Aunt Connie yelled, "Don't be so personal, Jo-Jo!" Then she turned to me and fired off a half dozen questions. "How old are you, Honey? Where are you from? Where are your people from? Is your mother upset that you are living in New York? What does your dad do? Where did you go to school? Are you dating anyone? What size underpants do you usually buy?"

Janice nudged me and cooed in a singsong tone, "Aunt Connie is going to surprise you with some expensive lingerie."

"Oh," I said to Aunt Connie. "You don't need to do that."

She smiled indulgently. "You come see me at Bloomie's. Second floor. I work weekdays. We'll fix you up with a nice set for when you go on a date."

Maria stabbed a ravioli and shook it in the air. "Damn, Aunt Connie! Do you have to be so crude? You're embarrassing Mickey!" Gramma made the F'Naples gesture at Mickey again. Mickey laughed again.

The meal was still going on three hours later. Mrs. Trussardi poured coffee and passed baskets of nuts and dried fruit. I took a walnut and reached for one of the nutcrackers on the table. Gramma eyed me suspiciously. She pointed to my mouth, "They your teeth?" she said.

"Yes."

She made a disgusted face and grabbed a walnut and bit down on the hard shell, cracking it open—showing me how it should be done.

"Wow," I said. "You have strong teeth. Mine aren't like that." I opened my mouth and pointed to a front tooth. "See this tooth. It's a crown. I chipped it on a jellybean." Everyone quieted now and were looking at me in anticipation. So I told this story. "A couple of years ago, I was helping my mother get out the Easter baskets ... you know for Easter morning ... and there was a black jellybean in one of them from the year before and I really love the black jellybeans and I popped it in my mouth and bit down on it. Which was so stupid. It was as hard as marble. It had petrified up there in the attic during the year. So my tooth chipped. My mother was so furious because I had to get a crown. And there—all the time—was a fresh bag of jellybeans—just waiting to be opened." I stopped talking and there was a strange pause. Everyone looked at me wide-eyed like I had just fallen out of my chair and hit my head really hard and then had quickly popped back into my seat again. And at that moment it occurred to me that I was turning into my mother. Mickey finally broke the silence. "You're a funny chick, Leanne," he said. And everyone started passing things and talking again.

Jo-Jo called down the table. "So Leanne, you got a boyfriend?"

"Yes," I said. "We're engaged."

Janice's mom said, "How lovely. What does he do?"

"He's a novelist."

Aunt Connie said, "No fooling? I'm a big reader. Would I know him?"

I nodded. "Maybe." Then I added, "Philip Roth."

Janice slapped the table. "SHUT THE DOOR! You're kidding!! You're engaged to Philip Roth?" And Maria said, "Oh god, you're a Liberal."

It took me a minute to understand how she made that connection, but I knew from my experience with the communists in Czechoslovakia, that some books, especially those that are funny and sexy, and the people who write them are very threatening to people who embrace authoritarian figures like Nixon. Because you have to be able to think critically if you want to write something funny. I kept my poise. "Yes," I said calmly, "I think of myself as an exasperated Liberal and an indignant citizen. But I vote Democratic ticket all the way."

Janice's dad said, "mother of God." Janice's mother put a nervous hand on his sleeve.

Then Connie shrugged and said, "Don't mind him, Leanne. I'm a liberal, too. It means we're open minded." She turned to Janice's dad. "Yes, open-minded, Vince. You should look it up in the dictionary. Liberal is a good thing. Very American." Then she added, "How anyone can continue to defend that bum Nixon. He's as crooked as a Chicago cop."

Mickey laughed and yelled, "Whoa!"

Janice's dad stood up at that point and threw his napkin to the floor. "I will not have the President of the United States disparaged by people eating food that I paid for at my table. I'm going to watch the ball game." He moved back to his chair in the living room.

Connie yelled, "I'm reading in the Times what they are finding out about your precious Nixon. Twenty-five grand from Nixon's reelection fund was deposited in those Watergate burglars' accounts. I'm telling you … This stinks to high heaven!"

Clara's father said nothing. His face was bright red. Janice's mother gave Aunt Connie a look and she changed the subject. She turned to me and said in a hushed voice, "So what's Philip Roth like in bed? You can tell me."

The front door now opened and two more people joined us: Janice's Aunt Anna and Uncle Richard. "We were in the neighborhood.... Oh, Clara—sorry ... you have company."

"No problem," said Clara. "I made enough tiramisu for a third-world country." More chairs were pulled up to the table. More conversation. More teasing. More wine. More yelling. Aunt Anna insisted that Janice switch places so she could sit next to me and question me about Philip Roth. Now I had an aunt on either side. Anna said, "I'm a big fan of Philip Roth. He's so funny. And smart! Is he always funny like that?"

"Yeah, I laugh all the time," I said and laughed.

Uncle Jo-Jo said, "Oh, c'mon, Anna. Like this little girl is dating Philip Roth! You're teasing us, right, Leanne? He's a Jew. What are you, Honey? Baptist?"

I was going to say atheist but caught myself. "I'm ... I'm Episcopalian."

Janice's father threw his hands up in the air and called from his BarcaLounger, "Oh, of course, you are. The most liberal religion in the world except for Buddhist. Which the Beatles are now. But I think they started out as Episcopalians."

Janice's mom stood and said "I'll get dessert. Maria, come help."

Mickey looked at me and said, "I read on the society page of the *Daily News* that your betrothed—you know Philip Roth —he's dating Barbra Streisand. Like they had dinner last week."

I shook my head. "I don't know anything about that."

"So can he get me Streisand's autograph?"

"I don't know," I said quietly.

Mickey stared at me, a cold stare. "I really want Streisand's autograph. I have a collection."

"Sure. I'll ... I'll ... uh ... tell Philip to get you one."

Connie clapped her hands, "Hey, guess who I saw at Bloomie's last week? Jacqueline Kennedy Onassis. Right there on the escalator. She had her bodyguard with her of course."

Janice's father yelled, "Rich whore."

Aunt Anna stood up and said, "Vince, what a terrible thing for an American to say about a former first lady. Shame on you."

He stood up. "She couldn't marry a Greek fast enough, could she?"

Now Connie jumped in. Her voice was shrill, "SHE IS PROTECTING HER CHILDREN! THEY ARE KENNEDYS—THEY HAVE A TARGET ON THEIR BACK. SUCH A CURSED FAMILY. I DON'T BLAME JACKIE AT ALL. ONASSIS GIVES HER PROTECTION."

Janice's father was on his feet. "HE'S A MOBSTER!"

I looked at Mickey and he shrugged and said, "Actually, I don't know that to be a fact."

Aunt Anna said, "Speaking of mobsters, are you all following the stuff about Nixon's campaign workers and the break-in at the Democratic Headquarters?" She stood and yelled, "HE'S A GODDAMNED TRAITOR, VINCE! I always knew...."

Gramma grabbed the sides of her face and yelled, "SHUT UP ABOUT WATERGATE!"

Then Maria entered the dining room and began to distribute the dishes of tiramisu. I tried to wave it off. Maria screamed "YOU HAVE TO EAT IT. MOM WILL BE HURT IF YOU DON'T." So I took the dish.

Suddenly Gramma moaned and fainted, her head falling back against the chair, her mouth open revealing the tiny nubs of her worn teeth. Everyone got quiet but no one looked alarmed.

Aunt Connie whispered to me. "Gramma's going into one of her trances. Quick. Give her your hand. She'll read your palm."

Aunt Anna whispered in my other ear. "She just does it for attention. But sometimes she's really on the mark."

Gramma opened her eyes and stared at my palm. "You are going to fall in love. "

"She's already in love, Ma," said Aunt Connie.

"Shhhh," said Aunt Anna.

"You love many men but only one is the right one. You will see. You will know. Your mother loves you. You will be starting a job on January 3, 1973."

Gramma fainted again. I stood up and excused myself. "I have to leave now. But this has been wonderful. Truly wonderful. Thank you so much for everything."

Janice and her entire family would become my close friends.

Chapter 27

Philip and I decided to spend the Christmas holiday right through the New Year alone together. Just us. No plans. No visitors. It felt luxurious to have him all to myself. Philip was as relaxed and happy as I had ever seen him. He worked half days and in the afternoon we took meandering walks in the fading sunshine and gathered pine cones and greens to decorate the mantels of our three fireplaces. After dinner, we cuddled on the couch and told stories from our childhoods. Philip, like me, had been raised with lots of love.

"This is my mother's favorite story about me, Leanne. I was probably around six and I was standing at the window in the kitchen. It was snowing and I turned to her and said hopefully, "Mother, do we believe in Winter?" We both laughed. Then I told a story about TJ. The twins were about five at the time. It was Easter. Mother was still in her Episcopal phase so we had gone to the service at Saint James that morning. The bishop was visiting our church for the first time in my memory. He was very majestic in his white-and-gold vestments and his tall crown of a head covering was visible above the heads of the choir and the clergy as he was led down the aisle to the altar. And then as he passed our pew, TJ jumped up and squealed, "Jesus Christ! The King is here!" Philip fell off the couch and lay on the floor laughing.

On Christmas Eve, we opened a lovely bottle of wine. I made us a dinner of Scallops Provencal and homemade pasta and set up a small table in front of the fireplace in the Stone Room. Philip had built an especially beautiful fire. It crackled and glowed and made the room warm as a hug. We exchanged gifts. I gave Philip a cashmere scarf and he gave me cashmere mittens. And then I said, "Okay, one more. Now close your eyes." He did and I quickly ran upstairs to the guest bedroom and returned with an open box. "Open your eyes." "KITTENS!" he said, with the delight of a child. Two little tiger-striped brothers with round blue eyes. Philip named them Mike and Ike. It was love at first sight.

The next morning I woke up to find Philip playing with the kittens in our bed. I watched how gently he handled them. Rolling them onto their backs and rubbing their tummies. Nuzzling their soft little heads against his chin. Philip tucked them in the pockets of his bathrobe and made us breakfast. Then he resumed playing with them on the floor of the living room. He took them with him the next day when he returned to work in his studio across the yard and they were with him every day that week until New Year's Eve. That evening he looked at me sadly and said, "You're going to have to find the boys a good home. I love them too much. I can't stop watching them or playing with them or touching them and if they disappear from my view, I panic. I can't work with that kind of distraction."

"Philip, you don't have to hold them all day. They would be fine alone in the main house until dinnertime. They are indoor pets."

"No, I would worry that they might get their heads stuck in a banister or fall into the toilet and drown … I'd always be running in to check on them."

I laughed. "Philip.... "

"I can't have them here, Leanne. I'm serious. I can't do my work."

"What are you going to do when we have kids?" I asked.

"Leanne, I don't know about having kids. I love children but if kittens distract me, I can only imagine what fatherhood would be like."

"Philip, I'd be here."

"It wouldn't matter. I would be unable to think of anything else. I'd never sleep."

"Honey...."

"I couldn't write, Leanne. I couldn't work. I would end up miserable."

"I'm afraid I won't be able to marry you, Philip. I would be miserable without children. I guess we are not meant to be."

ON JANUARY 3, 1973, I entered the Warner Elkins Advertising Agency and took my place in the Creative Department on the sixth floor. I was basically a secretary for the first few months, taking notes at brainstorming sessions, but I was learning a lot so I never complained even when Mr. Kenyon pointedly asked me how I liked the job. Then in March, I was given my first real assignment. The client was Funny Face, a new soda pop.

Funny Face came in five flavors—cherry, lime, grape, orange and root beer. And five colors—red, green, purple, orange and brown. But the color of the soda gave no indication as to the flavor. Let's say you like cherry soda and you select the red colored beverage, expecting it to be cherry favored. You would discover it was lime or grape flavored. And the purple colored one might be orange flavored. The green colored one could be root beer and so on. That was supposed to be fun for the consumer. It was supposed to make you laugh. Hence the name Funny Face. But there was an additional catch. Supposing you figured out that the cherry flavored soda is the green one so the next time you buy Funny Face, you load up on Green. But then you get home and discover that the green now tastes like grape. In other words there was no consistent correlation between the color and the flavor.

The team working on the roll-out of Funny Face included a serious young man named Steve Hengst and a wonderfully funny and smart guy in his mid-thirties named Tony Fitzpatrick. And, of course, me. At our first team session, Steve suggested that we tell the client to make the combinations of color and flavor consistent so that once people had played along and found the one they liked, they would have solved the mystery and could be confident that there would be no more surprises. But we soon learned that the client had already produced thousands of bottles of this stuff and they had to sell that before they made any changes to the formula. So Tony, Steve, and I spent a long afternoon strategizing a way to make this concept appealing to someone older than ten.

Tony said, "Hey, how about this? We target the 'freshman male de-mographic'—kids still living on their parents' dime but who want to look rebellious." He grinned, "The ads will show a guy in a tie dye shirt with his tongue sticking out and it's got a big purple stain down the middle of it and he's holding up a bottle of the green soda. The tagline will be *FUCK YOU! It's Funny Face!*"

I laughed so hard I almost wet my pants. Steve said, "Okay, c'mon, guys. Be serious."

I smacked the table. "Hey, wait a minute! That's it! Lips and a protrud-ing tongue? You know like The Stones' *Sticky Fingers* album. We will do a variation on that. A big cartoon tongue with a rainbow of colors ... The kids will get the association. They will love it."

Tony clapped his hands, "A rainbow of stains on a big tongue! That's genius, Leanne!"

Steve shook his head vehemently. "Wait a minute. Wait a minute. Are you crazy? This is a family product. We'll offend mothers."

I ignored Steve and asked Tony, "We have to be careful ... run it by the lawyers first?"

Steve whined, "The client isn't going to like this, Leanne...."

I said, "We drop the Fuck You part of course. But the tongue will be playful and zany. Our market will be kids and teenagers and young twen-ty-somethings. And maybe a few mental patients." I laughed.

Tony stood up and grabbed a bottle of Funny Face and sang into it, "Brown Sugar ... how come you taste so gooooooood?"

To make a long story short, the client hated our idea. They wanted something safe. So Steve came up with something safe. A happy kid's birthday party with happy Mom and Dad looking on with delight as kids squeal with happiness at the Funny Face surprises. But the product didn't sell. And I knew why. No one was buying the sanctimonious images of the nuclear American family anymore. And the women in my generation didn't want to be represented by a stay-at-home mother in a shirtwaist dress hovering over her kids and husband. That wasn't the way Americans saw themselves anymore.

On top of that, humor was changing. America was becoming coarser. More vulgar. More cynical. We did interviews with customers to find out why the product Funny Face wasn't catching on and the most common response was "It's fucking stupid." And that was from the kids. The product was eventually reincarnated as a powder beverage like Kool-Aid, but it wasn't successful in that form either. By that time, it was no longer our client though, so we didn't care.

In late March, I came to the attention of a man named Paul Monroe. He was the Senior Vice President of Warner Elkins Advertising. I had spoken to him briefly on the elevator one morning and that afternoon, I got a call from Mr. Kenyon.

"Guess what, Leanne? Paul Monroe wants to meet you."

"Really? Why?"

"I'm sure he heard about your work on Funny Face."

"We lost that client."

"Yeah, but your impulses on that product were right. You seem to have your finger on the pulse of the new generation, Leanne. And you certainly made an impression on Mr. Monroe. He wants you to come to his office on Friday at three. I suspect he has a project in mind for you. This is a lucky break, Honey. He usually doesn't pay much attention to Creative. He's usually crunching numbers with the accountants."

I was actually thrilled. Other than Mr. Kendall, this was my first real acknowledgment at the agency and I anticipated that doors were going to open for me now. So that Friday at three, I went to the eleventh floor but it was deserted. Even the secretary stations were empty. It looked like all of the top brass had already left for the weekend. I was about to return to the sixth floor when a door opened and a middle aged man in a dark grey suit stepped into the hall and said, "Leanne? I'm glad you could make it. Come in."

Mr. Monroe motioned me to take a seat on a long white leather couch. Then he went to his personal bar and poured two glasses of wine from a bottle that was chilling in an ice bucket. He handed me one and lifted his glass in a silent toast. I did as well. Then he sipped his and I placed mine on the glass coffee table without drinking. And there it sat for the duration of our meeting, untouched. Mr. Monroe dimmed the lights and studied me silently; then he asked, "Have you ever heard of the *Carmina Burana?*" I shook my head. He walked behind his massive desk and took a seat. "It's a piece of music based on a collection of poems that were written during the 11th and 12th centuries by young men—young monks. The whole collection of something like 254 poems was found in 1803 hidden in a monastery in Bavaria. They speak of the lust men feel for young women. In springtime when life is so lush." He paused and I felt my stomach drop. Then he continued, "In 1936, a composer named Carl Orff selected twenty-four of the poems and set them to music. The piece has been performed many times by major orchestras and choirs around the world. But I feel the urge to listen to it every Spring. It makes me … feel." His voice trailed. We sat again in silence for a long moment. Then he resumed his monologue. "When I saw you on the elevator … I wanted to … experience this with you."

I took a deep breath and Mr. Monroe reached under his desk and pushed something and the room filled with the powerful opening drums of *Carmina Burana's* overture. For the next hour and a half I sat rigidly on the edge of the couch and counted the slats in the louvered blinds that covered the windows of Mr. Monroe's office. If I hadn't been so nervous I might have enjoyed the music, but I could feel his eyes traveling over me. Sometimes he would break into song—singing along with the recording in Latin or whatever language that was. But he never took his eyes off me. And while I was always aware of his gaze, I avoided looking back. As the music escalated in emotion, I was terrified for it to end. I wondered what he would do when it was over. Would he be in a state of such excitement that…. At one point, I thought, *Well, I'm just going to stand up now and leave. That's what I'll do. Then I'll run to the stairs and down the five flights. I'll hide in Robert's office. He'll protect me.* But I didn't. I remained frozen in place listening to the drumming of my own pulse.

When the music ended, we sat in silence for a full five minutes. The tension became so oppressive that I was on the verge of screaming when Mr. Monroe finally stood up and walked to the door of his office and opened it, indicating that I could leave. As I passed him on the way out, he said, "I want you here next Friday, same time." I nodded and took the stairs back to Creative.

Robert saw me entering my office and joined me. "Well?" he said. "What did you talk about?"

"Oh, he … he just talked to me about this music that he likes and he played the record for me."

"Oh, that's interesting. Did you enjoy it? Do you think you might use it in a commercial?"

"Umm … you know what? Actually it gave me a headache." I half laughed. I wanted to tell Robert everything but I was afraid he would confront Mr. Monroe. And end up in trouble, maybe lose his job. So I made up my mind just to get through this on my own.

The next Friday, I returned to the Tower and sat on the couch in Mr. Monroe's office and listened to the *Carmina Burana* again while his eyes moved over me. It was worse this time. His stare was bolder. I couldn't help but think of my body as he was seeing it. And that made me feel embarrassed. Embarrassed to be naked in front of a man I didn't know and didn't especially like.

I would have to endure two more Fridays with Mr. Monroe. Throughout he never touched me, but I felt thoroughly violated. I didn't tell anyone at work because I didn't think anyone would find any fault in his behavior. I mean, he didn't touch me. I had no case. The last time I saw Mr. Monroe was on a Tuesday after the last Friday I had spent with him. He had told me that I didn't have to return, but suddenly there he was again, standing in front of my desk on the sixth floor. I looked up and felt the blood rush out of my face. He spoke softly but firmly. "Leanne, I'd like to talk to you privately."

I followed him into the hall and then he opened the door of the Janitor's Closet and motioned for me to enter. It was a small room with wooden shelves, laden with cleaners. A couple of buckets were stacked on the floor. Everything smelled of disinfectant and Mr. Monroe and I had to stand so close together in the tiny space that our sleeves touched. I held my breath and waited for him to kiss me. Instead he said, "I have instructed Payroll to give you a nice raise. Please don't tell anyone. President Nixon has imposed a wage freeze on corporations across the country to try to control inflation. Warner Elkins is of course complying. But you are...." For the first time, he smiled at me. "You are special. Thank you for spending time with me." *As if I had a choice.* And with that, we emerged from the closet. He went back to the Tower and thankfully, I never saw him again.

I called Mimi that night and told her the whole story. Then I added, "I'm considering becoming a Muslim. Maybe moving to Saudi Arabia."

"Pour quoi, cherie?"

"Do you remember that time when we saw that woman who was completely veiled? You said she was a Muslim and probably from Saudi Arabia."

"Oui. I assumed that she was a Muslim. She was wearing the traditional Muslim veiling. It's called a burka. Everything is concealed."

"Well, I want to wear a burka."

"Are you sure? It signifies male dominance, actual possession of women. Mon dieu, Leanne—you of all people wouldn't stand for that. Especially given that it is imposed on women in the name of god."

"Well, I think the joke is on the men, Mimi. I've thought a lot about this. The woman wearing a burka can still see everything. But no man can see her. If I wore one, I could stare at a man's ass for as long as I liked. I could stare at his crotch if I wanted, too. And he'd never be the wiser. But a man couldn't look at my ass. Or my breasts. I'd be invisible to him. I think it's the most transgressive clothing a woman can adopt. And it's funny as hell that men came up with it. It gives women the power of the gaze and takes it away from the men."

"I take it something is going on at work?"

I told her the whole story about Mr. Monroe. She listened and when I was finished, she said, "What do you suppose would have happened if you had simply said no and walked out? Would he have physically kept you in the room?"

"Probably not. But I would have been fired."

"You have Philip."

"No ... we have ended our engagement."

"Oh...."

"And that's not the point. Supposing I was just an average working girl."

"Well, shop around—try another agency. Isn't there one now that was founded by a woman?"

"Yeah. Mary Wells has Wells, Rich and Green. But I hear she's a bitch."

"Okay, what are you seeking?"

"What I want, Mimi, is an apology. I want Mr. Monroe to be so ashamed that he can only ease his pain by asking my forgiveness."

"Well, Leanne, I bet he suffers every time he thinks of you. But not because he humiliated you. If he is ashamed, it's because he defied Nixon and gave you a raise. All these older advertising execs? Believe me—I know from my father. They are all conservative. Uptight. Repressed. I mean who gets off on eleventh-century lust poems? Jesus … Did you know that Nixon's chief of staff, Haldeman—he is a former ad exec. He's there to manipulate the public perception of Nixon. He has packaged Nixon like some kind of national hero for the country, holding back the communists with one hand and giving the rich everything on their selfish wish list with the other. So for your Mr. Monroe to defy an order from Nixon himself and give you a raise just so he can sit across from you and fantasize about you … well, well, well, Leanne—you are really under his skin now."

"And he's under mine, Mimi."

"All right. Do you want to talk to a lawyer? Shall we get some advice from Pookie?"

I shook my head. "No, I don't want to sue him. I want an apology."

A couple of weeks after of my last visit with Mr. Monroe, the pretty model who appeared on the Ivory Snow detergent boxes—the gold standard of wholesomeness, the All-American young mother—yes, I'm referring to Marilyn Chambers—*she was exposed*—excuse the pun—as the porn actress who appeared in *Behind the Green Door*, the triple X-rated sex film that was making the rounds of main stream movie theaters that Spring. She singlehandedly almost brought down the P&G house of household products and the Warner Elkins Advertising Agency too. And here's the clincher. Marilyn Chambers never apologized. Quite the contrary. She spoke brazenly about how much she had enjoyed the experience of having sex on camera. And she was heralded in newspapers, including the *New York Times* as "shameless" and "unapologetic"—"an embodiment of the sassiness found in the new all-American girl." I'm sure Paul Monroe nearly had a heart attack.

April 12, 1973

Dear Diary,

I know it's no longer necessary to say you are sorry in America. In fact, it seems to be increasingly viewed as a sign of weakness. The coolest thing you can say about any public figure now is that he's "unapologetic." Like that's brave. Or strong. But I have decided to draw up a list of people to whom I owe an apology. And then I am going to apologize. Because it's the right thing to do. And I will feel better about myself. My list is not excessively long. I think I have for the most part been a kind person.

I'm going to start with Cindy. She was the girl whose bunny fur jacket I swiped when I was in kindergarten. I apologized at the time but it was insincere. My mother made me do it. Cindy was afraid of me after that. All through high school. Funny how bad that has made me feel over the years. So I will ask my old high school friend Lark to give me her number—they are still in touch. And this time I will apologize sincerely. I also need to apologize to Noah for getting engaged to him when I didn't love him and then lying that I was gay to get unengaged. It hurt him and he didn't deserve to be hurt. That apology will be a little tricky. I may have to lie again. I don't want to hurt him anymore. Let's see—I also want to apologize to my one time guru, Oric Bovar. Last I heard, he was losing followers at a rapid clip now since he told everyone to be celibate and I guess he is heartbroken. I heard he was moving to New York to gather his remaining disciples so that his dream of a Renaissance won't completely die. Maybe I can take him out to lunch, someplace that doesn't have peanuts, coffee, tomatoes ... I'll tell him I appreciated The Work and that I'm sorry it ended the way it did.

More than anything, I have to find a way to apologize to the young security guard at the bank. Perhaps I can set up a scholarship in his memory. Or send his parents a letter telling them how nice he was. I could lie and say that he and I had been friends. I'd just as soon not lie but sometimes it's just necessary if you want to be kind.

I've considered apologizing to Bert Heckel. Not that he wasn't awful to me. I mean he hypnotized me and I still blame him for the bee attack on Daddy ... but I really terrorized him that morning when I unleashed my Witch performance on him. I suppose it's time to let bygones be bygone.

I WENT HOME TO see my parents one weekend that April. I hadn't seen them since Thanksgiving. Mother and I went to the movies in Pennswalk that Saturday night and saw *The Heartbreak Kid*. During the Coming Attractions, Mother suddenly grabbed my hand and whispered, "When you were born, Annie, I was so overwhelmed with love for you that I was terrified I would die and not be around to raise you. I tried to teach you everything I knew about survival as fast as I could." She paused and sniffed. Then she continued, "I made mistakes. Terrible mistakes. Babies don't come with instructions. And even if you had come with instructions, they would have been useless. You have always been so unique. But I never meant to hurt you." She patted my hand. "Anyway, I just want you to know, Honey, how much I love you. I always have and always will. And I admire you more than anyone I've ever known. And I hope you will forgive me because I'm so very sorry for making you believe that I didn't think you were good enough just as you were. You are more than good enough. You are perfect." I squeezed Mother's hand and heard her quietly sobbing. I cried, too. And then I said, "I forgive you, Mother. I love you, too."

I will be honest here. I never did forgive her. Not really. But I accepted her apology. It was sincere and I respected that. And I knew enough by then that people are unreliable. Good people can do bad things. And we all have a tendency to lie to ourselves. Although I don't. I mean I lie a lot, but not to myself. I know myself. I'm spoiled. But I'm kind. And I deserve to be loved.

Philip arrived at my apartment the following Wednesday, carrying a large bouquet of roses. I opened the door and he walked in, fell to one knee and said, "I love you. And I miss you and I'm sorry. Please marry me, Leanne. I promise to be a faithful and adoring husband and a devoted father to our children. I want to make a home with you."

ON WEDNESDAY, MAY 17, 1973, Philip and I were married. Our families joined us at the Farm for an early dinner of steak and salad. Corn on the cob. All the late Summer harvest favorites. Philip's brother, Sandy, and his wife Trudy did the grilling. Daddy kept them company. Mother and Bess oversaw the rest of the menu and my brothers set the table. Philip's dad went through our record collection and picked out some Jo Stafford records for dinner music. Soon her beautiful voice filled the house. *Long ago and far away....*

Mimi and Olivia confided in Philip and me that they wanted to have a wedding, too, later that Summer when the current Theater of the Deaf tour took a pause. Philip and I immediately offered them the Farm for their reception. And I volunteered to officiate. It wouldn't be legal in the eyes of the government, but who cared what the government thought anymore? Even my mother offered her services as a wedding planner.

After dinner the local Justice of the Peace arrived and we all gathered in front of the fireplace in the Stone Room. Philip and I had written our vows to be read that day. So Philip began. "I used to think that love brought you together in a soul embrace that made you literally feel like you were one entity. The Platonic ideal. But when we fell in love our hearts opened so fully that they fractured in two. We thought that was real love and we each gave each other a half of our heart to hold close on the journey ahead. And ours has been a long journey. At each stage, we were awakened anew to how strong and yet how fragile we were as halves of this relationship. At times we were afraid that we would lose each other in the traffic and busyness of life and we actually did come apart at one point. We thought now our hearts would remain forever broken. But we came to understand as every other couple eventually does that you must create a world in which your hearts can fully mend. And that world has to hold everything you love—not just each other."

Here I took over the reading, "And so this world began to take shape. A place where we could insulate ourselves from cruelty and sadness. Our world would be kind. Our world would provide warmth on snowy days. And sunshine even when it was raining. Our world would be quiet when we needed sleep. But ebullient with music when we wanted to dance. Our world would be generous. We would always welcome our friends and family to share our world. We would cultivate flowers in our garden and feed the songbirds so there would always be beauty. Trust would flourish in this world and our hearts would be returned to us. Whole again. And then we would create new love, and we would experience more than we ever thought possible."

We had dessert after the ceremony. A yummy wedding cake, custom made at a local bakery. And iced tea and champagne. Then we all settled in around the TV to watch the first meeting of the Senate Select Committee on Presidential Campaign Activities on our local public television station. There would be fifty additional meetings broadcast over the next six months, ending on November 15, 1973. It would soon become known simply as The Watergate Committee and it would lead to Nixon's resignation on August 8, 1974.

On that Spring night, as Philip and I climbed into bed as husband and wife, I curled up in his arms. I felt overwhelmed with joy and an optimism I had never before experienced. I felt that in some sense my personal happiness that day was a reflection of the fact that at long last the country was finally righting itself. That there was a reckoning happening across the land and that America would emerge wiser and truer to its founding ideals. I said, "Philip, do you think Nixon is feeling deep shame right now? Do you think he will apologize for cheating?"

And Philip said, "Oh my god, Leanne, let's hope so. When the day comes that we as a nation have a President who doesn't feel shame, we will have elected a sociopath. And that will be the beginning of the end for America."

Afterword

an Autumn day in 2020

Well, we created our own worlds, didn't we, Philip? We retreated behind the doors of our privilege and lived in our worlds of material comfort and safety as long as we could. While the outside world simmered with fury and grievance. And now the madness has coalesced and threatens everything we worked so hard to establish in the 60s and 70s. In just four years, we see the damage that has already been done.

It's November, Philip. I'm back in the year 2020. I am 72 years old now, having had a birthday in August. COVID is still threatening our communities—that we can't escape with privilege. The COVID vaccine won't be ready by Christmas as was hoped. So we are still wearing masks and avoiding personal contact. The death toll has been frightening. And speaking of frightening, the election is next week. I feel confident that Trump will be defeated this time. He's been appallingly inept not to mention vulgar and corrupt. But I'm also confident that he will refuse to leave the White House, so who knows what kind of craziness lies ahead.

Regardless of who ends up heading our government—I'll be honest with you, Philip—I don't think there is a fix for America. America is simply too fractured now. There are two Americas. That's been the case for years … actually since the Civil War. The South never healed and now a political party has fully embraced their cause. Maybe the solution is to accept that reality and simply break apart. Into two separate countries. We retire the name America. We all start again. It is not unimaginable if you consider the history of the world. Wars and revolutions occur with regularity. And natural disasters like famine, fire, and flood—look at the impact they have had on the map of the world. Look at how people have always been on the move, in flight for their lives or to find "a better life," however they define that. Empires rise and fall. Countries are conquered and swallowed up by the victors. Languages disappear. History is rewritten to serve the Powerful. And people adapt. Are we Americans so special, so unique that we can escape the inevitability of Change? Change is Life. Change is a part of everything.

I don't think it would be altogether a mistake to let America split into two pieces. Two separate countries with their own laws and budgets and education systems. I'm not being cynical, Philip. It would release the furious disappointment we all feel. It would free all of us to reimagine our homeland, less naively, more realistically. We've had a taste of what the opposition has in mind. We can all choose now which side we want to be on. We could live among the like-minded—in peace. Hopefully we split up amicably without war. Maybe just have a vote on it? At this point, I don't think the MAGA people who are demanding secession will get any pushback from the rest of us. In fact, it might actually alarm them—to see just how easily we let them go.

You know what's crazy? My kids agree with me. And they are the next generation on deck. My husband, on the other hand, is still holding on to a *United* States. I don't argue with him. I love him. He is a wonderful man, loving and generous—a good husband and father—but he is fragile. It pains him to see America coming apart. I, on the other hand, have moved on—I guess I have more imagination than he does. After all, I'm a writer. It doesn't pain me anymore to consider having America split in two. In fact, I think it's a healthy conclusion to America's run as an empire. I am thinking about publicly proposing that America have a cordial and civil separation from itself. I'd do it on Facebook or Twitter. That's how we get big ideas into the popular discourse these days. Maybe I will become an Influencer.

What else did I want to tell you? Both of my parents are dead, Philip. I'm sure that doesn't surprise you, given my age. Mother went first. Her lung disease finally overwhelmed her. She was brave and optimistic, but, in the end, she didn't know Daddy anymore. That broke our hearts. She adored him all their married life. They had a wonderful marriage and I took note. Daddy died several years ago, just before his ninetieth birthday. He just let go. I miss them both. I think about them every day. I'm grateful that I was lucky enough to be raised by them. I think they did a fabulous job, don't you? Look how neat I turned out. Ha! I can hear you laughing. But it's true. I like myself.

My brother John died ten years ago, Philip. It was so sudden. Heart. He had such a gentle heart. I know … it breaks my heart, too. And my darling Mimi. This one always makes me cry. She died in 2018—the same year that you died. If there is any way to reach her wherever you are, please tell her she's alive in my memory. She will like that.

As are you, dear Philip. You are alive in my imagination. Thank you for everything.

Well, I better go. It's starting to get dark and snow is predicted this evening. Winter's coming. But I will return to the lake in the Spring. And I will reach out to you here at our spot. Of course you might be able to contact me yourself if you try. Please feel free to do so —I mean, if you ever want to talk....

Don't be a stranger.

Acknowledgments

I've enjoyed writing this book. But it took more than two years and I might have drifted away from it at any point were it not for the steady love and support and maybe more importantly the genuine interest of my wonderful friends and family. In particular I want to thank Dulcie Arnold who read new pages and old pages and rewritten pages every single week and met with me every Monday afternoons for two years via FaceTime. She was my editor, my cheerleader, my grand inquisitor, and she remains my loving friend. I owe you so much, Dulcie. I owe you this book and my everlasting loyalty. And a bottle of wine or two.

Katie Kraemer was my other nearly daily companion on this journey. She read the crazy thing in and out of order and sat over long dinners and discussed and questioned the emerging story always in her gentle albeit cunning way. She gave me praise that gave me confidence, even when it maybe wasn't warranted. She even took it along on her travels through

Europe and texted at regular intervals to let me know she still loved it. Oh, how I thank you, Katie!

Cathy Fuller was the first to read the opening section of the story. She was so enthusiastic that she even recorded early chapters, reading with her rich melodic voice, so that I could hear what she heard. Thank you, dear Cathy. There were others. Paul Meshejian who has been my champion for thirty years. I love you, Paul—always have, always will. And Luigi Salerni who wraps me in a hug every time I question myself. Even when I don't. And Andre Bergeron who brought me to the finish line. Smart, sensitive and generous. And dear friends—Barb Snow, Signe Pretzel, Tess Kissinger, Tara Guy, and Jenni Runte. You all made me feel like this story was worth sharing. Thank you for that.

And Carolyn Whitson, whose beautiful artwork on the cover of this book is the icing on the cake. I also want to thank Tom Jenks for giving me an early thumbs up. And thank you, Wendell Ricketts and FourCats Press, for making this story a book. And making it available to my friends and family.

I want to thank my sister Sally Bagshaw and my cousins Russ West and Sue Doran all of whom encouraged me every step of the way. And my beloved children—Amy, Jason, Sam, and Michelle. And … drum roll please … my wonderful husband, Fred Reasoner who still tells me I'm smart and beautiful even after forty seven years together. I think he's smart and beautiful, too.

Finally, I want to thank Philip Roth. Boy, I'm going to miss you, Philip.

About the Author

Nancy Bagshaw-Reasoner spent thirty-five years on the professional stage as an actress, producer, and playwright. Then she spent fifteen years overseeing construction and facilities-maintenance at a Minnesota state university. Then she retired and figured out what she really wants to do with her life. She wants to write novels. *Philip Roth Loves Me* is her first. Nancy lives in Saint Paul, Minnesota, with her husband Fred Reasoner and their border collie, Jack.

Made in the USA
Middletown, DE
21 October 2023